Storm of Ghosts
Surviving the Dead Volume 8

By:

James N. Cook

COPYRIGHT

FIRST EDITION

Library of Congress Cataloguing-in-Publication Data has been applied for.

Epub Edition © JUNE 2017

Also by James N. Cook:

Surviving the Dead Series:

No Easy Hope
This Shattered Land
Warrior Within
The Passenger
Fire in Winter
The Darkest Place
Savages
The Killing Line

Monsters are real, and ghosts are real too. They live inside us,
and sometimes they win.

-Stephen King

ONE

Caleb,

Parabellum

At around 0300 on a Saturday morning in the first week of June, I found myself lying on a hillside in Northern Arkansas. I had been lying there since sundown and was losing hope I would move my legs again before dawn. So when my earpiece crackled and my old friend Tyrel Jennings spoke, I was grateful.

"All stations, Sierra Lead. Confirm targets acquired. Over."

There were eight other snipers positioned around the walls of the small community nestled in a natural hollow roughly two hundred yards below. From where I lay, I could smell the smoke of cook fires preparing breakfast for the marauders who ruled the town. Orange lights glowed from glassless windows, mostly candles and oil lanterns, only a few buildings in town boasting electricity. What power was available was provided by a large generator near the central plaza.

The buildings connected to the limited grid belonged exclusively to the Storm Road Tribe. There was no infrastructure in place to provide power to the rest of the town, even though doing so would not have been difficult. A twenty-man work crew and a halfway knowledgeable electrician could have done the job in a week, provided they had the necessary resources. Which the Storm Road Tribe most certainly did. However, in the three weeks the Blackthorn Security Company had been surveilling the area, the man in charge had made no effort to improve his town's

1

infrastructure. Nor did it appear likely he would. Perhaps it was his way of establishing a sense of privilege among his men while simultaneously reminding the peasants of their place in the pecking order.

"Sierra One, target acquired."

"Sierra Two, target acquired…"

On it went until Gabriel Garrett's rumbling baritone informed Sierra Lead, AKA Tyrel Jennings, that Sierra Eight had acquired his target.

I keyed my radio. "Sierra Nine, target acquired."

"All stations, Sierra Lead, acknowledged. Stand by."

My right eye peered through the reticle of a night vision scope. The crosshairs followed a man walking the catwalk on the southern wall of the compound. He was one of twelve guards on the outer perimeter: eight on the catwalks, four in the towers. The roving patrol on the south wall and the southwest tower were my responsibility.

The rover I watched stopped by the guard tower, pulled something from his belt, took a drink from it, replaced the container, and stood staring southward for a few seconds. Then he turned and began walking toward the other tower. I shifted aim toward the southwest tower, positioned the crosshairs center-of-mass on the tower guard, and began counting backward from sixty-two.

Over the last couple of hours, sixty-two seconds was the average time it had taken the rover to walk from one end of the wall to the other and turn around. If Tyrel gave the order to fire during that time, the tower guard would die first, then the rover. If the order came down after sixty-two seconds, I would take out my targets in reverse order. The second option was not my favorite. It meant there was a chance the tower guard would see the rover go down and sound the alarm. There would be less chance of that happening in the next minute while the rover had his back turned.

"All stations, Sierra Lead. Coordinate fire on my mark."

"'Bout damn time," I muttered.

"Three, two, one, *mark*."

I squeezed the trigger and felt the rifle thump against my shoulder. A suppressor on the end of the converted SCAR 17's barrel dulled the report to a muted crack. Through the NV scope, I saw my target stiffen, but he did not fall. I fired twice more and watched him twitch with each impact. Finally he collapsed.

The tower guard must have made a noise because when I switched aim to the rover, he had stopped, turned around, and was peering through the darkness at the watchtower. He put his hands around his mouth to call out, but the words never made it. I fired twice. The shots took the marauder in the chest at a diagonal, sending two gouts of dark liquid spraying behind his far shoulder. He stumbled backwards, fell on his ass, and clutched his chest. Before he died, he looked at his hands, no doubt seeing them covered in blood. I had a moment to wonder what he was thinking in his last few seconds of life before the radio crackled again.

"Sierra One, tango delta."

'Tango delta' was the call sign for 'target down', meaning Sierra One had killed his bad guys without incident. If he had said 'tango Charlie', meaning 'target compromised', things would have gotten hectic. Thankfully, the rest of the confirmations came quickly, including mine, all stations reporting tango delta.

I took a few big breaths and let them out slowly, willing my heartrate to decrease. I did not get the shakes. My hands were steady.

I was seventeen the first time I killed someone. Two someones, actually. Afterward, I got the shakes bad enough the paramedics wanted to take me in for observation, which I refused. In the years since, my reaction to fighting and killing had gradually diminished. I likened it to the Doppler Effect, the noise of a loud object passing close by at first, then diminishing like the drone of an engine fading into the distance. It had been over five years since those first killings, and the noise was dim now. I wondered how long it would be, how many more faces I would see in the dark when sleep refused to come, before I would hear it not at all.

Tyrel's decision to attack at three in the morning was not random. At that hour, most people in the settlement were asleep. The townsfolk, lacking electricity and therefore unable to light their homes without running the risk of burning them down, had mostly turned in after sunset. The marauders stayed up later, but not excessively so. Even criminal scum need to rest before a late watch. The pattern had been the same the last three weeks. Tonight was no exception.

So when the ladders went up and nine squads of highly-trained Blackthorn operators scaled the walls of Parabellum, it seemed there was no one around to observe them. All the marauders on the wall were dead, and the others were still in their barracks with the lights out.

Someone, however, must have been awake because the assault teams had no sooner reached the ground and set out for the center of town when, from somewhere near the east wall, a bell started ringing.

My earpiece crackled. "Bravo Lead, Sierra Lead, all teams proceed on mission. Acknowledge, over."

"Acknowledged, Sierra Lead. Proceeding on mission. Over."

"Sierra Two, who the fuck is ringing that bell? Over."

"Got him, Sierra Lead. Wait one."

A moment later the ringing stopped.

"Sierra Lead, Sierra Two. Tango delta."

"About fucking time. All right gentlemen, the ball is up, but the plan hasn't changed. Stay focused, provide fire support where you can, and make sure you don't shoot anyone dressed like a Blackthorn."

We didn't bother with acknowledgments. There was no time. I hunched down over my rifle and searched the area of town I could see. A few people came out into the streets, none of them armed. I held my fire. From the east part of town the unmistakable rattle of an AK-47 tore into the night. It was answered by several M-4s. The AK went silent. I scanned the streets again. Still no gunmen, and no sign of the assault teams.

I shifted focus to the center of town. A few dozen marauders had exited their barracks and formed into fire teams, each one moving to a different street accessing the central plaza. One of them, a four-man team, had taken position directly in my line of sight. I put the scope on the guy who looked like he was in charge, let out half a breath, and squeezed the trigger. The shot took him high in the back, likely hitting a major artery. Dead or not, he was out of the fight.

There was a moment of panic as the rest of his fire team saw him go down. One moment he was standing there giving orders, the next he had a hole in his chest and was spitting up blood. The delay gave me enough time to line up another shot and take it. Another marauder went down. The last two broke and ran. I tried to sight in on one of them, but he went around a corner and out of visual.

At other points around the central plaza, panic was taking hold. Shots poured in from all sides, their source invisible to the men on the receiving end. All they knew was they had been awakened and now stood in the darkness taking heavy fire. But they couldn't hear any reports or see any muzzle flashes. It was useless to return fire because they could not tell where the shots were coming from. They were more likely to hit each other than the enemy.

After a few more seconds, the defenders broke. Panicked men left their posts and fled down streets and alleyways and ducked into buildings. I shifted focus to the largest building in town. The marauder's leader lived there. He had been seen going in and out of the building numerous times over the last few weeks. At night, he went in and stayed. I checked the windows and doorways. No one. The balconies were deserted as well. To all appearances, the place was abandoned. No lights, no movement, nothing.

Strange.

Back to the southern part of town. What few people had been in the streets before had now sought shelter indoors. Smart. It was not a good time to be outside. Too much chance of getting shot at.

5

Since I had nothing else to do at the moment, I switched comms channels and listened to the assault teams' radio chatter. They moved with speed and efficiency, keeping conversation to a minimum. Several teams met small pockets of resistance and crushed them without mercy. None of our guys had been hit so far.

Less than five minutes from the time their boots hit Parabellum soil, the teams reached the central plaza. A few of them advanced on the barracks while the rest stormed the leader's mansion. They met no resistance. In fact, they met no one at all. The building was empty.

The assault teams reassembled and began to sweep the town building by building. At each doorway, they announced themselves and gave the inhabitants a chance to come out. Most did. A few houses contained people too sick or injured to stand up. The assault teams entered and cleared, but did so carefully. Our rules of engagement were very firm on one particular point: we were to minimize civilian casualties. The mission was to liberate these people, not kill them. The teams took their time and did things right.

A few houses turned up marauders trying to hide out from the assault teams. Most of them went quietly, but one took a hostage and started shooting. The teams did the smart thing: they waited until he was out of ammo and then moved in. Within seconds of the first dry trigger pull, the marauder was face down on the ground, pinned in place by about five hundred pounds of armored whoop-ass. His hog-tied form being dragged into the central plaza marked the last gasp of resistance from the Storm Road Tribe.

The radio emitted static and Tyrel started talking again, but he abruptly stopped when several thumps reverberated through the ground. I was confused for a moment, then realization dawned and I felt my heart sink.

Explosives.

The radio was loud for a while until it was determined no one was hurt. The explosions had come from underground. I keyed my radio.

"Sierra Lead, Sierra Nine. Looks like Sierra Eight's theory was correct."

Tyrel ignored me. "Bravo Lead, can you confirm if those blasts came from tunnels?"

"Affirmative. Just found the entrance to one in the mansion. Nothing but a pile of rubble now."

"Any chance we can get our guys in there and give chase?"

"Negative. We'd need an excavator."

A few seconds passed. I could just imagine Tyrel scraping a hand over his close cropped hair and cursing in frustration.

"Bravo Lead, can you confirm the town is secure?"

"Affirmative. Last team just reported in."

"Good. I'm calling in air support. Those raiders have to come out somewhere. Maybe the helo can find them. All sierra stations, maintain posture. Report contact, but do not engage. Wait for backup. Bravo Lead, keep everyone on the clock. This might not be over."

"Copy, Sierra Lead. Staying frosty."

I sat up, put my back to a tree, and took a long pull from my canteen.

"Tunnels," I muttered to myself. "Sneaky bastards."

TWO

With dawn came hope and frustration. Hope for the townsfolk, and frustration for the Blackthorns.

The civilian population of Parabellum was now being tended to by an Army support platoon and a few doctors from the Phoenix Initiative. The extra troops and the docs had come in via Chinook a couple of hours ago. A field hospital had been set up and medical supplies flown in. There were a lot of people in need of medical attention.

I did my part to help, but stayed wary while I moved among the townsfolk. Most people were acting grateful now, but this had been a marauder settlement for a long time. The only reason we were being welcomed was because we were less of an oppressive presence than the Storm Road Tribe had been. And not everyone was happy to see us. More than a few of the people in the plaza would be facing criminal charges before the end of the day. Brothel owners exploiting underage children, slave traders, dealers in stolen goods, and others. A few federal law enforcement types were cutting the criminals from the herd, conducting interviews, and gathering evidence.

Gabriel found me and motioned for me to follow him. I put down the box I was carrying and went over.

"Any sign?" I asked as we walked.

He shook his head. "Birds searched all over the damn place. Didn't see anything. Sons of bitches could have come out anywhere. No telling how long those tunnels are or where they lead."

"Tyrel's not happy, I'm guessing."

"If you fed him a horseshoe right now he'd spit nails."

We made our way through the swarm of people in the plaza toward a low-slung restaurant repurposed as a command center. Tyrel stood beyond the open doorway under a single Coleman lantern. Several folding tables sat before him, awash in maps. A tired looking radioman in a Blackthorn uniform sat in a chair nearby, his equipment in front of him. He pecked away at a laptop while Tyrel stared down at the table, hands on his hips, face in shadow. He turned his head as we walked in.

"Tell me you have good news."

Gabe wiped sweat from his forehead. It was stiflingly hot in the room. "I could, but I'd be lying."

A curse. "You were right all along about the tunnels. I should have listened."

"Nothing for it now," Gabriel said. "How many did we get?"

"Of the estimated hundred and sixty three marauders comprising the Storm Road Tribe, we managed to kill thirty-three and apprehend eleven. So forty-four all together."

"And the rest scattered to hell and gone."

I took a step closer to Tyrel. "You forgot an important statistic."

He looked at me. "What?"

"Zero casualties on our side."

A reluctant smile parted the clouds around my old friend's face. "Well, not exactly. Florian sprained his ankle."

"He's a Blackthorn. Give him some whiskey and tell him to walk it off."

A round of laughter. Even the radioman joined in. I smiled at Tyrel and slapped him on the arm. "Relax, brother. File this one under mission accomplished. We'll get the rest of 'em down the line."

9

Tyrel had work to do, and we had nothing further to report, so we left him to it.

"Other than mollifying Tyrel," I said to Gabe, "is there a reason you pulled me away from the plaza?"

"Yes. I'd like to get my trade back, except some Army prick isn't letting any Blackthorns into the warehouse. Thought you might be able to help."

"Let's see."

We approached a large wooden building which, up to that point, I had only seen from a distance. It was bigger than I thought it would be, and taller. And unlike most of the ramshackle buildings in Parabellum, this one looked well-constructed. The wood used to build it had been properly cured, the walls and doors were straight, and the ground it sat on looked to have been carefully leveled prior to construction. By contrast, the drinking hole down the street was comprised of blue tarpaulins, saplings tied together with old rope, and a crude sign out front that said, 'BOOZE'. The bar itself was a wooden plank supported by two rusted steel barrels.

We approached one of the large openings that permitted wagons inside. The barn doors that secured it had been thrown open and I could see soldiers moving around inside. A pair of armed sentries blocked the entrance. We stopped in front of them. One was a specialist, the other a sergeant.

"Can't let you in right now," the senior man said. His nametag read Shaw. He had red hair and freckles and could not have been more Irish if he tried.

"I need to speak with the officer in charge."

"He's busy."

I took a half step closer and pitched my voice low. "You know who I am?"

"No. And I don't care."

"I'm the appointed liaison to the Blackthorns for this mission. Appointed by General Phillip Jacobs, I might add. Personally. So when I tell you I need to speak with the officer in charge, you fucking go get him. Are we clear?"

The sergeant glared, but complied. A minute or so later a big first lieutenant came out and blinked in the sunshine. He was a few inches taller than me and built like a linebacker. Probably played football somewhere before the Outbreak. His gaze settled on me and he stepped closer. His expression was not a happy one.

"What do you want?"

I kept my expression neutral as I reached into a shirt pocket, removed a leather ID case, opened it, and handed it to the lieutenant. He looked at it, paled, and swallowed.

"Sir, this man has a federally authorized recovery claim," I said. "Gabe, could you show the lieutenant your paperwork?"

Gabe dropped his assault pack, withdrew a slim metal tube, uncapped it, and removed a sheaf of papers. He handed the paperwork to the lieutenant.

"There's a manifest and identifying information. I'll personally see to it he doesn't take anything not on the list."

The lieutenant sifted through the papers, eyes scanning. I sincerely doubted he had ever seen a recovery claim before. After a while, he handed the papers back. Gabe rolled them up and put them away.

"We'll need you to get your men out of here, Lieutenant," I said. "I'll let you know when they can come back in."

The lieutenant hesitated. "We're supposed to inventory all this stuff. Central is waiting for a report."

"Yes sir, I understand. But they can wait a little longer." I looked at Sergeant Shaw. "Excuse us."

Shaw looked at the lieutenant. He flicked a hand. "Go on. Move."

Shaw moved. Gabe and I proceeded inside the warehouse. Behind us, the lieutenant snapped off a couple of orders and he and the two sentries started the process of clearing the warehouse.

11

"What the hell was that?" Gabe whispered, eyes alight with amusement.

I gave a small shake of the head. "Later."

THREE

Heinrich,
Outside Parabellum

Heinrich squatted in the darkness, earthen walls pressing in around him, and fumed with rage.

For two months, Parabellum had been his. He had enjoyed good food, ample booze, a steady supply of young girls, and the respect and admiration of his tribe. His wealth had grown, as had his reputation. Raider chieftains from all corners of the wastelands came to Parabellum to trade in his town, and he always took a cut. And now, in one night, everything he had worked for had been stripped away.

Not everything, he thought. *I still have the tribe. Most of it, anyway.*

He keyed his radio. "All stations, this is your chief. Report. Over."

Heinrich listened in the oppressive stillness, fingers pressed to his earpiece. Above him, a receiver took his message and routed it to an above-ground antenna hidden among the thick forest surrounding the settlement. Radio waves propagated from one receiver to another, and responses began pouring in. Most of his men had made it out and were now at the rally points. Some had chosen to stand and fight.

Idiots. Should have run when they had the chance.

Nevertheless, Heinrich was grateful they had stayed behind. Whatever meager resistance they offered would slow the Blackthorns down and increase Heinrich's chances of escape.

"All right, men," he said into his radio. "At this point, everyone who's getting out is out. We lost some people. It happens. Let's try not to lose any more tonight. Officers and squad leaders, get your men topside and blow the tunnels. Call it in when you're done."

Heinrich turned, gave a signal to one of his men, and climbed out of the tunnel. He emerged into the pre-dawn darkness under a thick canopy of trees. It was humid and warm, the smell of rotting vegetation thick in the air. The rest of his men joined him, twenty in all, what remained of his personal retinue. The last man out was Maru, his second in command.

Maru trailed a wire behind him that disappeared into the tunnel opening. He connected its two bare copper ends to a detonator switch, told everyone to stand back, and pressed a button. A distant thump echoed in the darkness, followed by a shuddering of the ground. Seconds later, a great gust of air and dust blew upward from the tunnel, forcing Heinrich and his men to shield their faces. Maru waited a few seconds for the air to clear, then tossed the switch down the hole.

"Let's move," Heinrich ordered. "Got a lot of ground to cover and not much time to do it."

*****

Heinrich had learned about Parabellum's tunnel network from a traitor.

The traitor had worked for the town's former ruler, Necrus Khan, and harbored a vendetta against his boss. Heinrich never asked what Khan had done to the traitor, and the traitor had never volunteered the information. But whatever it was, it compelled him to ferret out the full size and scope of the tunnels and where they could all be accessed from. His only request was that Heinrich use

14

the information to kill Necrus Khan. When he had the maps in hand, Heinrich thanked the traitor by plunging a knife into his heart.

No sense leaving loose ends lying around.

Upon seizing the town, Heinrich's first order of business had been to review Khan's files and journals. He had found that in addition to the tunnels, Khan had also set up secret caches of weapons and supplies in the event he ever had to evacuate. Heinrich knew this was valuable information, and took steps to make sure it never got out by dividing his men into groups and assigning a tunnel and supply cache to each one. Consequently, the men he was with only knew about the tunnel they had used to escape, and the supply cache they were headed toward. The same applied to the men in other groups. This way, if any of his men were captured, there was only so much information they could give up. The other groups would be safe.

Two miles of frustrating travel through dense, dark woodland brought Heinrich and his party close to their cache. Maru had kept them on track using a compass and a map Heinrich had given him from his bug-out pack. Now that they were close, Heinrich ordered his men to split up into pairs and search for the stack of river stones that marked the entrance to the underground chamber where the supplies were hidden. After several minutes, someone gave three short, sharp whistles.

The group converged on the source of the whistles, whispering to each other in the dim blue light of early dawn. The man who had found the cache was busy brushing leaves and dirt from the hatch. He soon had it open, and Heinrich and his retinue climbed down a short ladder to the dirt floor within.

Other than a pale shaft of light through the opening, the cache was utterly dark. Heinrich felt his way along the wall to his left until he reached a support beam. His right hand went up and found the beam where it crossed the ceiling, followed it, and touched an oil lantern.

"Maru, got your knife on you?"

"Just a second," the big Maori said. He drew his fighting dagger, unscrewed the bottom, and removed a thin quiver of matches held together with a small rubber band. Heinrich took the matches and used one to light the lantern, then gave the matches back to Maru.

"Okay. We got light," Heinrich said as he rehung the lantern.

The golden illumination from the lantern dispelled the eerie gloom the men had felt over the past half hour as they had marched away from Parabellum. Heinrich surveyed his surroundings, taking inventory. There was ten days' worth of food for thirty men, as well as weapons, ammunition, and travel kit for all of them. Heinrich's party was only twenty strong, but everything in this room would be going with them. What they didn't use, they could trade. But first, they had to survive the coming day.

"First things first, somebody close that fucking hatch," Heinrich said. "Don't want any infected dropping in on us."

One of his men did so, the creak of rusty hinges loud in the enclosed space. With the hatch closed, it felt as if the room were its own small, sealed world. The sound of wind in branches and the scuttling of small animals in the brush went silent.

"Anybody in here claustrophobic?" Heinrich asked, grinning. His men laughed nervously. "If so, you better get over it. We're stuck here for a while. Anybody remember how long?"

One of his men raised his hand. Heinrich pointed at him.

"Protocol is twenty four hours, sir."

"That's right," Heinrich said. He kept his tone light, like a parent comforting a child. "The Blackthorns probably won't look for us here. It's a big forest out there, and this place is hard to find. They'll send out patrols, but they won't have enough men for a thorough search, so they'll use helicopters. Helicopters have FLIR. Not much use during the day, but great at night. That's why we won't move until tomorrow morning."

"You think the Blackthorns will be gone by then?" a man asked.

"Probably not, but the helicopters will be. They're too valuable to leave on station for long. They'll do a sweep and then head back

16

to wherever they came from. We'll have to be careful, but I'm confident we can slip by any Blackthorns we come across. Any other questions?"

No one spoke.

"All right. Everyone grab a bedroll and let's move this shit to the back of the room. Stack it high enough and we should all have space to bed down."

When the supplies were moved and his men were snoring in their bedrolls, Heinrich lay awake long into the morning. His mind played over the hardships he had faced to become leader of the Storm Road Tribe, to grow their ranks, to build enough wealth to take Parabellum and hold it. And now, after starting with nothing but an axe and his will to survive and fighting his ass off to build a small empire, he was back to sleeping in the dirt. Back to running and stealing and fighting. He clenched his fists and ground his teeth in frustration.

The Blackthorns. Always the fucking Blackthorns, dogging my trail.

He thought it had been bad when a Blackthorn had taken two of his fingers. Now, they had taken far more. And as always, he had run from them. That was how it had been from the beginning. Always running, always hiding, fighting only when he had the advantage of overwhelming numbers.

No more.

The time for running was over. The time for retribution was at hand. Tyrel Jennings and his men believed they could strike with impunity. Believed they could hit whoever they wanted without retaliation. They were about to find out differently. It was time for the Storm Road Tribe to go on the offensive.

It was time to go to Colorado Springs.

FOUR

Caleb,

Parabellum

Gabriel managed to recover fifty-eight barrels of incredibly valuable salt. The weapons, ammunition, and other trade taken by the Storm Road Tribe were nowhere to be found.

"Probably traded away a long time ago," Gabe said as we stood looking at the steel barrels arranged in the town square.

He'd made the statement without preamble, but I knew what he meant. Despite the wealth arrayed in front of him, he had lost nearly a fifth of the net worth he'd earned during his time in Hollow Rock. Losing that kind of trade in a business deal is one thing, but losing it to marauders has a far worse sting.

"Maybe you should have just taken the insurance payout," I said.

Gabe shook his head. "Price of salt doubled since the attack. FTIC only pays out the value at the time of loss. At least this way I come closer to breaking even."

"Went through a hell of a lot to get it back."

"Yep."

18

I sat down on one of the barrels and looked eastward. There was a convoy inbound to haul away Gabe's salt barrels, the Blackthorns, the goods seized from the warehouse—less what the Army troops had pilfered—and the people set to face trial in Colorado Springs.

"What are you going to trade all this for?" I asked.

"Land, horses, and cattle."

I looked at him skeptically. "You starting a ranch?"

"Yep."

"Didn't know you did that kind of work."

"I don't. But I know someone who's willing to do it for a cut of the profits."

From the east, a distant, low rumble of engines added its voice to the morning chorus of birdsong flitting among the trees. The land around us was green, verdant, and alive with the vibrancy of early summer.

"Sounds downright entrepreneurial," I said.

Gabe grunted and sat down next to me. The rumble of approaching vehicles grew steadily louder, the day growing hotter and more humid as the sun neared its zenith.

Shortly before the convoy arrived, Tyrel walked over to us, dropped his rucksack, and sat down heavily on the barrel to my right. There was weariness etched in every line of his face.

"So what's the news?" Gabe asked.

Tyrel took off his headscarf, wrung sweat out of it, and put it back on his head. Between the three of us, we smelled bad enough to knock a buzzard off a pile of shit.

"Town's under martial law until they can hold an election," Tyrel said. "Plan is to turn the place into an Army garrison and kill or capture any marauders who come around looking to trade."

"Gonna be tough to pull off if word gets out," Gabe said.

"Army's got this place sealed up tighter than a nun's ass. No one comes in, no one goes out."

19

"Marauders will find out," I said. "They always do."

"Maybe," Tyrel said. "Doesn't matter much. With all the intel we've got, we can track down damn near every major marauder group west of Colorado. Gonna be a busy summer."

"And profitable," Gabe said.

Tyrel nodded. "That too."

The first vehicle in the convoy reached the main gate and stopped. Army troops manning the massive, crane-like mechanism used to open the gate began urging horses tethered to a rotating wheel into motion. The wheel turned a series of gears that slowly, inexorably parted the large wooden doors to the compound. I had to admire the imagination and expertise that had gone into the contraption. Its components were primitive, but taken in aggregate, it was quite a feat of engineering.

Several more troops positioned throughout the streets signaled the various vehicles where to go and park. One of them, a large HEMTT, stopped close to the town square. A civilian contractor leaned out the passenger window and shouted something to a soldier below. I could not hear the soldier's reply, but the fact he pointed in our direction made the truck's purpose obvious.

"Looks like my ride's here," Gabe said.

"Looks like." I stood up and walked toward a building at the northeast corner of the square. After making sure no one was in earshot, I removed a satellite phone from my vest and called a number programmed into it. After identifying myself and going through security protocol, General Jacobs' voice sounded in the earpiece.

"So how'd we make out?"

"You haven't gotten any reports, sir?" I asked.

"Of course I have. But I want your take on it."

"I'd say we did pretty well. Got forty-four marauders, couple dozen criminal types from the local populace. Everyone else is playing nice for the moment."

"What about the other marauders? I thought there were over a hundred of them."

"Escaped. Turns out Gabriel's theory about a tunnel network was right."

The general cursed softly. "No matter. We'll run them down eventually."

"Yes sir."

"Jennings' report said no casualties. That correct?"

"Blackthorn sprained an ankle. Other than that, it's a win for the home team."

"Very well. Consider your mission complete, Sergeant. Hitch a ride back with the convoy."

"Yes sir."

He hung up.

Gabriel and the two civilian contractors had finished loading the salt barrels into the HEMTT and were locking the rear doors when I got back. I asked Gabe if he was finished, and he said he was.

"Follow me," I said.

A small fleet of Humvees occupied a broad boulevard on the north side of the central plaza. I approached a junior officer standing around trying to look important and showed him my ID.

"I'll be needing one of these vehicles," I said.

The officer hesitated. "We only have enough for the men we brought in."

"There's plenty of room in the trucks." I pointed to several deuce-and-a-half transports on the other side of the plaza.

The officer sighed and handed me back my ID. Twenty minutes later, Gabe and I had a Humvee to ourselves and were trundling out of Parabellum with the rest of the convoy, headed north.

"So," Gabe said as we jostled and bounced over deep ruts and potholes. "What's the deal with that ID you keep flashing?"

I grinned. "You've heard the story of Alexander the Great cutting the Gordian Knot in half, right?"

"Yes."

I patted my shirt pocket. "Does pretty much the same thing. Only instead of rope, it cuts through red tape and bureaucracy."

"Damn. Where do I get one?"

"You'd have to ask General Jacobs. Knowing him, there'd be strings attached."

Gabe's face darkened. "Forget I asked."

We drove an hour in silence before Gabriel spoke again. "It's not the same doing this stuff without Eric."

"No, it isn't."

"You were in the Springs last week, right?"

"Just for a couple of days."

"Any word from him?"

"He's still there."

Gabe scratched his chin and settled back further in his seat.

"Good to hear."

FIVE

Caleb,

Colorado Springs,

Mid-April, Six Weeks Earlier

A runner found me in my room at the bachelor officer quarters (BOQ) at Peterson Army Air Base, formerly Peterson Air Force Base. The facility's name had changed almost two years ago when the Air Force and Marines were disbanded and absorbed into the Army.

I was not an officer yet, although General Jacobs assured me a field commission was in the works, but as a show of good faith he let me room in the same building as the brass. I got some funny looks, and was stopped in the hallway several times by officers demanding to know what I was doing there. A few flashes of the black ID card identifying me as a federal emissary—a detachment of JSOC (Joint Special Operations Command) operators and federal marshals (of which I was the former) answerable only to the president and her designated appointees—quickly put those questions to rest. No one bothered me anymore.

The runner had two envelopes for me from the Federal Refugee Intake Center. Back in the early days, the Intake Center had originally been established to process Outbreak survivors into the Colorado Springs Safe Zone. But now it did much more, one of those functions being to maintain the Missing & Deceased list, or M&D as it was commonly called.

Another function, one which generated revenue to offset the Center's meager federal funding, was to employ a cadre of runners to deliver messages on a fee basis. When I first arrived in the Springs, after traipsing across Missouri and Kansas, I had paid a deposit at the Intake Center and given a clerk a list of names. If any of the people on the list showed up on the M&D, dead or alive, I wanted to be notified. I also paid to have any messages addressed to me from the free community of Hollow Rock delivered in person. I got both on the same day.

The first was an impersonal hand-written message with several spelling errors informing me that Gabriel Garrett, Elizabeth Stone, Sabrina Garrett, and Eric Riordan had arrived safely in Colorado Springs, along with their trade and livestock. They knew I would want to see them, so they gave the name of their hotel and asked if I could call upon them at my earliest convenience. I fully intended to do so.

The second letter was a typed telegram from Hollow Rock. My hands shook as I opened it and unfolded the letter within. It read:

Caleb,

I can't tell you what a relief it was to get your message. Knowing you are alive and safe in the Springs is like a weight off my chest. I was so worried. I'm sorry about what happened to the caravan, and I'm proud of you for helping those prisoners.

I know what you're wondering, so I won't keep you in suspense. The answer is yes. I'll move to Colorado to be with you.

It was unseasonably hot that day. I was standing in my small barracks room with both the window and the door open to allow a cross breeze. I was wearing a pair of athletic shorts and nothing else. Despite the heat, I felt cold and dizzy and had to sit down on my bed and breathe deeply for a minute or two before I could read

24

on. If anyone before that moment had told me relief could be painful, I would have laughed at them. Now I knew better.

The letter continued:

That being said, there are a few logistical concerns which will delay my departure. You see, Eric more or less left me in charge of G&R Transport and Salvage. Great Hawk handles the salvage work, and Johnny Greene is a big help around the store, but there's also the farm co-op, and real estate investments, and rental properties, and tax paperwork, and the philanthropic stuff, and military contracts, and all the other things Eric has his fingers in. I don't think there's a business or a farm in town that isn't in debt to him. And with just the three of us, it's a lot to manage. We're all working sixteen hour days, but we're barely keeping up.

I want to be with you more than anything in the world, but here's the thing: Eric saved my life. He rescued me from the Free Legion, and I owe him for that. It's a debt I can never repay. So I hope you understand when I tell you I can't just pick up and leave. That would just leave Great Hawk and Johnny to run the business, and they can't handle everything on their own. I asked Great Hawk to hire some new people, but he refused. He said that's Eric's job. Problem is, Eric isn't here. And you know as well as I do how productive it is to argue with the Hawk. Might as well shout at a brick wall.

So for the time being, I have to stay here. When Eric gets back and hires some more people to help out, I'll tender my resignation and send word to you. I'm not sure how I'm going to get out there, so I'm hoping you can help me out with that when the time comes.

The thought of starting a new life with you in Colorado is exciting beyond anything I can describe. I love you Caleb. More than I have ever loved anyone. You are my soldier, my heart, my warrior-poet. I will count the days until we can be together again.

Love always,

25

P.S.—Maybe you could talk to Eric the next time you see him? Maybe explain things, kind of smooth the road for me? I would really appreciate it. In fact, I know you will do it so I'll go ahead and say thank you and I love you and tell Eric to get his ass home. His wife worries for him, and his son is growing like an adorable little weed.

I miss you. Be careful.

The telegram fit neatly back into its envelope. Getting Miranda out here would not be a problem. All it would take would be a satellite phone call to Captain Harlow at Fort McCray, and she would be on her way to FOB Tecumseh in Missouri via Chinook within 24 hours. From there, another Chinook could take her to the Wichita Safe Zone with perhaps one or two stops for fuel. The WSZ had its own airstrip with transport planes coming and going regularly. Getting her on a direct flight to Peterson AAB would be no trouble at all. Would it be an abuse of my authority? Yes. Did I care? Not in the least. I lay back on my bed and put the letter on my chest and smiled as a gentle breeze stirred the thin white curtain bordering the window.

*****

Later that evening the sun relented and the weather cooled. I was off duty, so I dressed in civilian clothes, threw a few things in a small backpack, armed myself with a combat knife and a Beretta 9mm in a drop holster, and left the base on foot. Across the street from the main gate there was a line of people clustered around all manner of vehicles clamoring to give me a ride. An orange line painted on the sidewalk was their admonition to stay on their side of the street, a rule enthusiastically enforced by the guards on duty.

I scanned the crowd. There were bicycle taxis, donkeys, mules, horses, small carriages drawn by a variety of livestock, and even a few gas-powered vehicles that looked like the automotive equivalent of Frankenstein's monster, pieced together with whatever parts the operators could scrounge to keep them running. I did not waste time scanning the cars. They were too expensive; the cost of gasoline alone ensured that. The government had gotten a few refineries online, but supplies were still limited. If I'd been in a hurry and had a long way to go, I might have considered renting a car. But I was in no hurry, so I didn't. Instead, I motioned to an old man sitting in a small open-top carriage powered by a healthy looking ox.

"Where you headed?" he asked as I approached.

"Mountain View Hotel. Know where it is?"

"Sure. Climb on up."

"What'll it cost me?"

He told me. I didn't have the trade he wanted, but I did have some spare ammo of various calibers and a few mini-bottles of pre-Outbreak hooch. He said he would take a mini of rum. I told him that was a lot for a ride across town. He agreed and wrote me a receipt with credit for two more rides, redeemable at any time, so long as my destination was inside the safety perimeter surrounding the city.

The old man, like most people in his hardscrabble trade, was outside the gate to the Army base pretty much every day. I had sold my horse a few months ago, so it would not be long before I needed another ride somewhere. I figured it was a fair deal and climbed aboard.

The Mountain View Hotel was posh by post-Outbreak standards. Solar panels and windmills on the roof provided enough electricity to power a few overhead lights in the lobby and no more than one lamp per room, per the sign on the front desk. The hotel had a working ice machine, indoor bathing facilities, a barber on duty from 8:00 am to 6:00 pm, a restaurant in the east wing, and laundry service. Use of these services cost extra, of course, but at least they were available.

I told the pretty receptionist who I was looking for and gave her a room number. She quite surprised me by picking up a phone handset and dialing a number.

Don't see that much anymore.

"Hello, sir, this is the front desk," she said when she got an answer. "A Mr. Caleb Hicks is here to see you. Yes, of course. You're welcome, sir."

She regarded me with wide brown eyes. "Mr. Riordan will be down to see you shortly. Please make yourself at home."

One delicate hand pointed at a few chairs and couches behind me. The lobby was not large, but it looked comfortable. I sat down and realized it had been a long time since I had planted my ass in a padded armchair. It was a feeling I could quickly get re-accustomed to.

Within a minute, I heard feet pounding down the stairs. Eric Riordan appeared at the bottom of the staircase. He was a little shorter than me, longish blonde hair, lean and wiry, little crinkles at the corners of his eyes, deep parenthetical lines around his mouth that emphasized a strong chin and jawline, and a pair of dark blue eyes that stood out in contrast to the sun-darkened skin of his face. He shook my hand with a surprisingly strong grip, smiled broadly, and slapped me on the shoulder.

"Well look what the cat dragged in. How the hell are you?"

"Can't complain. You?"

"I could complain a lot. Last couple of weeks have been pure shit."

"I heard a rumor about that. Some kind of trouble in Dodge City?"

He shook his head. "A story best told over drinks, and lots of them. Short version, stay the hell out of Dodge. No pun intended. Now come on, the girls want to see you."

Elizabeth was as beautiful and graceful as ever, and Sabrina even gave me a hug before she called me an asshole for not

28

coming to see them sooner. I explained I had duties that required my attention.

"Fuck your excuses," she said, demonstrating her usual eloquence. "We were worried about you. You should have sent a goddamn runner or something."

"You're right. I should have. Sorry about that."

A punch on the arm. "Try using a couple of fucking brain cells next time."

"I will so endeavor."

Eric rescued me by grabbing a bottle of moonshine and a bucket of ice. Three ice cubes went into each of four tumblers, along with a generous measure of hooch and a squeeze of freshly cut lemon.

One of the glasses went to Sabrina. Before the Outbreak, I would have been put off by the sight of a girl on the cusp of her fifteenth year drinking hundred-proof booze. But I had seen Sabrina drink enough times to know she could hold her liquor. Besides, in the post-Outbreak world, if you could reach over the counter, you were old enough to drink.

I rattled the ice in my glass and sniffed at the lemon. "Living the high life are we?"

"Hey," Eric said. "In these dark times, you take pleasure where you can find it."

"I'll drink to that."

We all sat down, the girls cross-legged on the room's two beds, and Eric and I in a pair of chairs by the window. I asked where Gabe was, and Elizabeth told me he had taken a job with the Blackthorn Security Company and was attending orientation. I raised an eyebrow at this, but upon reflection, did not find it surprising.

"Expect him back soon?"

"Probably in the next hour or so," Eric said.

I gave a short nod. "So what have the rest of you been up to?"

29

"I took a job with the Department of Justice," Elizabeth said. "Apparently they're hurting for US attorneys. Doesn't pay much, but it keeps me busy."

I sipped my hooch. It wasn't bad. The lemon added a nice flavor. "I heard the attorney general is kind of a prick."

"He is," Elizabeth said. "But he sort of has to be. With the president and the new congress rewriting the Constitution, everything's sort of in limbo right now. We're sticking with the old laws until something else gets passed, and there's a lot of people not too happy about that. And most of them have the word 'representative' or 'senator' in front of their names."

I shook my head. "Politics."

"The economy here is growing," Eric said. "And the politicians are fighting to be first in line to graft the shit out of it. The AG and a few senators who actually give a rat's ass about regular people are trying to keep them from fleecing the public too badly."

"Good luck to 'em," I said.

Elizabeth sipped her moonshine. "Yeah. They're gonna need it."

The conversation went on for another hour or so. I didn't say much. I usually don't. But it was nice to hear my friends' voices again, to catch up on their lives and be in good company with people I trusted.

The warm camaraderie got me thinking about my buddies in my old unit, the First Reconnaissance Expeditionary. Specifically First Platoon, Delta Squad. I wondered how Ethan Thompson, Isaac Cole, Holland, Page, Cormier, and Smith were doing. I thought about Fuller, his sense of humor and wit, and how he used to keep us entertained on long marches and cold nights in the wastelands. He was gone now, but at least he'd died a soldier's death. And then there was Justin Schmidt, who had left us to join the Phoenix Initiative. I wondered how he was doing. I wondered if I would ever see the guys from my old squad again. The ache in my chest when I thought about them surprised me. I had not joined the Army voluntarily, and from the beginning had told myself I was not there to make friends. The plan was to serve my time, keep my head down, and stay alive. But despite my best efforts, friendships happened anyway. And now my brothers-in-arms were in Tennessee, I was here, and I doubted anyone had told them yet that I would not be coming back.

There was a knock at the door. Sabrina yelled to come on in. The door opened and Gabriel Garrett stepped into the room. At six foot five, he had to duck a little not to hit his head as he entered. He noticed me sitting by the window and a rare smile creased his face.

"Hicks. The hell you doin' here?"

I stood up and shook his hand. "Gave Jacobs the slip. Figured I'd stop by and make sure y'all weren't making trouble for yourselves."

The smile left Gabe's face. "Jacobs? General Jacobs?"

"The same."

He was quiet a moment, then said, "We'll talk later."

I gave a single nod. "You cut quite a figure in that uniform."

"Looks good on me, doesn't it?" Gabe said, taking the change of subject in stride. He held his arms out and looked down at the distinctive dark tactical fatigues of the Blackthorn Security Company.

"Don't encourage him," Eric said, pouring Gabe a drink. "Guy's been strutting around like a damn peacock all week."

"I think he looks very handsome." Elizabeth stood up and gave Gabe a peck on the cheek. "You have to admit, it's very stylish."

"So were the uniforms for the SS," Eric said.

I glanced between Eric and Gabe, sensing tension there. Gabe did not seem perturbed.

"Eric doesn't like that I'm a security contractor again."

"Security contractor." Eric's voice dripped with sarcasm as he handed Gabe his drink. "Pretty phrase, that. But let's face the facts, Gabe. You're a mercenary. Again. How'd that work out for you last time?"

"Apples and oranges, Eric. The Blackthorns aren't Aegis. They don't do that kind of work."

"Not yet."

Gabe frowned at him. "This coming from the guy looking to start his own security outfit."

"Yes, so I can provide protection to caravans at prices that don't cut their profits down to zero. Unlike your employer."

"We charge a lot because we're the best."

"Sure you are. That's why Spike and all his people are dead and the trade you brought from Hollow Rock is currently in the hands of a bunch of marauders. Because the Blackthorns are so damned good. There were two Blackthorns in that caravan, if you recall. You warned both of them about the ambush, and neither did a damn thing about it."

"Because Spike told them not to." Gabe's voice was growing heated. "He was the client. His contract insisted he be in charge. They couldn't override his orders. And even if they'd tried, Spike's people wouldn't have listened. The only person they took orders from was Spike. And besides that, you saw how many raiders were in that ambush. They would have taken down a convoy of Marines, much less a bunch of civilians."

"Gabe, you just made my case for me," Eric said. "Is that how you want to end up? Dead because some dumbshit caravan leader was too stupid to listen to the experts?"

"In case you forgot, Eric, the only reason any of us survived that ambush is because of me. And as I recall, you were one of the people telling me I was being paranoid, that there was nothing to worry about. So no, I don't think I'm going to end up dead because of someone like Spike not listening to my advice. I'll quit the company before I let that happen."

Eric sat back down. He seemed to have lost his enthusiasm for the argument. I had the feeling this was not the first time the two old friends had quarreled over the subject.

"Don't let Hadrian Flint or Tyrel Jennings hear you say that," Eric said. "They'll throw you out on your ass."

The mention of Tyrel's name sent a jolt through my stomach. I had known him since I was a little boy. He was a good friend of my father's, the two of them having worked together back in my old life in Houston. Tyrel had had almost as much of a hand in raising me as my father, along with Mike Holden and Blake Smith.

My father and Blake were dead now, both killed in an attack by Army deserters, and Mike was in Oregon waging a guerilla war against the Republic of California. But Tyrel was right here in Colorado Springs, one of two people left from my old life. I knew I should go and see him, but I was hesitant. Our last meeting had not been under happy circumstances. I had just faced trial for felony assault and had been sentenced to four years in the Army. Tyrel visited me in jail where I was still recovering from the effects of severe alcohol withdrawal. Over two years had passed since then, and I had made no effort to contact Tyrel. I could have written a letter or sent a telegram, but was too ashamed of myself to do so. Whether or not I would receive a warm reception from my old friend was a question I wasn't sure I was ready to explore.

"Is anybody else hungry?" Sabrina said. Eric and Gabe stopped glowering at each other and turned toward her.

"I could eat," I said.

"How about we all head down to the hotel restaurant?" Elizabeth suggested. The palpable intensity in the room dissipated.

"Sure," Gabe said. "Sounds good."

Sabrina was the first one out the door.

SIX

An hour later, after dinner, dessert, and a round of exorbitantly expensive instant coffee that I would not have fed to a pig before the Outbreak, Sabrina and Elizabeth announced they were retiring to the movie theater.

"They have a movie theater here?" I asked.

"Well, it's more like a conference room with a wall projector connected to a DVD player," Elizabeth said.

"What's playing tonight?"

"*The Help.*"

"Yeah, I think I'll have to pass on that one."

Elizabeth turned to her husband. "What about you?"

Gabe held out a hand. "Hi. Gabriel Garrett. Have you met me?"

A smile. "All right, tough guy. Don't stay up too late. And take it easy on the drinks. You have to work tomorrow."

Gabe looked at me. "See what happens when you put a ring on their finger? They think they own you."

"As I recall," Elizabeth said as she stood up, "*you* proposed to *me.*"

"I suppose I did. Enjoy your movie."

"I will. Have fun, boys."

Sabrina stopped to kiss her father on the temple. "Love you, Dad. See you later."

Gabe's face softened so much he looked like a different person. "Love you too, sweetheart."

I grinned at him. When Sabrina was out of earshot, I said, "Dad? Sweetheart?"

"You got a problem with it?"

"Nope. Just never seen that side of you before."

"Contrary to popular belief," Eric said, "Gabe is not heartless. Merciless in his anger and ruthless in his rage, yes. But in his better moments, not completely incapable of basic human compassion."

Gabe raised an eyebrow. "Did you just give me a compliment?"

"Sort of. It was a bit underhanded, and I used a lot of big words to make it sound better."

"I guess the Ivy League education wasn't worthless after all."

"Touché."

"When you two old hens are done pecking at each other," I said, "I got something I want to talk to you about."

Gabe rolled his eyes. "Ah, Christ. Here it comes. The hell does Jacobs want this time?"

We were interrupted by our waiter stopping by to see if we needed anything else. I asked if they had any pre-Outbreak hooch. He apologized and said they had run out two weeks ago, and there had been none on the auction markets since then. From this, I gathered that the salvage trade around the Springs was getting to be just as sparse as back in Hollow Rock.

"I assume you have moonshine?" I asked.

"Yes sir. Very good quality."

"Anything I might have heard of?"

"Out top shelf is Stall's Reserve, out of Tennessee. Have you heard of it?"

The three of us looked at each other and burst out laughing.

"You mean as in Mike Stall?" Eric asked. "The distiller?"

"Yes sir." The waiter looked surprised. "You're familiar, I assume?"

"Familiar?" Eric said. "Hell, the bastard took me for a box of .308 rounds last time we played Texas hold 'em."

Gabe pointed a finger. "Don't forget about the Henry rifle he won from you."

"Oh, believe me," Eric said. "I haven't."

The waiter's smile had gone rigid. The restaurant was busy and he had other tables to attend. "Would you like me to put in a drink order?"

"Yes," I said. "Put it on my room tab, please."

"Of course. And your dinner?"

"That too."

"For the entire party?"

"Yep."

"I'll be back shortly with your drinks, then."

We watched the waiter walk away. Gabe leaned back in his chair and laced his fingers across his chest. "Feeling generous?"

"I have an expense account."

"The bean counters are going to be pissed at you."

"When the bean counters get off their asses and spend some time in the field, I might consider giving a shit what they think. Until then, they can lick the sweat off my balls."

"Well stated," Eric said.

Gabe smiled a little, but his gaze remained steady. "So you're working for Jacobs now."

"He's the guy I answer to, yes."

"I heard things are changing over at Cheyenne Mountain. Some higher-ups being shifted around."

36

I regarded Gabe closely for a second and reminded myself who I was talking to. His Kentucky accent and surly, blue-collar attitude were only a front. Beneath that veneer was one of the most brilliant minds on the face of the earth. He missed little and forgot nothing. His ability to analyze and glean conclusions from extremely small subsets of data was unmatched by anyone I had ever met. I would gain nothing by lying to him, or trying to conceal information. He'd figure out whatever it was regardless. So I opted for the direct approach.

"Yes, some things have changed."

"Haven't heard any announcements."

"They're in the pipeline. The president and joint chiefs are still working things out." I lowered my voice. "Just to get it out in the open, anything we say from here on out is classified. If you talk, I'll deny we had this conversation."

Gabe nodded impatiently. "Duly noted. Let's try not to spend all night stating the obvious."

Our drinks arrived. I took a pull from mine as soon as the waiter left. "Tell me what you heard, and I'll tell you what I know."

"Why?"

"You know why."

"And me?" Eric asked.

I nodded. "Same."

Eric tossed back his drink, put down his glass, and stood up. "Whatever it is, the answer is no. I've got some business deals to work out, and then I'm going home."

I held up a hand. "Eric, please-"

"No," He said sharply. "I've had it with this shit. I'm not a goddamn soldier, or a spook, or an operator, or whatever the hell you people call yourselves these days. I'm a business man with a wife and son. I took a few jobs for the government out of self-interest, not patriotism. I wanted to protect my home and the people I love. That's it. The Alliance is gone, and Hollow Rock is as safe as it's going to get. I've done my part and then some. From

37

here on out, whoever the hell needs to be killed, it's someone else's problem. I'm out of it."

The dark blue eyes were not angry, but they were intense. I knew it would be pointless to argue.

"Okay," I said. "I'll let Jacobs know you're out."

Eric gave a short nod and left without another word. I looked at Gabe.

"I notice you're still here."

"That I am," he said.

I let out a long breath and drank some more moonshine. "So what have you heard?"

"I heard ASOC is going away and the president is reviving Joint Special Operations Command."

I nodded. "Yep."

"And General Jacobs is going to be heading it up, only with two stars on his insignia instead of one."

"Also true."

"And they need operators."

"Obviously."

"And they picked you."

"Not 'they'. General Jacobs, personally. Had to overcome some objections to do it."

"Let me guess. You're not SF, SEALs, MARSOC, or Delta, so they didn't think you had the goods."

"Pretty much."

"And Jacobs convinced them otherwise."

"Convinced is probably too strong a word. More like they indulged him. If it doesn't work out I'll be dead, and they can give Jacobs the old told-you-so dance."

Gabe tapped his finger on the rim of his glass. "I guess that explains the black ID card."

"Yes."

"What's your title?"

"Officially, I'm a federal emissary."

"Which is just fancy speak for JSOC operator."

"Not entirely. There's a civilian equivalent. Law enforcement types. You see, with all the survivor communities so spread out, jurisdiction has become a real problem. What's left of the FBI, ATF, all those guys, it's not enough. Too many laws, too many restrictions, too much getting in the way of them doing their jobs. And you've seen what it's like for local cops."

"Not good," Gabe said.

"Not good at all. So the president appointed someone, and before you ask I don't know who, to be overall in charge of national law enforcement. Someone above even the attorney general. Not just the feds, but all of it, all the way down to the local level. The civilian emissaries will officially be federal marshals. But much like JSOC operators, they'll pretty much have carte blanche to do whatever it takes to restore law and order."

Gabe snorted. "Gee, I can't see that going wrong at all."

"I didn't say I thought it was a good idea."

"No. You didn't. Sorry, I've been in a mood lately."

"You okay?"

"Yeah. Just getting used to things, you know? New city, new job…"

"New wife, new daughter."

A tired smile. "That too."

"I was married once." The pronouncement startled me. I had not intended to broach the subject; it just came out on its own.

The serrated sharpness of Gabe's eyes lessened. "I didn't know that."

"I never said anything about it. Her name was Sophia. She was seven months pregnant when she died. A little girl. I was out on a salvage run with Tyrel Jennings when it happened. I had the bodies cremated, and me and some guys on my salvage team and some folks from our neighborhood had a memorial service. We were living in the refugee district back then. It wasn't so bad in those days."

"What did you do afterward?"

"You know, I don't really remember much of it. I think mostly I tried to drink myself to death."

"Jesus, Caleb."

"You've seen my file, right?"

Gabe furrowed his brow. "Yeah. Why?"

"You know how I ended up in the Army?"

"Yes."

I finished my drink. "Well, now you know why."

Neither of us spoke for a while. I looked around the restaurant. It had been built after the Outbreak, everything constructed of wood and scavenged materials. The tables and chairs all matched, probably built by the same carpenter. The bar was stained and polished, the walls dark and welcoming in an earthy sort of way. There was dim electrical lighting, and I heard the low hum of a generator from somewhere outside the building. The waiter came by and I ordered another drink. Gabe declined.

"So anyway," I said finally. "I got a mission for you if you're interested."

"I already have a job. A good one. I'm not hurting for trade."

"I know. And General Jacobs knows that too. He's offering a quid pro quo arrangement."

Gabe went still. "Please elaborate."

"The trade you lost to the Storm Road Tribe. He's offering to help you get it back."

The big man laughed quietly. "Assuming it hasn't been spent already. Damn raiders have had it for weeks. Who knows how much is left?"

40

"Quite a lot, according to the people Jacobs has watching the raiders who took it."

The smile left his face. "The GPS trackers. The ones I planted on their wagons."

"Exactly."

"Where are they?"

"Marauder settlement down in Arkansas. Locals call the place Parabellum. The Storm Road Tribe took it over not long after the rescue mission."

Gabe looked away and drummed his fingers on the table. "Sons of bitches. So it's all in one place?"

"What's left of it, yes. They spent some of it."

"How much?"

"Hard to say. The operators watching the place counted more than fifty steel barrels in a warehouse matching the description of the ones on your recovery claim."

"Fifty." Gabe muttered. "A lot less than what I left with, but still…"

"It ain't chicken feed."

"No, it certainly is not." He looked up at me. "So what's the catch?"

I told him as much as I knew. He listened quietly, gaze wandering around the room. I knew Gabe listened with his ears and not his eyes, and I knew he wouldn't miss a single word. When I was done, he did not speak for a while.

Finally he said, "Tell Jacobs I want to talk face to face. And whatever we agree on, *if* we agree on anything, will need to be in writing."

"I'll relay the message."

41

SEVEN

The Mountain View Hotel had a rooftop patio with a bar and a stage for live music. Being a weeknight, the live music was a young woman with a violin playing slow, mournful instrumentals of old folk songs. Eric was sitting alone at the bar nursing clear liquor in a glass with two small ice cubes. I took a seat next to him.

"No," he said.

"No what?"

"You know exactly what I mean."

"The mission? I'm not here to talk about that."

He turned to me and blinked. He'd had two drinks after dinner, and I was guessing he was well past his third. Probably past his fifth or sixth.

"Well, what do you want?" he asked.

"If you're not sober enough for a serious conversation, I can wait until tomorrow."

He put down his drink. "I wouldn't want to operate a motor vehicle at the moment, but if I stop now I'll be fine."

"So you'll remember the conversation?"

"Yes. What's on your mind?"

The bartender came over and asked what I wanted. I asked if he had anything other than liquor.

"Yeah. Beer," he said.

"I'll have a beer then."

He poured one from a white oak barrel and set it down in front of me. I tried it. It wasn't bad.

"It's about Miranda," I said.

Eric's face grew concerned. "What about her? She okay? You get a message or something?"

"She's fine." I held up a mollifying hand. "But yes, I got a message from her today."

"What about?"

I took a moment to organize my thoughts before responding. "The job General Jacobs has me doing is a permanent assignment. I'll be stationed in the Springs for the rest of my time in the Army."

Eric is a lot of things, but dumb is not one of them. Even slightly inebriated, he quickly put the equation together. One of his elbows rested itself on the bar and he put his forehead in his palm.

"So where does that leave you two?"

"She wants to move here."

Eric folded his arms and laid his head down on them. He stayed that way for a solid minute. The bartender came over with a pinched expression on his face. I waved him off. He did not look happy, but he let us be for the moment.

"You still with me Eric?"

"Yes." His voice was muffled, but steady.

"You gonna say something?"

He sat up and stared at the line of sharp mountains to the west. The sun had just sank behind the peaks, casting the distant range in hues of fiery orange and neon pink. The sky darkened as it stretched away from the sunset, fading from cornflower blue to dark cobalt. Nightfall was not far away.

"What is there to say? She's in love with you. Any idiot can see that. She wants to be with you. I want her to be happy. I'm guessing we both have that sentiment in common."

"Eric, it's not that simple and you know it."

He picked up his drink and sipped it delicately. "You see, that's where you're wrong. It is *exactly* that simple."

"You saved her life. More importantly, you gave her back her freedom. You helped her through the kind of trauma most people don't survive. She cares about you. She feels like she owes you."

"She doesn't owe me anything."

"Good luck convincing her of that."

Eric turned in his stool so he could face me. "If you're worried I'm going to get upset, don't be. Miranda is a free woman. She can do whatever she wants. I'm not going to pretend I'll be happy to see her go. In fact, I don't know what the hell I'm going to do without her. She pretty much runs my business for me."

"That's what's got her concerned. She doesn't want to leave you in the lurch."

"When is she leaving?"

"Not until you get back and hire some more people."

Eric pondered that. "She'll need to train them. Might take a few weeks."

"Tell her to take her time. There's no rush. I'm going to be busy the next few months anyway."

"Your mission?"

"Missions. Plural."

"Just out of curiosity, who are you going after?"

"I can tell you the first mission is for Gabe. We're going after the Storm Road Tribe."

"No shit?"

"No shit. We've got a fix on them. They're holed up in some shithole marauder settlement in Arkansas. There's a pretty good chance we'll be able to recover some of the trade Gabriel lost."

Eric laughed. "I bet Gabe about shit his dick when you told him that."

"He expressed a keen interest."

"And what does he have to do in return?"

"The other mission."

"Which is?"

"If you're not in on it, I can't tell you."

"No dice, Caleb. The answer is still no."

"Then I can't talk to you about it."

Eric stifled a yawn and turned back toward the bar. His hand was steady as he picked up his drink.

"I guess I'll just have to live with that."

EIGHT

The headquarters of the Blackthorn Security Company was a large facility.

When the company was founded, they had set up shop in a couple of abandoned hotels near the airport. Since then, as they had grown in size and wealth, the original headquarters was insufficient to their needs. Consequently, they had purchased the US Olympic Training Center from the federal government. It had survived the Outbreak mostly intact, and what damage was done had been repaired by the government back when they were using it as a refugee shelter.

After the refugee district had been built and the refugee population relocated, the Center had sat unused for over two years. The Blackthorns got a pretty good deal on the purchase; I think the government was just glad to get the place off the books. BSC was still in the process of relocating their operations and personnel to the new facility, but the main office was up and running in a building that had once been a communications and marketing center for the University of Colorado Health.

A tall chain link fence topped with concertina wire had been erected around the training center grounds, complete with a rolling gate manned by armed guards. There were two watchtowers behind the main gate, both with snipers and machine guns, and other towers spaced along the fence every few hundred feet. Beyond the gate, I saw a small fleet of vehicles—everything from Humvees to armored personnel carriers—sitting in a sizable parking lot toward the northwest corner of the perimeter. The vehicles were painted charcoal black and bore the BSC logo. I decided my previous perception of BSC's success had been a gross underestimation.

The guards stopped me at the gate and asked me for ID. I handed them my black card. They recognized what it was, and what it meant, and handed it back to me.

"What can we do for you, sir?" The guard in charge asked. He looked to be in his late thirties, darkly tanned face, and a hardened look about him that suggested he was no stranger to violence. However, he knew BSC was still subject to federal oversight, and if I wanted to come in, he would be ill advised to stop me. Not that he couldn't if he wanted to, but if I went back and reported that I had been refused access to the facility, BSC's management would be getting a very angry visit from someone with the authority to put them out of business. So for now, they were being polite.

"I'm here to see Tyrel Jennings," I said.

The guards looked at each other. "Sir, he's usually pretty busy. Do you have an appointment?"

"No. But trust me, he'll want to see me."

The guards looked uncertain. I gave them a reassuring smile. "Look, fellas, I'm not trying to get anyone fired here. I'll have a seat on that bench over there. Talk to whoever you need to, and when you've gotten clearance, let me know. Fair enough?"

The lead guard looked relieved. "Sounds good. Be with you shortly."

He walked toward a small shack with a radio antenna sticking up from the roof. I saw him pick up a handset and speak into it. There was a wooden bench on the lawn just in front of the fence line under a maple tree. Judging by how uncomfortable it was when I sat down on it, I guessed it was more for decoration than actual use. A minute or two later, the head guard shouted for me and motioned me over. Someone was already rolling the gate open.

"Do you know where to go, sir?" the guard asked.

"The old UC Health building, right?"

He looked surprised. "Yes sir. Just check in at reception and they'll help you from there."

"Thank you."

"Thanks for being civil with us. Not everybody with a black card is."

I nodded once and walked through the gate.

It was not a long walk to the BSC corporate office, but I found myself approaching slowly. I normally don't suffer much in the way of anxiety, even in combat. Being even-keeled is kind of my thing; I was known for it in the First Recon. Cole used to jokingly call me Iceman, and it caught on after a while. But I didn't feel like an iceman walking toward Tyrel's office. I felt like a puddle of useless goo. Finally I stopped and stared at the front entrance. Something my father once said to me popped into my head:

Son, when you've got a job to do, best just to get it done. Even if it scares you. Most of the time, you'll find the fear of a thing is worse than the thing itself.

I took a deep breath, told myself to stop being such a candy-ass, stood up straight, and walked into the building.

The receptionist was no surprise. Tyrel liked women. The prettier, the better. I would not have gone so far as to call him a chauvinist, but he definitely had some antiquated notions regarding the female of the species. I approached the front desk and smiled politely.

"Hello. I'm Sergeant Caleb Hicks here to see Mr. Jennings."

The receptionist smiled back. If I weren't so in love with Miranda, I may have been dazzled. "Yes sir, he's expecting you. Down this hall, all the way at the end. His name is on the door."

"Thank you."

I walked down the hall and realized my skin was cool. I had broken a light sweat on the walk to BSC headquarters, and now it seemed to be evaporating. There was a moment of confusion, and then it dawned on me what I was feeling was air conditioning. I stopped under a roof vent and closed my eyes. A sigh escaped me.

General Jacob's office had a small air conditioner in the window, but he never turned it up very high. Here, I was in the presence of central air conditioning set at what I guessed was about seventy-two degrees. What luxury. I had forgotten how good it felt.

After a few seconds, I remembered why I was there and proceeded to the door at the end of the hallway. It was made of dark, heavy wood with shiny brass letters on a wooden plaque attached to the door with screws. The plaque read:

Tyrel Jennings

Chairman and CEO

I raised a hand to knock, but the door opened before I could. Tyrel stood in the doorway.

I froze.

His face was as hard and angular as I remembered. He was shorter than me, medium build, but obviously very fit. He had shaved his beard and his hair was cropped close to his head. There was a bit more gray lining his temples than there had been the last time I saw him. At a glance, he seemed unremarkable until you looked at his eyes. Black as obsidian, and about as merciful as a tiger shark. I'd seen armed soldiers tremble under his glare. He favored me with a blank look for a few seconds, then his face split into a smile and he opened the door wide.

"Get your ass in here, kid. Let me take a look at you."

I found myself smiling back and did as he asked. Tyrel shut the door, stepped in front of me, and looked me up and down.

"You look a hell of a lot better than the last time I saw you. You've filled out, put on some muscle."

"About thirty pounds."

"Jesus, kid. You must have been in bad shape back when they locked you up. How long ago was it, two years? Three?"

"A little over two."

"Damn. I tell you, when you get to be my age, the years pass like seasons and the months pass like weeks. A day takes about twenty minutes. The longer you live, the worse it gets. Come on in and have a seat."

I sat down in a padded leather chair lined with little brass studs. The carpet in the room was dark green, there was a wet bar on one wall, a leather sofa and two armchairs complete with a coffee table on the other. The walls themselves were paneled in hardwoods stained almost black, and several paintings had been hung around the room. I did a double take at the one on the wall to my left above the sofa.

"Is that an original Monet?" I asked.

A grin. "I've always admired his work."

"Jesus."

"Don't think he was a painter. So what brings you here, kiddo?"

I shrugged. "I'm not here on official business. I just…"

"You wanted to see me."

"Yeah."

Tyrel tilted his head. "You say it like you've done something wrong."

"It's been over two years, Tyrel. I haven't written, or sent a telegram, or anything."

"And?"

"And, well, I feel bad about it."

"And you thought I was going to be upset."

I shifted in my chair. "I was a little worried, yes."

Tyrel leaned back and laughed loudly. His eyes crinkled up and he had to grab the arms of his chair to keep from tipping over. When he had control of himself again, he wiped his eyes and said, "How long you been in the Springs, boy?"

"Um…about a week or so."

"I bet you been stewing over this the whole time, haven't you?"

I felt myself flush. "Pretty much."

Another laugh. "You ought to see yourself. Tall as a tree, broad-shouldered, scars on your face, and eyes like a stone-cold killer. Killed two men before you were eighteen, and God only knows how many since then. I've seen you drop ghouls at a hundred yards with nothing but iron sights, and yet here you sit, twisting your hands together and shuffling your feet like I just caught you stealing from the cookie jar."

I smiled at my old friend and felt the embarrassment evaporate. "Hey, I did not shuffle my feet."

Tyrel stood up and came around the desk, arms open. "Come here, you idiot."

*****

The Robber Baron was the first honest-to-God steakhouse I had seen since the Outbreak. A revival in the beef industry over the last two years had seen the cattle population, which were nearly wiped out during the Outbreak, make a dramatic recovery. Beef was still in short supply, and was highly expensive, but for someone like Tyrel, price was not an issue.

I cut into a piece of filet mignon that cost as much as two whole goats and tried not to moan. The cow it came from had been grass fed, and the steak was seasoned and cooked to perfection.

"My God," I said. "All I need is a good lay and I can die happy."

"Can't help you there," Tyrel said. "Prostitution is illegal in town. But go outside the wall and you can get whatever you want."

I made a face. Surrounding Colorado Springs was a collection of slums the rival of the poorest places anywhere in the world. Over the years, real estate prices and rents in the city proper had risen steadily and driven the poorest people outside the wall. At first, according to those who'd witnessed the process, it had not been that bad. People built simple houses, planted gardens, raised chickens, that sort of thing. The Army did a good job of keeping the undead away, so life had not been bad.

51

But as time went on, and more and more people were forced to live outside the wall, things quickly deteriorated. When it got bad enough, the government stepped in and forced the people who, up to that point, had been living in the shadow of the wall, to pick up stakes and move half a mile from the city. A fence had been built and laws passed to keep the slums away from the Springs. As a result, a barren no-mans-land of empty ground now stood between the crippling poverty of the Slummers, as they were called, and the city dwellers.

"No thanks," I said.

"I was just kidding, Caleb. You tried to go there, I'd knock you over the head and lock you up somewhere. Only thing you'd find in the slums is a knife in the back."

"Is it really that bad?"

"Yes, it is. People only go there in numbers, and armed. Otherwise, you're a victim. And don't even think about trying to blend in. You'd stand out like a sore thumb."

"How so?"

"You don't look starved, or dirty, or riddled with disease. You stand up too straight, your clothes aren't rags, and you look like you eat at least once a day. Slummers would mark you in a heartbeat. Probably fight over who got to kill you first."

I shook my head sadly. "Does the government try to help at all?"

"They used to. But they got tired of sending aid workers in only to have them disappear along with whatever food or medicine they brought with them. President tried sending in the Army as escort, but that only caused riots and even more bloodshed. Finally they gave up."

"So they're just left there to starve and die."

"It's not really like that. Slummers can come and go in and out of the city as they please. They can look for work here, buy property here, do what any other citizen is allowed to do. Cops keep a close eye on them, but there are strict non-discrimination laws in place. On top of that, there's still plenty of good land available in Kansas. Anyone can apply for a land grant, and most applications get approved. And if they don't like Kansas, there's nothing stopping them from getting together and building homesteads elsewhere, they just have to protect themselves from infected and marauders."

"You make it sound so easy."

"I know it's not. And I know it's a bad situation all around. But what can anyone do? The Slummers know their options. The reason the live where they live is they either lack the knowledge to run a homestead, or can't get enough people together to make it work. Either that or they can't find work in town. And then there's the folks who just plain don't want to do for themselves. That's why they run whorehouses and sell cheap booze and buy opium from the drug runners out of Mississippi and Alabama. Opium addiction is getting to be a big damn problem around here."

"I didn't know that."

"Well, now you do. And if you find yourself in the refugee district, watch your back. Half the junkies in town live there. Fuckers will kill you for your boots."

"You know, Tyrel, whatever problems the Slummers have, those problems are going to make their way into the city. It's only a matter of time."

"I know. It's already started. You can't have two populations living this close together without making trouble for each other. Especially with all the animosity going around. There's some powerful folks lobbying Congress and the Senate to pass laws making it so only citizens with a registered address can be issued IDs."

"What would that accomplish?"

"Be a way to keep the Slummers out."

I snorted. "What the hell good would that do? If the Slummers want to get in, they'll find a way in. Law be damned."

"You know that, and I know that, but the lobbyists don't. And even if they do, they don't care. If it was up to them, they'd have the Army carpet bomb the slums and be done with it."

"That's the most disturbing thing I've heard in a long time. And that's saying something."

"I'm with you on that one, son. Look, I know all about being poor. I'm the youngest of four kids. My family lived in a tarpaper shack in western North Carolina until I was eleven. One day my father packed his few belongings and told us he was going down to Asheville to look for work, and if he couldn't find anything there, he'd head down to Charlotte. He was gone eight months. We thought he wasn't coming back. If not for welfare and food stamps, we'd have starved to death. Momma took to drinking, and I'll give you one guess how she got the money to buy her booze."

"Dear God. I'm sorry, Tyrel. I didn't know that."

He waved a hand. "Probably 'cause I never told you. Anyway, dad showed up one Saturday morning in a rental car. He was wearing new clothes, and he looked healthier than I'd ever seen him. He told us he'd found a good job and rented a place where we could all live down in Asheville. I looked at my mother, and I swear to God she looked like she'd seen a ghost. My oldest brother, who was seventeen at the time, pulled all us kids aside and told us if we didn't keep our damn mouths shut about what momma had been up to he'd peel our hides with a dull knife. And we believed him. So we all drove down and moved into a double-wide trailer on the outskirts of Asheville. I thought it was paradise. I mean, the place had a furnace. It was winter in the Appalachians. I was so used to freezing, I'd forgotten what it felt like to be warm."

"Tyrel…"

He raised a palm. "I know what you're gonna say, and I appreciate it. But you got to understand, this was all a long time ago. I've put it in perspective and moved on. Now do you mind if I finish the story?"

"Sorry. Go ahead."

"Things were all right for a while. But it didn't last. Momma wouldn't let Dad put his hands on her. At first he thought she was mad at him for being gone so long. He apologized about a thousand times until she couldn't take it anymore. Conscience got the best of her. She told him what she'd done. Dad got real quiet and told her she needed to go see a doctor. So they did. Turned out she had syphilis. It was still in the early stages, so they were able to clean it up with antibiotics. Dad had the rest of us tested too. He told Mom it was to make sure she hadn't passed it on to us by accident. But I don't think that was the truth. I think he was worried she'd been turning us out. She hadn't been, so we all tested clean. My folks stayed together after that and eventually patched things up. But it was never quite the same between them."

Tyrel went silent, eyes far away. I let him be for a while and quietly ate my steak. My appetite was mostly gone by then, but I didn't want to waste Tyrel's money. His story played through my mind a few times until I realized he'd left out a vital detail. At first I didn't want to ask, but curiosity finally got the best of me.

"Mind if I ask you something?"

The dark black eyes focused on me. "Shoot."

"What did your father do while he was gone those eight months?"

"Guess I forgot to mention that, huh? Turns out he found work in Asheville right away. Problem was, the job was washing dishes in a diner. Couldn't raise a family of six on five bucks an hour, even back then. So he got a second job loading sodas onto trucks at a distribution center. While he was doing all this, he made a plan. When he had enough money, he took a bus down to Charlotte, rented a cheap apartment, and put himself through truck driving school. Couple of months later he had a class A license and headed back to Asheville. Got a job with a carrier there. Guy that owned the restaurant he used to work for let him sleep on a cot in a storage shed so he could save money. Couple of months after that, he finally had enough to rent the double-wide. Then he came up and got us."

My steak was mostly gone. The potatoes were untouched, but I figured I'd done enough. Tyrel's plate looked to have gone cold. He realized it and tucked into his meal.

"Well, enough of that depressing shit," he said. "What's new with you?"

NINE

"So let me make sure I got this straight," Tyrel said half an hour later. We had left the restaurant and were walking through the wealthiest district in the city. "The ROC has moved every American they could get their hands on into internment camps. They're holding them hostage so the Union doesn't attack."

"Yes," I said.

"Mike Holden is leading the Resistance. The government is helping him by providing supplies and special operations support."

"Correct."

"And the president and joint chiefs have cooked up a plan to bring down the ROC, but you don't know what it is."

"Not yet."

"Of course not. So General Jacobs wants you to go out there as a military liaison for JSOC, and he want's Gabriel to go with you."

"That's right."

"He wanted this fella Eric Riordan too. But he ain't having it."

"Unfortunately."

Tyrel looked at me. "What's so great about this Riordan guy? He's just a civilian, right?"

"He never served in the military, but Gabriel and a few other very qualified folks trained him and turned him into a certifiable badass. He's saved my life a few times, and I've done the same for him. We've been on missions together."

"What kinds of missions?"

"I'll give you an example. You may have noticed the Midwest Alliance is conspicuously absent from the list of our nations enemies lately."

"I have so noticed. Heard there was some kind of coup up in Illinois. All the leaders were killed, and the Alliance fell apart."

"That's the official story."

Tyrel stared straight ahead. "Which is utter bullshit."

"I can neither confirm nor deny."

"You were there. There weren't no damn coup, those leaders were assassinated. Who was with you?"

I casually looked around and kept my voice low. "Gabriel, Eric Riordan, an ex-SEAL contractor, and a bunch of Green Berets."

"Jacobs sent a civilian with you?"

"Eric is no ordinary civilian. He's as good as they come."

"As good as you?"

"Put it this way. I wouldn't want to be downrange of him."

We were quiet for a while as we walked. Tyrel was deep in thought, and I did not want to interrupt him.

I observed the city around me and was struck by how much this part of town had changed. It was a far cry from the bombed out ruin it had been when I first arrived here in the early days after the Outbreak. Where once was rubble and ashes and artillery craters now stood newly constructed buildings, oil-fueled street lamps, and warm lights shining through the windows of successful establishments and upper class homes. The potholes and craters had been repaired, there was a strong police presence, and people walked the streets unafraid. Couples strolled hand in hand, children ran around getting underfoot, groups of laughing, boisterous men and women flitted from one tavern to the next in a constant swirl of hormones and flirtation. I liked the atmosphere of the place. It felt like civilization.

We kept walking away from the restaurant towards a livery nearby. Tyrel's personal carriage was there. Unlike his office, there was nothing ornate about it. The carriage was well-constructed, comfortable to ride in, and pulled by a sturdy draft horse. It was not in any way ostentatious. From what I had gathered about Tyrel so far, with the exception of his training facilities, he did not believe in flashy displays of his newfound wealth. I didn't blame him. No sense making a target of himself for those desperate enough to make a run at him.

When we reached the livery Tyrel asked the stable boy to bring his carriage around. When he ran off into the barn, I noticed the kid had a small clipboard stuck in his waistband at the small of his back. I asked Tyrel about it.

"It's for tips," he said.

"Tips? What do you tip people with around here?"

"Federal credits. Most places around here accept them these days."

My eyes widened. "Really?"

"Yep. There's six exchanges in town now, all of 'em pretty well stocked. It's easier than bartering. Just give a few credits and let people buy what they want."

"Sounds an awful lot like a monetary system. You know, like money."

"Seems to be the direction things are headed."

I laughed skeptically. "Maybe here. Out in the wastelands, you better have something to trade or you're up shit creek."

"Give it time."

Tyrel sounded confident, so I didn't bother arguing with him. But I did not necessarily believe him either. I had the feeling maybe he didn't get out of the Springs enough.

The stable boy brought the carriage around, Tyrel tipped him, and we rode back toward Peterson AAB. Tyrel offered to let me stay in one of his guest rooms, but I had to turn him down. I had a meeting with General Jacobs in the morning.

"About that meeting," I said. "Would you be interested in coming?"

Tyrel's face remained neutral, but his hands tensed on the reins. He didn't say anything for almost a full minute. The carriage wheels clattered over the pavement, punctuated by the clip-clop of the draft horse's iron shod hooves. Pedestrians noticed us and casually got out of the way. These were people accustomed to sharing streets with horses and carriages and wagons. I felt as though I were glimpsing a fragment of the past, long before the invention of the automobile. It made me wonder if the streets of the future would resemble the narrow, winding lanes common in old European cities.

"And what would be my interest in going?"

"Gabe lost a lot of trade to the Storm Road Tribe."

"I know. He told me."

"We've got a fix on them."

Tyrel glanced at me, then returned his attention to the road. "Gabe told me that too. Jacobs is offering to help get his trade back in exchange for Gabe's professional services."

"That's about the size of it."

"Well, since Gabe works for me, I guess the Blackthorns will have to render assistance. For a small fee, of course. Otherwise, I'm afraid Gabe will have other obligations that will prevent him from assisting the government against the ROC."

"Don't think you'll get too much pushback on that. The government's got plenty of trade, but they're short on troops right now. Big recruiting push isn't going so well. Retention is low. Jacobs will probably be glad for the help."

"They're not so hard up they need Gabe for Jacobs' mission. Why is the general asking for him?"

"They need operators with the right kind of experience. Gabe fits the bill."

"Bullshit. JSOC has plenty of people who could do the job just as well."

"True. But Jacobs doesn't want to send them."

"Why not?"

"He hasn't said. My guess would be plausible deniability. If the mission fails, there's no proof he sent Union forces to challenge the ROC. The president could blame the whole thing on Resistance fighters."

"Maybe," Tyrel said. "Or maybe he wants people he can count on to keep their mouths shut."

"Jacobs doesn't know me that well, and I'm going."

Tyrel gave me a level stare. "And just exactly how important do you think you are to him?"

"Important enough to warrant a black card."

A shake of the head. "That don't mean shit, Caleb. He can give a black card to anybody he wants. Face the facts, kid. He says the word, and you're out of the Army. And you know what that means."

I didn't say anything, but I knew exactly what Tyrel meant. With the stroke of a pen, General Jacobs could have me sent to prison. It was leverage, plain and simple. I realized I had been pretty naïve to think Jacobs would bring me on board without some way of keeping me under control.

The fence around the base came into view ahead, the main gate lit by electric streetlights. The carriage stopped in front of the gate. I remained in my seat and looked over at Tyrel.

"So?"

"What time?"

"Ten hundred, in his office. I assume you know where it is."

"Yeah." My old friend heaved a sigh. "Fuck it. Tell him I'll be there."

"Okay. See you tomorrow."

"See you."

I jumped down from the carriage. "It's good to see you again Tyrel. Been too long."

He smiled thinly. "Yeah. Have a nice night, Caleb."

TEN

Caleb,

The Wastelands,

June, Present Day

We spent four days and nights on the road.

Convoys make a lot of noise, and noise attracts the infected. Ergo, the trip back to the Springs was not a leisurely one. Rather, it was a stark reminder of the dangers still inherent in the wastelands.

Six times we ran into large hordes and had to stop, send up a drone to get a birds-eye view of the enemy, hastily deploy into defensive positions, and kill the dead. Two of the HEMTTs in the convoy were full of ammo; nearly a million and a half rounds altogether. I thought it was overkill at first, but after spending hours firing round after round into the heads of ghouls—most of them Grays, which I found immensely worrisome for reasons I could not quite name—the plentitude of ammo was a comfort.

Rifles were another problem. One can only put so many rounds through a weapon before it needs a cool-off period. Shooting heats up the barrel and internal components, and letting a gun get too hot is a good way to ruin it.

Beyond that, the M-4 carbine, which was what we were using, has a limit to its service life. It is made of moving parts, and those parts sometimes break. Additionally, the direct gas impingement system that operates the weapon necessitates it be cleaned regularly to maintain good operation. Otherwise, it will eventually foul up and jam. So while guys like me were standing on top of Humvees and other vehicles shooting for everything we were worth, there was another entire cadre of soldiers running around with ammo and fresh weapons. If a gun jammed or began to overheat, or if a soldier ran out of ammo, he or she raised a hand and someone came over to help them.

One of the hordes was over eight-thousand strong. If the convoy had been fighting company strength, we would have worked in shifts. But we were not fighting company strength. In fact, we were barely over platoon strength. So once the battle was joined, there were no breaks until it was over. There were only a hundred and ten of us in the convoy. It was a good thing we had plenty of fuel and bullets.

After four days of sleep-deprived hell, when the ring of slums around Colorado Springs came into view, I was glad to see them. It was the first time I had approached the city by land since first arriving here over two years ago. Back then, there had been flat, barren plain all the way to the outer perimeter. Now, an endless shanty-town populated by hostile, gaunt figures occupied the plains as far as the eye could see.

Ahead, beyond the slums, the wall, and the city within, the Rocky Mountains were a sudden, massive contrast to the flatness of eastern Colorado. As we drew closer, soldiers went topside on their vehicles to man M-240s and fifty caliber machine guns. I heard the rattle and clank of someone loading a MK-19 automatic grenade launcher behind us (MK in military parlance being pronounced 'mark').

"Fuck's sake," I said. "Is all this really necessary?"

"It is," Gabe said. "Slummers like to throw pipe bombs and molotovs at convoys. A few warning shots are usually enough to make them keep their distance."

I shook my head. How could the government be so inept as to let things get this bad? I suppose, considering human nature, I should not have been surprised. Compassion is well and good when there is nothing on the line. But let the plight of the downtrodden conflict with moneyed interests, let it stand in the way of the insatiable addictions of greed and influence, and one sees quickly which strata of society holds the reins of power.

I could never be a politician. I'm too temperamental, and too quick with a gun.

*****

There were showers on base, but I did not feel like waiting in line. After arriving with the convoy and sending a runner to notify General Jacobs that Gabe and I were back, I took a carriage to an inn near the caravan district. There were no caravans in town at the moment, so I had the bathing facilities to myself. I showered, and then sat in a tub of heated water for nearly an hour. The water was kept warm by a small fire burning underneath it. A layer of bricks protected the tub from getting too hot. The tension in my muscles slowly faded to a dull ache.

Dressed, shaved, refreshed, and poorer by a handful of .22 rounds, I headed back to base. A runner had slipped a letter beneath my door. It was from General Jacobs, telling me to be in his office by no later than 1000 hours the next morning. But otherwise, I had the day off.

I did not need to be told twice.

It was late afternoon, so I hopped a carriage to The Sixgun, a bar and grill I had discovered not far from Base. Not many military types frequented the place because of its high prices, but I still had most of the trade Eric had paid me for traveling with him from Hollow Rock. I wasn't worried about going broke any time soon.

The place was busy. I took a seat in the bar area at a table for two. I had a couple of beers and ordered some roasted chicken and grilled vegetables. The food was good, and the beer, which was stronger than I thought it would be, gave me a dull glossy feeling.

A girl seated at the bar was eyeing me as I ate. She was petite, had straight brown hair, was about my age, slender, and very pretty. A couple of equally attractive girls, probably her friends, flanked her. I made eye contact and she smiled at me before looking down.

The part of me that notices whether or not women are attractive sat up and demanded attention. Not that I wanted it to, it just happened. Men are wired that way. We notice an attractive woman and our brain says, *Hey, stupid, look over there.*

So I looked, and then returned my attention to my meal. My libido said something along the lines of, *Hey, what the fuck? Go talk to that girl!* I told it to consider a few things. First, how did I know she was not a prostitute? The counter argument was that if she was, one of the drunken and clearly horny bastards at the bar would already have made off with her by now. Not to mention she was with two other girls, all of them dressed in expensive clothes. So chances were pretty good she was just a single girl out on the town, and not a whore paying her way through life on her back.

My second argument was I was spoken for. More to the point, I was in love. The little voice in my head told me what Miranda didn't know couldn't hurt her. I replied that *I* would know, and it would hurt *me.* My libido cursed me for a fool and finally left me alone.

The waitress saw I was finished and came over to see if I wanted anything else.

"No, thanks. What do I owe you?"

"How are you paying?"

"Federal credits okay?"

"Sure."

She told me how much. I had expected a high bill, but I still grimaced a little as she handed me the clipboard and I signed my name to the slip of paper. The girl at the bar was now staring at me openly. She caught me looking and smiled again. This time she did not break eye contact. I nodded to her and hurried out the door.

My feet carried me through the merchant district, past an affluent new housing development, and then northward on Academy Blvd. I looked up as I reached East Platte Avenue and stopped. I had walked over two miles from The Sixgun, and it was a little more than a three mile walk back to Peterson AAB. Before the Outbreak, that would have seemed pretty far. Now, it was nothing. People walked farther than that to go to work in the morning. Back at Fort McCray, twelve-mile training marches were considered recreation. Running eight or more miles in full battle gear across rough terrain was just a way for our platoon sergeant to kill an hour or so when there wasn't anything else going to do. The soldiers of Echo Company, to a man, ate like horses and never gained any body fat.

So I wasn't worried about the trip back. I could run it at almost a sprint if I had to. But there was no reason for me to go any further. There was a bench nearby. I walked over and sat down on it, gazing up the street.

Ahead of me was an empty, bulldozed swath running from I-25 in the western part of town all the way to the southern edge of Cimarron Hills to the east. The undeveloped space ran northward from East Platte Avenue to Galley Road, nearly a half mile wide and six miles long. The ground was flat, the asphalt and concrete in good repair, the spaces for stalls and parking and government vehicles all clearly marked and carefully delineated. Planes and other aircraft could land here, troops could assemble, festivals could be held, farmer's markets set up—any function requiring an abundance of open space.

On most days, as long as no government functions were occurring, people did not even need a permit. They just showed up, and as long as the event dispersed by sundown, the cops left them alone. Caravans often set up shop in the massive thoroughfare during the spring and summer, and traders would come from as far away as the Kansas plains. It was here that the fall harvest festival was held every year. Nearly the entire city turned out for it, from what I understood, and no one had to fight for elbow room.

Beyond the wide stretch of open ground known simply as The Strip stood a distant chain-link fence. Past the fence was an empty field of crumbling houses, burned-out businesses, and abandoned vehicles of every sort, all slowly sinking into the ground. The grass was head high, trees and bushes competed ruthlessly for space, and the chatter of birdsong and the buzzing of insects was audible even at this distance. No building permits were ever issued by the city for this area. It was a dead zone, a no-man's-land where any kind of development was forbidden. The official reason for this was that eventually, once the area had forested over, it would be turned into a large public park. But I knew better. The field was a barrier, a screen preventing the wealthier parts of the city from having to gaze upon the results of their selfishness and desire for exclusivity.

I had once lived beyond that field when The Strip was still being bulldozed and the fences around it built. Back then, the government had not bothered with explanations. They hadn't needed to. People were too frightened to ask questions in those days. I know, because I was one of them.

Past The Strip and the fences and the field was a warren of shipping containers and other detritus converted into living quarters. I remembered being there when it was first constructed. The containers were placed on the foundations of abandoned houses that had been ripped apart and hauled away by work crews of terrified refugees. Little did they know, those refugees were clearing land for the place they would soon call home.

The government gave them assignments and soldiers took them to their designated spots. Minimal public services kept piss and shit from running in the streets and provided a couple of gallons of fresh water per day, per household. Most of the people the government dumped off in the district never left.

I looked toward the refugee district, the place where I had once built a life with a young woman I loved, a woman who later died giving premature birth to a child that also did not survive, and thought about how the subconscious mind is a mysterious and powerful thing.

It had not been my intention to visit the refugee district. It had certainly not been my intention to align myself directly with the street that ran in front of the blue shipping container I had once shared with Sophia. I had not been thinking about my old life when I got dressed to go out to dinner. But now that I considered it, I was wearing pants I had found on a salvage run that looked like casual wear, but were actually designed to be tactical. I was wearing a plain brown button-down shirt over a white t-shirt. It was a little warm to be wearing layers.

68

My hands searched my torso, and sure enough, my Beretta was in a shoulder holster underneath the over-shirt. There was a Sig Sauer P225 in a concealed holster at the small of my back. Both pistols had threaded barrels. Suppressor slots were connected to the shoulder holster, one for each gun. I touched my ankle and discovered a short-barreled Ruger .357 five-shot revolver.

"And just in case..."

I felt along my beltline past where the Sig was holstered. A SOG combat knife rested comfortably across my lower back. I did not remember donning any of the weapons. I did not remember tying my shoes either. It had been a product of habit, my mind elsewhere while my body went on autopilot. Except normally, a pistol and a knife were all I carried. It was rare I needed anything more in an urban environment with a strong military and police presence. Furthermore, in the nicer, more genteel parts of Colorado Springs, it was considered crass and unfashionable to carry weapons of any sort, even concealed. Open carry was simply unheard of.

Not that the people here were unaware of the dangers facing the world. The inhabitants of the Springs were Outbreak survivors, after all. They knew the realm outside the city's defenses was a dangerous place. However, they considered their little corner of the earth one of the last bastions of true civilization. A place where people could live in peace and not be afraid to walk the streets at night. Instruments of death were an ugly reminder of a cataclysm they wanted to forget as much as possible. I did not blame them, nor did I think less of them for their attitude toward weapons. In all honesty, I wished everywhere could be like the merchant district. But that was not the world we lived in.

And I knew now why I had armed myself so thoroughly. I had not realized it at the time, but the course of action I was about to take was like a command hidden in my subconscious mind, an executable program dormant in the code. I was not sure what set it off, but I knew with unflinching certainty there was no stopping what was about to happen.

I was going to the refugee district. Alone.

ELEVEN

The street looked much the same as it had the last time I saw it.

The shipping containers were still there, albeit rusted and more heavily modified. People sat outside on buckets and salvaged lawn furniture as well as hand-made chairs and benches slapped together with whatever materials were available. Makeshift canopies of tarps and discarded fabric hung from poles and rooftops to provide shade from the merciless sun. There were no trees to be seen, nor lawns. Only pale clumps of stunted weeds poking up amidst lifeless patches of barren ground.

Large plastic containers stood in silent ranks in front of each residence: red ones for urine, black ones for shit, and tall green ones for garbage. The sight brought back a strong memory of the stench of the shitwagon coming around every week to carry waste to the fertilizer yards, and the public works trucks delivering precious gallons of fresh water.

Most men were shirtless in the heat, their tanned skin overlaid with a thin sheen of sweat. The women covered themselves enough to maintain modesty, if only barely. Barefoot children dressed in rags ran like flocks of birds from one street to the next, screaming for all they were worth. Not one person I saw possessed any excess body fat.

The double-doors of most containers stood wide open to allow the afternoon breeze to flow through sweltering interiors. People only went inside if they needed something. Otherwise, they stayed in the open air where it was cooler.

At a glance, the district did not look so bad. Poor maybe, but not hostile. Neighbors talked and laughed, people arriving home from other places shouted greetings to friends and family, and the smell of wood smoke and food cooking permeated the air. There was a general sense of community and good humor about the place.

But that was only at a glance.

If one looked closer, the subterfuge did not hold. At several homes I passed, people laid on cushions with elongated pipes held over strange, cone-shaped pieces of glass with fires burning within.

Opium lamps.

The lamps sat on simple metal trays arrayed with a wide variety of hand-made tools: pipe bowls, spittoon shaped pots the size of shot glasses, thin metal rods similar to needles, little pairs of scissors, brushes made from animal hair, and what looked like narrow putty knives in a myriad of shapes. I watched as people extracted stamp-sized rectangles of a black, gooey substance from wooden containers the size of ammo boxes.

As I passed one doorway I saw an old man using the little tools on his tray to roll the black substance—opium, obviously—into a ball about the size of a pill over the opium lamp. His fingers worked skillfully and deftly, and he seemed to be taking special care not to overheat the little black ball. There were three people around him, all lying down. He was the only one handling the drug paraphernalia.

From what I could tell, the smoking of opium was a somewhat complex process that required a certain amount of practice to accomplish skillfully. The goal seemed to be to shape the black stuff into a small sphere, heat it to the right temperature, and then inhale intoxicating vapors through the long stem of a pipe. The people lying around the lamps did not seem stoned to the point they could not move. Rather, it appeared they chose to recline because it was easier to put their pipes over the lamp that way. If anything, the drug users seemed mildly energized by the experience. The old man doing all the work must have been an attendant of sorts.

The more residences I passed, the more I realized this theory was most likely correct. There seemed to be a place every couple of blocks—dens, for lack of a better term—where people gathered to smoke opium. No effort was made to conceal the actions of the people within. Each den seemed to have at least one person tasked with assisting the smokers, and at least one other person tending to their other needs. The dens were dimly lit, cloth hangings keeping air movement from disturbing the opium lamps.

I came to within a few blocks of where I once lived in this district. My steps slowed involuntarily. I kept my face blank, but maintained a high level of alertness. Since arriving in the district, I had noticed groups of young men covered in crude tattoos standing on corners conversing, usually under a shade of some sort. Young boys and even a few girls approached them and handed them small cloth bags. One of the young men took the bags, disappeared into a shack, and came back out with the bags empty. He gave each kid a small box, an empty bag, and sent them on their way.

Street gangs selling opium.

Booze was also a common theme. Not everyone seemed into the drug scene, but those who weren't had no problem drinking moonshine. I saw children as young as ten or eleven doing shots with their parents. Troops of teenage girls giggled and squealed around packs of teenage boys with bottles in their hands and leers on their faces. Many of the boys had similar tattoos to the young men hanging out on the corners. It did not take a genius to grasp the neighborhood dynamic.

My old place was a few lots up around a curve in the street. I walked toward it until I was staring at the doorway. My feet felt rooted to the ground.

The container had some rust on the outside. Someone had painted it with illegible symbols and pictures I could only assume were gang tags. Four young men were sitting around a plastic table under a wide patio umbrella playing cards, bottles of clear liquor at their elbows, the smell of marijuana thick in the air. A couple of girls who could not have been a day over fifteen sat with the boys,

73

both of them on someone's lap. The boys treated them like accessories, something to be displayed. I wondered how long it take the girls to wind up pregnant.

Looking past them, I saw the interior of my old home. Gone was the bed, the chairs, the small dinner table, the cookware hanging from the ceiling. There were a few ratty couches and boxes of various trade items. It was clear the youngsters at the table did not live here. It was a place to hang out and store trade, nothing more.

I thought of all the nights I had spent here with Sophia, the two of us sitting by the light of a single candle trying to convince each other things would work out somehow. I thought about all the exhausted evenings listening to Sophia make a meal of whatever meager food we had, and her gentle hands as she tried to massage the soreness from my back after hours spent working on the city's outer wall. I thought about how we had shared a bed in that cramped space, my hand cupped around her pregnant belly at night, a small new life moving under her skin, and dreaming about a future that would never come to pass.

And now, the place where all these precious memories had been created was nothing more than a clubhouse where street punks drank, got high, and fucked underage girls. My gaze shifted back to the boys at the table. They seemed to have noticed me. One of them got up and began walking in my direction.

"You looking for somethin'?" he asked. Not hostile, just curious.

"I thought I was."

The young man's eyebrows came together. He was about my height, slender as a cane, covered in tattoos and scars, and had bright hazel eyes turned old by hardship and violence. I guessed his age at nineteen or twenty, just a kid when the Outbreak happened.

"The fuck does that mean?"

I shook my head. "Nothing."

74

He looked at the other guys at the table, then back at me. "Whatever you need, son, we got it. Shine, dream, smoke, pussy, whatever."

"Not here for that."

He surprised me by laughing. "You must be new here, son. I seen you watching us play cards. Gambling your thing? We got places for that too. Craps, blackjack, hold 'em. Hell, there's motherfuckers around here play Russian roulette."

I stared at him and said nothing. The pounding of my heart was loud in my ears. A slow coldness started in my belly and spread outward through my limbs. The young man in front of me stepped closer, head tilted, looking at me like a particularly interesting bug.

"Hello? Anybody home?"

My fists clenched.

A hand waved in front of my face. "Yo, you fucking retarded or something?"

This elicited a round of laughter from the table. The girls looked at me condescendingly, their soft faces twisted in youthful scorn.

I don't know why the next few sentences came out of my mouth. Maybe it was old, nearly forgotten pain coming to the surface after being submerged for so long. Maybe it was the irrational anger I was beginning to feel toward the kid in front of me and his buddies for desecrating the one place in this whole damned town I had ever had a moment's happiness. Or maybe I just needed an outlet and I didn't care who caught the heat.

I said, "I used to live here a couple of years ago. Neighborhood was a lot nicer back then. No drugs, no little shitbags like you lording over the place."

The kid's face went blank, his skin reddening. "The fuck you say?"

I met his eyes. "You heard me."

The boys at the table put down their cards and bottles. They didn't even bother telling the girls to move, they just stood up. The girls took the hint and scrambled away. The three gang members produced knives as if by magic and fanned out as they approached.

"You just fucked with the wrong one, son," the kid in front of me said.

His hand moved toward his back. The others were within ten feet now. I did not have much time. Nevertheless, I felt a smile crease my face. My heart rate increased even more as I felt the warm flow of adrenaline hit my veins. The world seemed to slow, the movements of the gangbangers impossibly sluggish.

"Let's see about that," I said.

My feet were planted firmly. The swing came up from the ground, through my hips, and out my shoulder like a whip. My left arm shot out straight, all two hundred and twenty pounds going into the punch. There was a meaty *thunk,* and the kid talking to me went down like he'd been shot. The other three stopped.

"Anyone else?" I said looking at the others, still grinning like a madman.

They came as one, trying to encircle me. I went straight at them. The first one, a short little guy no older than eighteen, tried a deft little upward thrust at my groin. I sidestepped it, caught his hand, and nailed him in the orbital socket with an elbow. Bone crunched and skin split, splashing both of us with blood. The kid screamed, dropped his knife, and went down clutching his face.

The other two were faster. One came high, the other low. I leapt sideways, rolled, and popped to my feet. When I came up, I had my knife in my hand. The boys hesitated, then came on again. Rather than wait, I threw my knife at the closest one's face. I am no expert knife thrower, but I usually hit what I'm aiming at. This time was no different. The knife hit pommel first just above the gangbanger's upper lip. He stopped, spit out a tooth and a mouthful of blood, brought his hand to his mouth, and ran in the other direction. The other boy paid no attention and attacked, probably figuring I wouldn't be able to handle him barehanded.

He figured wrong.

His blade came at my face, then switched directions toward my arm. I dodged sideways and lashed out with a kick at the side of his knee. He was off balance, too much weight on the leg. There was a crunch and a scream before he fell. By the angle of his leg, he would probably never walk right again.

I drew my Sig, screwed on the suppressor, and calmly walked away.

*****

The girls must have run straight to the gang member's friends.

There were eight of them positioned along a cross street as I headed southward. Looking past them, I saw no other enemies waiting. That did not mean they weren't there, but I had a feeling whatever gang I had just offended had decided to wait for me at the edge their territory. And unlike the punks at my old hovel, these shitweasels had guns.

To their credit, they tried to keep it low-key. There were no shouts, no challenges, no tattooed thugs running toward me shooting wildly. I had been kind of hoping they would. Dangerous for the residents around here, but the commotion would work in my favor. When bullets start flying, chaos ensues. People start running. A panicked crowd of bystanders would make it easier for me to slip away. Sadly, the gangbangers weren't that stupid.

When I was half a block away, I decided to force their hand by turning left through a yard full of people getting roaring drunk. A few of them looked about to say something until they saw the gun in my hand and the expression on my face. Whatever they saw there caused them to raise their hands and back off.

"Hey, easy man," someone said. "Don't want no trouble."

I ignored them and kept walking. The crowd watched me pass. I turned right again, double-backed the way I had come, and hunched down behind a heap of junk piled against a container's metal wall. Angry voices and rapid footsteps approached. I let them pass, turned back, and ran to the next block over, glimpsing

77

between containers as I went. People noticed me, but so far no one was shouting. That wouldn't last long.

When I finally found a spot where I thought no one could see me, I tossed the Sig on a rooftop and followed it up. Then I lay flat, gun in hand, waiting.

"Hey, you. Where the fuck did he go?"

"What?" The voice sounded drunkenly confused.

There was a distinct crack of hand meeting face at high speed. "The blond motherfucker with the gun, dumbass! Where did he go?"

"Fuck, man." The voice was alarmed now. "He went that way."

More pounding footsteps. I slid to the edge of the container and peeked over the edge. Four of the eight street toughs I had spotted earlier were coming uphill toward me, all carrying handguns. Not the lean, tactical kind like I had, but rather gaudy, nickel-plated abominations only useful to someone trying to keep up an image. The gangbangers were young, maybe early twenties at most. I had a brief pang of conscience and wondered if there might be a way out of this without bloodshed.

The tattooed thugs stopped and interrogated an elderly man and his wife. The leader asked the old lady a question she could not quite hear. When she asked the thug to repeat himself, he pistol whipped her in the face. Then he turned and did the same to her husband.

Okay. Bloodshed it is.

They were less than twenty yards away. I had the high ground. The shipping container would not provide any cover; the metal was too thin. However, being uphill from the gangbangers gave me a tactical advantage. It is almost always easier to shoot downhill than up, and requires the shooter to expose less of a target profile.

I stayed in the prone position, took aim, and fired once. The leader's head snapped back with a neat hole in his forehead just above the bridge of his nose. A spray of brain matter and blood splashed the young men behind him, causing them to stop and shout in dismay. The elderly couple scrambled for cover.

Before the other thugs could regain their wits, I fired four shots. Double-tap, shift, double-tap. Two more gunmen went down, each hit center of mass. The last one, finding himself without backup, tried to run. I led him a little with the sights and fired three times. The first two missed, but the third caught him in the lower torso. From the way he fell and screamed, I surmised the bullet had gone through him sideways, probably tearing a swath through his guts. Hollow points are dangerous like that.

Four to go. Maybe more.

The slide on the Sig had locked to the rear on an empty mag. I removed it, stashed it in a pocket, slapped home eight more rounds of 9mm, and released the slide. A round went into the chamber, the hammer still back. I eased down the hammer so I would not accidentally shoot myself and slid off the container.

As I hit the ground, another tattooed figure came around the corner to my right and raised a weapon. I fell over backwards as he opened fire. His bullets shot past where my head had been a fraction of a second before. I flattened my legs so I wouldn't shoot myself and pulled the trigger twice, both rounds taking him in the chest. He dropped his gun, staggered a few steps away, clutched his chest, and hit the pavement.

I got up and headed around the corner. Stopped. Looked around. No more gangbangers. Plenty of screaming. The suppressed fire from my Sig had probably gone unnoticed, but the shots aimed at me had been full volume. The whole damn district probably heard them. Which meant any friends the dead gangbangers had were on their way, and quickly.

I ran west another block and then cut south again. Stopped at a corner. Listened. People had left their homes in this area, and, rather stupidly I thought, gone in the direction of the gunfire. Unexpected, but it worked in my favor. No more witnesses.

There was another shipping container across from me and several more on either side of it, facing the opposite street. Which meant I was in the back yard of everyone who lived on this block. If I moved fast and kept quiet, I might be able to escape unnoticed.

A quick peek around the corner showed I was alone. I sprinted to the next container. Another look around. Still no one. Another sprint. The process repeated three more times. I was beginning to think I might get out of this without killing anyone else.

Finally, I reached the street where the gangbangers had originally been waiting. Unfortunately, they had left one guy behind to keep an eye out for me. I spotted him before he spotted me, leveled my weapon, and fired. The bullet took him in the side of the head. He fell, and someone screamed.

I ran as fast as I could and didn't stop for five blocks. People saw me go by, but showed no more interest than if I were an errant squirrel. I skidded to a halt, put my back against the side of a container, and looked behind me. No one was following me.

Deep breaths. Calm down. Put the damn gun away.

The suppressor was still warm to the touch as I unscrewed it and stashed it under my shirt. The Sig's mag had six rounds left and one in the chamber. With a start, I realized the hammer was still back from the last shot. I cursed softly and told myself it was a damn good thing I had kept my finger off the trigger. Pretty hard to run with a bullet in your foot.

I lowered the hammer and holstered the Sig. To my right, there was some light pedestrian traffic. To my left, the street on the other side looked empty. In both directions, no one was paying me any attention.

It took me half an hour cross back over The Strip and hail a carriage. The ride back to the base cost me the remaining six rounds in the Sig's magazine. Once there, I got a couple of sugar packets from my trade stash in my barracks room and hopped another carriage to Tyrel's house. His maid opened the door. Unlike most of Tyrel's female employees, she was long past the age when she might have been considered attractive. Her clothes were made from practical homespun material and she wore a white apron around her ample waist. A pair of dark brown eyes regarded me suspiciously.

"Can I help you?" She had a trace of a Mexican accent.

"Name's Caleb Hicks," I said. "Mr. Jennings here?"

"One moment." She closed the door and locked it.

A minute or two later, Tyrel appeared. Night had fallen, and I realized I must have looked a mess standing there covered in sweat, my clothes rumpled and dirty.

"Jesus, Caleb," he said. "The hell happened to you?"

I handed him a small bag with the Sig in it. "Could you hold on to this for me, hide it someplace?"

He stared at the bag a few seconds before taking it. "You smell like cordite. Who you been shooting at?"

"No one important."

The black eyes narrowed. "Caleb, what kind of trouble are you in?"

I opened my mouth to tell him not to worry about it, but stopped myself. Of course he would worry about it. I show up in the dark of night and ask him to hide a gun for me, and he's not supposed to ask questions? Stupid.

"Some guys made a run at me in the refugee district," I said.

He blinked at me. "The refugee district? What the flying fuck were you doing there?"

I let out a breath. "Went to see my old place. Don't know why, just wanted to see it. Some gangbangers were there, hanging out, drinking. Didn't care much for that. Long story short, I had to shoot some people. Might come back on me, might not. Either way, probably best if I don't have the murder weapon in my possession."

"Oh, yeah, sure," Tyrel said. "Just give it to me, make me an accessory. No trouble at all."

I looked him in the eye. "I'd do it for you."

Tyrel started to say something, then closed his mouth. "Yeah. You would."

"Thanks, Tyrel." I turned to leave.

"Hey."

I stopped. "Yeah?"

"Come on in and get cleaned up. I'll have Roberta wash your clothes. You can go back to base in the morning."

A part of me wanted to refuse, but logic won out. Tyrel was right. Probably best if I stayed off the street for a while, and staying with him would make it harder for the police to find me.

"Don't worry about the cops," Tyrel said, as if reading my mind. "Gangs won't tell 'em shit. But whoever you pissed off will probably come looking for you sooner or later."

That gave me pause. "If they do, I don't want you getting caught up in it."

Tyrel shook his head. "Not your call. If you're in it, so am I. If the situation were reversed, what would you do?"

I knew exactly what I would do. So I said, "You really think they'll come looking?"

"Probably. If they do, we'll deal with it. There's a solution for that kind of thing."

I stayed still a few seconds. People passed me on the sidewalk. I looked down the street and saw maelstroms of insects swirling in the light of streetlamps. The merchant district was calm and hushed, most of its residents having turned in for the night. I blended in here about as well as a scorpion on clean sheets.

"Okay."

I went inside.

TWELVE

I got back to my barracks room at 0800.

The loudspeaker outside my window announced a ninety-percent chance of rain and advised all base personnel to prepare accordingly. At 0945, while on my way to General Jacob's office, the dark gray clouds lurking overhead opened up and began pouring down rain. I was in uniform, my poncho rolled up in my right hand. Most of the troops and civilian contractors scurrying around me obviously had not heeded the warning.

I stopped under the awning in front of the entrance, shook off as much water as I could, and entered. A young private at the front desk took my poncho and hung it up for me. I told him I had a ten-hundred meeting with General Jacobs. He told me the General was waiting for me.

Gabe was already there when I walked in. I nodded to the General and said, "Hope I'm not interrupting."

"No, Captain, you're not. Just in time."

I stopped and looked behind me for a second, then back at the general. "Captain?"

Jacobs opened a desk drawer. "Guess the runner I sent didn't find you. Your field commission went through. Congratulations."

He handed me a sealed brown 8 ½ by 11 envelope. I opened it and scanned the contents. It was indeed a field commission promoting Sergeant Caleb T. Hicks to the rank of captain in the

83

United States Army. I read carefully to make sure it was not contingent upon extending my service beyond my initial enlistment. It was not.

"Anything to say?" Jacobs asked.

I almost said I was expecting to be a second lieutenant, but decided not to look the gift horse in the mouth. "Thank you, sir. I appreciate it."

"Good answer, Captain. Now have a seat."

I put the papers back in the envelope and did as ordered.

"We were just wrapping up negotiations," Gabriel said.

"Don't you have to ask your boss first?" I asked.

A voice from the doorway said, "He already has."

I turned. Tyrel walked in and offered Jacobs a hand. The general stood and shook it. "Thank you for coming Mr. Jennings."

"Always a pleasure, General." Tyrel took the last seat. "So what am I here for?"

"One moment." Jacobs stood up and shut the door. There was a gray panel beside it. He opened the panel, typed something on the keypad, closed the panel, and sat back down behind his desk. I may have been imagining it, but I thought I heard a faint electric hum emanating from the walls.

"We'll have complete privacy for the remainder of the meeting," Jacobs said. "Needless to say, our conversation will be classified and no one is to repeat anything said in this room to anyone, ever, without my express authorization. Agreed?"

We all acknowledged.

"All right then. Here's what we're dealing with…"

Jacobs laid out the situation as he had explained it to me when I first agreed to work for him. Gabe and Tyrel stayed quiet, listening. Jacobs dimmed the lights, brought up a map on a projector, and aimed it at the wall to my left.

"The ROC has claimed territory as far north as Vancouver. However, based on our satellite data and intel from the ground,

84

most of their forces are concentrated in four regions." Jacobs activated a laser pointer. "The first and largest is here, around Humboldt Bay. This is where the Flotilla initially landed and where, over the course of a few months, they offloaded their supplies and equipment."

"Question." Gabe said.

"Yes?"

"Why didn't the Navy stop them?"

Jacobs scratched the back of his head and let out a long breath. "When it became clear the East coast was a total loss, the Navy evacuated as many ships and personnel as they could to the West Coast before the Panama Canal closed. As you can imagine, this was not a smooth operation. But we managed to get most of our ships through. Those that didn't had to sail around the horn of South America. Not all of them made it. While all this was happening, most of the West Coast Navy was assisting with humanitarian efforts and evacuating vital government personnel to Hawaii and Guam. Afterward, the Navy was ordered to port all remaining vessels in Hawaii, the Mariana Islands, and a few other classified destinations. By the time the Flotilla arrived, the Navy was short on supplies, fuel, and basically everything a modern navy needs to operate. All we could send were a few nuke submarines, and for reasons unknown, when they were halfway to California, the president ordered them to turn around and head back to Hawaii."

"So what's the state of the Navy at this point?" I asked.

"Not very good. We have exactly two battle groups up and running. Which means two carriers, four destroyers, four cruisers, two supply ships, two submarines, one amphibious assault ship, and a small fleet of fast-boats. MK 5s, RHIBs, LCACs, etc."

"So," Gabe said, "in other words, a fraction of the old fleet. What about aircraft?"

"Managed to save most of those. Sadly, in order to maintain the capabilities we have at this point, we're cannibalizing everything not currently in service. Ever seen an aircraft carrier stripped for parts?"

Gabe shook his head.

"Let me tell you, it's a sad damn sight. Now, are we ready to move on?"

"Sure."

The laser pointer came on again. "The other three areas where enemy forces are concentrated," Jacobs said, "are here near Crescent City, California, here just east of Eugene, Oregon, and here in Castle Rock, Washington. There are dozens of outposts spread out between Humboldt Bay and Castle Rock, but those are only manned by a few hundred troops each. We'll see to them in due course. Our primary concern is the four main bases and the internment camps."

"So how many internment camps are there?" Tyrel asked. "And where are they?"

"There are eight of them, six in Oregon, the rest in Northern California. The biggest one by far is here in the Klamath Basin. The detainees at this camp are being used as slave labor to grow food for ROC forces. Mostly potatoes and grain, as far as we can tell."

"And the others?" I asked.

General Jacobs pointed them out. They were located in areas with fertile farmland and grazing land available for livestock.

"So where will we be going?" Gabe asked.

"The Klamath Basin," Jacobs said. "Nearly half of the detainees are being held there. That's where most of our forces will be concentrated. Resistance fighters and special operations forces will coordinate to liberate the other camps as well."

"How do we plan to do this?" Tyrel asked.

"You'll be briefed on the particulars when you meet up with Resistance forces in Oregon. The less you know for the time being, the better for operational security."

The three of us nodded. It was no less than we expected. If we were somehow captured between Colorado and Oregon, the less we knew, the less the enemy could torture out of us. A morbid precaution, but sensible nonetheless.

"So what happens now?" Gabe asked.

"For now, I'm going to give all of you papers to take to medical. The docs will give you a checkup and a few inoculations. God only knows what diseases those North Koreans and who-the-hell else brought over with them. After that, you'll have five days to get your affairs in order. Then you'll report here and wait for orders to deploy. Fair enough?"

Gabe inclined his head. "Fair enough."

Jacobs stood up. "Well, that's all for now gentlemen. Mr. Jennings, if you could let me know who you'll be sending by tomorrow morning, I would appreciate it."

"I'll tell you now," Tyrel said, getting to his feet. "I'm going."

My head snapped around. "What?"

Tyrel held up a hand for silence. It was an old gesture, one he had been using to shut me up since I was six years old. It must have had some kind of Pavlovian effect because my mouth closed immediately.

General Jacobs regarded Tyrel, eyebrows slightly raised. He spoke with deliberate calmness. "I'm familiar with your record, Mr. Jennings. I'd be happy to have you along."

"Good," Tyrel said. "Then it's settled. See you in five days."

Tyrel and Gabriel left first. I stood immobile, staring down the hallway. After a few seconds, General Jacobs cleared his throat. The noise startled me.

"Captain, is there anything else?"

"Um, no. No sir."

"Very well. You're dismissed."

"Yes sir."

I started to shut the door on my way out.

"Oh, Captain, one more thing."

I stuck my head back in. "Yes sir?"

"I'll be sending someone around to see to your uniforms. Feel free to wear civilian clothes until they're returned to you. Just make sure you keep your black card on you. And don't forget to turn in your commission paperwork to personnel. Have them make a copy for your records."

"Yes sir. Anything else?"

"That will be all."

I shut the door and left.

THIRTEEN

Five days.

I did not have any regular duties at Peterson AAB, and the only person I answered to was General Jacobs. All he asked was I let his secretary know where a runner could find me. Otherwise, I had nothing to do.

I didn't care for it.

Back at Fort McCray, they kept us busy. Training, cleaning, PT, eating, more cleaning, more training, patrols. Occasionally, we got to shoot at something. Usually it was infected, but sometimes we were called upon to clear out raiders and bandits along the trade routes. When things were peaceful, we had nights and weekends off unless we pulled watch.

But the Springs was not Fort McCray. I had no fellow soldiers to hang out with, no drinking buddies, no camaraderie, and worst of all, no Miranda. I could have dealt with the boredom if she were around. But without her, and without the friends I missed far more than I thought I would, I was going stir crazy.

On the second day, after deciding there was only so much entertainment to be found at the public library, I visited with Gabriel and company. They had moved into a house in the same district where Tyrel lived. The house was a newly-built four bedroom with a workshop in the backyard, a fireplace in each bedroom, a woodstove in the kitchen, two washrooms complete with stoves, buckets, and clawfoot tubs, and a privy next to each bedroom that emptied into the city's sewer system. There were no electrical lights, but the walls and ceiling were lined with hooks for lanterns and sconces for candles. Gabe told me he planned to install solar panels and run wires so he could have LED lighting and a few small appliances.

I found myself staring out one of the big windows that allowed light into the sitting room on the second floor. Gabe stood beside me, gazing down onto the bustling street in front of his house. The window was five feet tall and nearly four feet wide. There was a gentle breeze blowing through it, the swarming bugs outside kept at bay by a mesh screen.

I thought about Miranda. I thought about where we would live when she moved out here. There was a small fortune in trade sitting in a storage building in Hollow Rock that I had accumulated over the year and a half I had been stationed there. I thought about how best to convert it into something small, valuable, and portable, and have it shipped to the Springs. I thought about Echo Company and how they would soon be rotating back to Fort Bragg. Hollow Rock wouldn't be the same without them around. Not that I would be going back any time soon.

"Something bothering you?" Gabe asked.

I could hear Sabrina and Elizabeth downstairs. Sabrina had tested out of high school and was absently studying Gray's Anatomy while sharpening her impressive arsenal of knives. Elizabeth was cutting vegetables and a pork shoulder. Dinner would be carnitas on flatbread with fresh vegetables. I doubted I would be staying for it.

"Thinking about the future," I said, realizing it was the most I had spoken all day.

"Miranda?"

I grunted in acknowledgment.

"When's she coming out here?" Gabe asked.

"Not sure yet. Wants to wait until Eric gets back and hires some people."

"Eric's just about done here. Probably be leaving in the next week or so."

"What's he been up to?"

"Not sure. You'd have to ask him."

"Whatever it is, I'm sure it'll be lucrative. He's got a mind for business."

"That he does."

A farmer in homespun clothes pushing a cart full of vegetables turned onto the street in front of us and headed toward the nearby farmer's market. It was Saturday morning, and the street had been shut down for three blocks, running right in front of Gabe's house. The man with the cart was a latecomer. Elizabeth had already been shopping, as had most people who lived in the neighborhood. I wished the farmer luck.

"I got a bad feeling," Gabe said.

I looked at him. "You too?"

Gabe's countenance was even more grim than usual. "Something isn't adding up."

"Like how they plan to take out the ROC troops at the internment camps without getting the hostages killed?"

The big man glanced at me. "Yes. I guess that's one of those 'particulars' we'll be briefed on when we get to Oregon."

"There's also the matter of the visit to medical," I said. "Did someone follow you to your appointment?"

"Yep. Fella thought he was slick. Spotted him as soon as he started tailing me."

"He know you saw him?"

"Nope. Took off as soon as I left the clinic. I'm guessing you were followed too."

"I was. Ran a detection route after I left to see if he was still tailing me."

"And?"

"No dice. I went back to the hospital and asked if anyone had been there looking for me. Told the nurse I was supposed to meet a friend there. She said someone stopped by and shoved a black card in her face and asked if I had been given my inoculations. Lady seemed real sorry about it, kept apologizing for giving up information about a patient. I said it was no big deal but she probably shouldn't talk about it, and left."

"Jacobs," Gabe said.

"Yep."

"Why? What's so important about those inoculations?"

"More importantly, what was in them?"

"Tracking devices?"

I shook my head. "Doubt it. Easier just to tell us up front. Why would we refuse?"

Gabe stepped closer to the window, hands on his hips. "There's something he's not telling us. Something important to the mission."

I laughed quietly. "Why should this time be any different?"

*****

Day three.

The Colorado Springs Chamber of Commerce Semi-Annual Job Fair took up close to half a mile of The Strip. There were tables and tents, and the smell of food cooking and charcoal burning was strong in the air. I got a pulled pork sandwich on honest-to-God bread that tasted remarkably close to sourdough. The beer I chased it down with was warm, but still good. A crowd of people, most of them men of varying ages recently discharged from the Army, wandered from tent to tent speaking with representatives of the city's many employers.

I found Eric near the food stalls. It was a good strategic location. He had rented a big tent and several plastic folding tables.

92

A few signboards identified his company, the newly founded Great Hawk Private Security, LLC. A man I didn't recognize stood next to Eric in front of a board proclaiming him the managing director of Delaney Bowyers, a subsidiary of G&R Transport and Salvage.

Out-of-work veterans crowded in front of Eric while he stood on a small platform and explained the hiring process, expectations, pay, and benefits of Great Hawk Private Security. A schedule printed on a small sign said this briefing would be given every two hours. Since it was noon, Eric was giving it for the third time. When he finished, a dozen or so men signed their names on a sheet and Eric gave them a small brochure. I could only imagine how much he'd paid to have brochures printed. Such things were not cheap anymore.

When Eric finished, it was the bowyer's turn. He was a short, muscular fellow with graying red hair, a thick beard, and hairy arms burned red by the sun. His face was pinched and wrinkled from too much squinting, and a pair of shrewd, gray-green eyes peered out from narrow slits. He spoke plainly with a Mid-Western accent (Wisconsin I was guessing), and identified himself as Arlo Delaney. He said he'd run Delaney Bowyers as a small sole proprietorship until Eric Riordan, investor and entrepreneur, approached him with the idea of scaling up his operations. I had seen Eric make sales pitches before. His confidence, charisma, and the sheer palpable force of his will made him a difficult man to say no to.

Delaney said he wasn't looking for men with carpentry experience, but it wouldn't hurt anyone's prospects of getting hired. What he needed were men willing to work hard, learn a task, do it properly, and be comfortable with the idea of repeating that task over and over again. Anyone who could not overcome tedium would not last long at Delaney Bowyers.

When asked why, he said Delaney Bowyers was going to become the first mass production bowyer since the Outbreak. Which meant assembly line work, and lots of it. Someone asked him what a bowyer was. He said it was people who made bows and crossbows. Someone else asked him what about arrows. He said they would make those too, and bolts for the crossbows. There were more questions, but I did not stick around to listen. Eric had finished with the most recent batch of applicants and was walking toward the food stalls. I caught up with him on the way.

"Nice pitch," I said. "Looks like you've generated some interest."

"Yeah. Saw you lurking around in the back of the crowd. What gives?"

Eric got in line with people waiting for chicken sandwiches. I waited with him.

"Lurking is a strong word," I said.

"Whatever. If you're here about the mission, the answer is still no."

"Not here for that."

"Then what?"

"Gabe says you're leaving town soon."

A nod. "That's the plan."

"How went the business pursuits?"

The line moved. We both took a couple of steps forward. "Better than I expected. Got plenty of recruits for the security company. Hired some contractors to build training facilities out in Kansas."

"What about trainers?"

"Pilfered some guys from the Blackthorns, signed a few Special Forces types. Once I free up Great Hawk's schedule, he'll be out here to oversee things."

"Blackthorns aren't going to like that."

"Fuck 'em."

"They have clout around here."

"Fuck 'em harder."

I shook my head. Tyrel Jennings was a formidable man, but if there was anyone who could find a way around him, it was Eric.

The thought of my two friends locking horns was not a pleasant one. Chances were good I'd get drawn into it sooner or later.

Problem for another day.

"What about the bowyer thing?"

"Shouldn't be much trouble getting Delaney's factory up and running."

"Delaney's factory?"

"He'll be in charge, along with a guy used to be an automotive engineer."

"An automotive engineer."

"Yep."

"To build a factory for bows and arrows."

"Crossbows and bolts too."

"Okay, I'll bite. Why?"

"Knows all about mass production. Me and Arlo gave him a basic outline of what we wanted, and in two days he was writing schematics. Had some great ideas. Impressed the hell out of me, so I hired him to design the factory and help Arlo run it."

"And where do you fit in all this?"

"I'll be providing the venture capital. Got a damn good lawyer drawing up the partnership agreement right now."

"Elizabeth."

"Yep."

"Thought she specialized in criminal law."

"Her father worked in contract law, let her help out at his firm for a while. She's no dunce on the subject."

The line shifted again. We were tantalizingly close to the girl taking sandwich orders. The pulled pork I'd had was good, but I am a big eater. A chicken sandwich or two was looking, and smelling, like a capital idea.

"So," Eric said. "You're not big on social visits. I assume you went through the trouble of tracking me down for a reason."

"I did."

"So what's the reason?"

I looked at him. "You ever notice how many sentences you start with the word 'so'?"

"So fuck you. How about that?"

I laughed a little. Eric wasn't smiling, but I could tell he had amused himself. "So I need to ask you for a favor."

"So what is it?"

"You can stop that now."

"We both should. It's annoying."

I took a small envelope out of my hip pocket. "Give this to Miranda for me."

Eric glanced at the envelope, then took it and examined it. "Mind if I ask what it says? Not the details, just the gist of it."

"Why do you ask?"

"Because if it's something that's going to upset her, I'd like to know ahead of time."

"I don't think she'll be upset."

"Tell me anyway."

The line advanced again. There was now only one person ahead of us. "Mostly it just asks her to wait until I send word before leaving town, and that I don't know how long I'll be gone. If I don't come back, she should stick with you and Great Hawk. You'll take care of her. That and the usual lovey-dovey stuff we say to each other."

"Something about you being a warrior-poet?"

"Her words, not mine."

"But you don't hate it."

I let myself smile. "Been called worse things."

Eric put the envelope in a shirt pocket. "Consider it done."

"What do I owe you?"

"Nothing. This one's a freebie."

"Thanks."

"Don't mention it. And I mean that literally. Word gets out, people will come out of the woodwork asking me to do shit for them."

"Understood."

The chicken sandwiches were served on plastic plates with an admonishment from the clerk to put food waste in the compost bin and return the plates at the other window. We promised obedience. I paid for both meals with my diminishing stock of federal credits and we retired to Eric's tent. Arlo was sitting at the front desk speaking with job applicants. Eric put a sandwich on the table next to him, and the two of us sat down in a pair of folding chairs.

"On a lighter note," I said, "how do you plan to get home?"

"Got a flight leaving next week."

"A flight? On what?"

"C-130."

"How'd you swing that?"

"The usual method."

I scowled. "Bribes."

"Don't hate the player. Hate the game."

There was much I could have said on that subject, but it would have been a waste of time. The military does not always attract the best and brightest. A certain amount of corruption in such a large and powerful organization is unavoidable.

I said, "Where's the flight taking you? Wichita?"

A nod. "Be hitching a ride with your buddies' replacements from there. Should be home before the end of the month."

97

I finished my first sandwich, drank some water Eric gave me, and started on the second one. "What are you going to do when Captain Harlow leaves? With the First Recon back at Bragg, you won't have anyone left to bribe."

"I'll cut a deal with the next guy. Harlow already set up a meeting."

"Awfully nice of him, considering he hates you."

"Feeling's mutual. But he's a pragmatist, and he knows how hard I could have made his life if he hadn't played ball. Same applies to his replacement."

"Even with the new mayor?"

"What's he got to do with anything?"

"I'm not stupid, Eric. Elizabeth helped you more than you like to let on."

He gave a shrug. "The new mayor won't be a problem."

"What makes you so sure?"

The left corner of his mouth twitched. "Who do you think paid for his campaign?"

I paused. Eric looked smug. "You supported Will Laurel over Sarah Glover?"

"Actually, no. I contributed to both campaigns."

I stared hard at him. Typical Eric. "So no matter who won, you had a mayor in your pocket."

"Politics is a dirty business."

"On that," I said, "we agree."

FOURTEEN

Day five came and went. Our orders were to stand by.

Tyrel and Gabe were given rooms in the BOQ down the hall from where I slept. They said it was a step down from the Blackthorns' standard accommodations. I decided when I was done with the Army, private security might not be such a bad idea.

We were free to go off base as long as we left word with Jacobs' secretary where to find us. I thought this was redundant being we all had satellite phones, but complied anyway. The general's offices were on the way to the main gate, so it was no trouble to stop by.

Gabe stayed on base for the most part, having already said goodbye to his family. He'd set them up with plenty of trade and had signed over a letter of credit and power of attorney to Elizabeth from G&R Transport and Salvage. It was worth about half his fortune still in storage in Hollow Rock, along with any future distributions commensurate with his remaining twenty-percent stake in the company. Meaning if he didn't come back, it would be a century or so before his wife and daughter would have to worry about going hungry.

A runner found us on the seventh day and we met Eric at the big airstrip on the western side of Peterson AAB. He informed Gabriel he had gotten his business expansions up and running and hired people to oversee them. Further, he had appointed Elizabeth as regional director of operations, meaning if she said jump, everyone

99

in the chain of command would be compelled to ask how high. Gabe agreed Elizabeth would ensure their mutual interests in the region were well looked after.

"You're not going to be around for a while," Eric said. "The mission and all."

Gabe shrugged. "Jacobs held up his end. I got to hold up mine."

Eric nodded and looked down the runway. Behind him, a C-130 was loading troops and equipment and preparing for takeoff. Eric had a large duffel bag, a much smaller assault pack, and was strapped down with weapons. I could only imagine how much it had cost him to book passage on a military transport flight.

"Somewhere in Colorado Springs," I said, "a senior officer is greedily counting how many credits he can get for whatever you paid him."

Eric noticed me looking at the C-130. "I miss my wife and son," he said. "The faster I'm home, the happier I'll be."

"Couldn't have been cheap," Gabe said.

"It was worth it."

I reached out a hand. Eric shook it. "Probably won't see you again for a while," I said. "Take care of yourself, amigo."

"You do the same. And watch out for this guy." He hooked a thumb at Gabe. "He's nothing but trouble."

Gabe snorted. "Pot, kettle, black."

The two men clasped hands and slapped each other on the back a couple of times. Eric looked at both of us, cast a glance around at the city of Colorado Springs and the mountains and plains beyond, and said, "Not a bad place. I think you'll be all right here."

And with that he gathered his gear and headed toward the transport plane. Before walking up the ramp he gave a final wave. Gabe and I returned it. Eric walked on and disappeared from view.

Shortly thereafter, the props sped up and the lumbering giant of an aircraft gained momentum. It looked painfully slow at first, but quickly sped up. In a far shorter stretch of tarmac than I would have guessed it needed, the nose tipped upward and the C-130 gained altitude. Minutes later, it banked eastward and flew higher until only the drone of its engines remained. That too eventually faded.

*****

My satellite phone rang when we were three blocks from the main gate. I answered it.

"We're on," Tyrel said.

"Got it," I said. "On our way."

"Be quick about it." He hung up.

"That who I think it was?" Gabe asked.

"Tyrel. Time to go to work."

We doubled-timed it the rest of the way. Despite Gabe being twenty years older and outweighing me by at least thirty pounds, I had to open my stride to keep pace with him. I could only imagine what he must have been like at my age.

I showed my black card at the gate and said Gabe was with me. The guard checked my ID carefully but let us through without comment. We hoofed it immediately to General Jacobs' office.

A short, stocky man with captain's bars and a Special Forces rocker met us in the lobby. When he saw Gabe, he grinned broadly.

"Long time no see," the short man said. His nametag read Grabovsky.

Gabe smiled back and the two men shook hands. "The hell you been hiding?" Gabe asked.

"Oh, here and there. You?"

"Tried being an honest businessman for a while. Did pretty well, but got bored with it. Now I'm with the Blackthorns."

"Worked with some of those guys. Nice outfit. Good pay. Man could do a hell of a lot worse."

"True. I could have your job."

"Fuck off. How's the Ninth TVM doing?"

"Hanging in there. Most of 'em stuck around. Lost a couple."

"Infected?"

"And raiders."

A head shake. "Fucking raiders. Soon as we get done with the ROC, they're our next order of business."

Gabe tilted his head. "I assume by 'we' you mean SF?"

"And then some. Probably be seeing more of each other in the not-too-distant future."

"Always good to stay busy."

Grabovsky glanced at me. "Who's the kid?"

"Captain Caleb Hicks," I said. I did not offer to shake hands. SF types, in my experience, did not generally treat other people like human beings unless they did something to earn it.

Grabovsky looked skeptical. "He with us?"

"Yep," Gabe said.

"Any good?"

"One of the best."

The shorter man's eyes widened a little. "Serious?"

"Serious."

Another appraising glare. "Where you coming from, kid?"

"First Reconnaissance Expeditionary."

"No shit. What platoon?"

"First."

"Lieutenant Jonas still the platoon commander?"

"Last I heard."

"Huh. Small world. You get back there, tell him Raymond Grabovsky said hi."

"Be glad to, except I won't be going back," I said.

Grabovsky was about to say something else when the door opened behind me.

"Where's Jacobs?" Tyrel asked as he strode into the lobby.

"Don't know," Gabe said.

"You won't be seeing him," Grabovsky said. "He's headed out of town. I'm your point of contact from here on in."

Tyrel stopped next to me and stared hard at the Green Beret. "I feel like I know you from somewhere."

"You look familiar too. You ever with JSOC?"

"Years ago. Long before the Outbreak."

Grabovsky snapped his fingers. "Coronado, joint exercise, couple years after we invaded Iraq. You were one of the instructors. Remember that?"

"I'll be damned," Tyrel said. "Forgot all about it 'til you just said something. You were enlisted back then."

"I was." Grabovsky held out a hand. "Glad to see you made it."

Tyrel shook. "Same to you. So what's next, Captain?"

Grabovsky's demeanor shifted. He was all business now. "First things first, you fellas need to gear up. General Jacobs told me one of you has a black card."

"That would be me," I said.

"We need a vehicle. Something with plenty of cargo space."

I walked behind the reception desk and picked up a radio handset.

"Coming right up," I said.

FIFTEEN

A sergeant driving a deuce-and-a-half stopped in front of the headquarters building. I identified myself and showed my black card. Grabovsky looked at me with newfound respect.

"How long you been in?" he asked.

"Coming up on three years."

"Three?" he said incredulously. "That's it?"

"It ain't the years, it's the miles."

I climbed into the passenger's seat and shut the door. The others filed into the back of the truck. As they went, I heard Grabovsky talking to Gabe.

"He fucking serious?"

"Yep."

"He wasn't in before the Outbreak. How'd he make captain?"

"Field commission."

"From who?"

"General Jacobs."

I watched in the side-view mirror as Grabovsky turned and looked at me. Probably didn't think I could hear him.

"Who the fuck is this guy?"

"Not sure," Gabe said. "Hardly ever talks. But he's good, I can attest to that."

"You worked with him?"

"Lots of times."

Grabovsky shook his head. "I been in twelve goddamn years. Took a silver star and a recommendation from a general to get me a field commission. And they give a black card to a fucking kid? Unbelievable."

The truck rumbled to life and the quiet sergeant drove us toward the south side of the base. I stared out the window as we rolled along, watching servicemen and civilians passing by. No one looked our way. A transport truck going past them was so common as to not warrant attention. I had certainly ignored my fair share.

I wondered if the people around me ever thought about the ROC, or marauders, or infected, or what the world used to be. If I was honest, I tried not to think too much about those things myself. And I was one of the few people in a position to actually *do* something about it. Most people were not. They simply went about their lives and hoped those with the guns and the troops and the power acted in their best interests. It was not a misplaced hope, mostly, as long as the interests of the people and the interests of those in power were aligned. For now, we had common enemies. But if we took care of the ROC, made the highways and trade routes safe from marauders, and exterminated enough infected to prevent another major outbreak, what then?

One more thing I didn't like to think about.

I told the driver where to turn. The truck turned off onto a gravel track leading to a set of four cinder-block buildings in an open field. According to General Jacobs, this was where Peterson AAB kept the lion's share of its supply stock.

By the look of the buildings, they had been built post-Outbreak. A tall chain-link fence topped with concertina wire surrounded them on four sides. There were eight guard towers, all manned with machine guns. The gravel road gave way to a series of concrete highway dividers set in a serpentine pattern to prevent vehicles from rushing the gate. There were two more machine guns guarding the gate—fifty caliber M2s—and several guards with M-4s and grenade launchers. A Humvee parked near the gate had an automatic grenade launcher on the roof turret. I was willing to bet a month's pay that each of the guard towers had at least two LAW rockets.

A guard held up a hand and stepped into the middle of the narrow lane. The driver stopped. I climbed out of the truck, held up my hands, and approached the guard.

"Stop," he said. One of his hands rested on a carbine hanging from a tactical sling, the other was held palm-up toward me.

I stopped.

"Captain Caleb Hicks," I said. "Here on authority of Major General Phillip Jacobs."

"Turn around," the guard said.

I did.

"Walk backward toward my voice."

A dozen or so careful steps. The last thing I wanted was to trip and fall on my ass. Hard to look dignified and official when you're picking yourself up off the ground.

"Stop."

I obeyed.

"Keep your hands where I can see them."

"Okay."

"Are you armed?"

"No."

I heard footsteps approach and someone searched me. They used two hands, so I figured I wasn't about to be shot.

"Keep your hands up and turn around."

I did.

"ID?"

"Left breast pocket."

The guard reached a hand in and removed the leather case holding my black card. He opened it, examined it, compared the picture to my face carefully, and handed it back.

"Sorry, sir. Protocol."

"No worries. Just doing your job."

"Anyone with you other than the driver, sir?"

"One officer and two civilian contractors."

"Can you ask them to step out of the truck please?"

I turned and shouted for them. Gabe, Tyrel, and Grabovsky climbed out of the truck and approached.

"Follow me, please," the guard said.

"What about the truck?" I asked.

"It'll have to stay here, sir. Just until we get authorization."

"Fair enough."

Our quartet followed the guard through the gate. A tension that had been building in my shoulders eased once I was past the business end of the perimeter defenses. It is hard to relax with fifty-cals and grenades ready to end one's existence in spectacular fashion.

The guard led us to one of the buildings and knocked on the door. There was a pause, and I heard an electric *clack*. The guard opened the door and led us inside.

We walked into a foyer with another door at the end. The guard shut the outer door behind us and I heard the lock engage automatically. He approached the other door and waited. Another *clack*, and we went through.

The building was a wide, single-story affair with exposed steel rafters and a smooth concrete floor. There was fluorescent lighting, shiny ventilation ducts overhead, cables and wires running along the bare white walls, and I heard the muffled hum of a generator. Tall rows of steel shelves packed with boxes and crates of all sizes marched off toward the far end of the building. There was airflow, but only enough to keep the interior under eighty degrees. Before

107

the Outbreak, I would have said it was stuffy and uncomfortable. Now, I thought it was a nice break from the relentless heat outside.

There was movement to my right. I turned my head and saw a master sergeant exit a small office with a wide window looking out onto the warehouse floor. He looked first to the guard and handed him a writing pad and pencil, one hand hovering near a sidearm on his right hip. The guard wrote something on the pad and handed it back.

"Okay, sir," the master sergeant said, relaxing as he addressed me. He had a strong Southern accent, was about my height, graying hair cut high-and-tight, lean and strong-looking, and had a hard face turned permanently leathery by the sun. His nametag read Hoffman. "What can I do for you?"

The guard left without being asked. I looked to Grabovsky.

"Got a list for you," he said, pulling a set of papers from a pocket. He unfolded them and handed them to Master Sergeant Hoffman. The sergeant shuffled the papers and scratched his head.

"Sir, I need a requisition form to give you all this."

"Got it right here." I handed him my black card. He looked at it.

"Oh. Right. Well, give me just a minute to get some help-"

"Negative," Grabovsky said. "We ain't above grunt work."

Hoffman nodded. "Fair enough, sir. I'll tell the guards to let your truck through."

*****

Grabovsky got a call and excused himself.

"So much for not being above grunt work," Gabe said. Grabovsky gave him the finger as he walked away.

The rest of us, along with Sergeant Hoffman and a couple of guys he called over for assistance, loaded the rest of our gear onto the truck. It was hot outside, the noonday sun beating down without regard to who it roasted. Shimmering waves of superheated air drifted up from the parking lot, making an already unpleasant day downright miserable. The crates and bags were heavy, and my uniform was soaked through with sweat.

Grabovsky's surprisingly long list had included radio equipment, MRE's, machine guns, explosives, lots of ammunition, night vision equipment, generators, fuel, and enough medical supplies to make even Gabe raise an eyebrow. I was glad I had opted for a large transport and not just a Humvee. I would have had to request additional vehicles.

"Bird's waiting whenever we're ready," Grabovsky said. "You guys got your own gear, right?"

"We do," Tyrel said.

"Where at?"

"Storage building over by the BOQ," Gabe said.

"Hicks," Grabovsky said, "how about you grab three or four bodies and we'll head over there."

"Sure. What do we need the extra men for?"

"What do you think? You wanna unload all this shit by yourself?"

I pointed a finger at him. "Got it."

Hoffman wasn't happy about it, but knew better than to argue with a black card with captain's bars. He fetched us four stout-looking troops, all privates who had probably been in the Army for roughly fifteen minutes each, and told them to go with us. I assured Hoffman I would have my driver return his men when we were done with them.

"Thank you, sir," he said. He did not look grateful. Neither did the men going with us.

The BOQ was a short drive away. I told the driver to keep the truck idling while we handled our business. I swung by my room and put away a few possessions I had left out that morning. Then I grabbed a duffel bag and filled it with two pairs of spare boots (both already broken in), four sets of dark combat fatigues with no insignia, a small case of body paint used for camouflage, extra socks and underwear, my Beretta and its suppressor, and a personalized wilderness survival kit.

Next I unlocked the closet and took out my sniper rifle, a SCAR 17 modified for long-range work. The SCAR was a recent acquisition, and not one I had paid for.

Upon receiving my black card from General Jacobs, he had instructed me in its use. Being a federal emissary granted me access to almost every government facility in the country, as well as the authority to requisition or commandeer anything I needed from within the military or federal law enforcement community. Which, being stationed in the Springs, was great. However, if I went anywhere without a military installation nearby, my black card was worth precisely jack shit.

But since I *was* in the Springs, and likely would be for the next couple of years, I decided the one thing I would always need would be a good sniper rifle. So off I went to a building set aside for JSOC operators and other special ops types where they could outfit themselves with weapons and equipment not normally available to your average infantry grunt. Having been the aforesaid infantry grunt for over two years, walking into the local JSOC armory for the first time was like walking into a candy store. This was the kind of gear I could only dream about in my previous assignment.

I spoke to the guy in charge of the place, a scarred Navy SEAL master chief who looked like he ate anvils for breakfast, and explained what I was looking for. He was cold at first, but when he realized I was knowledgeable and not some idiot there to drool over cool-looking guns, he brightened up and said he might have something for me.

The two of us spent the next hour building my ideal semi-auto sniper system from the ground up. When we were finished, he let me borrow a Leupold scope and took me to test the rifle at the sniper range. After zeroing the scope, I was able to group .5 minute-of-angle shots at a hundred yards. In other words, at one hundred yards the shots all landed within half an inch of one another. At two hundred yards, they hit within 1 inch, an inch and a half at three-hundred yards, and so on. Since the SCAR fired powerful NATO 7.62x51 cartridges, I tested it out to 700 yards. Same result.

"This'll do nicely," I said to the master chief, whose name was Grumley.

"You're never returning it, are you?" he replied.

"You can have the scope back," I said, smiling.

"Very generous of you."

"Not really. Got my own. Nightforce one to nine power, thirty millimeter."

"In that case, fuck you very much."

I made sure to bring the rifle with me every time I had occasion to visit Master Chief Grumley. The gesture significantly mitigated his hatred toward me.

Before I left my room, I stripped the sheets from the bed and put them in a laundry cart at the end of the hall. The maids had been by earlier in the day. The floor had been swept, the bathroom had been scrubbed, the small kitchen I never used wiped spotless. No dust, no dirt, and other than the locks on my dresser and closet, no sign anyone lived here. My duffel bag was in one hand, my rifle hanging over my shoulder.

I wondered if I would ever see the place again.

SIXTEEN

"At least it's a dry heat."

I turned to look at Grabovsky. My sunglasses dialed down the harsh glare of the Nevada sun enough to make it tolerable, but the heat was a different matter.

"It's still fucking hot," I said.

"'Bout a hundred and fifteen," Gabe said.

Grabovsky consulted his tablet. "I'll be damned. It's a hundred and seven, heat index one-fifteen."

Gabe nodded. He and Tyrel were wearing wrap-around sunglasses like mine, along with weather-beaten keffiyehs wound over their heads and loosely across their faces. The big greenish scarves had checkered patterns to break up their wearer's outline and sheer see-through stripes that could be worn over the eyes if necessary. I had seen Iraq and Afghanistan veterans wearing similar garb before. Sometimes they called it a shemagh instead of a keffiyeh. I didn't know the difference. All I knew was I was tired of wind-blown dust caking my head and neck and wished I had one. The scarf in my possession was of the narrow winter variety. Good for protecting my mouth and keeping out bits of ghoul flesh when need arose, but not much else. And because of its thick fabric, it was too damned hot to wear at the moment.

"How long do we have to wait here?" I asked.

"The fuck should I know?" Grabovsky flipped the cover closed on his tablet and slipped it into his assault pack. "Get here when they get here."

The four of us were seated at a lone picnic table next to a trash can, and, of all things, a charcoal grill. The tiny picnic area faced a cracked, sun-bleached parking lot with crudely painted symbols designating it as a helipad. It was a mile away from the airstrip at Army Air Station Fallon, formerly Naval Air Station Fallon.

Since there was not much left of the Navy, I doubted any of their people had complained when the Army took the place over.

The C-130 that flew us to Nevada had touched down around 1400 hours. We exited the plane to find a major with an arm patch identifying him as part of the Army Expeditionary Corps, formerly the Marine Corps before they were disbanded and absorbed into the Army (which went over about as well as a turd in a hot tub), who ushered us into the back of a deuce-and-a-half. Our gear was loaded in afterward and someone drove us to the helipad.

Upon arrival, another crew of soldiers was waiting to help unload our gear. Once done, they piled in the truck and retreated to a set of tents around a field barracks a few hundred yards away. As best I could tell, we were the only people around.

I knew our next destination was FOB Winnemucca. I knew after arriving there we would wait until after nightfall, and then a Chinook would fly us and our gear to an undisclosed location near the Oregon border. This gave me a few things to consider. First was the Army's definition of the word 'near'. Near could mean a few feet, or it could mean fifty miles or more. My guess was we were looking at something closer to the latter. The second consideration was the Chinook itself. With the amount of gear we were bringing, I figured the bird could make it four-hundred nautical miles, maximum, before it would need to refuel. And, according to the encrypted message on Grabovsky's tablet, we were to expect a fuel stop along the way. Bearing this in mind, I took a highway map out of my pack and began tracing it with a measuring compass.

"Where'd you get that?" Tyrel asked.

"Bought it," I said.

"From who?"

"A guy in the Springs."

"The compass too?"

"Already had that. Comes in handy, so I keep it in my pack. Don't you have one?"

"Well yeah, but…"

"But what?" I looked up at Tyrel. "I'm too young and inexperienced to think ahead?"

My old friend reddened. "That's not what I meant, Caleb."

I waved a hand. "Figured since the mission was out this way, it wouldn't hurt to have a backup map. Especially seeing as Central didn't see fit to send any along with us."

"I got our maps," Grabovsky said.

Figured as much. "Mind if I take a look?"

"Give 'em out when it's time."

"Which means we're not supposed to see them yet."

A shrug.

I went back to my map.

"Got something there?" Gabe asked. He turned around so he could see the map laid out on the table. His sunglasses did not let me see his eyes, but I could tell from his posture he was curious.

"Chinook can go about four-hundred nautical miles before refueling. As the crow flies, that's about four-hundred-fifty or so regular miles. They're supposed to refuel, but I'm thinking that's just to get 'em back to Winnemucca." I circled an area on the map in the center of Northern California, directly south of the Klamath Basin. "Which probably puts us somewhere around here in the Tulelake National Refuge. I'm guessing probably thirty or forty miles from the target area."

Grabovsky stared at me in silence for a few seconds. "Goddamn, kid. I thought you were regular Army."

"Was. Not anymore."

He leaned closer and touched a finger to the map. "Grunts don't do this kind of shit. Not since the Outbreak. They go where they're told to go and shoot what they're told to shoot. Thinking's not part of the job description."

Tyrel chuckled. "Caleb ain't no grunt."

Grabovsky glanced at him, then back at me. "So who trained you?"

I tried to give Tyrel a stern look but stopped myself. Not much point with the sunglasses on. Nevertheless, he got the message and stayed quiet. Gabe, for his part, looked on curiously. To him, this interaction was just another piece of the puzzle. He knew I used to live in the Springs, knew I'd been married, knew how I ended up in the Army, and he knew Tyrel had a hand in raising me. It was only a matter of time before he figured me out, assuming he had not already.

"So what you're telling me," I said, countering Grabovsky's question, "is I'm right."

"Didn't say that."

"Come on, Grabovsky. We're all in this together. What's with the secrecy?"

"Orders. That's what."

I let it go. I knew what made guys like Grabovsky tick. When the president had ordered all troops to report to duty stations back during the Outbreak, I was willing to bet Grabovsky had not hesitated. I doubted the idea of deserting had ever entered his mind, even when things were falling apart and it looked like there was no hope. Grabovsky was a soldier. It was not just his job, it was his identity. Moreover, he was a Green Beret. Or Delta Force, more likely. My father had been in Delta Force. It takes a certain kind of person to do that job, and in that regard, Grabovsky was a poster boy. Which meant if his orders were to withhold information until a certain point in time, he would do so regardless of anyone's feelings on the subject.

115

I folded the map and put it away. The compass went back into its side pocket. I took off my hat, ran a hand across my forehead, flicked an inordinate amount of sweat to the ground, and replaced the hat. The band encircling my head felt warm, wet, and gritty with dust and salt. I took a pull from my canteen, swished it around, and spit it out. My mouth did not feel any better.

"Shouldn't waste water," Grabovsky said. "We're in the desert."

I took another sip, swished it around, and spit again. Grabovsky got up, grabbed his pack, and walked toward the field barracks.

"You don't like him much," Gabe said when Grabovsky was out of earshot.

I took a drink. "What's to like?"

"You don't know him. I do. He helped me train the Ninth Tennessee Volunteer Militia a few years ago. We fought together against the Free Legion. He's a good man."

"We'll see."

"My word isn't enough?"

"I'm sure he's tough as nails and brave as a mongoose. But the fact you like him doesn't stop him from having his own agenda."

Tyrel adjusted his sunglasses. "Gotta say I'm with Caleb on this one."

Gabe stared out at the desert. "Point taken."

*****

Winnemucca was depressing.

I was not sure what to expect when we landed there. I knew the Army had come through two years ago and set up an FOB in the remote town. I knew they had cleared out the infected and opened the place up for settlement. A few hardy folks had even registered claims and gave it an honest try.

116

They'd come with supplies, tools, wagons, plows, seeds, building materials, everything needed to run a successful farm co-op. The aquifer and irrigation network that had kept the town alive before the Outbreak was still intact. Clean water for drinking and irrigation was not a problem. In fact, it was downright plentiful. There were settlements in far gentler lands to the east that could not say the same.

As for undead, the FOB sent out regular patrols, but rarely encountered anything. The area had been sparsely populated before the Outbreak, and federal extermination efforts had been thorough. Northern Nevada was the closest thing to a ghoul-free zone one was likely to find. But as it turns out, living in a desert climate during the summer without air conditioning is an exercise in abject misery.

The settlers came in early autumn. By late summer the following year, they had all left.

The news hacks on civilian radio made a big deal out of the failed settlement for a while. Federal inefficiency and all that, as if a bunch of civilians biting off more than they could chew was somehow the government's fault. Then some crisis or another came along and everyone forgot. Everyone except stodgy dorks like me, that is. I thought the story was fascinating when I first heard it, but being here made it all too real. The heat, the dust, the empty sky, the unrelenting sun, the feeling of lifelessness about the place; I could only imagine the settlers dismay when the temperate winter faded and the harsh reality of this hellish land made itself evident. I would have fled too.

The troops stationed in the area seemed to share the ill-fated settlers' sentiments, but were forced by circumstance to remain. I found myself re-examining my own service in the Army and the hardships thereof. There had been a time when I thought I had it pretty rough. A sweltering day in the harsh glare of the merciless Nevada sun was enough to disabuse me of this notion. My fate could have been much worse. I could have been stationed in Winnemucca.

After the Chinook dropped us off outside the FOB, an open top truck and a few troops met us and helped us load our gear. When

117

we finished, the troops climbed into the truck with us for the ride back to base. Tyrel tried to strike up a conversation with a young sergeant, but got only a grunt and a sour look. We made a brief stop at the gate where a surly contingent of officers and senior NCOs looked us over and checked our IDs. If my black card impressed them, they gave no sign. When the captain in charge was satisfied we were not enemy troops, he ordered the guards to let us through.

As near as I could tell, the troops were all men. No women. That by itself would have been enough to challenge my sanity, but it got worse. The town itself was deserted. What hadn't been burned down had been thoroughly looted. All that remained were scorched lots, cracked and broken streets, empty businesses, and houses waiting to collapse. No civilians meant no restaurants, no bars, no taverns, no festivals, no farmer's market, no music, no culture, and certainly no entertainment. There wasn't even a brothel. I pointed this fact out to Tyrel.

"How bad's a place gotta be even whores won't go there?" he said.

"Pretty damn bad. You'd think this place would be a hooker's paradise. No competition, no regulations, no cops, Army base full of swinging dicks with nothing better to do. It's a goddamn gold mine."

"Ain't enough, apparently."

I looked around again. "Even the weeds look miserable."

The FOB was pretty standard. Four long walls, watchtowers, tents, Quonset huts, and a few cinder-block buildings with metal roofs. The perimeter walls were chain-link fences topped with concertina wire and reinforced with earth-filled HESCO bastions. Beyond the fence was a tall earthen berm and a deep trench where the ground had been dug up. The surrounding area was flat and open, providing an excellent field of fire. No one would be sneaking up on FOB Winnemucca anytime soon.

The driver cruised toward the north side of the base, pulled around behind a building that smelled of food cooking, and stopped.

"Chow's being served," the driver said as we disembarked. He was already walking away. I thought about reminding him to say 'sir', but decided it wasn't worth it.

"Friendly place," Gabe noted dryly.

"May as well get a bite to eat," Tyrel said. "No telling when we'll get another hot meal."

I followed the others into the chow hall. It looked like every other post-Outbreak chow hall I had seen. Low ceiling, exposed rafters, corrugated metal roof and walls, long wooden tables and benches, food served buffet style at one end of the building, big window for dirty dishes and flatware at the other end. I got a plate and walked the chow line. Peas, beans, rehydrated chicken, dried fruit, flatbread, and not a scrap of flavor to be found. The beverage of the day was water. Something told me that particular menu item never changed. I fervently hoped in the near future a few enterprising souls from somewhere tea and coffee could be grown once again found their way to American shores.

We took our plates to an unoccupied corner and ate quietly. The chow hall was hushed and oppressive. Only a few people engaged in muttered conversation, the words loud enough for the parties involved to hear and no more. The atmosphere made me uneasy, and by the looks on their faces, the others in my group felt it as well. This was not right. A chow hall was a place to relax, a place to enjoy a meal with friends and tell jokes and laugh loudly and forget about the drudgery of military life for a little while. Here, there was no such respite. It left me to wonder what relief these men had from the daily indignities and frustrations all soldiers suffered. These men needed an outlet, and from what I could tell, they had none available.

I did not know what the time-on-station requirements were, but I hoped they were short. FOB Winnemucca felt like a powder keg. And when it went up, I hoped I was far away.

SEVENTEEN

Heinrich,

The Wastelands

After leaving Arkansas, Heinrich and what remained of the Storm Road Tribe trekked westward for over a week until they reached Highway 59 in Oklahoma. It was a difficult and costly journey, the infected dogging their trail the entire way and claiming eighteen of Heinrich's men. The terrain was rough and hilly with few places to rest. Several times they were forced to march through the night on narrow back-country roads in order to avoid being overrun. Worse, they could not use firearms to fend off the infected due to low ammunition and the fact that if they did, the noise would attract far larger hordes. The only strategy left to them was to utilize humanity's greatest advantage over the undead—speed.

Those who lacked the endurance to keep up were left behind. Heinrich paid lip service to the sad necessity of their loss, but inwardly, he did not care. He detested weakness, and there were always men willing to take up with a successful tribe. What was lost could be replaced.

Upon reaching Highway 59, Heinrich urged his men onward until they topped a hill and saw the waters of Lake Eucha beneath them. A long bridge spanned the narrow waterway leading to yet more rugged hill country to the north. This was good. The hills bordering the north and south shores of the lake would act as a natural barrier against the undead. The lake itself would protect them to the east and west, and the bridge was easily defensible with the resources on hand. Once there, it was a simple matter to fell trees and build a makeshift fort where the tribe could rest a few days.

During this time, Heinrich took stock of his situation. Excluding himself, he was down to a hundred men. He liked that. 100 was a nice round number. A good place to start. The thought made him smile. Less than two weeks before, he'd been cursing his luck at being chased out of Parabellum. Now, he was enjoying himself. It was an enlightening moment. For so long, Heinrich had thought his future lay in securing a stronghold and lording over it. But now that he was back on the road, he realized how much he had missed nomadic life.

That aside, there was still the matter of the tribe's morale to consider. While Heinrich may have been taking things in stride, his men were not. They were tired, sore, and nearly beaten. The rest was good, but they needed something more, something to energize them, get their minds off what they had lost. For Heinrich, the answer was not hard to come by. Supplies were low, enough for two or three days at most even with careful rationing. This, at least, was a problem the men could do something about.

Heinrich divided the tribe into two groups. One was tasked with searching the immediate area for anything useful: guns, ammo, game trails, wild edibles, fishing tackle, boats, etc. The other group he tasked with hunting for meat. He did not particularly care what kind.

As it turned out, there was a game refuge to the west accessible by the lake. Heinrich's men found several canoes and small fishing boats, as well as a plentitude of fishing tackle in nearby abandoned houses. They went to work hunting and fishing, and within a few days, the bridge was covered with small fires and wooden racks of drying meat.

The tribe remained on the bridge for twelve days. While they rested, some of the men came to Maru and quietly suggested maybe the valley wasn't such a bad place to settle down. Maru brought the idea up to Heinrich, but he would not hear of it. Why work and hunt when there were plenty of victims out there to do it for them? All the tribe had to do was find them and take what they wanted. Farming was for sheep. The tribe were wolves.

The idea, however, was gaining momentum. Faced with this new challenge, Heinrich reached into his bag of tricks and pulled out two of the oldest motivators known to man: greed and fear.

He told the men the area was not sufficient to sustain them long term. Furthermore, there were no women, no booze, and no crops. Eventually, they would hunt the area out, overfish the lake, and suffer malnutrition from a lack of fruits and vegetables. People could not survive solely on meat, after all. The lake was a good place to rest and resupply, but soon they would have to move on. And besides, did none of them ever want to fuck a woman again?

It was enough to compel the tribe into action.

When they had stocked enough supplies to last a couple of weeks, Heinrich announced it was time pack up and move out. A few scouting parties rounded up what materials could be found and constructed crude carts to load the food onto. It was an unwieldy way to travel, but the only other option was to starve. So the men bent their backs to it and made it work.

Two days northward, the tribe reached the broad waterways of the Neosho River. They encountered only a few infected along the way. This part of Oklahoma was, ostensibly, the edge of federally patrolled territory. But in truth, the government hardly ever sent troops this far south. Not since Operation Relentless Force, anyway. Despite the lack of a federal presence, the undead population was very low in the region. It had not been heavily populated before the Outbreak, and the architects of Relentless Force had sent more than ten thousand troops into Northern Oklahoma to ensure the undead there would not find their way into Kansas. Their efforts were still paying dividends.

Maru informed Heinrich the men wanted to build another camp on the bridge and rest a day or two.

"No," Heinrich said. He stood on the roof of an abandoned fast food restaurant, a pair of binoculars up to his eyes, scanning the edges of the waterway. The area had once been home to a prosperous community of upper-crust lake dwellers and the businesses that catered to them. Now, it was a burned out ruin pocked with artillery craters, bullet holes, and strewn with heaps of rubble and ash. The restaurant was one of the few buildings still standing.

"You want us to cross and camp on the other side?" Maru asked.

"No."

Maru narrowed his eyes. "Then what's the plan?"

Heinrich lowered the binoculars and pointed toward the shoreline. "Every house on this side of the peninsula has a boat house. Over there to the east, you see that floating dock?"

"'Fraid not, Chief."

"Here." He handed Maru the binoculars. "See it now?"

"Yeah, I do. Wait…those boats…"

"Look pretty good, don't they?"

"Yeah. The motors are in good shape. I bet they even work. Somebody's been taking care of them."

"You have any idea how much it costs in time, energy, parts, and fuel to keep a boat running these days?" Heinrich asked.

Maru shook his head. "Just the fuel alone is a small fortune."

"You see anybody guarding them? Any sign someone's been there recently?"

"Hard to tell from here, but no. I don't think so."

"Exactly. So tell me, who has enough trade to pay for boats like that and not give a fuck if someone steals them?"

The binoculars came down, and Maru showed his teeth. "Smugglers."

"Get the squad leaders together. We have planning to do."

*****

Four days passed.

Heinrich began to think the smugglers were not coming back. Perhaps they had found a new route, or were captured or killed. Any scenario was equally likely. His prime motivation for staying and waiting had been the condition of the boats. They were in good working order, something one almost never saw anymore. He doubted they had been left to rot; someone was coming back for them, and soon.

That had been his thought, anyway. Now, he was not so sure.

He and Maru and a few other high-ranking tribe members had taken up residence in several abandoned lake houses out of sight of the shoreline. The rest of Heinrich's men were spread out along the lake front keeping an eye out for anyone approaching the boats. This had been the situation since Heinrich discovered the boats and resolved to intercept their owners.

Despite the frustration of waiting, there were factors working in Heinrich's favor. Chief among them was the fact the tribe now had working radios. They had brought the radios with them from the supply caches outside Parabellum, but had, until now, lacked the ability to charge them. The day they arrived at Lake Neosho, during their reconnaissance around the lake, a team of searchers had found a house with operational solar panels. The panels needed cleaning, but once that was done, they charged the house's bank of deep-cycle batteries to 100%. Heinrich immediately ordered a charging station set up and selected a cadre of men to act as runners. The runners, for their part, had found several bicycles in decent condition, only needing to re-inflate the tires. Twice daily they visited the central supply cache and, under Maru's supervision, swapped out dead batteries for charged ones and delivered rations to the men keeping watch over the lake.

"Two more days," Heinrich said thoughtfully. He sat on the front porch of the house in the late afternoon drinking hot water and picking his teeth with a fish bone.

"What's that, Chief?" Maru asked. He sat in a chair on the opposite side of the porch.

"We'll wait two more days," Heinrich said. "Then we'll take the motors off the boats and move on."

Maru stood up and leaned against one of the columns supporting the second floor balcony. In front of him, a flat expanse of trees and waist high grass stretched westward toward the lake a quarter of a mile away. Birds chirped and squawked. Insects buzzed and fluttered their wings in the still air. A grasshopper jumped onto the porch railing next to him. Maru flicked it away with one thick finger.

"Won't have much to trade when we get to the Springs, way things are going," Maru said.

"Don't worry. Something will come along. It always does."

Maru stayed silent for a while. When he tired of standing he walked back to his chair. "What if it doesn't? Way I hear it, trade routes are better guarded now. Seems what we did to that big caravan a while back got people's attention."

"So what? They'll be more vigilant for a while, and when nothing happens, they'll go back to the way things were. Ain't the first time, won't be the last."

"Sure. But that don't help us now."

Heinrich felt his irritation growing. "What are you getting at Maru? Don't fuck around with me. You got something to say, say it."

The big Maori looked at his chief, then down at the boards under his feet. "Don't know what I'm saying, if I'm honest. Letting doubts creep in, I guess."

Heinrich settled back into his chair. "Well knock it off. We got two more days of this shit, and if nothing happens, we move on. We'll find a caravan sooner or later. And if we don't, worst case scenario is we go up north and raid some farms. It's only June, Maru. We got plenty of time to store up supplies for winter."

Maru nodded. The sun descended the horizon as another hour passed. The two men did not speak to each other. Just as the sky was beginning to turn purple to the east, Heinrich heard the sound of tires crunching over gravel. He stood up, climbed the stairs inside the house, grabbed his binoculars, and stood on the second floor balcony. One of his runners was inbound, pedaling for all he was worth on a pink bicycle decorated with white kittens. Maru met the runner at the driveway.

"We got something, sir," the rider called out.

Heinrich walked downstairs and came out onto the porch. "What?"

"Sixteen men, all armed, driving wagons, headed toward the lake."

"Coming from the south?" Heinrich asked.

"Yes sir."

He paused to think. "How many wagons?"

"Four."

"Livestock?"

"Horses. Two per cart."

"Any idea what's in the carts?"

"No sir. They're covered."

"What kind of weapons?"

"Assault rifles, mostly. Pistols and shotguns too."

"Explosives?"

"Not sure, sir. Couldn't tell."

"All right. Give me your radio."

Heinrich sent out a message to all squad leaders and told them to pass it down to the men. When he finished, he added, "And remember: don't shoot the goddamn horses. They're valuable. We need them. Heinrich out."

He gave the radio back to the runner and motioned for him to leave. While the man pedaled away, Heinrich smiled at Maru. "See? Told you something would come along."

The big Maori nodded assent, one hand resting on his machete. "Right you are, Chief."

EIGHTEEN

"They're meeting someone," Maru said.

Obviously, Heinrich thought. "No other reason to stay on the island."

"We got eyes up north, Chief?"

"I sent Locke and his crew this morning. Should be in position by now."

Maru brought up his binoculars. "Seems like north is where they'll come from. Why else meet here at the river? Could meet on land anywhere they want. Gotta be from up north."

Which is why I sent an entire squad to look for them, idiot. "If they do, our guys will spot them."

Before Maru could state the obvious again, the radio crackled.

"Chief, Six Lead. How copy?"

"Lima Charlie, Six. What do you got?"

"Boats, Chief. Five of them, hidden in a barn, all in good shape."

"Roger. Back off and keep eyes on them. Leave no trace. Call in if you see anyone coming."

"Copy, Chief. Six out."

"Three and Seven, move to positions designated Sierra and India. One and Two, proceed to position Zulu. All other squads, round up the canoes and land them on the western bank of area designated Tango. Once on land, move the boats to the southeastern shore. Move quietly and stay out of sight, but make sure those canoes are in position by nightfall. All stations, acknowledge and repeat."

The other six squad leaders repeated back the orders given to them.

"Very good," Heinrich said. "Chief out."

"Time to go?" Maru said.

"One second."

Heinrich looked again through the binoculars. The men that arrived the previous day had split into two groups. One group had driven the wagons to the northern shore of one of several peninsulas jutting into the winding river. There, they had waited for the other group to drive the boats to a covered dock nearby. The wagons had then been offloaded and their cargo transferred to the boats. Afterward, twelve of the smugglers landed the boats on a narrow stretch of beach on the western side of the island, then dragged the boats ashore to keep them from floating away on the strong river current. Four men had remained behind on the peninsula to guard the wagons and livestock.

Four men weren't much of a challenge for Heinrich and Maru alone, much less the entire Storm Road Tribe. The other twelve smugglers now camped on the western shore of the island would not be much trouble either. The only wild card was the party approaching from the north. Heinrich wanted eyes on them before he made a move. Until then, he had to wait.

*****

The smugglers on the northern shore pushed their boats into the river an hour after nightfall. It was full dark now, a haze of clouds turning the sky opaque. The four men left behind to guard the

129

wagons were still on the northern peninsula, sitting around a fire roasting fish they had caught earlier in the day. This was good news. Staring into the flames would ruin the smugglers' night vision, whereas The Storm Road Tribe, having spent the last hour in darkness with their eyes adjusting to the night, had no such handicap.

Heinrich keyed his radio. "Six, Three, and Seven, this is Chief. Hold position. Anybody comes your way that isn't tribe, take 'em out. All other squads, prepare to begin assault. Sound off assignments by numbers. Over."

"Chief, One. Position Zulu, northern shore. Eyes on the docks. Over."

"Chief, Two. Hundred yards southeast of One. Over."

"Chief, Four. Location Tango. Over."

"Chief, Five. Hundred yards south of Four. Over."

"Acknowledged. I'm sending Maru to One. Two, converge on One's position. Over."

"Chief, Two. Wilco. Over."

Heinrich turned to Maru and handed him a radio. "Take charge of squads One and Two and deal with the rear guard. Do it quietly. I'll go up on overwatch."

"Right, Chief." Maru took the radio and slipped soundlessly into the night.

When his second-in-command was well out of earshot, Heinrich belly crawled out of the ditch he lay in, slid down a shallow embankment, grabbed his pack and rifle case, and set out northeast at a fast jog.

The road he followed led to a group of lake houses positioned on the northern shore of the peninsula. As he ran, he passed a wide road leading to a parking lot that once served the boat dock where the four smugglers still on the peninsula had struck camp. Heinrich kept running. In another thirty yards he turned northward on a tree-lined driveway leading to a massive lakefront house.

130

The front door was open. Heinrich had come by earlier in the day to make sure of that. Once inside, he climbed the stairs to the top floor, entered a bedroom overlooking the river, put his gear down on a dusty, long-unused bed, and opened a window. That done, he went back downstairs and retrieved a chair from the dining room. He sat down so he could see out the bedroom window and brought up his rangefinder.

"Two-hundred twenty yards," he muttered.

Heinrich opened the rifle case and took out his M-110. The semi-automatic sniper system was equipped with his secret weapon, a forward looking infrared (FLIR) long-range scope. He checked the batteries and found they were at full charge. Heinrich turned off the scope and picked up a magazine loaded with 175-grain match-grade 7.62x51 NATO cartridges. There were ten rounds in the mag, more than enough to suit his purposes. Heinrich seated the magazine and pulled back on the charging handle. When he released his grip, the bolt carrier group went forward and a round went into the chamber. He checked the suppressor to make sure it was seated properly, then flicked the safety off.

Next, Heinrich reached in his pack and pulled out an Army issue aiming stick. The stick had a telescoping handle that stretched as tall as six feet and collapsed down to two feet. At its top was a padded, Y-shaped rest where he placed the fore-end of his rifle.

Now the waiting began. Heinrich checked his watch. His men would most likely need six to seven minutes to get into position. He decided to give them ten. The night was young. No need to rush. No need to wait too long either. Too much waiting made people paranoid and sloppy. Warm muscles became cold and stiff, empty bladders filled with piss, fatigue and boredom set in, hunger and thirst became distracting annoyances, and the anticipation of battle made otherwise stern minds uneasy. Best to get his men moving while they were still fresh and aggressive.

Ten minutes passed. Heinrich picked up his radio. "All stations, Chief. Status."

The reports came in. His men were in position.

"All stations, Chief. Stand by."

Heinrich's breathing steadied. His hands moved with deliberate precision. The aiming stick was at the right height, the scope set to the proper magnification, the contact paper he'd put on the trigger a rough texture under his fingertip. He centered the reticle on the only target facing him and adjusted for the difference in elevation. All four of the men at the dock were sitting around the fire. Perfect.

"Point Man, Chief. Engage."

"Copy, Chief," Maru whispered into the radio. "Moving in."

Heinrich waited. The four smugglers sat and talked and made small gestures. They spoke quietly and were careful not to let plates, pans, and other items clank or thump, a sure sign of people accustomed to traveling through infected territory. But at the moment, they were not expecting trouble. The river protected them on three sides, and any undead approaching from the south would be heard long before they arrived. The smugglers had no reason not to relax. Or so they thought.

The man facing Heinrich sat up straight. The raider chief could not make out the smuggler's face in the washed-out FLIR image, but he could tell by the man's posture he had heard something. Even relaxed, these men were still alert. Heinrich repositioned his scope and felt a small pang of regret. Not at the impending loss of life, but at the fact these men would have made good additions to his tribe. Sadly, this was not a recruiting drive. It was a raid. He needed trade, and livestock, and wagons, all of which these people possessed. And they were not likely to give any of it up willingly.

Heinrich watched and waited, willing his heart to beat slowly. His breathing became shallow, his finger tight around the trigger. The man in his sights stood up and swiveled his head from left to right.

"Point man, Chief," Heinrich said. "You've been heard, but not made."

"Copy, Chief. You got eyes on him?"

"Affirmative. Move in, but tell those bastards with you to be fucking quiet."

"Copy, Chief."

The image of the smuggler shifted as he walked to the outer edge of light cast by the fire. Not a smart move. Even without the scope Heinrich would have been able to see his silhouette against the backdrop of night. As Heinrich watched, the man turned and began speaking to his friends.

Now or never.

Heinrich squeezed the trigger. The rifle made a muted *crack* similar to dropping a wooden board on concrete. The smuggler jerked, stumbled backward, and fell on his ass. Heinrich began to shift aim but stopped when Maru and sixteen other men emerged from the darkness ringing the campsite. The three remaining smugglers had enough time to stand and face their attackers before the raiders were on them.

Heinrich watched Maru slug a man in the jaw and then swing his machete in a horizontal slash. The man clutched his throat and went down, lifeblood pulsing from his neck. Maru looked for another target, but the other three men were already down, bludgeoned and punctured by a dozen weapons.

"Chief, Point Man. All targets down."

Heinrich scanned the four bodies. In seconds, they were still. Maru and his men had managed to get very close before being heard. Impressive, but not perfect.

"Copy, Point Man. Hide the bodies and have four of our guys guard the loot. The fuckers on the island might have eyes your way. If they look, I want them to see four men sitting around a fire acting like nothing's wrong. Got it?"

"Affirmative, Chief."

The men moved quickly and efficiently, just as Heinrich had trained them to. He allowed himself a small smile and a moment of satisfaction. Perhaps losing over a hundred of his previous number was a good thing. The strong survive, and the cream rises to the

133

top. At least that was what his father had always told him. Life had thus far given him no reason to disagree.

When the scene of the fight looked the way Heinrich wanted it to, he notified Maru he was inbound and ordered him to have his men prepare to assault the island. When they departed for the peninsula's northern shore, Heinrich returned his rifle to its case, grabbed his assault pack, and headed northward.

"At best count, we're up against two dozen enemies," Heinrich said when he reached the two squads waiting for him. His men were hunkered down behind a treeline that thinned out to scrub grass, and beyond that, a narrow beach of gray river stones. Seven small boats waited on the slender bank, a scavenged collection of canoes and fishing skiffs. Not exactly an armada, but enough to get Heinrich and his men across the roughly four-hundred feet of shallow water to the island immediately northward.

"Six, Three, and Seven are going to stay on the northern bank," Heinrich went on. "If anyone tries to escape, they'll probably head north. Our boys will be there if they do. The rest of you are with me. Four and Five will approach from the west. Their job is to get the smugglers' attention. Once they're engaged, we'll flank them from the south. Everybody clear?"

The men nodded and grunted assent.

"Good. When we hit the island, break up into fire teams. I want five yard intervals, squad leaders hanging back with radios. Squad leaders, keep your men on track. I don't want anyone getting lost in the dark. Understood?"

"Yes sir," the squad leaders said quietly.

"I want a shooter in three of the boats in case we come under fire. Squad leaders, pick your best marksmen. Marksmen, if you hear shots, aim for the muzzle flashes. And no matter what, keep fucking rowing. When we hit that beach, we do it together. No running, no hiding, no letting other fire teams take the heat while you lay in the dirt like cowards. Remember your training, keep your head on a swivel, and stay in the fight. Any man caught slacking will answer to me. Do I make myself clear?"

The men nodded. They had all seen what happened to people who failed to meet Heinrich's expectations, and were duly solemn.

"Squad leaders, have fire team leaders take charge. Move out."

While his men obeyed orders, Heinrich keyed his radio and notified the squads on the opposite side of the river it was time to start the assault.

"Copy, Chief. Six, Three, and Seven holding position."

"Acknowledged. Four and Five?"

"Moving out now, Chief. Will advise when we have a beachhead."

"Copy. Chief out."

Now for the hard part, Heinrich thought.

NINETEEN

Before heading out, Heinrich stashed his M-110 and retrieved his pistol and Chinese AK-47. He hated leaving his sniper rifle behind—he had kept it close to him since the day he found it—but the fight ahead required close-quarters work.

The raider chief sat in his room and placed a hand on the M-110's case, regarding it like a talisman. He understood now why ancient cultures had placed so much value on well-made weapons, going as far as to name them and ascribe them supernatural powers. Heinrich harbored no such superstitions, but he nonetheless felt an attachment to the rifle. Taking time to grab it before fleeing Parabellum had nearly cost him his life, but in retrospect, he was glad he had done it. Losing the M-110 would have been like losing a limb.

Heinrich stood and checked his equipment. The small assault pack contained water, a first-aid kit, and a spare battery pack for his radio. His tactical vest was configured for spare rifle ammo, a fighting knife, small flashlight, multi-tool, and a machete.

Next he checked his rifle. He had only fired it a few times, but it had thus far proved reliable. He'd used others of its kind in the past and had not encountered any failures. Chinese manufacturing may have been shoddy in other areas, but the commies knew how to make a rifle. Heinrich's vest contained six extra magazines. Counting the mag in his weapon, he had 210 rounds.

Last he examined his pistol, a Glock 17 he had owned since before the Outbreak. It was clean and lubricated and ready to go. Heinrich inserted a magazine, chambered a round, dropped the magazine, and replaced the chambered round from his meager supply of spare ammo. The Glock went into a drop holster along with two spare magazines. Fifty-two rounds for the pistol and 210 for the rifle gave him 262 total, which was most of the loadout he had brought with him from the supply cache. His men were similarly equipped.

This raid better produce something, Heinrich thought. *If we don't re-stock soon, we're in deep shit.*

Heinrich left the house, boarded a boat, and sat quietly while two of his men paddled for the island where their intended victims awaited.

*****

The shooting started before Heinrich could see more than a flicker of light from the smugglers' camp.

"One and Two, this is Chief," Heinrich radioed. "Double-time, but maintain intervals. Do it now."

"Chief, One, Copy."

"Chief, Two, Copy."

"Point Man, Chief. Take your fire team and swing around north."

"Copy, Chief. On my way."

Heinrich crouched and increased his pace. The three-man fire team in his charge followed suit. As he moved, the radio crackled in his ear.

"Chief, this is Four. Roving patrol spotted one of our teams on our way in. Had to engage early. Over."

Heinrich choked down his anger and kept his voice even. "Acknowledged. What's your disposition?"

"Landed the boats northwest of the camp. Smugglers are about forty meters off the water, just inside the treeline. We're holding position on the western shore. Five is up north of us. We've got 'em in a crossfire, but it's hard to see anybody in the dark."

"Copy, Four. We'll come in from the east and hold off at thirty meters. Five, on my order, move in and hit 'em with frag."

"This is Five. Copy, Chief. Be advised, we're taking heavy fire."

"Acknowledged, Five. Watch out for our guys coming from the east."

"Copy, Chief."

"One, Two, Point Man, move north until I give word to stop."

A round of acknowledgments came in. Heinrich turned his fire team in the appropriate direction and followed as they darted from tree to tree. The occasional stray bullet careened overhead, ripping wood chunks loose and turning them into high-velocity shrapnel.

When Heinrich had covered what he estimated to be a hundred yards, he took cover and scanned the smugglers' camp. From where he stood, he was directly in line with the campfires to the west. He hissed at his fire team to hold position and keyed his radio.

"One, Two, Point man, stop and proceed toward enemy camp. Hold off at thirty yards and engage."

More acknowledgements. Heinrich waved his fire team closer and set out at a run.

Squads four and five were doing their jobs. As he came within visual of the camp, he saw muzzle flashes spread out over a roughly fifty yard area, all focused westward. The camp itself was empty but the fires still burned, illuminating a small circle of forest.

"One, Two, Point Man, hold up and engage from cover. Four, cease fire. Five, hit 'em with everything you got. Keep 'em distracted."

"This is five lead. Copy, Chief."

Heinrich found a thick tree and took cover behind it. The island was mostly covered with old growth trees and little in the way of brush, meaning there was cover but very little concealment. The ground was loose and rocky, making lying prone painful. Heinrich ignored the discomfort and was grateful he had chosen to attack at night. With the lack of brush to hide in, a daytime raid would have meant heavy casualties, something he could not afford right now.

To his right, Heinrich's fire team hit their bellies, leveled their rifles, and opened fire. Across from their position, squad four ceased fire and the fusillade of stray rounds overhead ceased for the moment. Gunfire erupted all across the raiders' eastern skirmish line as squads one and two joined the fight.

Heinrich shoved aside all thought and scanned the battlefield. He heard screams erupting from the direction of the smugglers, telling him his renewed assault was claiming victims. By constantly shifting the direction of attack, Heinrich had put his targets off balance.

All according to plan.

"Five, this is Chief. Move in and hit 'em with frag. One and Two, direct your fire southwest."

Heinrich saw a muzzle flash in the night and heard bullets impacting trees inches over the heads of his fire team. He came up to one knee, aimed low at the muzzle flash, and squeezed off four rounds. The flashes stopped, as well as the bullets. One of the fire team gunmen looked Heinrich's way and nodded, grinning. Heinrich gave him a thumbs-up, went back to his belly, and rolled to his left, stopping behind another tree. His men followed his example and began firing again. Heinrich approved. Not only would changing position frequently make it harder for the smugglers to hit his men, it would make it seem as if there were more of them than there really were. An overwhelmed enemy was a sloppy enemy, and a sloppy enemy was a dead one.

Above the gunfire, Heinrich heard the smugglers shouting to one another. He could not make out what they were saying, but their tone was decidedly panicked.

Good.

"Five, Chief. Where's my goddamn frag?"

There was no response for a few seconds. Heinrich keyed his radio and asked again. Still nothing. Then his earpiece clicked twice, the signal for acknowledgement when the enemy was close enough to hear if one of Heinrich's men spoke. The raider chief settled down and waited. Less than a minute later, a smuggler stood up and ran screaming toward the western shore. He got three steps before being cut down. As he fell, an explosion rocked the night and Heinrich felt a familiar thump come through the ground and into his torso. The feeling was oddly sexual. There were more screams and more explosions, seven in all.

When the Storm Road Tribe had left Parabellum, there had been enough fragmentation grenades in the emergency caches to outfit his men with two each. Squad five had just exhausted half their supply.

Heinrich risked coming up to his feet to look around, keeping his body bladed behind a tree. The grenades had taken a heavy toll on the smugglers. He heard screams and moans from their direction, and saw a few severed limbs that had been blown into the ring of firelight. No more than eight rifles still fired at his men, all of them focused eastward. "One, Two, Point Man, cease fire," Heinrich radioed. "Four and five, move in and engage."

There were no acknowledgements. Nor were there shouts or challenges or battle cries. His men stayed low and quiet and kept behind cover as much as possible. As they neared the campsite, they held up hands to signal one another. A few smugglers tried to resist and were quickly put down. The rest threw down their weapons and surrendered, begging for mercy. Heinrich ordered squads one and two to reconnoiter the island for survivors. Then he radioed the squads on the northern riverbank and asked if any boats had left.

"Chief, Six. Negative. Be advised, we can't see the southern side of the island."

"Copy, Six. Two, send one of your fire teams to the south shore. Make sure our boats are still there."

"Roger, Chief. En route."

The last of the smugglers were now bound with zip ties and being dragged into the light of the campfires. Heinrich stood up, stretched, and motioned for his fire team to follow.

"Hard part's over, fellas," he said. "Let's see what we got."

The men chattered excitedly as they followed their chief toward the smugglers' blood-spattered camp.

*****

"Casualties?"

"Two," Maru said. "One of Rourke's men took a shot to the leg. Through and through. He'll be all right in a few weeks, long as it don't go septic."

"And the other?"

"Took one in the head. He's done."

Down to 99. "Give him a proper burial."

"Will do, Chief."

Heinrich watched Maru walk away for a few seconds, then turned his attention to his other lieutenant, a red-bearded giant of a man named Ferguson. "What's the story on the cargo?"

"Come take a look," Ferguson said.

He walked over to a stack of white five-gallon buckets lined with trash bags and topped with weather-sealed lids. There were six buckets. Ferguson unscrewed the lid from one and opened the plastic bag within. Heinrich looked down at the contents.

"The fuck is that?"

Ferguson reached down and picked up a dark brown rectangle of dense, sticky resin and squeezed it. The substance resisted being compressed. "Opium. Uncooked."

"Uncooked?"

"The raw stuff. Dry resin. Didn't boil it or filter it much.

"Guys from down south brought it?"

"Looks like."

"Worth anything?"

"Oh, hell yeah. We find a buyer, we got a fuckin' fortune on our hands."

Heinrich walked over to a pile of crates his men had stacked nearby and kicked one. "And what were they trading for?"

"Seed grain. Enough for about five-hundred acres."

Heinrich gave a low whistle. "Son of a bitch. Is it in good shape?"

"No mold or rot, near as I can tell. Have to keep it dry to trade it."

"What about supplies?"

"These guys packed light. Probably didn't figure being on the road more than two weeks. Last us a day or so."

"Better than nothing. Weapons? Ammo?"

"Military M-4s, mostly. Stole 'em or bribed 'em off somebody. 'Bout two-thousand rounds of 5.56."

"Anything else?"

"Few pistols, different calibers. Porn mags, booze, weed. Usual shit."

"What kind of booze?"

"Moonshine. Decent stuff."

"How many bottles?"

"Found twelve so far. Guys are still looking."

"One of them is mine. And one each for you and Maru. You two did most of the hard work, you deserve first pick of the spoils."

"Roger that, Chief."

"The rest we'll trade. Ask around, see if anyone knows where we can sell the opium."

"Will do."

"Any women?"

A frustrated sigh. "Sadly, no."

"What about survivors?"

"Three of 'em. Say they're dope smugglers out of Mississippi."

"I'm curious about that opium. Find out what they know."

"No problem."

"And ask them about the men they were trading with. I want to know who they were and where they came from."

Ferguson nodded.

"I'll leave you to it, Ferg. Anybody needs me, I'll be on the waterfront."

"Sure thing, Chief."

Heinrich left the forest canopy and walked to the shore of the island. The first light of dawn shone through the cloud cover overhead, washing the river and surrounding countryside in shades of blue. The air was damp and heavy with the promise of a hot day ahead. Heinrich sat down on the rocky beach and crossed his legs and listened to the morning. Birds sang in the trees and insects buzzed along the riverbank.

Tired as he was, Heinrich was glad he was awake. The early hours when most of the world was asleep and the new day was still opening its eyes had always had a calming effect on him. He took a deep breath and let it out slowly.

"Something always comes along," he said, nodding to himself. "Something always comes along."

TWENTY

Caleb,

Northern California

The Chinook flew off and left us with a big pile of the olive-drab fiberglass crates the US military is so fond of. I looked at Grabovsky and made a show of indicating the four of us.

"Exactly what the hell are we supposed to do with all this?" I asked. "We'd need half a platoon and two trucks to move it."

Grabovsky flipped up his NVGs and consulted the readout of his tablet. "Nothing to worry about. Someone will be along to collect it."

"Collect it? Who?"

"Friends. Let's get moving. We got a lot of ground to cover."

I looked at the stacks of guns, ammo, medical supplies, food, and communications equipment, and then at Grabovsky. He was already marching northward with NVGs over his eyes, rifle hanging at the ready. Tyrel touched my shoulder as he passed.

"Better get moving, son."

Gabe muttered something under his breath, gave the equipment a long look, and followed. My choices were to either stand there, or go along. So I activated my NVGs and went.

Half a mile passed under my feet before I realized how tense I was. My hands were tight around my rifle, my shoulders hunched, my jaw clenched. I took a long, slow breath and focused on relaxing.

There were a lot of things bothering me. I didn't care for the extreme secrecy surrounding this whole thing. I did not like being in enemy territory and still not knowing the full parameters of my mission. Most of all, I did not like being forced to trust Grabovsky, despite Gabe's endorsement of his character.

I also knew it did not matter what I liked or didn't like. No one had put a gun to my head and forced me into this. I could have turned General Jacobs down when he offered to make me a federal emissary. I could have backed away from this mission when it was offered to me and rejoined the First Recon back in Hollow Rock. General Jacobs had made it clear from the beginning he did not want conscripts in his service, he wanted volunteers. If at any point I did not want to work for him anymore, I need only resign my commission and turn in my black card.

Furthermore, in the last two and a half years, I could have deserted the Army whenever I wanted and started a new life in any of the multitude of communities between Tennessee and Colorado. Plenty of people far dumber than me had done exactly that. Federal records were not what they used to be, and while there was an extensive file on me in the Archive, a simple name change and establishing myself in a community where I was unknown would make it next to impossible for a federal agent to find me. Assuming one was sent for me at all. I doubted that would happen. The feds had bigger problems than tracking down a lone deserter fleeing a felony rap.

But I had not refused to work for General Jacobs. I had not turned down any missions. I had not deserted the Army, nor did I intend to. On the march northward through the Cascade Mountains, I examined my reasons for this.

145

The first question was why I had not left the Army. My time in service had been an unending parade of dangers and near-death experiences. So why had I stayed? I could have left at any time. I was not afraid to face the world on my own. Fear did not factor into the equation. So what was it?

Another mile passed. The pine forest around me grew taller, the land steeper and more difficult to traverse. We were at high altitude and the air was cool, but I was still sweating from the effort of carrying my heavy gear and weapons. The others looked to be having the same difficulty. Even Gabe, with his near inexhaustible endurance, stopped occasionally to fill his lungs before continuing.

It's the altitude. We're not used to it.

We climbed a natural switchback trail along the southern face of a low mountain and then followed a ridgeline westward. Another couple of miles passed. The ground underfoot became increasingly rocky, slowing our pace. Even with NVGs to see our way in the dark, it was nearly impossible to exercise noise discipline. Any infected within half a kilometer had undoubtedly heard us and were inbound. It was bad enough we were traveling at night in an area with a high infected population, but add to this the fact we were also in enemy territory with limited ammunition and no air support, and it was a recipe for disaster. I just hoped Grabovsky knew where he was going.

The ground leveled off and the going was easier for a while. Ahead of me, Grabovsky signaled a halt, consulted his tablet, and then indicated for us to follow him northward. Less than a hundred yards later, the forest opened up onto a narrow, back-country stretch of crumbling asphalt.

Normally, I would not have been enthusiastic about traveling along a road. Roads are magnets for infected and marauders, and I had always made a point of staying away from them whenever possible. If I had no choice but to follow a road, I paralleled it from a safe distance. In this instance, however, since I was running on just a few hours of sleep, very little food, and facing an open-terrain march of indeterminate distance, I was willing to make an exception.

For the first couple of kilometers, the forest rose high to my right, obscuring the country to the north. After a while, though, the road curved down a hill and the forest fell away along a steep embankment. I flipped up my NVGs and peered through the FLIR scope on my sniper rifle. Gabe covered the distance between us and stopped next to me.

"What do you see?" he asked.

"Take a look."

I handed him my rifle. He used it to gaze northward. A few seconds later, he grunted and handed the weapon back.

"I believe that's Mount Shasta up there," he said.

"Yep. Which means if we're on the road I think we're on, we're about seven miles from I-5 and about fifteen from the 97."

Gabe flipped up his NVGs and raised an eyebrow at me. "'The' 97?"

"Isn't that how Californians refer to highways, prefacing numbers with 'the'?"

"Back in the day, yeah. How'd you know about that?"

"Born in San Diego. Dad moved there with my mom after the Army. Got stuck in the habit, always referred to highways as 'the' something when most people just called them by their numbers. People thought he was from California."

"He wasn't?"

"No. Wyoming."

Gravel crunched to my right. I looked over my shoulder to see Grabovsky standing close by.

"When you two are done gazing into each other's eyes, we need to get moving."

I flipped down my NVGs with a middle finger and motioned for him to lead the way.

The road curved northward again and eventually intersected with a larger, less dilapidated highway. I cast a glance behind me as we turned and regarded the old two lane we were leaving. The

147

asphalt was breaking apart into sections large and small, potholes dotted the surface every ten feet or so, and grasses, flowers, small shrubs, and trees were pushing their way up through the cracks. Not twenty yards from where I stood, a pine sapling nearly five feet tall occupied the center of the eastbound lane. In another five years, I would have to dig under the deepening layer of dead vegetation to find asphalt.

"Look on my works, ye mighty, and despair."

Gabe was walking beside me and stopped when he heard me speak. "*Nothing beside remains 'round the decay of that colossal wreck. Boundless and bare, the lone and level sands stretch far away.*"

I looked at him. "You've read Shelley."

"Just that one."

"Not a fan of romanticism?"

"Not particularly. Writers from that era were long on angst and short on experience."

"Hell, you could say that about any poet."

"True." Gabe jerked his head in Grabovsky's direction. "Better get moving. Unless you want a lecture on noise discipline."

I started walking. "Why is Grabovsky in charge, anyway? Never got any orders about that."

"You know where we're going?"

"No."

"There's your reason."

I could think of no good argument, so I kept my mouth shut.

*****

Dawn was near.

Grabovsky called a stop in a clearing at the bottom of a steep valley. Two mountains rose up on either side of us, their peaks lost in the haze of morning mist above. I sat down on a boulder halfway sunk into the gravelly earth. My pack was heavy on my shoulders, and the tactical sling tethering me to my rifle had begun to chafe my neck. I adjusted it so it rested on my shoulder. Gabe sat down next to me. The boulder was just big enough for the two of us. Tyrel took off his pack and lay down with his back against it.

Gabe looked at me. "What's on your mind?"

"Why do you ask?"

"You look preoccupied."

I shrugged. "I was contemplating whether or not to take off my pack. It always feels good to drop it, but putting it back on is a bastard."

A quiet laugh. "My advice, keep it on. Damn things get heavier every time you take 'em off."

"Yes they do."

Grabovsky dropped his pack and sat down on it. His legs were short enough that doing so was not uncomfortable for him. I would have looked like a spider taking a dump if I'd tried the same thing. It wasn't until then I realized how short Grabovsky was, maybe five-foot-eight in his boots. But what he lacked in height he made up for in mass. His shoulders were broad and rounded, his hands big and brutal-looking, and his legs were thick as tree trunks. He took off his helmet to wipe sweat away, revealing a shaved head and a bull neck with wider circumference than the base of his skull.

"You hear that?"

I looked at Tyrel. He was sitting up straight, head erect, eyes fixed to the south. I stood up and held my breath, ears straining. There was nothing at first, then a low, keening howl drifted into the valley like a tendril of fog.

"Shit," Gabe said. "Didn't think they'd catch us this soon. Damn things must be getting faster."

"Or were close by when they heard us," I said.

"That too."

Grabovsky remained sitting. "Relax. Sound carries different here 'cause of the mountains. Ghouls are over a mile away."

"You sure about that?" I asked.

"C'mere. I'll show you."

I walked over and kneeled so I could see the tablet's screen. I had used similar tech before with the First Recon, but Grabovsky's device was a highly ruggedized version designed for special ops use. The screen was smaller, the resolution higher, and the battery larger than the tablets used by regular infantry. I examined the screen and pointed at several blobs of green on a topographical map.

"Infected."

"Yep. Four groups. Two south of us, one west, and one up north."

"And this is us." My finger tapped an icon blinking in the saddle of two mountains on the map. According to the distance scale, the closest horde was nearly two miles away. I did not find this comforting. The undead are slow, but steady. They cover ground a lot faster than people think they do.

"We should get moving," I said. "Don't want them to catch up."

"Don't sweat it. We're near the objective. Dead won't bother us there."

"You say that like you've been there before."

Grabovsky made a shooing motion. "Go on, kid. I got work to do."

I walked back over to my boulder while Grabovsky's fingertip darted around the screen. If I had to guess, I'd say he was probably relaying our position and status back to Central. It's what I would have been doing, anyway. The last thing we wanted was to get stranded in the open with no support. The more Central knew about our disposition, the better off we would be if things went pear-shaped.

A few minutes later Grabovsky stashed the tablet and re-slung his pack with annoying ease. His gear was at least as heavy as mine, but he did not seem troubled by the weight. I decided if things ever came to blows between us, I would be well served to keep the squat operator at range. I doubted anything good would come of letting him get ahold of me.

"Let's go," Grabovsky said. "Need to reach the objective before dawn."

"Where exactly is our objective?" Tyrel asked.

"You'll see when we get there."

Tyrel started to say something else, and I could tell by the look on his face it was something sharp, but he bit down on it. I approved. Grabovsky would spill his secrets when he was ready and not a second before. Antagonizing him would not help.

We marched northwest for another few miles until we came upon a low, wide mountain with a sprawling plateau at the top. The mountain's southern face was heavily forested with tall evergreens, the ground beneath covered sparsely with scrub grass and stringy bushes.

"We head northeast from here," Grabovsky said, pointing. "'Bout two more klicks."

I welcomed the news. We had been hiking for hours, and I had not slept much the last couple of days. I needed rest, and by the looks of them, so did the others.

The terrain we covered sloped gently upward. At the base of the high plateau we turned sharply westward and marched through increasingly dense forest. The sun had topped the horizon, but was still below the mountain peaks to the east. Long stretches of lemon colored illumination lanced between the shoulders of the Cascades, casting the treetops in stark relief. It looked like the kind of thing Miranda would want to paint. I wished she were there to see it.

Focus on the misson.

There was a tap on my shoulder. "Hey," Tyrel said. "Look at that."

I turned and looked where he pointed. Gabe did the same. Where we stood was halfway up a steep slope leading to a plateau above. There was a clearing directly behind us, allowing a broad view of the valley beyond.

To the south, a writing swath of dark shapes lurched and tottered around a bend in the hills we had just traveled through. The hungry wail I'd heard earlier became louder. They were less than a mile away now.

"We've been spotted." Tyrel said.

Gabriel took a swig from his canteen. "Be after us like flies on shit."

"All the more reason to move your asses," Grabovsky called over his shoulder.

We stopped talking and moved.

TWENTY-ONE

"Shit."

Grabovsky stopped walking and stared at the path ahead of us. We were on a narrow dirt cutoff winding through the dense woodland. Above us, a canopy of thick limbs provided shade from the harsh glare of the morning sun.

"What's wrong?" Gabe asked.

Grabovsky pointed. "That."

I stepped around him and looked up the hill. The ruts of the dirt road terminated in front of a cabin nestled against the mountainside a hundred yards up. The cabin was probably attractive once, judging by the lone wall still standing. The rest of the structure, however, was covered in several hundred tons of dirt and boulders. A long gash of freshly exposed sediment marred the mountainside above.

"Landslide," I said.

"No shit."

Grabovsky took off at a run. The rest of us followed. Behind me, the wails of the infected grew unrelentingly louder. The squat soldier stopped at the base of the massive pile of rubble, his face a mask of frustration.

"Fuck me running."

Gabe stopped next to him. "Ray, what's the problem?"

153

"It's covered. We can't dig it out in time."

"What are you talking about?"

"The objective. There's a survival bunker right here. Guy that used to live here before the Outbreak put it in. Resistance has been using it for a safehouse. This is where we're supposed to wait."

Gabe regarded the rubble. "Well, that ain't happening. Got a plan B?"

Grabovsky ripped off his helmet, wiped his face, and slung a handful of sweat to the ground. "No. Guess we gotta come up with one."

"We can't stay here," I said. "Those ghouls back there got a fix on us."

"Bunker's the only safe place for miles," Grabovsky said. "Unless you want to hide in a tree for a couple of days."

I looked at the pile of dirt. A few logs from the cabin poked up through the wreckage like broken matchsticks. "How long will it take to dig out the entrance?"

"Fucking hours. We don't got that long."

I dropped my pack and handed Gabe my SCAR. There was an M-4 lashed to the back of my rucksack. I untied it and began removing the mag pouches fitted for 7.62 ammo from my MOLLE vest.

"Gabe, I need your ammo."

There was no arguing or hesitation. He dropped his own pack, laid my SCAR down on top of it, and began removing 5.56 pouches from his vest.

"The fuck are you doing?" Grabovsky said.

I thought about not answering, but remembered Grabovsky did not know how extensively Gabe and I had worked together in the past.

"Gonna draw the infected off while you three dig."

I could tell by the look on his face Grabovsky did not like it. But he didn't have a better idea, so after a few seconds, he nodded. "We'll get out of sight," he said.

"Make sure the dead are far away before you start digging," I said. "Don't want stragglers doubling back."

"Ain't my first rodeo, kid."

I was getting really damned tired of Grabovsky calling me 'kid', but let it go for the moment. The ghouls nipping at our heels were a far more pressing concern.

"Take this," Gabe offered me a suppressor.

I put the cylinder over the M-4's muzzle and cinched it in place. Next, I inserted a magazine, pulled back the charging handle, and released it. The weapon was clean and well oiled. The bolt carrier group slid forward easily and chambered a round with a satisfying *clack*. I handed the rifle to Gabe while I affixed mag pouches to my vest. As I worked, I saw Tyrel cast nervous glances toward the sound of approaching ghouls. I wondered how long it had been since he'd faced a horde without a platoon of Blackthorns behind him.

When the last mag pouch was attached, I took the M-4 back from Gabe, dropped my helmet, tapped my radio, and nodded at Grabovsky. "Comms check."

He turned on his handset and keyed the mic a couple of times. I did the same.

"Check, check."

My voice came through the speaker in Grabovsky's hand.

"Put your earpiece in," I said.

"Right."

I put in my own earpiece and gave my gear a last check. "Okay. Heading out. Let me know if you have to relocate."

"Which way you headed?" Tyrel asked.

I looked at Grabovsky. "You know this area?"

"Yeah. Take 'em north. Hard climb a ways, then it levels out. There's a dry streambed about half a klick east of here, can't miss it. Lead 'em down that and then climb the bank on your right as you're heading south. You'll see a cliff in the distance. You want to be up on the bank about two hundred yards before the cliff. The dead won't be able to climb it. Just lead 'em to the edge and let 'em fall off."

"Got it. Stay quiet for a while."

The others said they would. I checked to ensure my M-4's safety was on and set out northward at a steady trot. I was hot, tired, hungry, and not in the mood for this shit. But it needed doing, and since I was the youngest and the fastest, I was the best guy for the job.

Story of my life.

*****

The terrain flattened after a tough incline, and I found myself running across an open plateau. The ground was rocky and covered in fine dust, the forest having thinned out a hundred yards back. Thankfully, there was little in the way of undergrowth to trip me up. I stopped for a few seconds to get my bearings, and then headed eastward.

The undead were a raucous din behind me. I had stopped a few times along the way to jump and wave my arms and shout for the undead to follow. It would have been better to draw my pistol and fire off a couple of rounds, but that was a no-go in enemy territory. Infected were bad enough, the last thing I wanted was to bring ROC troops down on my head.

Ahead of me, the plateau sloped downward toward the streambed Grabovsky said I would find. The dirt at the bottom of the ravine was dry, telling me it had not rained recently. At my current elevation, it was unlikely I would run into a flash flood.

One less problem.

The walls of the streambed were steep and grew taller as the ravine descended the mountainside. Once I was in, the undead would be an unstoppable river of dead flesh barring the way back. The only way to get clear of them would be to climb the walls of the ravine. I would have to be careful here. If the walls got too high or too hard to climb, I would be in serious trouble.

The ghouls topped the rise behind me and tromped steadily in my direction. The faster ones moved out front, outpacing the slower, more mechanically injured ones. If I looked down from a hundred feet up, the horde would look like a giant teardrop.

I brought up my M-4 and looked through the ACOG. It was clear and unbroken, the reticle sharp and distinct. I took a small pair of binoculars from my vest and scanned the horde. The first thing I noticed was most of the infected were Grays. That was bad. Unlike ghouls that had not yet shed their skin, Grays could heal. All they needed was a little meat. They were also somewhat faster than their non-alien looking brethren, and had denser bone tissue. Which meant they had thicker skulls than other infected. This was a problem up close and personal, but the 5.56 greentips in my M-4 would bust their heads with no trouble.

Shooting, however, was not my goal. I had a limited supply of ammo and I did not want to waste it on infected. I would be better served to follow Grabovsky's advice and let the harsh landscape of the Cascade Mountains do the work for me.

To that end, I waved my arms in the air and let the vanguard of ghouls close to within sixty yards. It did not take long. Most of the horde was over the rise now, maybe a few hundred at most. I had dealt with bigger hordes under worse circumstances, but it did not pay to get complacent. One bite, and I was a dead man. Even a small horde could be lethal if I was careless.

I started down the ravine slowly at first, allowing the horde time to account for my change of direction. Rather than swing wide and enter the streambed the same place I had, they simply swiveled in my direction and lurched onward, oblivious to the drop they were headed toward. I backed off another hundred yards and waited.

Finally, the horde reached the edge of the ravine. I watched the faces of the first few Grays as they stepped into empty air and face-planted in to the ground four feet below. As they fell, their milky, lidless eyes remained fixed on me, mouths open, hands outstretched, fingers bent into claws. A couple went down and started trying to get up, but were stopped by additional skeletal bodies falling off the same ledge.

The pile of bodies grew taller and longer as other ghouls reached the ravine and fell in. The ones on top struggled to pull themselves in my direction while the ghouls beneath wriggled uselessly against the weight pinning them down. After a while, the pile was level with the ravine and a few ghouls managed to stand up and make their way toward me. I flicked the safety on my M-4 to semi-automatic and slowly backed away.

Over the next half hour, the horde slowly regained its feet as ghouls on top of the pile reached level ground and the ghouls pinned beneath them managed to get up. I realized I had not fired the M-4 I was holding and figured now was a good time to test it. Hopefully the zero on the ACOG was good.

The stock was adjustable. I have long arms, so I stretched it out to its maximum length. Then I pulled the rifle into my shoulder, grabbed the foregrip near its end to stabilize the barrel, peered through the ACOG, and centered the reticle on a ghoul's sinus cavity. A slow squeeze of the trigger elicited a muted *crack*. The suppressor absorbed most of the report. The ghoul's head snapped back and it slumped to the ground.

Then something unexpected happened.

Two ghouls behind the one I shot stopped, crouched over the fallen body, sniffed it like lions on a kill, and tore into it with their teeth.

"What the fuck…"

My hands and face went numb. My legs felt rooted to the ground. I stood and stared, uncomprehending, a river of ice-cold confusion washing over me. The ghouls ate perhaps a dozen mouthfuls each, then got up and resumed their march toward me.

Something important is happening, a voice in my head told me. *Watch.*

158

The ghouls that ate part of their dead friend were both Grays. The ghoul I shot was also a Gray. As I watched, most of the horde continued on past the corpse. But a few—ghouls with broken bones or wounds or sections of muscle missing—stopped, hunkered down, and feasted on the fallen revenant. Some ate only meat, while others chewed up chunks of bone and swallowed them down. After a while, there were so many undead surrounding it I could no longer see what was happening.

"This doesn't happen," I told myself aloud. "Ghouls don't fucking eat each other."

Well, now they do.

A howl hit me like a glass of water to the face. I looked up and saw a Gray reaching for me less than ten feet away. My hands reacted before my mind did, bringing the rifle up and firing two rounds. The ghoul went down, but there were more coming.

Time to move.

I turned and ran, counting steps in my head. My legs are long, and I knew a running stride for me was about six feet. When I reached fifty, I looked behind me. The lead ghouls in the horde were fifty yards or more back. I looked around and realized the sides of the ravine were over my head now. Not good. In the distance, the streambed ended at a cliff with nothing but open air visible beyond.

I had passed the point where I should have climbed out of the ravine.

But there was nothing for it now. A wall of hungry, monstrous corpses barred my way back. I sincerely doubted they would step aside if I asked them nicely. My only option was to climb.

My first step on the loose shale bordering the streambed ended in a near fall as the rocks under my boot tore away. I ran to another section and tried again. Same result. My feet could gain no purchase, and anything I grabbed pulled free in my hand.

"Shit. Not good."

I kept running and attempted to climb in other places, but the walls of the ravine were just too unstable. Rocks and dirt kept coming loose, sending me skidding to the ground. While this was happening, the ghouls grew relentlessly closer, forcing me to travel farther and farther toward the cliff. The walls grew higher and looser as I went. Finally I gave up on climbing and simply ran.

I stopped at the edge of the cliff and looked down. The ground fell away in a flat escarpment directly beneath me, worn away by flood waters. The walls of the plateau to my left and right swept outward more gradually. Far below, a thin line cut through the dry landscape as the terrain sloped southward.

At best guess, I was somewhere around two hundred feet from the base of the cliff. I had five-hundred feet of paracord in a bundle on my vest. A glance behind me revealed the horde less than a hundred yards away. Whatever I was going to do, it would have to happen fast.

"Come on, Hicks. Think."

I looked left. The cliff face hung outward overhead, comprised entirely of the same loose scree I had been unable to climb elsewhere in the ravine. The wall on my right was no better. I looked back at the horde again.

Inspiration struck.

Moving quickly, I placed my M-4 on the ground, removed the paracord from its pouch, drew my fighting knife, and cut the paracord into a trio of roughly ten-foot sections. Then I tied slipknots in the ends of the sections and stretched them out so they formed wide loops. That done, I stashed the rest of the cord, picked up my rifle, and ran toward the infected.

When I was twenty yards from them I stopped, dropped the cord, took a few deep breaths, and scanned the horde for the biggest ghoul I could find. Near the front, I spotted a tall one that must have been a huge man in life, long limbed and broad shouldered. Now he was a gray, skinless monstrosity. I shot him in the head and sprinted toward his body. He lay only a few yards from several other ghouls, all turning to vector in on me. I grabbed both of his ankles and hauled backward for all I was worth. For his size, he was surprisingly light. When I reached where I had left the paracord, I bound one of the three line sections around his ankles.

Two to go. I selected another ghoul and repeated the process. The horde was much closer now. For the third one, I didn't have even to run forward, just stood up and fired. As the ghoul went down, I emptied the rest of my magazine to give myself a little breathing room. This beat back the leading edge and caused the ones following to slow as they tripped over corpses, but it was only a temporary reprieve. Nothing short of a bomber strike was going to stop the wave of undead marching in my direction.

With three ghouls tied at the ankles, I slung the M-4, wrapped the cord around my hands, laid it over my shoulder, and hauled. It took a few seconds and a lot of straining to get the things moving, but move they did. I pulled harder and we went faster, the loose, dry sand acting as a kind of lubricant. I managed to push myself into a slow run, torso almost parallel with the ground, lungs heaving and legs burning as I grunted and dug my boots into the dirt. Finally, I reached the edge of the cliff.

Glancing backward, I saw I had maybe three to four minutes before the horde would be on me. Not only did I have to get to the bottom of the cliff, I had to get down there and get out of the way. A little thing like a two hundred foot drop was not going to stop the ghouls chasing me. If I didn't want to be flattened by falling corpses, I needed to be elsewhere when they began raining down.

I had left my climbing harness with my rucksack, so I was going to have to do this the hard way. I took the three sections of paracord binding the ghouls' ankles and tied them in a modified water knot, two cords on one side and the third on the other. A hard tug and the knot was secure. Then I took the remaining cord from my vest, grabbed the bitter end, and tossed the rest down the cliff. Working as fast as my arms could move, I doubled the cord until the second end was a few feet from the bottom. Good enough. Using the doubled cord, I tied a bowline knot around the cord binding the ghouls and cinched it. A bowline probably wasn't the best knot I could have used, but I knew it well and could tie it fast. As my father had once told me: when in doubt, go with what you know.

I looked up. The horde was less than fifty yards away now and closing fast. Moment of truth. I picked up the doubled paracord, stepped toward the edge of the cliff, and leaned back. The three ghouls tied together shifted a little, but didn't move. It would work.

The next part was going to hurt. I was wearing shooting gloves, which were better than nothing, but not designed for what I was about to do. I wrapped the doubled cord around my left hand, lay down on my stomach at the edge of the cliff, and slowly slid my legs over. Every nerve ending and synapse and sentient aspect of my mind screamed at me to STOP! STOP! STOP! But I didn't. A sense of vertigo hit me as I let my hips slide down the edge of the mountain and caught a glimpse of the void beneath me.

Goddammit, don't look down. You've done this kind of thing before, plenty of times.

When I was a kid, my father insisted I learn mountaineering. He told me I might never need the skills I learned, but if I did, I would be glad I had them. As usual, he was right.

I was completely over the edge of the cliff now, clinging desperately with both hands and dangling in open space. The ghouls' corpses held my weight, the force of my body pulling on the cord insufficient to overcome their static inertia.

No wonder the rotten bastards were so hard to drag.

I wrapped my boots around the cord and let my weight settle onto them. They would be doing most of the work now. Finally, I unwrapped the cord from my left hand and allowed it to pay out.

The side of the cliff slid past my face as I descended, slowly at first, then faster. Ten feet went by. Twenty. Thirty. My grip was beginning to cramp around the narrow lines and I did not know how much longer I could hold on, so I let myself down even faster.

Heat flared against my palms as friction rapidly warmed the pads of my gloves. I knew the thin sheep-leather protecting my hands wasn't going to hold up much longer, and when it gave way, the nylon cord would cut directly into my skin. Still, I went faster.

I bumped and bounced off rocks and boulders as I went down and down, falling debris pelting me on the head and shoulders. I didn't care. The only thing that mattered was escaping the burning in my hands and the cramping in my muscles. My jaw ached as I grunted in pain from between clenched teeth. The last few layers of leather were giving way. Soon my flesh would be the only thing keeping my descent at a survivable pace, and I had no idea how much further down the bottom of the cliff was. I refused to look. Instead, I focused on maintaining my grip and not letting go of the thin cords. It didn't matter if I fucked up my hands. As long as I survived, I could heal. Death, however, was a permanent injury.

Just as the cord cut through my gloves and laid directly into my palms, I hit the bottom hard enough to collapse my legs and fall on my ass. I let go of the lines and flapped my hands frantically to cool them, the sound of my own guttural cursing loud in my ears.

Congratulations, Hicks, you made it. Now get up and run!

With the heat in my hands subsiding, I felt the M-4 digging into my back and hoped I hadn't broken the ACOG or damaged the suppressor. Groaning, I rolled over, lurched to my feet, and risked a look toward the top of the cliff. For a second there was nothing, and then a foot stepped out and a thin, sticklike body hurtled over the edge.

"Shit!"

I ran as hard as I could parallel to the cliff face. Lucky for me, I didn't need to go far. The ravine above was narrow, only about thirty feet across, and I was directly in the middle. It only took me ten frantic, half-slipping lunges to get a safe distance from the falling ghoul. Behind me, I heard it hit the ground with a sickening thud. When I looked over my shoulder, there was a plume of dust rising up from where it landed.

My instinct was to stop and stare, but my training reminded me that in my current situation, I was not necessarily safe. Just because I had escaped one horde did not mean I hadn't just dropped into another one. Not wanting to go from pan to fire, I unslung the M-4 and scanned my surroundings. I was in a clearing about a hundred yards across, dry grasses and small shrubs underfoot and tall pines ringing the edges. I dug out the small binoculars on my vest and looked through them, scanning for movement. I saw none. For the moment, I was okay.

Now I looked. The ghouls in the ravine above were coming down faster, one after another, each one stepping off the cliff and hurtling face-first to smack hard into the ground two hundred feet below. After a few minutes, the bodies began to form a pile. As the pile grew, I realized that with the number of ghouls in yon lofty horde, they might just pile up high enough to allow some of the undead base-jumpers to survive. Maybe even a lot of them.

"Time to go, Hicks."

I went.

TWENTY-TWO

Lacking a map and not knowing exactly where the others were, I had only one option: follow the base of the mountain and keep my eyes open for sign. Eventually I would cut across our backtrail and could follow it to the others.

But before that, I needed to check a few things. I was back in the shade of the pine forest at this point, having trekked a couple of kilometers from where I left the horde. There was a fallen tumble of boulders nearby, left there by a long-ago rockslide. I took a seat on one of them and removed my gloves.

The damage was not as bad as I had feared. A thin, diagonal line of burned tissue seamed each palm. There was raw flesh showing in the creases, but the wounds were not deep. Hurt like a bastard, though. Burns always do, especially on the palms where there are lots of sensitive nerve endings. I cleaned the wounds with iodine from my first aid kit and bandaged them with gauze and tape.

Next I examined my shooting gloves. Each one had a slit cut into the palm exactly mirroring the burns on my hands. I slipped them back on and patched the slits with more medical tape. Not perfect, but field expedient.

After stowing my medi-kit, I did another sweep with my binoculars. Nothing to see. Not yet, anyway. I hoped there were no ROC patrols in this region. If there were, and they came anywhere near this mountain, my team and I were in for a fight. Our trail was obvious; the swath of crushed shrubbery left behind by the infected pursing us was pretty hard to miss. If they followed the trail, they would find the pile of dead bodies I had left behind at the cliff. Logic dictated if they did, they would climb the mountain and find the corpses on the plateau that had unmistakably been killed by gunfire. Not to mention the paracord I had left behind. Some secret mission this was turning out to be.

I checked my rifle. The ACOG and the suppressor did not appear damaged. I looked through the optic and picked a spot on a tree about fifty yards away and fired a shot. The zero on the ACOG was good, and the bullet did not strike the baffles within the suppressor. Things were looking up.

Still, I had no food, no water, and hadn't slept in over twenty-four hours. The sleep deprivation I could deal with. Military life is not kind to one's circadian rhythms. Hard experience had taught me how far I could push myself in that regard.

No food wasn't much of a problem either. Life had been good when I was stationed in Hollow Rock, but before that, the First Recon had spent years roaming the wastelands looking for survivors. I came along for the last year of it. Our platoon stayed constantly on the move and was always short on everything: food, ammo, medical supplies, even clothing. We scavenged most of what we needed, even though technically, as a matter of regulation, we were not supposed to. Whoever wrote the no-salvage rule had never marched for six days straight with nothing to eat. I had, so I knew I could go a long time without food. That part did not worry me.

What did worry me was not having any water. Life on the march had taught me how quickly my body uses up fluids when I exert myself. Sweating and urinating is bad enough, but the body also loses a great deal of water through respiration. Up here in the Cascades, the air was dry and hot. Not a good recipe for moisture retention.

I did not recall seeing any water on the way out here. No streams, no rivers, no ponds or lakes, nothing. And from the look of the landscape, it had not rained in quite a while. Which meant my best course of action was to get moving and find my way back to the others as quickly as possible.

I headed north. Several miles passed under my boots, the sun grew higher and hotter, and toward midday, I still had not detected our trail. The terrain remained unfamiliar. I needed a break, so I climbed a tree and scanned with my binoculars. I spotted a small herd of deer about two hundred yards away and quite a number of birds and squirrels, but no infected and no people.

Another two or three miles of searching led me up a shallow slope. The slope flattened out at the top and I saw a thin strip of head-high brush ahead of me. The trees were evenly spaced on either side of it, limbs hanging over. It was the first spot of high brush I had seen for miles. My pace picked up as I hurried to examine it.

As I suspected, the brush had grown over a narrow dirt trail that had once seen regular vehicle traffic. The trees had been cut back to permit cars to pass, so the space allowed sunlight down into an area that otherwise would have been covered by forest canopy. Before the Outbreak, passing cars had kept the weeds from growing too high. Then civilization ended and five years went by. Hence the brush.

Moving the grass aside, I could see the two rutted indentations dug by long-ago tires. Someone had used this road often back before the Outbreak. Grabovsky said the cabin he brought us to was the only shelter for miles. We had used a similar trail to find it. The math wasn't difficult.

The trail ran east to west. West led away from the mountain, so I went east, increasing my pace to a quick jog. The rifle in my hands became a hindrance, so I slung it across my back. As I'd hoped, the trail went up the mountain in a meandering switchback for about a mile and then turned southward.

The brush grew thinner as the canopy overhead thickened and the trail flattened out. After hiking another half-mile south, the dirt road intersected with the trail Grabovsky had followed to find the cabin. Stepping onto it, I looked up the slope and examined my surroundings. The area looked familiar. Figuring there was no need to hurry, I slowed to a leisurely pace.

167

When I rounded the bend leading up the last section of trail, I heard the sound of metal striking dirt. Ahead, Gabe and Grabovsky had fixed the spades on their entrenching tools and were digging furiously. Tyrel was on patrol. He spotted me immediately and waved a hand for me to approach.

"Where the hell you been?" he asked angrily.

I stopped and narrowed my eyes at him. "Leading the horde away. The fuck do you think?"

"You lose your radio?"

I blinked. "What?"

He pointed to his earpiece. "Did. You. Lose. Your. Radio."

My hand slowly came up and touched the spot on my vest designated for a radio. It was there. I looked down and saw the earpiece cord dangling along the outside of my magazine pouches.

"No. No I didn't."

Tyrel glanced over his shoulder. Gabe and Grabovsky had noticed us, marked my return, and gone back to work. They were out of earshot. My old friend stepped closer and lowered his voice.

"You all right?"

"Yeah, I'm fine." My hand was still absently holding the earpiece cord. I blinked a couple more times. How the hell could I have forgotten about my radio?

"What happened out there? You take a shot to the head?"

"No, nothing like that."

Tyrel looked confused. "Then why didn't you call in?"

I let the hand holding the cord fall to my side.

"Would you believe I forgot?"

"Ordinarily, no." Tyrel looked me over with concern in his eyes. "But you look just about beat. When was the last time you ate?"

"Same as you."

A nod. "Water?"

"Been a few hours."

"Sleep?"

"Again, same as you."

"Yeah. And I feel like hammered shit. Go get some water, son. We'll keep this between the two of us."

"Thanks."

I walked toward my rucksack, retrieved my canteen, and drained it. When I finished, I wiped my mouth and wondered precisely what the fuck was wrong with me. In all my years of training, salvaging, and soldiering, I had never once made such a boneheaded mistake. My radio had been right there the whole time, right where it was supposed to be. I had even made Grabovsky do a radio check before setting out to divert the horde. How the living hell did I forget about it?

"Hey, sunshine," Grabovsky called out. "When you're done daydreaming, how about you give us a hand over here?"

I pondered Grabovsky's accent. He was from somewhere up north. New York? Jersey? Massachusetts? No. Not enough long vowels. Speech too clipped. Maybe one of the Midwestern cities? I glanced at him.

"Chicago," I said quietly. "Gotta be."

"What?" Grabovsky said. "I can't hear you. You gonna help or what?"

I looked down and noticed I was swaying.

For fuck's sake, Hicks. Get it together.

"Just a sec," I said. "Let me get my shovel."

169

TWENTY-THREE

Around nightfall we finally dug out the entrance to the bunker. When we were done, Grabovsky searched the bases of a few trees until he found a rock that turned out to be a key hider. From it, he took a small red pennant with cord around it and tied it to a tree.

"What's that for?" Tyrel asked. He had stayed on patrol the entire time and was standing nearby.

"Lets the Resistance know we're here."

"Might also let someone else know we're here," I said. I was rapidly losing patience with the sloppy way this mission was being conducted. "As if that horde out there and the big hole we just dug weren't enough."

Grabovsky shook his head wearily. "No ROC patrols out here. They know better."

The squat man weaved a little as he approached the bunker. I wanted to argue further, but seeing his weariness reminded me of my own. I stood aside, shovel in hand, and breathed hard while sweat ran down my back. Grabovsky worked the combination dial to open the hatch. After what seemed like hours the lock finally clicked.

"In we go," Grabovsky said.

"Want to leave someone up on overwatch?" Gabe said.

"Not necessary. Told you. No patrols out here."

Gabe and I looked at each other. I could tell we were both thinking the same thing—we weren't willing to bet our lives on Grabovsky's assessment.

"It's all right, Ray. I don't mind." Gabe said.

"No. Trust me, Gabe. You don't want to be up here when the Resistance arrives. Safer if you're down below."

Gabe didn't like it, but he went along. I was too tired to argue anymore, so I went too. Tyrel followed last.

Inside the bunker the air was stale. Sunlight coming through the hatch provided the only illumination. What I could see of the place looked pretty typical of other bunkers I had seen throughout the wastelands. The interior had a rounded ceiling and walls, suggesting cylindrical construction. We stood in a small foyer with rubber flooring, beyond which a wide doorway led to a large room with four bunks in it. Past that I could see a galley-style kitchen and another doorway, this one closed. The details of the room were lost in shadow.

"Keep the hatch open a second," Grabovsky said, tromping inside. He disappeared beyond the far doorway, grunted to himself a few times, and with no warning, a bank of hidden lights came on in the ceiling. Clear white light bathed the room, reflecting off the stainless steel in the kitchen and eggshell colored walls throughout.

"Okay. You can close it now. Turn the wheel all the way to the right to lock it. You'll hear it click."

Tyrel did as instructed. The door locked with a clear metallic *whack*.

"Pick a bunk, fellas."

We dragged our rucksacks down with us. Grabovsky thumped his down beside one of the bunks and took a seat. I noticed the bunks had sheets, pillows, and blankets. *Hello, lover.*

The walls, rather than being covered in finished sheetrock, were overlaid with some kind of thin plastic. There were 120 volt outlets with USB ports. The kitchen was pre-Outbreak modern with stainless steel appliances and faux granite countertops. The floor beyond the foyer was carpeted in gray.

"This place have a bathroom?" I asked.

Grabovsky pointed with a thumb. "Through that door on your left. Composting toilet. Turn the handle when you're done."

"Will do." I started toward the door.

"Place has running water," Grabovsky said. "Use it sparingly."

"How's that work?" Gabe asked.

"Cistern up the mountain feeds into it. Not sure how full it is right now."

"Where's the juice coming from?" Tyrel pointed at the lights.

"Solar panels around the same place. Resistance comes by and cleans them once in a while. They use this place to charge batteries and stuff."

"Sounds good to me," Tyrel said, throwing his ruck on the bunk over Grabovsky. Gabe took the opposite bottom bunk leaving me to sleep above him. Fine by me. The less I saw of Grabovsky the better.

*****

I got a good night's sleep, a couple of meals, and plenty of water. It always amazes me, no matter how weary I am, how much better those simple things make me feel.

The next morning, with nothing to do, I inventoried my gear. First order of business was to clean the M-4. The AR platform is a solid performer so long as the weapon is well maintained. Direct gas impingement, the operating system used by AR pattern rifles, makes for lightweight, accurate weapons. It also makes for lots of gunk and carbon fouling in the chamber. Which is not to say M-4s cannot take a beating—they can. But if you have the time and the resources to give your weapon a thorough cleaning, it is always a good idea to do so.

That done, I checked the SCAR. I hadn't used it yet on this mission, so it was good to go. I checked the other things in my

172

pack, rearranged them a couple of times, and wound up putting everything back the way it was to begin with. There was a hand operated washing machine in the bunker, so I washed my clothes from the day before, spun the excess water from them in a little rotating basket operated by a foot pedal, and hung them up to dry. I bathed in the tiny bathroom with a bucket, a washcloth, and a small bar of soap I'd brought along. I dug rocks out of my boot treads with the tip of a 5.56 round. I cleaned my pistol even though it did not need it. I unloaded and reloaded my magazines to make sure they had the correct number of rounds in them. I sharpened my fighting knife. I wished I had my spear so I could sharpen it too, but I had left it behind in Colorado. I wished I hadn't done that. Gabe had his falcata and bowie knife, and Tyrel and Grabovsky had those government-issue MK 9 ghoul choppers that look like Chinese war swords. All I had for a hand weapon was my Ka-bar.

By mid-afternoon my clothes were dry. I was already dressed, so I folded them and stowed them in my ruck. It was the last productive task I could come up with.

"Think somebody ought to go up on patrol?" I asked Grabovsky.

"Nope," he said. He was lying on his bunk with his eyes closed. Gabe and Tyrel were playing cards at a small table in the kitchen. I don't much care for cards, but if I got any more bored, I was going to have to reconsider that option.

"Right." I lay back on my bed. At least it was comfortable. If I was lucky, I might grow drowsy and pass a few hours in this claustrophobic little coffin that way. I thought about submarines and the sailors who manned them. From what General Jacobs had said, there were still a couple in service. It boggled my mind the kind of person who could stay submerged in an oversized beer can for months on end. I'd been doing it for less than twenty-four hours and I was ready to kill something. I'm a country mouse. I need open spaces and fresh air.

I closed my eyes and focused on keeping my mind blank. Thoughts of Miranda kept trying to intrude, but I shoved them away. Homesickness and sexual fantasies were the last things I needed. Eventually, I dozed.

"Hey, wake up."

I startled and sat up in my bunk. "What is it?"

"Somebody's here," Tyrel said.

From somewhere above the bunker, I heard a rumbling, crunching sound. "Are those vehicles?"

"Sounds like."

"Trucks probably," Grabovsky said. He was sitting up on his bunk tying his boots. I hopped down and began doing the same.

"About damn time," I muttered.

"It's probably our guys," Grabovsky said, picking up his weapon. "But all the same, let's be careful."

I hefted my M-4. Gabe drew his sidearm. Tyrel had an old Marine Corps M27 Infantry Automatic Rifle, or IAR. The IAR looks similar to an M-16, but operates on a gas piston and can fire from the open bolt, which allows it to fire more rapidly than a closed-bolt M-4. Which means, essentially, the IAR is a light squad automatic weapon that can use standard magazines just like a regular service rifle. Except Tyrel did not have a standard magazine. He had a specially made dual-drum magazine loaded with a hundred rounds. Knowing how well he could shoot, I did not want to be downrange of him if he ever had occasion to fire that thing.

Gabe put in a pair of earplugs. I did the same, and the others followed suit. We all hoped to walk away from this situation without violence, but if kindness failed, I didn't want to go deaf when the shooting started. Not that we were likely to survive such an encounter, considering our tactical position. If the troops above us were with the ROC, all they had to do was blow the hatch and toss down a handful of grenades, and we were done for.

"Everybody stay cool," Grabovsky said. "Let me do the talking. I know these guys."

"I'm cool." I looked at Tyrel. "You cool?"

He grinned. "Yeah. I'm cool."

I looked at Gabe. "You cool?"

"Brother, I was born cool."

I turned a smile at Grabovsky. "Looks like the only one ain't cool is you."

He tried to glare at me, but couldn't suppress a laugh. "Fuckin' asshole."

All laughter died when three booming strikes hit the hatch. There was a pause, and then four more.

"That's the signal," Grabovsky said. "Keep your weapons down. I'm gonna open the hatch."

He laid his rifle down and climbed the ladder. The hatch opened and he looked up.

"Well you're a sight for sore eyes," he said.

"Come on out," said a voice above. "You got friends with you?"

"Yeah, three of 'em."

Grabovsky motioned for us to put our weapons down. We did and followed him out of the bunker.

It was late afternoon outside, the sun beginning its slide behind the mountains. There was a strong breeze, and the air was cool after the stuffiness of the bunker. I took a deep breath and enjoyed it for a scant moment before turning my attention to our new associates.

At a quick count, there were sixteen of them. They had arrived in four trucks, all Toyotas outfitted for off-road use. Most of the men had full beards, some were long-haired, and they all wore what looked like old surplus Army fatigues. Most of the men carried the same loadout: M-4 rifle, Berretta M-9 pistol, frag grenades, and a vest with spare ammo and other gear. Three of the men carried M-249 squad automatic weapons, or SAWs, and three men had M-203 grenade launchers fixed under their carbines.

Looking at the trucks, two of them had M-240 machine guns mounted to them, and one had a MK-19 automatic grenade launcher. The last truck had an RPG launcher and a duffel bag full of RPGs. I figured the US ordnance had been donated by the

Army, while the RPGs were probably seized from ROC troops no longer among the living.

"Damn good to see you alive, Romero," Grabovsky said, shaking hands with a man who appeared to be in charge.

"Same to you. How are things in Colorado?"

"Better than out here, that's for sure."

Romero smiled. "And yet you keep coming back."

"I'm a glutton for punishment. Let me introduce you to some people."

Grabovsky pointed to Gabe. "This is Gabriel Garrett, Marines. Scout sniper. We worked together in Tennessee putting a militia together. I can vouch for him."

Romero shook hands. "Nice to meet you."

"Likewise," Gabe said.

"And this is Tyrel Jennings, former Navy SEAL, JSOC operator, and founder of the Blackthorn Security Company."

"So you're the famous Tyrel Jennings," Romero said. "I thought you'd be taller."

"That's what they all say," Tyrel said, "till they see me with my clothes off."

Romero's men gave a low roar of amusement.

"And this is Captain Caleb Hicks," Grabovsky said. "Works for General Jacobs. Black card type. Other than that, I don't know shit about him. But Gabe and Jennings know him."

Romero stepped in front of me and looked me over. I did the same to him. He was black, a little taller than me, beard streaked with gray, long hair tied in a multitude of braids held back under a brown headscarf. He was possessed of a lean, strong build, and there was something distinctly feline about the way he carried himself.

"So what's your story?" Romero asked. "You look too young to be doing this shit."

176

"Got lost on the way the college," I said.

Romero stared blankly for a moment, then humor creased his face. "Seriously. I need to know who I'm working with."

"Used to be with the First Reconnaissance Expeditionary. Won some medals, impressed some people, got headhunted by General Jacobs. Now I work for him directly."

"Ever done any covert work before?"

"Not officially."

A smile. "Good answer."

Romero looked at Grabovsky. "Got any gear to bring along?"

"Yeah, a little bit. You know if Sullivan ever picked up those supplies I left for him? 'Bout ten miles south of here."

"Yeah, he got 'em."

"Good," Grabovsky waved toward Gabe, Tyrel, and me. "Come on, fellas. We need to go."

We went back down in the bunker long enough to retrieve our gear. Each of us picked a truck, tossed in our belongings, and hopped in the back. A couple of Romero's men covered up the bunker hatch and did their best to make it look like no one had been there. They did not do a bad job, although there was no hiding the tire tracks.

At a signal from Romero, the four vehicles turned around and headed down the mountain.

TWENTY-FOUR

Romero called the highway we traveled on 'the 97'. After a half day of driving, I began to wonder if 97 was the highway's designation, or if it represented the number of fallen trees blocking the road. It seemed we could not travel more than a few miles before having to stop and clear the highway.

"If the roads are this bad after just five years," I said to Gabe as we worked, "imagine what they'll be like in ten more."

"Won't hardly be any roads by then," Gabe replied.

We continued on a slow trajectory to the Oregon border. I was somewhat startled by the shift in scenery when we left northern California and crossed into the southern reaches of the Klamath Basin. The landscape abruptly shifted from brown and dusty to green and verdant. I leaned my head in the open back window of the truck and asked the driver what caused the difference. He shrugged and said it had something to do with irrigation and volcanic soil and he wasn't a goddamn farmer so maybe just shut up and let him drive.

It was a rough trip of just over forty miles. Once we crossed into Oregon, the drivers changed course westward such that we paralleled the border for a long stretch. We kept on in that direction for another twenty miles or so until we reached a small dirt side road and turned onto it.

At this point, Romero's men, who had been relaxing in their trucks, suddenly became alert and manned their weapons. I took a cue from them and checked my SCAR to make sure it was ready to go. One of the Resistance fighters gave my rifle a long look and leaned over to speak to me.

"You know how to use that thing?" he asked.

I replied with a flat, contemptuous glare. The man grinned broadly and went back to staring up the road.

The forest around us grew denser the farther we proceeded. After fifteen minutes of driving through the thick greenery we emerged into a clearing with a small white building in the center. The building was roughly sixty feet square with a metal roof and aluminum siding on the outer walls. The entrance was a garage door, currently closed, big enough to drive a truck through. There was a smaller security door next to it for foot traffic.

The dense trees around the building were so green they almost hurt my eyes. Their limbs hung over the roof, and the walls of the building were streaked with rust stains and mildew. Tall grass and ferns grew everywhere except the narrow drive where our short convoy traveled. The air was warm and damp and I felt wet just from being there. Looking up through the hazy grayness of the place, I could not see the sky through the boughs of fir trees and broad leafed hardwoods overhead. The thickness of the tree trunks and profusion of undergrowth made the landscape feel primordial, a place so ancient it took no notice of men invading its grounds. To this realm, our existence was fleeting and inconsequential.

We pulled in front of the building and I saw Romero speaking into his radio. A few moments later, the garage door opened and several armed men stood in the entrance. One of them walked along our line of trucks, gave Grabovsky, Tyrel, Gabe, and me a slit-eyed examination, and then changed channels on his radio and spoke into it out of earshot. He got a reply in short order, turned around, and waved at the guards to let us inside.

Romero's truck led the way, tires crunching over gravel and black dirt. There were several parking spaces marked off with spray paint on the far end of the building. The four drivers parked the trucks and indicated for all passengers to follow Romero.

I hopped out of the truck's bed, put on my rucksack, and looked around. The building was mostly empty, the floor unmarred except where the trucks' tires had left muddy tracks. There was a small office just past the garage door, a few crates and barrels on one wall, and a table and chairs near the office. The floor was bare concrete. Someone closed the garage door and locked it shut. Narrow banks of windows on two of the walls provided the only light in the room. The air was close and stale, and I felt sweat break out under my shirt.

I followed Romero to where the table and chairs sat on a large Afghan rug. Two of Romero's men moved the table and chairs and flipped over the rug. Beneath it was a seamed, rectangular section of floor. Romero said something into his radio, and beneath my feet, I heard a rumbling, grinding sound. The seamed section of floor slowly raised up on one side and stopped, a few inches of gap separating it from the surrounding concrete. Romero's men lifted it the rest of the way, revealing a narrow set of steps leading down a dimly lit stairwell.

Grabovsky turned in my direction. "You know all those questions you been asking me?"

I glanced at him. "Yeah."

"You're about to get your answers."

*****

"What is this place?" I said to Tyrel, speaking in a low voice. My old friend shook his head, eyes wide.

"No idea."

"Ever seen anything like it before?"

"Sort of. Did a mission briefing at Area 51 once, back when I was with JSOC. Building they put us up in looked kinda like this place."

We proceeded down a dimly lit corridor. The stairwell we had entered took us three stories underground in a narrow concrete shaft. At the bottom, Romero unlocked a door, let everyone stream past, then locked it behind him. Above us, I heard grinding and rumbling again as the entrance shut on its own.

The corridor was painted white with a smooth, dusty floor. What little light there was came from LEDs mounted in recessed fixtures in the ceiling. There was a space for a light every ten feet, but I would have been amazed if even half of them were on.

The hallway ended at a large double door. Romero paused at the entrance, one hand on a doorknob.

"I probably don't have to tell you this," he said, taking time to look at Gabe, Tyrel, and me in turn. "But everything we're doing is as classified as it gets. Nothing said or seen today is to be spoken of outside this facility, not even amongst yourselves. That includes anything regarding this building, its location, and any of the people and things in it. Is that clear?"

"In other words," Gabe said. "This place doesn't exist and we were never here."

"You got it."

Tyrel and I both gave a word of agreement. Romero turned and opened the door. I felt my eyes go wide and Tyrel and I spoke simultaneously.

"Holy shit."

Romero laughed quietly and walked through the door. I followed on numb feet.

The room we entered was huge. After a moment's consideration I decided 'room' was not a fitting descriptor. It was more like an underground warehouse. The ceiling was twenty feet above our heads, exposed wiring, air ducts, and metal rafters visible despite the dim illumination. A faint hum of machinery sounded from somewhere, and I felt a slight breeze as I walked beneath one of the vents in the overhead ventilation ducts. The air was cool, but did not have the crisp bite of air conditioning. I guessed there was a fan unit active somewhere keeping the air in the facility from going stale.

As I walked inside, I followed the others down a broad central lane with the two halves of the long rectangular warehouse on either side. There were shelves on both sides stacked floor to ceiling with boxes, crates, and barrels of innumerable goods. Each shelf had a metal placard at the end detailing what was kept on the shelves in that particular section. The shelving sections were numbered, and each individual shelf utilized an alpha-numeric system corresponding to the items stored there. One of the sections I passed near the entrance had only one item listed. It read: Ammunition Cartridges, 5.56x45 NATO M855.

I examined the shelves as I passed. The ammo was in green fiberglass crates roughly three feet square and four feet tall. I did the math in my head, operating on the assumption the ammo in the crates was stored in standard green metal cans of 840 cartridges each, the cans being roughly five inches wide, twelve inches long, and ten inches high. Which put each can's volume at 600 square inches. The dimensions of the crates were 36 by 36 by 48, which put each one's capacity at around 62,000 square inches. Not an exact figure, but close enough. Dividing 62,000 by 600 I came up with 103 and some change. Since my measurements were estimates and not precise, I rounded that down to one hundred. From there, the math was simple. 100 cans multiplied by 840 rounds each.

There were approximately 84,000 rounds per crate.

This place is a gold mine.

I kept reading placards as I passed them. There were six sections of shelves full of ammo crates. Each section had crates in the hundreds. I realized I was looking at somewhere north of one hundred million rounds of ammunition, an enormous amount of wealth. The thought was a little dizzying.

The ammunition section also included shelves of 7.62x51, 9mm, and a few other cartridges primarily used in sniper weapon systems. There were racks stacked ceiling high with M-4 rifles, most of them brand new looking, as well as bolt action sniper rifles, M-110s, SAWs, grenade launchers, M-240s, fifty-caliber heavy machine guns, portable miniguns, and the equipment necessary to mount the heavy ordnance to vehicles. Beyond that were artillery shells, mortars, large caliber machine gun cartridges, grenades, LAW rockets, mines, plastic explosives, detonation cord, and even shoulder-fired anti-aircraft missiles. I noticed quite a few of the missile and explosives crates had been opened and the contents removed.

The rest of the warehouse was dedicated to food, medical supplies, repair parts for a variety of machinery, printed manuals on a broad range of topics, radio equipment, fuel, and the list went on. After a while, I stopped trying to keep track of it all.

When we reached the opposite end of the warehouse we came upon a large room with a bank of windows reinforced with wire mesh. The space beyond looked like a large conference room complete with a chalkboard, drop-down screen, chairs arranged in rows, and an electronic projector. Two men were waiting inside. I almost stopped when I saw who they were.

Romero opened the door and he and his entourage filed in. Grabovsky followed them with Gabe and Tyrel close behind. I went in last.

"Welcome to Oregon, gentlemen," General Phillip Jacobs said from the front of the room. He looked at me directly, eyes alight with amusement. "Bet you weren't expecting to see me here, were you?"

I couldn't bring myself to speak, so I simply shook my head. The general's presence was enough to give me pause, but it wasn't him who had taken my ability to vocalize. It was the man next to him.

He was tall, about my height. His hair was long and tied back, and a thick beard covered his face. When I had last seen him, he was clean-shaven and the hair was dark brown with a few scattered flecks of gray. Now it was all gray, even the eyebrows. He had lost at least forty pounds. It had only been a couple of years, but he looked to have aged by about a decade. I looked at Tyrel. He was staring at the same man, a pained expression on his face.

"Hey there, Mike," Tyrel said. "Fancy seeing you here."

183

Mike Holden, leader of the Resistance and one of the men who raised me, walked forward until he was standing in front of us. His face was tanned and leathery, the lines in his skin deep and sharply refined. His gaze went back and forth between us a few times. Slowly, he broke a smile and embraced Tyrel. The two men slapped each other on the back a few times and then stood apart. Mike turned to me and the smile faded.

"I was starting to think I'd never see you again, son."

I still couldn't talk. There was a knot in my throat and my vision had gone somewhat blurry. The old man put his arms around my shoulders and pulled me in. I squeezed back and wondered exactly what the hell I was supposed to say to him.

TWENTY-FIVE

Heinrich,

The Wastelands

The first challenge Heinrich faced after seizing the smugglers goods was trading them for wagons, livestock, and supplies. If the seed grain they had stolen had been their only commodity, this would not have been a problem. He could just make the long trek to the nearest trading post and cut deals with passing caravans. But he'd seized more than just seed grain; he had stolen a king's ransom in opium. A few of his men used a hanging scale to weigh the stuff in batches, and the weight came out to over thirty kilograms.

According to Ferguson, this was a huge shipment, valuable enough to outfit his tribe with everything they needed and have quite a few kilos to spare. Heinrich had never trafficked in the stuff before, being that it was a fairly new commodity, so he was willing to take his gigantic henchman's word for it. The problem he faced now was offloading the narcotics at a decent price.

As he thought about this, Heinrich sat around a fire with Ferguson and Maru and waited while his men loaded the boats in preparation to debark the island. The three of them were eating a breakfast of dried meat with roasted cattails when they heard footsteps and saw two men approaching. One of them was Locke, a surviving member of the original tribe, and the other was a recently acquired troop named Horton.

"Found someone who can help you," Locke said, nodding to Horton.

Heinrich regarded his tribesman. He was a light-skinned black man with a ring of bushy hair surrounding a bald crown set off by a thick beard. While not very tall, he had a lean, powerful build and gave off the vibe of a dangerous man. His face was broad with strong features, a heavy brow, and the blank, dead eyes of a prowling shark. Heinrich saw potential there.

"Locke tell you what I need?" Heinrich asked.

"Yes sir. Said you lookin' to sell that dream we took."

"Dream?"

"Slang for opium," Ferguson explained.

"Good to know." Heinrich looked back at Horton. "So?"

"You heard 'bout a place called The Holdout, right?"

Heinrich thought a moment. "Up near I-44 towards Missouri. 'Bout fifty miles from here."

"That be the one."

Heinrich looked away, his face pensive. Horton remained quiet. Like most of the Storm Road Tribe, he knew better than to interrupt his chief when he was ruminating.

"That might work," Heinrich said finally.

He had heard of The Holdout, and knew its reputation and history. It had originally been an Army FOB, but most of the troops there had been reassigned after Operation Relentless Force cleared the majority of infected from the area. Only a small contingent remained, less than two hundred troops total. The Union would have preferred to leave a larger force—The Holdout was near a major caravan route—but the people living there had never signed an official treaty with the Union. They tolerated Union troops living among them because they helped keep ghouls and marauders at bay, but it was an uneasy truce. The Army did not interfere with the doings of the general public, and in turn, the public let the troops enjoy the safety of the walls.

The town had a mayor, sheriff's department, and city council to handle civic affairs, and did not need the military to help them run things. But they didn't mind taking the soldiers' trade. Army garrisons, even small ones, were a good source of income for local businesses. Especially bars, restaurants, brothels, and, surprisingly, performing arts venues.

The most attractive aspect of The Holdout was the local vice trade. The Army garrison stationed there knew about the town's criminal element, but had neither the authority nor the inclination to stop it. Local law enforcement were also aware, but as long as they got their cut of the profits and the culprits left the town's decent folks alone, they allowed an acceptable level of corruption to persist. But as far as Heinrich knew, that only applied to things like prostitution, gambling, and dealing in smuggled goods. Crimes like extortion, kidnapping, rape, forced labor, human trafficking, fraud, and livestock rustling were treated with zero tolerance.

"How are the locals about drug trafficking?" Heinrich asked. "Cops gonna hassle us?"

"Not as long as we deal with somebody who pass it down the line," Horton said. "Pigs don't mind a dealer takes shit out of town, but we best not put that shit on the street. Bring the heat down real fuckin' quick. They see somebody using, they find out where that shit come from the hard way. Like brass knuckles and pipes and shit."

"So we need a dealer dialed in to the local scene. Know anybody who can help us?"

"Yeah, I know some people. Ain't gonna give us street prices, though. Strictly wholesale. Dream be illegal pretty much everywhere. Expensive shit to move."

A sigh. "Guess that's to be expected. Cops take a cut if they find out?"

Horton laughed. "Come on, Chief. They cops, ain't they?"

Heinrich nodded. "Right. We'll have to keep the cops out of it. So tell me, Mr. Horton. What's your plan? How do we do this?"

Horton held out his hands, shrugged, and tilted his head. "Might need some time to think on that. Give me till tomorrow?"

"I want a report first thing in the morning."

"I can do that."

Maru ladled rehydrated meat from the pot into a wooden bowl and handed it to Heinrich. The raider chief picked up a spoon and took a bite.

"Very well, Mr. Horton. Dismissed."

"Yes sir," Horton said and began walking away.

Heinrich let him take five steps, then called, "Hey Horton."

The man stopped and half turned. "Yeah, Chief?"

"You make this happen, I'll see to it you're well rewarded."

Horton grinned. "Oh, don't worry 'bout that Chief. I always come through with the goods."

You better, Heinrich thought as his henchman walked away. *You fuck this up and it'll be the last mistake of your life.*

*****

A week's hard travel brought the Storm Road Tribe to the gates of The Holdout.

The gates were shut, but there was a small access door allowing pedestrians and small carts in and out. People passed through the small portal, farmers, scavengers, and Travelers for the most part. Most of them looked haggard, underfed, and shabby. Heinrich suspected a few of the leaner, harder, and better armed people were Runners, members of a loose organization of professional couriers.

There were no caravans in sight, just Heinrich's tribe and the four carts and eight horses they had stolen. The opium was wrapped in scraps of cloth scavenged from houses back at the river and hidden inside the containers of seed grain. Unless the local inspectors dumped the crates on the ground, they were unlikely to find the opium. Heinrich was grateful drug dogs were no longer an issue. Most domesticated canines had died during the Outbreak.

Security at the gate was impressive. There were men with scoped rifles in a pair of watchtowers and four armed guards on the ground behind thick bastions of sandbags. A heavy machine gun sat front and center, a guard standing behind it. As the tribe grew closer, the guard checked the machine gun's chamber and took aim in their direction. One of the guards held up a hand, palm out, and blew three sharp notes on a whistle.

"Hold it right there," he shouted.

Heinrich signaled the tribe to a halt. "Wait here," he shouted, then jumped down from his wagon and approached the gate.

"That's far enough," the guard said when he was about ten feet away. The man on the machine gun trained his weapon in Heinrich's direction. Heinrich stopped and stood still, hands in the air.

"State your business."

"Here to trade," Heinrich said.

"For what?"

"Livestock and wagons."

The guard looked Heinrich up and down, then peered back at his convoy. "Lot of men you got there for only having four wagons."

"Like I said, that's why we're here. Got hit by raiders back in Kansas. Got us at night, kept us pinned down while a bunch of assholes snuck into our holding pen. Managed to fight 'em off, but they got away with most of our trade. Horses, wagons, all of it."

"How many people you lose?" the guard asked.

"Eleven dead, four wounded," Heinrich said, not missing a beat. "We left the wounded back near Spring River. Farming co-op there agreed to help 'em in exchange for some seed grain."

"Seed grain, huh. That what you're trading?"

189

"Yes sir."

"Let's take a look. Call the wagons forward, but tell your people to stay put."

Heinrich walked back to the convoy. "They're buying it so far," he said to Ferguson and Maru. "You two drive the first two wagons. Get Locke and Horton to drive the other two."

"What about you, Chief?" Maru asked.

"I'll walk. And don't fucking call me chief. We're supposed to be traders."

"Right. Sorry."

Heinrich followed as his men drove the wagons to the gate. When they arrived, the lead guard and one of his men climbed into the back of the first wagon.

"Open 'em up," the leader said.

Ferguson complied, prying the lid off one of the crates with a crowbar. The guard stuck his hands inside and moved them around. Heinrich kept his breathing steady and his face blank. His men did the same. They had all dealt with guards and cops and soldiers before, and knew how to maintain a poker face. It was why Heinrich had chosen them to accompany him for the inspection.

"This one's clean," the leader said. "Hit the other wagons. I'll finish up here."

"Got it," the other guard said.

Ten minutes later, the guards were finished. The crates were fairly large, the grain within tightly packed. After six or seven inspections, the guards grew bored of their task and simply went through the motions.

"Okay, you can button 'em up," the lead guard said. Ferguson nodded silently and proceeded to reseal the crates. The lead guard turned to his assistant.

"Daley, get Fortner and Pall out here. Check the wagons. Make sure there's no false bottoms or anything underneath the floorboards or in the axles or wheels or anything."

"Will do," Daley said.

The lead guard went back to his post and drank a ladle of water from a bucket behind a pile of sandbags. He watched with bored eyes while the other three guards checked over the wagons. Heinrich and his men stood aside looking equally bored, only this time they did not have to fake it. Now that the danger had passed, they were ready to get within the walls and find a place to rest for the night.

Twenty minutes stretched by before the guards gave their boss the all clear. He acknowledged them, then handed an empty sandbag to each man. They approached the wagons and ordered Ferguson to open a crate of grain.

"The hell for?" the giant rumbled, his ruddy face darkening.

The guards were not intimidated. One of them half-raised his rifle in Ferguson's direction.

"Because I fucking told you to," the lead guard said. "Unless you want to turn your little wagons around and fuck off to the next town. Shouldn't take you long. It's only about a hundred miles away."

"It's all right," Heinrich said, motioning for Ferguson to back off. "Let them take their cut."

The lead guard smiled and pointed. "Now there's a reasonable man."

Minutes later, their sandbags filled with half a crate of valuable seed grain, the guards finally opened the gate and allowed the tribe through. As they went inside, Ferguson leaned down so he could speak quietly to his chief.

"I'm gonna find where that fucker lives and skin him alive."

"Later," Heinrich said. "For now, we maintain a low profile. Once we offload the dope, you can do whatever you want. Until then, we don't do anything to attract attention."

"Might want to tell the men that."

"We'll have a tribal council as soon as we get settled in."

Ferguson stood up straight and gave a skeptical laugh. "That should be interesting."

TWENTY-SIX

"So here's how it's going down," Horton said.

Heinrich sat back in his folding chair. He and the rest of his tribe were camped in The Holdout's caravan district. They had been there for two days, and the men were getting restless. Heinrich had given them strict orders to avoid drunkenness, brawling, thievery, and excessive whoring. They were allowed to have a few drinks and satisfy their base sexual urges, but only in moderation. Heinrich had instructed them to travel in packs of no more than four men, and the senior man was to take charge and ensure no one got out of hand. So far, things had gone well. But Heinrich knew his tribe, and he knew the clock was ticking. Before long, someone would screw up and he would have to make an example out of them. He did not want this. Not that he particularly cared about hurting people, but his tribe was diminished and morale was already low. Disciplinary actions now were likely to inspire desertions he could ill afford.

"I'm all ears," Heinrich said. He could hear the relief in his own voice.

Horton grabbed a camp stool from the back of Heinrich's wagon and sat down close to his chief. He kept his voice low.

"I got a buyer lined up," Horton said. "But it ain't gonna be easy. He a cagey motherfucker. Agree on a price ahead of time, then offer half when you show up to make the deal. Say take it or leave it."

Heinrich nodded slowly. "How many men does he have?"

"Not too many. Maybe ten in his crew. Don't matter though. He got friends with the cops and the Army. Be a lot of heat, he decide to call it in."

"Where's the meet?"

"Warehouse next to the livery over on Market Street. The one across the street from the big hotel."

Heinrich knew exactly where Horton was referring to. The Holdout was not a large town, maybe twice the size of Parabellum. And like Parabellum, it was laid out in a grid pattern around a central plaza. The warehouse, livery, and hotel in question were well away from the plaza near the north side of town.

"When?"

"Whenever we ready."

"What's the buyer's name?"

"People around here call him T-Low."

Heinrich turned his head. "T-Low?"

Horton shrugged. "Hey, that's what they call him."

"Fucking Christ. This T-Low idiot have any family? Girlfriend? Anybody he cares about?"

"Don't know."

"Take Locke and Stanton and find out. Don't let him see you. I want to know everything about this guy. His friends, business associates, loved ones, places he hangs out, his favorite whore, all of it. You've got forty-eight hours."

Horton stood up. "I'm on it, Chief."

*****

The buy was at midnight.

194

Heinrich almost laughed when Horton delivered the news. What was it with these small time gangsters and their movie clichés? If this T-Low character was as connected as Horton said he was, why not just do the buy in the back alley of a restaurant or something? Heinrich had seen enough commerce in town to know the authorities mostly ignored business-to-business trade. They were too busy chasing petty thieves and cracking drunks over the head and settling domestic disputes. Who cared if a couple of traders exchanged nondescript boxes of uninteresting trade goods?

The answer seemed simple: T-Low didn't want anyone knowing about the exchange. Which meant whoever was really in charge around here would want a cut of his profits. Heinrich had taken this into account when formulating his plan for tonight. Not that he'd need the extra leverage; he had enough of that already.

The fact that T-Low desired secrecy also solved the problem of keeping the cops out of things, provided Heinrich's men did their jobs correctly. After the hard times his tribe had faced since leaving Parabellum, it was enough to make Heinrich think his luck was turning.

Ferguson, Locke, Maru, Horton, and a truly evil son of a bitch named Rourke followed Heinrich as he made his way to the warehouse. They walked down muddy streets strewn with garbage, piss, and the sleeping homeless. There seemed to be a lot of those in this place. It was a trade town. Not a lot of farming, logging, or manufacturing going on, which meant high unemployment. The only people who seemed capable of producing goods and services were the town's three fiercely competing blacksmiths, the innkeepers who brewed terrible whiskey, worse beer, and barely edible food, and the plentitude of whores.

Heinrich observed the buildings as he passed them. Only a very few houses looked well-constructed, obviously meant for the wealthiest members of the community. The labor must have been brought in from elsewhere, because everything else looked to have been built by a drunken ten-year-old. Whoever did the work evidently was unaware that freshly cut lumber needed to be cured before use. There was nary a straight board or plumb vertical line to be seen. Warped planks lined uneven walls, large gaps allowed in bugs and the stares of curious onlookers, and shingles dangled

195

precariously from wavy, uneven rooftops. He imagined the boomtowns of the old west must have looked something like this.

Ought to change the name of this place, Heinrich thought. *The Holdout doesn't quite do it justice. Should call it The Shithole.*

Given a choice between living here and dodging infected in the wastelands, Heinrich decided he'd rather take his chances with the ghouls.

Around a corner, the warehouse came into view. Like the structures in the more affluent parts of town, it did not look like it was about to fall over. Rather, it appeared sturdy and well built. Heinrich noted the security patrols. They were exactly where his men had said they would be. He stopped and turned to the crew with him, a half smile on his scarred face.

"You ready to go to work?"

Their fierce expressions were all the answer he needed.

The six men strode to the warehouse entrance, where a gun-toting guard stopped them.

"What do you want?" he asked, finger on the trigger.

"T-Low is expecting us," Heinrich said.

The guard looked him and his retinue over. "Wait here."

They waited. Several minutes passed. Heinrich knew he was being kept waiting for the sake of keeping him waiting. It was enough to make him shake his head. Amateurs always did stupid shit like this. It was a sign of insecurity, a weak man's paltry effort at establishing dominance. Heinrich wondered if it ever occurred to people like T-Low that a man who spent weeks at a time sleeping in the dirt, eating like a caveman, and crossing miles of ghoul-infested wastelands on foot would probably not chafe at having to stand and do nothing for a few minutes.

Stupid.

Finally the door opened. "Come on in," the guard said.

Heinrich and his men entered. The warehouse was dark except for a pool of light in the center. The warehouse was crowded with goods, preventing Heinrich from seeing the source of the light.

Piles of boxes, crates, barrels, and earthen pots were stacked high all around, but the layout was sensible and the path to the light was easy to follow.

Which was exactly why Heinrich didn't follow it.

The last man in was Rourke. As he passed the guard he suddenly turned, hit the man with an open-handed strike to the throat, and pulled him inside. Ferguson grabbed the man by the jaw and the back of his head, lifted him off the ground, and casually snapped his neck. Rourke pulled the door shut and put the bar in place. No one would be coming in from outside. Not through the main entrance at least.

Ferguson lifted the dead body easily and tossed it atop a pile of wooden boxes, then stood on tip-toe to look at his handiwork.

"He's out of sight, Chief."

"Good," Heinrich said. "Let's get to work."

He reached into the collar of his shirt, pulled out a radio earpiece attached to a cord, and turned the dial to activate the radio tucked into the small of his back. As he did so, he and his men moved deeper into the shadows, staying parallel to the light source.

"This is Chief," he said, keying his mic. "Lopez, what you got for me?"

"You're clear straight ahead, no obstructions," Lopez replied. He had entered the warehouse earlier in the day by scaling a wall in the back using a rope and grappling hook, then gained entrance by sliding his narrow torso through an opening in a wide, louvered window. Once inside, he had taken position in the shadows of the high rafters and waited. When he heard the guard explaining to T-Low that Heinrich had arrived, he activated the stolen night vision scope he had smuggled in with him and was now his chief's eye in the sky.

"Hostiles?" Heinrich asked.

"Four outside, three more inside, including T-Low. Fucker wants you to think he's alone, but he's got two guys with AKs on top of boxes set up for a crossfire."

"Positions?"

Lopez relayed where the gunmen were in relation to Heinrich's position. The raider chief turned to Maru and Rourke, who also wore radios and were listening in. He motioned for them to deal with the gunmen.

"Lopez, Chief. Let me know when the job's done."

"Copy, Chief."

Heinrich waved the rest of his men behind cover. They carried no firearms so as not to arouse suspicion with the guards, but did wear concealed knives. Heinrich knew Maru and Rourke were stealthy, and deadly with a blade. He did not expect to be waiting long.

"Chief, Lopez. Targets are down. Rourke and Maru got their guns."

"Maru, Rourke, this is Chief. Eyes on T-Low. Lopez, keep a lookout for anyone else entering the building."

"Copy, Chief."

Heinrich stood and motioned for Horton, Locke, and Ferguson to follow him. The four raiders walked toward the light source in the center of the warehouse. After a minute or two, they left the rows of stored goods and emerged onto a broad earthen walkway spanning the middle of the warehouse from one end to the other. In the center of this was a support column as big around as Ferguson's barrel chest. A burning oil lantern hung from a long metal hook bolted to the post, and beneath it, a man lounged on a plush leather recliner.

"Glad you could finally make it," the man said, smiling. He pushed the handle on the side of the recliner forward and stood up.

"So you're T-Low," Heinrich said.

"Guilty as charged." The man's smile remained in place.

Heinrich examined him. He was average height and build, and wore a tight-fitting shirt to emphasize the lean, whipcord muscles of his arms and torso. As he walked toward Heinrich, the raider chief could tell by the way T-Low moved he was not a man to underestimate. Heinrich had seen plenty of guys like him before: far stronger than they looked, fast as vipers, and ten times as mean. The kind of men who killed as easily as most people tied their shoes.

As T-Low drew close, Heinrich saw he had dark hair, olive skin, and a broad, slightly hooked nose. Italian, probably.

"So I hear you got something for me," T-Low said, speaking with a pronounced New Jersey accent.

"Only if you have something for me," Heinrich replied. It took everything he had not to laugh at the idiot in front of him. He had no idea what was coming.

"Come take a look."

T-Low pulled the lantern from the hook and began walking toward the other end of the warehouse. He moved with confidence, a man assured of his position of power. Heinrich looked over his shoulder and let one side of his mouth tilt up. His men gave him knowing looks and small smiles. They were enjoying this.

Heinrich was too.

"I see you got a radio," T-Low said as they walked.

Heinrich said nothing.

"Where you get tech like that? Don't see that kind of thing much outside the Army. You hit a military convoy or somethin'?"

"Anybody ever tell you it's not healthy to ask too many questions?" Ferguson said.

"Hey, just making conversation."

They reached the back of the building and T-Low hung the lantern from another long iron hook. The light revealed four long-bedded carts complete with buckboards, yokes, and harnesses.

"There they are. Your shiny new rides."

Heinrich looked where T-Low pointed. "There's only four. I asked for eight."

"This is all I could get."

"Bullshit," Heinrich said. "There's a whole goddamn dealership full of the things outside of town. I saw it on the way in. And where's the fucking oxen?"

"Your cows are in the livery next door. Eight of 'em."

Heinrich pinched his nose between his fingers. "I asked for eight carts and four oxen for each one. That's thirty-two oxen. You're short by twenty-four. You know how to fucking count, right?"

The smile left T-Low's face. His eyes drifted over Heinrich's shoulder and he very deliberately scratched the back of his head. Heinrich suppressed a smile.

"Listen fellas. I hate to give you the bad news, but the deal has changed. You see, wagons cost a lot and livestock is in high demand. So the price you offered me just isn't enough to get what you want. This is the best I can do for you."

"You're lying," Heinrich said. "You think I'm fucking stupid? You think I didn't send my men around to find the going rates for the shit I'm buying? The dream I'm selling you is worth twice what I'm asking for, even wholesale."

T-Low sighed. "Okay, fine. I guess the delicate approach isn't going to work. So let me put it to you another way." At this, his eyes grew hard and Heinrich saw the ruthless monster hiding under the surface. It almost made him regret what was about to happen. Under different circumstances, he could have used a man like T-Low.

"Here's the deal. You're gonna give me all the dream you got. I'm gonna be nice and give you these wagons and the cows, mostly because I can't do shit with them and I want you to fucking leave. That's the best deal you're gonna get. If it ain't good enough, I'll just take your fucking dream and sell the shit I'm fronting you, and have the cops haul your asses out of town. You see, we have a little arrangement. I help them out, they help me out. I need someone gone, they get 'em gone. And if you try to fight, the Army will hammer your asses into paste. Now, I'm trying to be reasonable here. I got a reputation to maintain. You give me what I want, you get the wagons and cows, and we all walk away happy. Give me any shit, and things are gonna get real bad for you." T-Low held out his hands. "So what's it gonna be?"

Heinrich looked at his men, and the mirth they had been holding in finally let loose. The four of them laughed loudly, tears running down their cheeks, hands on their knees. Ferguson had to squat down and put a hand on the ground to keep from falling over. The assured confidence on T-Low's face became strained and brittle.

"The fuck you laughing at?" he demanded.

When Heinrich could breathe again, he stood up straight, wiped his eyes, and smiled at T-Low. Whatever T-Low saw in that smile made him take a nervous step backward.

"Kid, you're so full of shit it's no wonder your skin is brown. Let me tell you what's going to happen. You're not gonna tell the cops a goddamn thing. Or the Army, or anyone else. And I'll tell you why. You don't want anyone to know we're here right now. Not that I give a rat's ass, but it makes me curious who's pulling your strings."

T-Low looked over Heinrich's shoulder again, made a little spinning motion in the air, and dropped flat on the ground. He lay there for several seconds, then looked up, his face a mask of incredulity.

"Jimmy!" he shouted. "Raw Dog! The fuck you doin'?"

Heinrich's grin broadened. Behind him, he could hear his crew chuckling. "I don't think they can hear you anymore, T-Low." He turned around. "Maru, Rourke, come on out."

The whisper of their footsteps crunched the dirt as they approached. After a few moments they appeared in the yellow-orange glow of the lantern's light. Maru's shirt was covered in blood, and Rourke's lean, angular face held a nasty grin. Both carried the guns they had seized from the men they killed.

Heinrich put a finger to his earpiece. "Stanton, Chief. Give me a status on the perimeter guards."

A chuckle came over the radio channel. "What guards? All we got out here is buzzard meat."

"Roger that. Chop 'em, bag 'em, and bury 'em somewhere out of sight. No witnesses." Heinrich looked down at T-Low. "Looks like you're all out of friends."

The raider chief took a knee in front of the still prostrate hoodlum. T-Low's face had gone pale, eyes wide in the firelight. The veins in his neck pulsed quickly and his breath came in shallow gulps. Heinrich leaned close so he could speak in a low voice.

"How's your sister, T-Low? Where is she tonight?"

The man went still. He neither moved nor breathed for several seconds, then came up to his knees.

"What did you do to her?"

Heinrich reached into a cargo pocket on his leg and removed a small bundle of black cloth. He handed it to T-Low.

"Oh, not much. Yet."

T-Low unwound the bundle with shaking hands. The cloth fell away and revealed a single severed finger. On the finger was a slim gold band with a heart-shaped ruby setting. T-Low's mouth worked soundlessly a few times, then he dropped the finger like it was on fire and scooted backwards on his hands and feet until his back hit a wagon wheel. He stayed there, breathing heavily and staring in anguish at the cleanly cut digit lying on the bare dirt floor.

"No, no, no, no, no. Not Marie. Not her. Please God no. She's all I got."

Heinrich stood up, walked over to T-Low, and sat down beside him so their shoulders were touching. "It's hard to take in, I know. But you have to see things from my perspective."

T-Low's gaze slowly shifted from the finger to Heinrich's face. Ferguson stepped forward and loomed over T-Low, his nearly seven foot frame blocking the lantern's light and casting the small-time gangster in darkness.

"I knew about your connections before I came here tonight," Heinrich said. "The cops, the Army, all of it. You see, we're not just a bunch of redneck traders hawking seeds and dream so we can buy enough food to get through the winter. That's what you thought we were, right?"

T-Low continued to stare wordlessly.

"It's okay, you don't have to answer." Heinrich patted T-Low on the leg. "As you've probably already figured out, we're a little more organized than that. Anyway, getting back to my original point, you have to look at things from where I stand. Going into this deal, I had a few options to consider. I knew you were going to try to fuck me. You're a cheap amateur hood, and that's what you small time assholes do. Problem is, you didn't know who you were dealing with. I did. And that's where the trouble started for you."

Heinrich stood up and paced slowly in front of where T-Low sat. Ferguson stepped aside to give him room.

"My first problem was your crew. Not much of a problem, really. I got close to a hundred trained killers in my tribe. Your little band of smashed dicks didn't stand a chance. But my thinking was after I kill them, and turn the tables on you, I still need you to procure my wagons and livestock. The dream is the only thing I have valuable enough to pay for that, and you have the connections to make it happen. I don't. Not here, anyway. And I doubt the local authorities would take kindly to me going around trying to buy shit with illegal narcotics. I can't spend the seed grain either because it's not enough to cover everything I need. And if I get rid of the grain, what would be my cover for going into Colorado Springs, right?"

Heinrich looked down at T-Low. The man's shocked expression had not changed.

"But you don't care about that part. Forget I mentioned it. Anyway, so the dream was the only way to pay for the wagons and everything else. What I needed was someone with enough working capital to buy my equipment in advance, and then let me pay them back with the opium. That's where you came in. And you know what? I was willing to deal straight. Last thing I need is an Army patrol catching me with a giant fucking shipment of dope. But then Horton," Heinrich pointed to his henchman, "came to me and told me what kind of player you were, how you like to cheat people. I had my guys look into you and, lo and behold, it turns out you have a sister."

Heinrich stopped pacing and held out his hands.

"In that moment, I had an epiphany. Why pay for the wagons and livestock at all? Christ's sake, I was starting to act like one of those sad chumps that actually deal with people honestly. Five years of robbing and stealing and taking whatever the fuck I want, and a few months of easy living got me acting like a humble shopkeeper. I tell you, I'm almost grateful I got chased out of Parabellum. It's been an eye opening experience. Reminded me of who I am."

Heinrich started pacing again. "But you don't care about any of that, and this isn't a therapy session. So let's get to the point. I got the lay of the land and figured, why not just kidnap your sister, keep the dope, and make you buy me the wagons and livestock on your own dime? And while I'm at it, why not have you throw in some weapons and ammunition? We're kind of low on bullets lately."

T-Low blinked a few times and Heinrich saw the wheels in his brain start turning again. He stood and held up his hands.

"Okay, look man, whatever you want. Just don't hurt Marie."

Heinrich pointed at the severed finger. "Little late for that."

T-Low closed his eyes and swallowed. "I mean, don't do anything else to her. Please."

"Well, T-Low…" Heinrich paused. "You know what, I'm tired of calling you T-Low. It's about the stupidest nickname I've ever heard. What's your real name?"

"Anthony Lorenzetti."

"Ah. T is short for Tony, which is short for Anthony. Low is short for Lorenzetti. I get it. Still a fucking stupid name, but I get it. Anyway, like I was saying, whether or not any further ill fortune befalls your dear sister is entirely up to you."

"I'll get what you want," Lorenzetti said. "But I wasn't lying when I said these wagons and the eight oxes were all I could get. It's all I had trade for."

"First of all, Anthony, it's *oxen*, not oxes. Read a fucking book or something. Second, how is that my problem?"

Lorenzetti's lip began to quiver. "Look, I swear to God, I can't buy what you're asking me for. I can if you give me some dream, though."

Heinrich keyed his radio. "Stanton, do me a solid. Go find Griffin and tell him to bring us another piece of the girl. Maybe a nipple this time."

"Copy, Chief. On it."

"Wait!" Lorenzetti screamed. "For fuck's sake, I'm telling you the truth. Please, just give me some of the dope and I can get you whatever you want."

Heinrich glared at the young man for a long instant, then turned to Ferguson. "You believe him?"

A shrug. "Probably telling the truth."

"Mr. Ferguson here knows a lie when he hears one," Heinrich said. He keyed his radio again. "Hey Stanton, belay my last. Leave her alone for now."

"Copy Chief."

"Horton, how much does he need?" Heinrich said.

"Probably 'bout six kilos."

"That work for you, Anthony?"

He nodded quickly. "Yeah, yeah, I can make that work."

"You have twenty four hours. After that, my guys go to work on your sister. We clear?"

"Yeah, I got it. I'll get your stuff, I swear."

"Good. I'm glad we had this talk." A click of the radio. "All stations, we're done here. Let's get some rack time. Busy day tomorrow."

Heinrich got a round of affirmatives. As he walked toward the front door of the warehouse, he called over his shoulder.

"I'd get started if I were you, Lorenzetti. Clock's ticking."

As Heinrich and his men emerged into the street, Ferguson fell into step next to his chief. "Gotta say, that was nicely done. You had that guy shitting his pants."

"Take it as a lesson, Ferg," Heinrich said. "You can get whatever you want out of people if you push the right buttons. It's all about leverage."

"You and Archimedes," Ferguson said.

Heinrich raised an eyebrow. Ferguson never ceased to surprise him with his knowledge of the classics.

"Give me a lever long enough," Heinrich said, "and a fulcrum on which to place it, and I shall move the world."

TWENTY-SEVEN

"What do we do with the girl?" Ferguson asked.

Heinrich looked up from the book he was reading. He was sitting in Marie Lorenzetti's small but comfortable living room. She lived in an undersized two-bedroom trailer that someone, most likely her brother, had hauled within the town's walls and set up on a spot of level ground. There was no electricity or running water within, but a wood stove had been installed in the kitchen, there was a privy outside, and it was a short walk to the municipal water supply.

"She still in shock?"

Ferguson gave her a kick. She writhed in her bindings, jaw and lips working against the duct tape covering her mouth. The ring finger on her left hand was missing. In its place was a blistered mess of black, cauterized flesh and protruding bone. Heinrich knew the pain must have been excruciating. It certainly had been when he'd lost two of his fingers to a Blackthorn's kukri.

"Looks like she's come out of it," Ferguson said.

Heinrich looked at his watch. "Your brother has ten minutes," he said to Marie. "After that, I'm afraid we'll have to get the bolt cutters and fire up the stove again."

Marie squeezed her eyes together and began weeping. Small, anguished sounds came from her chest, and her shoulders shook spasmodically. Heinrich watched her for a few seconds, then went back to his book. It was one of his favorites, *Robinson Crusoe*. The sound of the girl crying was a bit of an annoyance—Heinrich preferred to read in silence—but under the circumstances there was really nothing for it. He did his best to ignore her.

With two minutes left, there was a frantic knock at the door. Heinrich nodded to Ferguson, who drew a large bore revolver from under his black leather jacket and pointed it at the door as he opened it. The way he was positioned, the gun was invisible to anyone standing outside. But Ferguson could shoot them through the flimsy door if he needed to.

"I got it," Anthony Lorenzetti said, standing on the porch, chest heaving.

Heinrich looked to Ferguson. The big man gave a short nod, and Heinrich motioned for the young man to enter. Ferguson shut the door behind him and locked it.

"Where?" Heinrich asked.

"At your camp in the caravan district."

"All eight wagons?"

"Yeah, all of 'em."

"And all thirty-two oxen?"

"Yeah, I told you, I got it all."

"And the food, ammo, guns, fresh water, feed grain, all that stuff?"

Lorenzetti sighed. "I swear on my mother's grave, man, it's all there. Go see for yourself if you don't believe me."

"Got any dream left over?"

"Half a kilo," Lorenzetti said. "I gave it to that big Australian guy."

"You must mean Maru."

"Yeah, him."

"For the record, Maru is not Australian. He's Maori, and he's from New Zealand. If you like your teeth, don't ever call him Australian to his face."

Lorenzetti shook his head and made an exasperated gesture with his hands. "Yeah, sure, whatever. Can you cut Marie loose now?"

Heinrich stood up, stuffed the book in his assault pack, put it on, and stood in front of Lorenzetti. "Not yet. I'm going to leave you here with Ferguson for the moment. Rourke is skulking around outside, so if you're thinking about running, don't. If Ferg doesn't get you, Rourke sure as hell will. And believe me, you don't want that guy getting his hands on you. Ferg here is efficient. Gets the job done quick. Rourke, well…let's just say he takes pleasure in his work. And when he's finished with you, he'll come back here for Marie. Get the picture?"

Lorenzetti swallowed. "Yeah, I got it."

"Good." Heinrich patted him twice on the cheek and left.

Half an hour later he was back in the caravan district. A thorough inspection of the wagons, livestock, and cargo revealed Lorenzetti had been telling the truth. Between what the tribe had stolen in Oklahoma and what they had acquired in The Holdout, they now had twelve wagons, eight horses, and thirty-two oxen. Five of the wagons would be used for cargo, and the rest were purpose built for carrying personnel. As long as the trail was favorable, all his men would be able to ride to Colorado. Heinrich doubted the trail would be favorable the whole way. There would probably be a lot of walking and putting shoulders to wheels in the mud and rain and making repairs on the move. But it beat the hell out of being destitute, hungry, and low on ammo.

Speaking of ammo, Heinrich thought.

He went to a wagon loaded with long rectangular wooden crates. He opened one, and inside were twenty Colt M-4 rifles. Not the fully-automatic military kind, however. These were semi-automatic versions the Army had been loaning to communities under Union treaty for the last couple of years. Heinrich found this curious. The rifles had to have been manufactured before the Outbreak, and the government seemed to have a virtually limitless supply of them, not to mention ammo. It was as if, before the Outbreak, they had known something no one else did.

Not that it mattered now.

There were five crates, which meant enough rifles for all of his men. There were also a few medium sized crates of ammunition, each containing 8,400 rounds of military issue cartridges, and another couple of crates of standard metal NATO magazines. P-mags would have been preferable, but the less reliable GI mags would have to do.

Heinrich picked up one of the rifles and pulled back the charging handle. It came back smoothly and snapped back into place with a muted *clack*. He popped one of the takedown pins, opened the rifle up, and inspected the bolt carrier group. It looked brand new, had a stamp verifying it had been magnetic particle inspected and high-pressure tested, and was properly oiled. At the bottom of the crate Heinrich spied cleaning kits, solvent, and lubricating oil.

Heinrich put the rifle back in the crate and closed it up. There would be plenty of time to take inventory and issue weapons later. For the moment, he had loose ends to wrap up.

At his wagon, which he half-jokingly thought of as his command center, he opened a box and began taking out radio equipment. There was an antenna, an amplified radio frequency transmitter/receiver, a power inverter, and a charged deep-cycle battery. The battery weighed over a hundred pounds, so Heinrich left it where it was and connected a set of alligator clamps from the battery leads to an AC plug adapter. The AC plug connecting to the battery went into the inverter on the input side, while the power cable for the transmitter went into the inverter's output side. Heinrich put on the radio's headphones, picked up the handset, and double checked to make sure everything was connected properly. Once he started transmitting, the inverter would pull a significant amount of wattage from the battery. Not only did the battery have to power the radio, it had to power the inverter as well. And since the battery only had so many amp-hours before it had to be recharged, he wanted to keep things as brief as possible.

Once satisfied with the setup, Heinrich switched on the radio. The digital wattage readout on the inverter spiked for a moment, then stabilized. Heinrich keyed the handset.

"Mudman, Eagle. How copy?"

Rourke's raspy voice grated through the headset. "Lima Charlie, Eagle."

"We're done here. Button up and head home."

"Affirmative, Eagle."

"And make it quick. No dicking around. We need to get going. I want you and Big Red here in thirty mikes."

"Wilco, Eagle." Rourke sounded disappointed.

"Don't worry, Mudman," Heinrich said. "We'll go hunting soon enough."

"Copy. Mudman out."

There was a click as Rourke switched off his radio. Heinrich did the same and put away his radio equipment. According to the inverter readout, the entire exchange had used less than one percent of the battery's charge.

Good. Gonna need it over the next couple of weeks.

By the time Rourke and Ferguson returned, the tribe was ready to get on the road. Heinrich saw them coming and waved them over. The two men climbed onto Heinrich's wagon.

"You take care of 'em?"

"Yep," Ferguson said, tapping the base of his skull. "Blades. Quick and clean, no mess."

"And the bodies?"

"Dumped 'em in the outhouse pit. Doubt they'll be found for at least a few days."

"Good," Heinrich said. "Let's move out."

The tribe's convoy passed through the streets unhurriedly, the steady pace of people facing a long journey and not looking forward to it. Heinrich stayed alert, his sidearm positioned for a quick draw if need be. His wagon passed cops and laborers and bums and soldiers, and seemed to garner only perfunctory notice. Caravans coming into town were exciting. The bars, brothels, theatres, and restaurants regarded them as a source of income. Thieves and strong-arm robbers viewed them as potential victims. Gambling houses dusted off their tables and restocked their liquor shelves. But caravans leaving town were of no interest. They had nothing to offer but a trail of animal dung and more ruts in the muddy streets.

The Storm Road Tribe passed through the gates of The Holdout and once more ventured into the wastelands. Checking his watch, Heinrich realized they were leaving at about the same hour they had arrived a few days before. He also noticed there were only three guards on duty out front instead of four. The lead guard was nowhere to be seen. Heinrich turned to the red-bearded giant sitting next to him.

"Ferguson."

"Yeah, Chief?"

Heinrich pointed at the guards with his chin. "Your handiwork?"

A shrug. "Guy was an asshole."

"What'd you do to him?"

Ferguson smiled, and Heinrich felt the hair on his arms prickle.

"He was alive when I left him. But he ain't happy. Not one little bit."

Heinrich thought back to what Ferguson had said when they first arrived, how he was going to skin the pilfering gate guard alive.

"I think I might have an idea."

"Yeah?" Ferguson said.

"I've never known you to be a man of idle threats."

The giant laughed quietly, leaned back on the bench, and clasped his hands over his waist. Looking closely, Heinrich saw bloodstains etched into the creases of the man's thick fingers.

"That's why I like you, Chief. You're observant."

TWENTY-EIGHT

Caleb,

Southern Oregon

After introductions were made, General Jacobs informed us we would all get a full briefing in the morning. In the meantime, we would be shown to our quarters and meals would be provided. Living spaces had limited electricity and climate control, but ample access to fresh water. The hot water tank servicing the bunker was full, but we were admonished to use it sparingly. Once it was empty, it would take several hours to refill. I wanted to ask where the generators powering the bunker were so I could take a look at them, but refrained. Questions about the facility could wait. For the moment, I wanted nothing more than food and a place to rest.

When Jacobs dismissed the meeting, he, Mike, and Romero left through a door at the end of the room. Mike cast me a look over his shoulder on the way out. We had only exchanged a few words thus far, but I knew a longer discussion was in my very near future.

A few soldiers in the same nondescript fatigues I wore approached my group. Like the four of us, they wore no insignia, so it was hard to tell if we were dealing with officers or enlisted.

"Which one of you is Gabriel Garrett?" one of the soldiers asked. He looked to be in his late twenties, a little taller than

Grabovsky, obviously fit, with his hair and beard grown out in a way that told me he was no infantry grunt. Grooming standards did not generally apply to special operations types. His eyes and demeanor spoke of hard experience and an extremely low tolerance for bullshit.

"That'd be me," Gabe said.

The soldier gave him a brief nod and looked at a clipboard in his hand. "Captain Grabovsky?"

"That's me."

"Tyrel Jennings?"

"Right here."

The soldier looked at me. "You must be Captain Hicks."

I nodded once. His gaze stayed on me a few seconds longer than the others before he looked away. I figured he was either staring at my facial scars, wondering how a guy my age was already a captain, or both. My money was on the last option.

"Follow me please," he said and began walking.

The soldier led us away from the conference room, took us halfway across the warehouse floor, and then hung a sharp right between two racks of shelves loaded with multi-fuel generators. The salvager in me couldn't help but stare longingly at the profusion of valuable machines. The generators were a type used extensively by the Army since the Outbreak and the emergence of the Phoenix Initiative. They could be configured to run on ethanol, gasoline, diesel, kerosene, and even jet fuel. I had once personally watched my platoon sergeant pour several bottles of cheap grain liquor into one set up for ethanol, and it ran just fine.

"Through here," the soldier said, pointing to one of two doors set close together in the wall ahead. He opened it and went through. The four of us followed.

The hallway we entered was dimly lit like the one leading from the hidden stairwell down to the bunker. Only instead of unmarked cement, there were doors on either side of the hallway every twenty feet. The soldier stood aside and pulled a set of card keys

215

from a cargo pocket. Each one was small, roughly the size of a credit card, and aside from a black magnetic strip running across the back, marked only with a plain black number printed on both sides. He handed the first key to Gabe.

"You're number one." The next key went to Grabovsky, then Tyrel, and finally me.

"If you lose your card, pick up the orange phone on the wall and dial zero." He pointed at the aforementioned device halfway down the hall. "The phone might ring for a while, but stay on the line. Someone will get to you."

"Where's everybody else?" Tyrel asked.

"This is the officer's quarters," the soldier said. "Major Romero, Colonel Holden, and General Jacobs will be staying nearby as well, so you'd be wise to keep the noise down. As for the others, the door next to this one," he pointed at the entrance we'd just come through, "leads to the enlisted barracks. If you need to talk to somebody there, use the orange phone. Somebody will come and let you in."

"Fair enough," Grabovsky said.

"You have toilets in your rooms, but the showers are down the hall behind the green door. Try not to use up all the hot water."

As the soldier turned away, Gabriel said, "Didn't catch your name."

The soldier stopped and looked over his shoulder. "Staff Sergeant John Hathaway."

"Army?"

A shake of the head. "Marines, regardless of what they call us now."

Gabe nodded sympathetically. "Oorah."

"I read your file. Scout sniper, right? Did some time in Force Recon."

"Yep."

Hathaway pointed at his chest. "Phase five when the Outbreak hit. Visiting my folks in Augusta. Word came down for all military and law enforcement to head for Atlanta, so I drove down there and got picked up by the Georgia National Guard. Kicked around with the Army for three years before I wound up back in a Recon unit, just in time for the sons of bitches in the Springs to disband the Corps."

Gabe shook his head. "Black day, that one."

Hathaway was quiet a few seconds. "Anyway, you fellas need anything, you know what to do."

"Thanks for your help," Gabe said.

"No problem."

Sergeant Hathaway left.

"Catch you fellas in the morning," Tyrel said with a yawn. "I'm beat."

"Same here," Gabe said, and walked toward his room. I went toward mine. Grabovsky walked behind me to my door. I turned before swiping the key through the reader and stared at him.

"Need to talk to you," he said. No preamble, no small talk, no attempt at insincere pleasantries. Just a simple statement of intent. I approved.

"Fine."

I opened the door and went in. The room was dark, but a brief search revealed a light switch next to the door. I flipped it and a few LEDs came on overhead. The room was spacious by military standards, about twenty by thirty feet. The floor was covered in the kind of thin blue carpeting I used to see in office buildings before the Outbreak. The walls were plain, smooth concrete with no decorations. There were two beds on the far wall at the end of the room, both twins, separated by two low chests of drawers. In the space between the beds and the walls were two wardrobes, each one more than large enough for all of my uniforms and kit back in the Springs, much less the minimum loadout I had brought with me.

217

Beyond an open door there was a small bathroom with only a sink and toilet. To my right was a kitchenette with a small refrigerator, hotplate, toaster oven, sink, and cabinets. The countertops were off-white vinyl and the cabinets were the ugly yellowish color of plastic veneer attempting to pass for wood, and failing. The refrigerator did not hum, telling me it either had no power or was unplugged. Not that it mattered; I wouldn't need it.

I had been carrying my heavy rucksack in one hand since leaving the conference room. My arm was tired, my back was tired, and my legs felt like they were made of green sticks and rubber. I walked to one of the beds and set my ruck down against a wardrobe, then began removing my MOLLE vest and other gear. Grabovsky shut the door behind him and laid his pack against it.

"What's on your mind?" I asked.

He walked over to the small table in the kitchen, sat down, and pointed at the other chair. "Have a seat."

I thought about telling him to fuck off. This was my room, after all, and we were the same rank. He had no business ordering me around at this point. But the more reasonable part of my mind told me arguing with Grabovsky would run counter to him going the hell away, so I complied.

"You don't like me much," he said when I was seated.

"Is it that obvious?"

"Can't say I like you either."

"Glad we shared our feelings. Anything else?"

His gaze narrowed. "Got a few questions for you."

"Okay."

"You gonna answer 'em?"

"Maybe."

He shook his head. "First, how did you end up as Jacobs' personal bag man? Second, how did you get a goddamn black card? Third, how does an infantry grunt go from sergeant to fucking captain, and a federal emissary to boot? You guys in the

218

First Recon are tough, I'm not gonna question that. But you ain't SF, and you sure as hell ain't Delta. Who trained you?"

"As to the first three questions, all I can say is ask General Jacobs."

"You expect me to believe he didn't tell you?"

"I don't give a flying fuck what you believe, Grabovsky. You asked, and I answered. As for who trained me, I'm afraid you'll have to file that one under none of your damn business."

He stared for several long seconds. A cord twitched in his jaw and the cable-like muscles in his forearms moved like snakes in shallow water. I kept my breathing steady and shifted my feet so I could stand and dive away if I had to. Finally, Grabovsky stood up, walked to the door, grabbed his rucksack, and left without a word.

To his credit, he did not slam the door.

*****

I turned off the lights and lay down in the pitch darkness of the room. Unlike the cramped survival bunker back in California, this subterranean environment was surprisingly pleasant. A cozy silence enveloped me, broken only by a faint hum of ventilation. The air was cool and not at all stuffy. I could feel the walls around me and the earth overhead, thick and solid and impenetrable. My belly was full of tasteless but otherwise satisfying food. The bed was clean and comfortable and smelled of cheap detergent. My pillow was firm and unflattened, as if it had never been used. And, strangest of all, I was enjoying it. No nervousness, no jumping at sounds, no dread of sleep lest something come for me in the night. At first, I couldn't understand why I was so relaxed. But after a while, it came to me.

I felt safe.

It was an unfamiliar feeling, like a distant, fond memory of a place resurfacing after being away for a long time and coming back to visit. A smile crossed my face. The only thing that could have made the moment better was Miranda lying next to me. I rolled over on my side and got comfortable and let my eyes close. In a few short minutes, distorted fragments of dreams began to pull me down into the silky warmth of unconsciousness.

And then somebody knocked on the door.

Goddammit.

There was a small lamp on the table next to my bed. I turned it on, got out of bed, and threw on an undershirt and a pair of pants. My jaw creaked from yawning and my feet tried to break the concrete on the way to the entrance. I stopped at the door, let out a long breath, counseled myself to be patient, and turned the handle.

"Hey, son," Mike Holden said. "Sorry to wake you up."

The anger blew away like smoke on the wind. "Uh…no, no, it's fine." I wiped sleep from my eyes and blinked at the harsh light in the hallway. "What's going on? Is there trouble?"

"No, nothing like that. I was just wondering if you had a few minutes to talk. I know it's late, and I'm sorry to bother you, but…" he lifted his hands and shrugged. "I haven't seen you in a long time. I've missed you."

I stood and stared. Five years ago, Mike would never have been so frank. There was none of the old bluster and red-faced boisterousness I remembered from the Mike who had once entrusted me with his daughter's safety. This Mike had care-worn eyes that bespoke a man too worn down by life to engage in bravado or insincerity. It was hard to reconcile this lean, wolfish specter with the rollicking soul I'd known since my childhood.

"I've missed you too, Mike."

It wasn't my intention to speak; the words came out on their own. Mike gave a saddened smile.

"Maybe we could talk a while?" he said.

"Sure. Come on in."

I opened the door wider to allow him in, but he tilted his head down the hallway. "How about you come on over to my room? I got some decent hooch. Maybe we can have a drink if it ain't too late for you."

A drink sounded wonderful. A drink was a fantastic idea. Several drinks sounded even better. Maybe they would keep my hands from shaking when Mike finally asked what I knew he had been waiting years to ask.

"Let me get my shoes."

TWENTY-NINE

"I'm starting to understand the difference between junior and senior officers," I said.

The sides of Mike's mouth tilted up a little. "Not bad, is it?"

I looked around the room. It was roughly the same dimensions as mine, but much better appointed. Mike had his own shower, the carpet was thick and well padded, there were impressionist prints on the walls—blurred landscapes of France and Tuscany mostly—and the furniture and cabinetry were of vastly superior quality to mine.

Instead of two beds there was one twin with a thickly padded mattress and sheets with a thread count in the five digits. Where the second bed was in my room, Mike had a low wooden table flanked by two plush, leather-upholstered chairs. I sat down in one, and it was the most comfortable place I had parked my ass since the Outbreak.

Mike took the other chair. There was a lamp with a gold-colored shade and a bottle of Bushmills on the table. There were also two tumblers and a bucket of ice. I stared at the ice bucket with unashamed avarice. Like many things, ice is a pre-Outbreak luxury whose absence makes me appreciate how good things used to be, and probably never will be again. Bittersweet is the word that comes to mind, but somehow it doesn't seem to encompass the scale of pain and longing the sight of ice engenders in me.

"They treat me pretty good around here," Mike said as he placed a few cubes in both tumblers and poured three fingers of whiskey into each one.

"The hooch part of the deal?"

A chuckle. "I wish. Took this off a KPA patrol back in October. Found it in one of their rucksacks."

"KPA," I said. "So that's who they are."

"Yep. Some Chinese troops too, and a few Russians. I don't think the Russians were part of the plan from the outset though. I suspect they tagged along out of self-preservation."

My ears perked up. "What makes you say that?"

Mike put the bottle down, picked up his glass, and stared into it while he swirled the ice around.

"Probably don't make much sense what's going on here, does it? Folks back east only know what the government told 'em, and that ain't much. Been keeping a tight lid on this little war of ours. The more people know about it, the harder it'll be to take care of business. Too many chiefs and not enough Indians back in the Springs. Need to keep as many hands out of the pot as we can."

Mike went quiet again. Neither of us spoke for a stretch. I picked up my glass and sipped the whiskey. It was smooth and fragrant and went down like greased ambrosia. Compared to the moonshine I had gotten used to, it was like climbing out of a Volkswagen and hopping behind the wheel of a Porsche.

"Got some things I need to ask you," Mike said.

There was no getting around it, so I didn't try. "Sophia."

Mike sipped his whiskey and put it down. "Yep."

"You know what happened?"

"I do."

"Central?"

"Sort of. Jacobs looked into it for me after he first made contact with the Resistance. Show of good faith on his part."

I felt my heart rate pick up. Something was squeezing my chest and making it hard to breath. My hands felt hot, and I doubted I could have stood up without swaying.

"I'm sorry, Mike."

He reached out and patted my forearm. "It's not your fault, Caleb. You couldn't have stopped what happened."

I took a deep breath. The breath made the boa constrictor around my heart eased its grip, so I took another one. And another. I had expected to choke up and not be able to talk at this point, but to my surprise, I was holding it together. Perhaps once a man has shed enough tears over a lost loved one, it gets easier to talk about them without breaking down.

"I wasn't there when it happened."

"Tell me about it."

I looked at Mike. "What did Jacobs tell you?"

"Just the facts. She went into premature childbirth and died from blood loss due to complications. The baby didn't survive. You named her after your stepmother."

I didn't know what to say, so I just nodded.

"Jacobs told me where the ashes are buried. He also told me about what happened to you afterward. Not the details, but what was on the record. Said you damn near killed a fella in a drunken brawl, got hit with a felony assault charge, and had to choose between prison and the Army."

Another deep breath. "Yeah. That about covers it."

"If you ask me, you made the right choice."

I shifted in my seat. "Sometimes I wonder."

Mike looked away and drummed his fingers on the arm of his chair. "Jacobs also said you underwent treatment for severe alcohol withdrawal."

"That's right."

"You ain't no drunk, Caleb. I know you better than that."

I picked up my whiskey and drained it. The burn steadied me. "You ever seen that old movie *Leaving Las Vegas*?"

"Nicolas Cage and Elizabeth Shue, right?"

"That's the one."

"Most depressing damn movie I ever saw."

"Yeah, well, try living it."

Another silence. We both finished our drinks, and Mike poured two more. "For what it's worth, I'm glad you failed in that endeavor."

"For what it's worth, so am I."

"Now about Sophia…"

I sipped the whiskey again. "She was seven months pregnant at the time. They probably told you that already."

Mike nodded.

"I quit my job with the city when I found out we were having a baby. Tyrel was on a salvage crew. Wanted me to sign on. Put in a good word with the boss. Dangerous work, but it brought in trade, lots of it. We lived pretty well for a while. The day it happened, Sophia's friends were throwing her a baby shower. I wasn't invited, so I made plans. My crew wasn't scheduled to go out for another week or so, and I was bored. So me and Tyrel and a friend of ours named Rojas went to this little town outside the Springs, Woodland Park. Place is nothing but an empty patch of dirt, now. Army took everything, even the bricks and scrap lumber. But back then it was virgin pickings."

I set my empty glass down and poured more whiskey from the bottle. Mike made no protest.

"Long story short, we got ambushed by another salvage crew that made it there first. Fought 'em off, but Rojas got killed. When we got back to town, we stopped by the crew's company office to let our boss know what happened. He gave me a note one of Sophia's friends left for me that said she was in the hospital, and she was in bad shape. Fastest I ever ran in my life."

I put the glass down again. It was empty. I didn't remember draining it.

"Better slow it down, son," Mike said.

My face was hot and the burn in my stomach was low and steady. I looked at the bottle and decided Mike was probably right. So when I poured another one, it was only half as much as last time.

"You pretty much know the rest. They told me she passed. I had to identify her body. She didn't look dead. That was the worst part. I kept looking down at her face, and she looked so serene, and I kept expecting her to open her eyes and laugh and tell me it was all a joke."

I drained my glass in one gulp. "The folks at the hospital let me hold Lauren. Just once, and only for a little while, but I got to hold her. She looked just as calm and beautiful as her mother. She was so small, barely bigger than my hand, and her little skin was so cold. I asked the nurse to bring her a blanket, and that was when they took her out of my hands and led me away."

I put the glass down, and Mike gently confiscated it. My eyes burned, and when I reached up to wipe them, my cheeks were wet.

"I think that's enough for tonight, son."

I nodded. Mike went into the kitchen and came back with a thin cloth. I wiped my eyes and blew my nose and asked him what to do with the cloth.

"Laundry chute over there," he said, pointing.

I swayed and stumbled across the room. "Think I better go get some sleep," I said.

"Good idea. I'll go with you."

He held my arm, waited while I fumbled with the card key, helped me lay down in bed, and then arranged the covers over me.

"See you in the morning, son," Mike said on his way out. "I'll make sure you're up in time for the briefing."

"Thanks."

He left and closed the door behind him. I reached over and turned off the lamp and lay awake in the quiet darkness. The good, safe feeling I'd enjoyed earlier was now as distant as the moon.

There would be no peace for me in this emptiness. I'd made a terrible mistake. I'd bent my mind toward a black corner long ago quarantined, and with good reason. Only pain awaited me in that place. I had surrounded the path leading there with land mines and barbed wire and walls with locked gates and signs warning me to stay away.

Danger.

Here there be monsters.

But I couldn't stay away anymore. I had dodged the traps and picked the locks and entered the wasteland beyond the forbidden zone. And now there was no easy way out.

Sleep was not soon in coming. I learned that night that while I may not have any tears left for Sophia, I still had plenty for my daughter.

THIRTY

I should have been bright-eyed and bushy-tailed, but instead I was bleary and nauseated and wishing like hell the pounding in my head would let up. Which, in retrospect, says something about the content of the briefing. Because not only did I pay attention, I listened with rapt, wide-eyed interest.

The audience consisted of Romero and his men, about two dozen special operations types who arrived late the previous afternoon, and my team. We skipped introductions for the moment while Jacobs addressed us and asked us to be seated. At that point, Mike, or Colonel Holden as Jacobs called him, began speaking.

"Some of you have been here since the beginning," Mike nodded to Romero and several Resistance fighters seated around him. "Some of you have been helping out for a while now, and some of you just got here. Like General Jacobs said, this is a joint operation. The Resistance will provide the bulk of the troops needed, and you JSOC folks will take the lead on the final assault. But before we get into that, those of you new to the theatre need a brief history of the Resistance."

He nodded to a young man seated at a laptop controlling the projector. The lights dimmed and a map of a small coastal city appeared on the white screen.

"Humboldt Bay, California. As you all know, this is where the Flotilla set up its base of operations and began offloading its ships. When they arrived, there were somewhere north of seven hundred vessels all together. Not that the ships matter much now; they're a bunch of stripped hulks off the coast of San Francisco. But when they first got here, they were loaded for bear. A small fleet of car carriers, or roll on/roll off ships you might have heard 'em called, brought over most of the North Korean, Chinese, and Russian troops. Just over thirty thousand of them, at best estimate. The remainder of the Flotilla were container ships, warships, sixteen oil tankers, and various support vessels. Between them, the tankers were carrying over 25 million barrels of oil. For context, the entire United Kingdom only used about 1.6 million barrels a day back before the Outbreak. And that was for a country of 60 million people."

A collective mutter went around the room, accompanied by expletives and shaking of heads. Mike waited for it to subside, then continued.

"Not long after landing, KPA troops, civilian workers, and a few dozen engineers repurposed a warehouse into a refining facility using equipment brought in on the container ships. That was when the real trouble began."

Mike motioned to the man at the laptop. The map disappeared and an aerial reconnaissance photo came up on the screen. "By the time Flotilla forces mobilized, they had already made contact with pockets of survivors in the immediate area. KPA translators assured everyone they encountered that the new arrivals were nothing more than refugees fleeing the chaos pouring out of China. It wasn't too hard to believe at the time. Back before everything went dark, the news had been full of ghouls overrunning China's military. Not to mention the newsfeeds out of India, Southeast Asia, and the Middle East."

Mike took a sip of water and motioned for the next slide. A picture of the Pacific Northwest appeared with arrows pointing at familiar areas.

"Once the refinery was online, the invaders began a pacification campaign. KPA infantry consisted of roughly twenty thousand regular troops, about four thousand special operations personnel, five thousand aircrew and mechanics, and a thousand or so support staff, including senior officers. That's in addition to the eight

229

thousand civilians that crewed the Flotilla across the Pacific. On our side, the survivors in Northern California, Oregon, and Southern Washington were divided into pockets of a few hundred each, and those only poorly armed and barely able to hold off the undead, much less well-supplied, well-armed, highly-trained military forces. It wasn't even a fight."

Mike picked up a laser pointer.

"This here is the Humboldt Bay internment camp. It was the first, but it isn't the largest. Most of the folks here were rounded up in Northern California, but some of them came from Oregon as well. By the time this camp was built and the local populace put to slave labor, the other three main camps were already under construction. It's worth noting the North Koreans didn't build the labor camps. The prisoners did."

Mike put the water glass down and turned toward the assembled crowd.

"I won't bore you with the details because it's a long story and we don't have all day, but this is about the time me and some other folks formed the original cells that would become the Resistance."

Another hand signal, another slide, this one showing the parking lot of an abandoned big-box retailer littered with the smoking, wrecked debris of a few dozen helicopters.

"The first thing we did was take out their air assets. Most of the founding members of the Resistance were ex-military, so we knew how important air support would be to sustained operations. So aircraft were the first thing we went after."

The picture changed again, this time showing a civilian airport littered with the detritus of what used to be fighter jets.

"The North Koreans hadn't done too good a job hiding their aircraft, so it wasn't that tough to take them out. In less than a year, we had the sons of bitches grounded. Unfortunately, we became the victims of our own success. We'd counted on some sort of response from the KPA, but we hadn't counted on reprisals."

Mike put his hands on his hips and seemed to stare at each man in the room at the same time.

"Now I'll warn you. This next part is hard to watch. I know you've all seen some bad things, but it's something else entirely to see foreign invaders brutalizing your own people. Take a minute to think on that before we go on."

Mike sat down and closed his eyes and looked old and tired. It didn't take a genius to figure out he was not looking forward to the next part of the briefing. After a couple of minutes, he stood up and motioned to change the slide. A video began playing on the screen. There was no sound, but the footage was clear, obviously shot from a high-definition camera with a long-range zoom.

The footage showed a prison camp, complete with watchtowers, razor wire, machine gun nests, and two areas where buildings had been erected. One side of the camp hosted an administrative building, storage area, and several barracks. On the other side of the camp were longhouses situated in precise columns, no doubt for the prisoners. The whole setup looked disturbingly like old photos of Auschwitz.

As the video played, a man climbed a tower and started ringing a bell. Almost immediately, a few hundred troops poured out of the barracks and assembled on a broad parade ground. A short, stocky North Korean officer addressed his men via a bullhorn and began talking animatedly. When he finished, the soldiers stood at attention, saluted, and then headed toward the long, low-slung buildings where the slaves slept at night.

The soldiers rousted the terrified prisoners from their quarters and forced them onto the parade ground in their bare feet. It was winter, and the weather was cold, as evidenced by the cloud of steam put into the air by the slaves' rapid breathing and the way they shivered in their filthy rags. A few dozen soldiers began moving through the crowd, separating people seemingly at random and directing them to the far end of the parade ground. Very quickly, I figured out the separation of the prisoners was not random at all. The soldiers were counting to nine, and then directing every tenth person to move away from the others.

Decimation, I thought.

The word 'decimate' does not mean what most people think. It comes from an old Latin word meaning 'to reduce by one tenth'. It was a brutal form of punishment used in the Roman army for only the most egregious offences. Military units guilty of capital crimes were divided into groups of ten and forced to draw lots. The soldier on whom the lot fell was then beaten to death by his own comrades, who themselves were charged with carrying out the killing on pain of death. The killers usually performed their task with wooden clubs or thrown rocks.

The North Koreans did not bother with sticks and rocks. They simply forced the condemned to line up against the fence and gunned them down with tight, controlled bursts from their Kalashnikov rifles.

At least a fourth of them were children.

The survivors were horrified and enraged and attempted to overwhelm their captors through sheer weight of numbers. They very quickly learned the reality of what happens when unarmed civilians go up against armed, disciplined soldiers. By the time the slaves returned bloodied and weeping to their quarters, dozens more of them lay dead. The video ended.

Mike waved his hand wearily and the picture changed to another aerial map.

"Lights," Mike said.

The picture washed out as fluorescents came on overhead.

"What you just saw was not an isolated incident. Decimations like this one happened all over KPA territory, both in the prison camps and in occupied survivor communities. Up to that point, we'd been relying on a network of support from people the North Koreans either hadn't found, or agreed to leave alone so long as they did what was asked of them. But after the reprisals, support dried up. No one wanted to help us anymore. Everyone told us we should stop fighting before more innocent people got killed. Can't say I blame them. I had my own doubts at that point. In fact, I had just about decided to disband the Resistance when this fella showed up."

To my surprise, Mike pointed at Grabovsky.

"Captain Grabovsky, why don't you take it from here?"

"Yes sir," Grabovsky said, and stood up. Mike took a seat.

"When I was first briefed, what I learned was pretty much what Colonel Holden just said. Only part he left out was the Resistance had been in contact with Central Command for a few months, and Central had promised to send help as soon as they could. Now, you gotta remember, this was maybe two-and-a-half years after the Outbreak, and the government was still recovering. The only thing holding the country together was the military. We were still coming to grips with how to deal with ghouls, marauders, and all the goddamn insurgent groups popping up like fucking prairie dogs. Then came the Alliance, and Christ, you know what a mess that was. Anyway, I'd just gotten over some wounds I took helping this guy," he pointed at Gabe, "deal with some of those insurgents I mentioned. And no sooner am I back on my feet than does General Jacobs show up and ask if I'm interested in a special assignment. Offered me a field commission and told me I'd get to do some honest-to-God guerilla shit. I'll give you one guess how I answered."

A low hum of laughter went around the room. Grabovsky gave a small smile, and then his expression grew serious again.

"I was hyped for the mission, but I gotta tell you, I wasn't ready for what was waiting for me out here. I been a soldier a long time. Spent most of that time in SF and Delta. Iraq, Afghanistan, North Africa, The Philippines, you name the place, I probably put some poor bastard in the ground there. Saw a lot of collateral damage along the way. It's the nature of war. Shit happens. Learning to deal with it is part of the job. But what I went through before was always on foreign soil. It's a whole different thing seeing shit like that happen to your own people. It affected me more than I thought it would. So prepare yourselves for that."

Grabovsky paused. I may not have liked him very much, but I'll give credit where it's due—he could give a speech. There were distant stares and nodding heads all around. What he had said was sinking in and taking hold.

"Okay," Grabovsky said. "Enough with the sermon. Back to the topic at hand."

Grabovsky took a long drink of water before moving on. "So one night a plane HALO drops me close to the Resistance's mobile headquarters. I hit the ground, stashed my 'chute and gear, and the next thing I know, I got infected coming in on all sides. Only thing I can do is go up a tree. I'm sitting there wondering what the fuck to do when I remember we air dropped some sat-phones and encrypted radio equipment a couple of weeks earlier. So I call and Major Romero answers, and when I tell him my predicament, the son-of-a-bitch laughs at me."

Another low round of laughter. Grabovsky pointed a finger at Romero. "You see, I can say that 'cause you weren't commissioned yet."

"We'll hold off on the court martial for now," Romero said.

"Good. Had me worried a second there. Anyway, a couple runners show up and lead off the horde. Few other guys help me pick off the ones too slow to follow. Next thing I know, I got a black bag over my head, somebody puts me in a truck that smells like rotten beef, and I marinate in that stink for about an hour or so. Then I get out and somebody leads me inside a building. The black bag comes off and there sits our fearless leader." Grabovsky pointed a thumb over his shoulder at Mike.

"It was a long night. Colonel Holden told me what progress they'd made against the ROC. Also told me about the reprisals. Said they were thinking about disbanding and I might have come out there for nothing. I told him bull-fucking-shit. Nobody was quitting anything. I hadn't sweated my ass off in the desert for two weeks and jumped out of a goddamn plane just so I could go back to the Springs and tell General Jacobs we'd wasted our time. So the colonel here asks me what exactly I expected him to do. I said if those KPA dickholes were committing reprisals, then we'd make the motherfuckers pay ten-fold."

Mike stepped up next to Grabovsky. "As it turned out, once people got over being afraid, they were pretty pissed off about what the KPA had done. It's one thing to force people into labor, it's another thing all together to kill innocent women and children for something they had nothing to do with."

"First thing we did was a recruiting drive," Grabovsky said. "The Resistance back then was just Colonel Holden, Major Romero, and maybe a hundred other guys. And no offense, fellas, but most of you were too old for the shit you were doing."

He got no argument. Some of the older fighters in the room made rueful expressions, but I saw no anger there.

"War is a young man's game. What we needed were young men willing to fight. Problem was, most of the people we recruited were civilians with no training. So I came up with a plan. You see, the KPA hadn't seen hide or hair of the Resistance since the reprisals. Hadn't been attacked in months. The way I saw it, they must have believed they'd solved the problem. So I said fuck it, let 'em keep thinking that. Make it more of a surprise next time we hit 'em."

General Jacobs stood up and stepped forward. "The recruits were sent to Mountain Home, Idaho. There's a small Air Force base there that survived the Outbreak mostly intact. There was also a bunker like this one nearby with the supplies and equipment to train the new fighters. We sent civilian work crews, assisted by what was left of the Army Corps of Engineers and the Seabees, and built a facility to train them." Jacobs looked to Grabovsky and sat back down. I thought I detected a slight limp in the general's right leg.

"Took eight months to bring 'em up to speed," Grabovsky said. "The rest of us didn't spend that time sitting on our asses. We reconned every inch of ROC territory and mapped out the locations of all their bases, outposts, and patrol routes. Cross referenced it against satellite imagery and intel gathered by drones and decrypted message traffic between ROC bases. Central was kind enough to give us access to the supply cache we're in right now, as well as others in Oregon, Washington, and Northern California. We also established contact with every community that had KPA forces nearby and had them act as our eyes and ears. By the time the recruits made it back from Idaho, we knew our enemy's capabilities inside and out."

"The next phase was air drops," Mike said. "We had most of what we needed in the supply bunkers, but we were short on portable comms gear. Central took care of that for us. Also sent us some vehicles and fuel. After the spring thaw this year, we were ready to begin the assault."

Grabovsky motioned to the projector operator. The lights dimmed again and a collage of maps appeared with computer-drawn arrows pointing at red circles around key strategic areas.

"The first problem we had to deal with was the communities that hadn't been rounded up by the KPA," Grabovsky said. "We knew as soon as the fighting started, the KPA was going to haul every person they could get their hands on to the internment camps and confiscate everything not nailed down. The people in the towns knew it too. So we worked out a deal. First, we would hit the ROC with everything we had. Infantry would take out their tanks, artillery, APCs, and other vehicles. Central would send in drones to strike at their fuel depots and the main refinery in Humboldt Bay. Once we had 'em on the ropes, convoys of transport trucks with infantry and armor escort would move in and evacuate anyone who didn't want to stick around and join us. Nobody was exactly thrilled about having to leave their homes, but most people were smart enough to realize there wasn't much choice."

Mike picked up the laser pointer and aimed it at the screen. "The attack commenced at 0230 on the date listed. Some of you were there," he nodded toward the special ops guys, "so you know what happened. As for the rest of you, here's how it went down."

The pointer hovered over Humboldt Bay. "The drones moved in first and hit the refinery here, and the primary fuel depot here. From what I understand, it was a hell of a show. Captain Grabovsky led the forces that attacked this operating base here," the laser pointer moved again. "Hit 'em from the south with mortars and shoulder-fired missiles. Once they had the target softened up and the gates destroyed, they moved in with LAWs, grenade launchers, and truck-mounted heavy machine guns. Most of the KPA troops had been asleep when the attack started, and the ones on watch died in the initial attack."

Mike looked at Grabovsky. The shorter man nodded.

"I'll give the fuckers credit; they put up a fight," Grabovsky said. "But we caught 'em off guard and cut into 'em before they had a chance to get organized. Me and the best shooters we had held off the counter attack while the rest of our guys started hitting the motor pool. Some guys went around with LAWs and missiles shooting up the trucks and APCs, while others planted explosives with remote detonators on tanks, troop transports, and mobile artillery. Enemy officers figured out pretty quick what we were up to and changed strategies. Pinned us down with heavy suppressing fire and started evacuating out the north side of the base. Which, as it happens, is exactly what we wanted them to do."

The picture on screen changed again, showing dozens of blasted lumps of shredded metal with streamers of black smoke hanging over them on a long, two lane road.

"Before the attack, we planted IEDs and anti-tank mines on every road leading away from the base. When the last of the armor and other vehicles left, we triggered everything at once. The blast made my teeth rattle in my head, and I swear I almost shit myself, but it worked perfectly. After that, I gave the order to retreat."

"The same attack pattern was repeated at these locations," Mike said, moving the pointer over twelve more circles on the map. "Long story short, it was a success. All the planning, training, the long hours spent lying in the dirt baking in the heat or freezing in the cold, arguing with survivors, negotiating with politicians, all the times we went hungry, all the times we lost people to infected or disease or accidents, it all came to a head that night. And I will go to my grave saying it was worth it. All of it. Every sacrifice made, every life lost, and every nightmare we'll have from now until we're dead and gone. It was worth it to show those sons of bitches what happens when you hurt our people."

Mike stared at the air in front of him, eyes dark, jaw set in a hard line, muscles in his forearms tense from clenched fists. The room stayed quiet for several long seconds before Mike let out a breath and put the laser pointer down.

"We crippled them," Mike continued. "No armor, no aircraft, and only a handful of vehicles with barely enough fuel to last a few weeks. At best estimate, we took out eleven thousand KPA troops.

But it came at a price. Something close to four thousand Resistance fighters took up arms that night. Only about thirteen hundred of them lived to tell about it."

Another long silence ensued. General Jacobs ended it by motioning for the projector to be turned off and the lights turned on.

"And now we come to the crux of why we're all here," Jacobs said. "The internment camps. We couldn't hit them during the assault. Too much risk of collateral damage. We're trying to save our people, not sacrifice them. There were voices in Colorado arguing against attacking the ROC at all. Said the risk was too great. Wanted to seek a *diplomatic* solution."

Jacobs sneered and shook his head.

"I was tired of looking at photos of North Koreans burning piles of dead bodies. I think the president was tired of it too. When I explained to her and the Joint Chiefs the people in those camps didn't have time for us to spin our wheels negotiating with a ruthless, unyielding enemy, they listened."

Jacobs moved over to a stool and took a seat, still facing the room. I thought I detected the limp again and felt a frown pull at my face.

"As Colonel Holden said, we killed close to eleven thousand ROC troops. Over the years, they lost around four thousand others to disease, accidents, and the infected. The civilians the KPA brought with them had also been devastated by dysentery, influenza, and the gentle ministrations of their benevolent dictators for life. They hadn't been treated as bad as our people, but it was no picnic for them. Only about half of those who came over are still alive today. The KPA keeps them in Humboldt Bay doing all the industrial work their troops either don't want to do, or don't have the skills for. And from what our spies tell us, these people hold no love whatsoever for the KPA rank and file, much less their leaders. So we're going to try to save as many of them as we can. But make no mistake, our people take priority. If we have to sacrifice ROC civilians to save American lives, so be it. Everyone clear on that?"

The room echoed with acknowledgments.

"Anyone has a problem, now's the time to speak up. This mission is for volunteers only. If you don't want to be a part of this, or if you don't like the way I'm running things, you can leave right now. No questions asked."

General Jacobs waited a full minute. No one spoke.

"Very well," Jacobs said. "Doctor Faraday?"

A tall, thin fellow with a mop of brown hair streaked with gray, a shaggy beard, and rimless glasses stood up and walked to the front of the room. He wore the distinctive, dark blue coveralls of the Phoenix Initiative overlain with a white overcoat. I guessed his age at perhaps mid-forties, maybe older. The beard made it hard to tell.

"At this point, you should all be asking the same question," Faraday said. His voice was surprisingly deep, and marked by a faded British accent. "Anybody want to venture a guess?"

Seconds passed. A few people looked at each other and shrugged. Gabe looked around, rolled his eyes irritably, and put a hand in the air. It was his left hand, and I felt my eyes drawn to the missing finger he'd lost to a marauder's rifle over a year ago.

"Yes sir," Faraday said, pointing at Gabe. Everyone looked at him.

"How are we going to get the prisoners out of the camps without getting them killed?" Gabe said.

"Exactly." Faraday said, snapping his fingers. "And the answer to that question is very simple." Faraday held out his arms and paused for what I assume was dramatic effect.

"We don't."

Gabe's eyes narrowed and he leaned forward. He'd made no aggressive movement, but a hush fell over the room anyway.

"Excuse me?" Gabe said, his voice as quiet as a blade being unsheathed.

Faraday held up his hands and took half a step back. "Easy, now. Let me explain."

239

Gabe glared, but remained quiet.

"The problem is this—there's no way to get those people out of there as long as they're being watched by enemy troops. The KPA leadership realizes the prisoners are the only card they have left to play, and they're holding it tightly. The people we're trying to save are under constant surveillance, covered at all times by at least fifty riflemen and a minimum of ten crew-served machine guns. Not to mention the grenades ROC troops carry and the mortars zeroed on the longhouses where the prisoners sleep. So in order to rescue them, we have to take down the troops. But there are problems with that. One, they outnumber us. We could bring in reinforcements, but that would take time, and there's too much chance KPA long-range patrols might spot them coming in. If they do, it's game over. So that's out. Our second problem is these North Korean troops are absolute fanatics. If their commanders tell them to kill the hostages and prepare to fight to the last man, you had better believe they'll do it. Third, even if we could go at them head on, there's no guarantee we could save the hostages. So we were forced to come up with an alternative solution."

The lights dimmed again, and a picture of a stainless steel canister emblazoned with a biohazard symbol came up on the screen.

"Gentlemen, allow me to introduce A11-IM-38. Or, as it's known in the Initiative, the AIM-38 virus."

THIRTY-ONE

An hour later, General Jacobs dismissed the meeting and I went back to my room. I lay on my back with the lights off and absorbed the dark silence. A faint hum of ventilation was the only sound to be heard. I knew there would be a knock at my door, and I knew who it would be. When it came, I put my boots back on and answered.

"The General wants to see you," Mike said.

"Figures."

I followed Mike down the hall as he gathered Grabovsky, Tyrel, and Gabriel. Along the way, Faraday emerged from an unmarked door and joined us on our walk. I noted the door he came out of and filed it away for later reference.

No one spoke as we headed toward the conference room. Mike knocked on a door at the back and Sergeant Hathaway opened it.

"Come in, sir."

The office was a big one, about twice the size of my room at the officer's quarters. The walls were lined with tables topped with a variety of communications equipment, technical manuals, and tool boxes. There were also several workstations complete with computers, tablets, and piles of paperwork. Four maps were posted on the walls, each one scrawled on with red ink and perforated by multi-colored pins. I noticed the maps all depicted various regions of ROC territory.

At the moment, the office was empty except for Mike, Faraday, Sergeant Hathaway, and my group. General Jacobs sat behind an ugly metal desk painted the color of urine after a hard night's drinking. I stared at the bulky abomination and thought only the military would purchase something so hideous and force people to actually use it.

"Have a seat," Jacobs said. His face was drawn and gaunt, the lines in his forehead and around his mouth deeper than when last I saw him. Up close, I could see he had a day's growth of beard stubble, dark rings under his eyes, and his uniform looked like he'd slept in it.

There were enough chairs for everyone. I sat in one and stared silently at General Jacobs and reminded myself that if this man decided to do so, he could kick me out of the Army. If I got kicked out of the Army, I would be shipped back to the Springs and detained until a judge found the time to see me. When they did, they would determine that since I had not fulfilled my full four years of mandatory service, I had violated the terms of my sentence. From there, I would be sent to a prison camp for two years without the possibility of parole.

If they could take me alive, that is.

But this situation did not need to come to that. I could be as angry as I wanted to be. I could hate General Jacobs and the Army and the government as much as I wanted to. But right now, here in this room, I needed to keep it inside. Because it wasn't just about me anymore. I wanted a life with Miranda, and whether or not that would happen depended largely on the outcome of the conversation in front of me. So I told myself to put on my coldest exterior, dial down the outrage, overcome my doubts, put aside my objections, and listen carefully to what was expected of me.

"I'm sure you have questions," Jacobs said. Faraday positioned his chair so he was facing us. At a glance from Jacobs, Sergeant Hathaway gave a short nod and left the room.

"Gabriel, we'll start with you."

"Whose idea was this?" Gabe asked. He looked relaxed, but I could tell by the tension in his shoulders and the way he gripped the arms of his chair he was angry.

"It was decided by consensus," Jacobs said. "I can't divulge the names of everyone involved, but I can tell you I was one of them. Doctor Faraday was involved as well."

I turned my gaze to Faraday. The affable veneer he'd displayed earlier was gone. His eyes were steady, his demeanor calm and focused. This was an intelligent, calculating man. I couldn't understand why, but I had a feeling he was more dangerous than he looked.

Gabe looked at Faraday. "Tell me again the symptoms this virus causes."

Faraday sighed wearily. "I already discussed that at length during the meeting. I hardly think we need to-"

"Just fucking do it." Gabe's voice came out like a cracked whip.

Faraday paled and hesitated before speaking. "Well... within 24 hours after exposure, the subject will begin to experience flu-like symptoms. Fever, nausea, coughing, sneezing, that sort of thing. After six to eight hours, the symptoms recede, only to return with more severity shortly thereafter. Usually within one to two hours. This is the point at which the virus' replication accelerates and the subject experiences extreme lethargy in addition to the other symptoms. This lethargy lasts up to forty eight hours. If the inoculant is not administered within this timeframe, the virus goes into its next phase and begins attacking the central nervous system, including the brain. This results in permanent brain damage that disables the body's ability to regulate temperature. Soon thereafter, the body exceeds 107 degrees, at which point the enzymes inside the brain begin to denature. This, combined with the virus' attack on the subject's vital organs, results in seizures, severe heart palpitations, kidney failure, and, ultimately, death."

"So it literally cooks people from the inside out," Gabe said. His grip on the arms of his chair tightened.

"We're not going to let that happen," Jacobs cut in. "We have the inoculant on standby. I won't authorize the air drops unless I'm certain beyond doubt we can get it to the camps in time to save the prisoners. Once KPA forces have been neutralized, we'll administer the inoculant ASAP. Believe me, Gabe, I don't want this to go bad any more than you do."

"What about the old and the infirm?" Gabe said. "What about small children? Pregnant women? People who are malnourished, dehydrated, or sick? Do we know how they'll be affected?"

"Actually, we do," Faraday said. Gabe's attention shifted back to him. The man's thin hands shook a little as he sat up straight and resettled himself.

"And how, exactly, do you know that?"

Faraday adjusted his glasses and shifted uncomfortably. "Well, I'm not at liberty to discuss-"

"You know," Gabe interrupted, "because you've conducted experiments on people. On living human beings."

"Well...I..."

Gabe got out of his chair and squatted in front of Faraday so the two men were eye to eye, less than a foot apart.

"I'm going to name a few places. Places I was sent a while back when I worked for a company you've probably heard of." Gabe leaned closer. "A company called Aegis."

Faraday looked like he'd been kicked in the gut. His mouth opened a few times, but no sound came out.

General Jacobs' tone was a warning. "Gabriel..."

Gabe held up a hand to silence him. "Welam Village, outside of Erambo in Papua New Guinea. Ring a bell?"

Faraday said nothing. His posture reminded me of a mouse cornered by a housecat.

"Dolong, Indonesia. How about that one? Maybe Al Hait? Good cover up you guys pulled on that one, blaming the massacre on Al Qaeda. They were all good cover ups, come to think of it. But the one that really stands out in my mind is that little fishing village on the Changja River near the Chinese border. Place didn't even have a name. But if you drop me somewhere close, I bet I could find my

244

way back to it. And you know what I'd find there, Doctor Faraday? I'd find bones. Men, women, and children, all shot in the head. Sound familiar?"

Faraday wiped his face and attempted to stand. Gabe pushed him back down in his seat with a single finger to the chest.

"You made it, didn't you? You created it."

"Gabriel, that's enough." Jacobs said sharply.

Gabe ignored him. "Answer the question, Faraday."

The tall scientist took a deep breath and seemed to gather himself. "What are you referring to? AIM-38, or the Reanimation Phage?"

"I know you made AIM-38. I'm asking about the second one."

"Then the answer is no."

Gabe blinked. I had never met anyone in my life as good at sniffing out a lie as Gabriel Garrett. But from his expression, I could tell he had detected no deception from Faraday.

"Bullshit," Gabe said.

Faraday shook his head. "No bullshit. We didn't make it. We retrieved samples from the Outbreaks we responded to, and we conducted experiments to see how it worked, but as far as where it originated, we're as clueless as anyone else."

Gabe looked down, his expression lost for a moment. He stood up. "But you let it loose. You infected people in isolated parts of the world and watched to see what would happen."

"Yes."

"And afterward, you sent in operatives from Aegis to clean up the mess."

"Yes."

"And AIM-38. You know what it does because you did the same thing."

"It was never tested on Americans," Faraday said. His voice was hushed and weak.

"How very noble of you. Can you tell me how many people died in those experiments? How many lives were destroyed?"

Faraday cleared his throat. "We were careful about who we tested."

"You got a lot of fucking nerve. What about Atlanta? You have anything to do with the Outbreak?"

Faraday shook his head slowly. "No. It wasn't us. We have our suspicions about who might be responsible, but we had nothing to do with it."

Gabe fixed him with a level stare. "But all the other places. The smaller outbreaks. That was the Phoenix Initiative. You were behind it. All of it."

"We were working to prevent a larger catastrophe. And for the record, no, not all of those outbreaks were our doing. I'm not proud of what we did, Mr. Garrett. But we had our reasons."

"Reasons." Gabe's lip turned up, his face a mask of contempt. "There's always fucking reasons. I'm sure Hitler and Stalin and Chairman goddamn Mao had their *reasons*. What were yours? Stopping the end of the world? Preventing a global outbreak of the Reanimation Phage? Tell me something, Doc. How'd that work out for you?"

Faraday swallowed and looked down.

"Yeah. Nice work, you son of a bitch."

Jacobs stood up. "Mr. Garrett-"

Gabe stopped him with an icy stare. For a moment, no one moved. The general's face went a few shades lighter. Finally, Gabe strode angrily to the door and walked out of the office. After the latch clicked shut, the room remained silent. Jacobs slowly sat back down, smoothed his wrinkled shirt with his hands, and scraped a hand across his mouth.

"Mr. Jennings, what questions do you have?"

Tyrel let out a breath and crossed his feet. "Those inoculations you insisted we all get before we left the Springs. That was for AIM-38, wasn't it?"

"Yes."

"And the assholes that followed us to the clinic. Those your guys?"

Jacobs reddened. "Yes. Although perhaps they're not as well trained as I thought."

"So just to clarify, when those airbursts go off and people start getting sick, we'll be okay?"

"Yes. I've taken the inoculant myself, same formula given to you."

"Fair enough. That's all I got."

Jacobs nodded once. "Captain Grabovsky?"

"I'm good."

The general turned his attention to me. "Captain Hicks?"

I was silent a few seconds, thinking how best to say what was on my mind diplomatically.

"Just to be clear, we're talking about using a weaponized, lethal biological agent on American citizens."

"Yes. But they are not the intended target."

"Yes sir, I got that. The virus is intended to disable the KPA forces guarding the prisoners."

"That's right."

"Has anything like this ever been tried before?"

Jacobs looked at Faraday. The scientist shook his head. "No."

"Then how do we know it'll work?"

"We've used the virus against enemy forces before," Faraday said. "It works. And we know for a fact the inoculant works up to fifty hours after the virus enters the bloodstream. We engineered it that way, and it has been tested extensively."

"But nothing on this scale has ever been tried?"

"Well...no."

"Is AIM-38 contagious while the victims are infected?"

Faraday nodded twice. "Yes. It's an airborne virus. It'll spread much the same as any cold or flu would."

"Okay, so how long will these people need to be quarantined?"

"A week should be long enough."

"What about us?"

"The same."

"And since we have the inoculant already in our systems, we won't be affected by the virus."

"No, you won't. The inoculant will stop AIM-38 in its tracks."

"And once the inoculant is administered, how long until it takes effect?"

"The longest any test subject has ever taken to begin recovery is four hours. I think you'll find the inoculant works very quickly."

I let that soak in. I still didn't like it. "You said during the briefing it was possible the North Koreans had the formula for the inoculant. You didn't say how they got it."

"That's not important," General Jacobs said. "All that matters is some of them may have been inoculated, so we'll have to take that into account during the assault."

"Actually, General," Faraday spoke up, "it's probably best if they know."

The general looked displeased. "Why is that?"

"Because it may affect the extent to which they need to be cautious when searching for inoculated troops."

Jacobs clearly didn't like it, but he nodded anyway. "Fine."

"Prior to the Outbreak," Faraday said, "the Chinese directed a cyber-attack against the CDC and various other government agencies. This attack was the culmination of years of espionage carried out by Chinese and Russian spies. Luckily, the NSA detected the attack quickly and moved to shut it down, as did the CIA and other agencies. But certain data was compromised. The records for the AIM-38 inoculant were among them. However, the inoculant was incomplete at the time. It had not been fully tested and proven effective, although, admittedly, it was well on its way. It's not outside the realm of possibility the Chinese were able to glean enough information from what they stole to engineer the inoculant themselves. If they did, which I believe is very likely, there is a better than even chance they shared this data with the North Koreans."

"How long before the Outbreak did this happen?" I asked.

"Just over three years."

"And you think they could have completed the formula, or whatever, in that time?"

"It's possible, yes."

"It takes time to make vaccines, right? How much inoculant could they have made?"

Faraday tilted his head from side to side, weighing his response. "It took us two years to prove the inoculant reliable and effective. Manufacturing it took a few more months, but we were able to make enough for roughly ten thousand people. I realize that sounds like a lot, but you must realize it doesn't take much. You could fit everything we made in the back of a typical delivery truck."

"That's fine, but my question was about the Chinese."

"Oh, yes, of course. Well, there are a great many variables to consider. I doubt they would have been able to finish the formula, as you call it, nearly as fast as our teams. But if they did, considering their pharmaceutical manufacturing capabilities at the time, perhaps they could have made as much as we did, although I think that is unlikely. If it took them longer, they would have made less. It's hard to know, exactly."

"But they couldn't have made enough for all of them?"

Faraday shook his head. "That I highly doubt. If I had to guess, I'd say they only were able to make enough for perhaps two thousand people, maximum. I could be wrong, of course, but that is my best guess."

I gave a nod. "Okay. Next question. How is the virus going to be spread? I mean, you said it was weaponized. Weaponized how?"

Faraday looked to Jacobs. "Without getting too technical," the general said, "we load an aerosol laced with the contaminant into containers that spread it over a wide area via gas dispersion. The container is launched from a missile and can be precisely programmed where to detonate via a timed fuse. The container emits the gas as it falls to the ground on a forward trajectory, sort of like an unmanned crop duster. The people it hits will feel only a fine mist if they detect it at all. The container itself will fly well beyond the target area and break apart upon impact. Any remaining trace of the virus not in a living host will be dead in four hours. "

"Won't they notice the missile firing? The KPA troops I mean."

"Doubtful. The missiles will be launched far enough away they'll be over the horizon from the enemy's positions, and they'll be flying at fairly high altitude. On a clear night, if you just happen to be looking in the right direction, you might catch one of the missiles flying by. Otherwise, they're easy to miss. The guards on duty might hear the jets, but they're used to that by now. We've been flying regular sorties for months to get them accustomed to it. According to our spies, they think we're just conducting aerial reconnaissance. The North Koreans actually consider this a good thing. By their logic, our seeing the prison camps on a regular basis keeps us well in mind of what's at stake if we launch an all-out attack. They don't realize we're conditioning them to be less alarmed by aircraft."

The more I heard, the more uneasy I became. Jacobs and Faraday had said a lot of qualifying words like 'should' and 'I think' and 'doubtful' and 'might', the kinds of words people use when they're making suppositions and not stating known facts. I don't like unknowns. And I have a deep seated dread of chemical and biological weapons. The fact we were planning to not only use them, but use them against our own people, did not sit well with me. Not to mention the fact I would be exposed to the virus myself, and inoculated or not, I was not comfortable with that.

"I have to tell you, General. This seems like a bad idea."

"I know it does," Jacobs said. "And believe me, it wasn't my first choice. But we've run through every other scenario we can think of, and this is the one with the highest probability of success. I know you all have your doubts. I know you're worried about what will happen to the people exposed to AIM-38. All I can tell you is this—even if everything goes wrong, they won't be facing any worse of a fate than what's already in front of them. Make no mistake, gentlemen, most of the people in those camps will not survive the next winter. We have to act, and we have to do it soon, or there won't be anyone left to rescue."

I took a deep breath and let it out slowly. There was no choice, really. The decision had been made. General Jacobs was only fielding questions out of professional courtesy. The mission would proceed with or without us. And in my case, I had come too far to back out now. My only choice was to see this thing through.

"Well, I guess that just leaves one question."

"And that is?" Jacobs said.

"What do you need us for? You've got plenty of special ops guys to run this mission. Why put this team together? Why do you need *me*, of all people?"

Jacobs looked at Mike, then at Grabovsky and Tyrel. Finally his focus returned to me and he leaned forward and steepled his hands on the ugly, piss-colored desktop.

"We think we know who caused the Outbreak," he said. "We think we know why, and we think they may be able to get us closer to the ultimate weapon against the undead."

I blinked. "And that is?"

"A vaccine."

I felt my face go cold. My breathing became shallow. I was glad I was sitting down.

So that's what this is all about. He wants to keep this under wraps, so he handpicked a team he knew he could count on to do just that. Not because he trusts us, but because he has leverage. He could send me to prison. He could shut down the Blackthorns. He could end Grabovsky's career. Gabe owes him for helping recover his trade from the Storm Road Tribe. Mike wants the war to be over with. I wonder what he's holding over Faraday.

Jacobs talked for another half hour. We all listened without interrupting. He gave us photos and dossiers and told us who we were looking for and ordered us to take them alive at all costs. When he was done, he opened the floor to questions. There were none. I stopped on my way out and said, "General, Gabe will need to be briefed on this."

A nod. "I'll track him down and talk to him."

I could think of nothing else to say, so I went back to my room and sat alone in the darkness.

THIRTY-TWO

There was nothing scheduled the next day, so I explored the bunker.

It turned out to be larger than I first thought. The warehouse, conference room, barracks, and administrative offices were only about two-thirds of the underground complex. There was a separate wing for Phoenix Initiative personnel, a large mess hall complete with a kitchen and dishwashing area, an armory, a twenty-five-yard shooting range, and an exercise room with treadmills, free-weights, benches, racks, pull-up bars, and several punching bags of various sizes.

I hadn't done my regular PT in a few days, so I threw on comfortable clothes and a pair of running shoes I'd brought with me and started on the treadmill. Eight miles later, my blood was flowing and I felt a little better. Then came squats, dead lift, overhead press, power cleans, pull-ups, and twenty minutes of core work involving a medicine ball and a forty pound kettle bell.

There were hand wraps and sixteen-ounce gloves in a small locker near the punching bags, so I put in eight rounds, alternating between punches, kicks, elbows, and knee strikes. Last, I cooled down with fifteen minutes of stretching.

Back in the officer's quarters, I rinsed off the sweat and grime in the communal shower, shaved, and put on a clean uniform. A check of the time informed me I had only managed to kill half the day.

There was no one in the warehouse when I entered, so I checked the racks of weapons and ammunition and found they were not locked or secured in any way. I took an M-4 from a shelf and a box of 840 rounds from an open crate. I also procured two thirty-round magazines. The rifle did not have an ACOG, but it did have iron sights. Better than nothing.

The range was manned when I visited for the second time. A private about my age sat behind a small desk thumbing through a dog-eared paperback. His chair was tilted back, feet crossed on the tabletop. He sat up straight when he saw me come in.

"Good afternoon, sir."

I was wearing no insignia, but somehow he knew I was an officer. "Word travels fast around here, huh?" I asked, smiling.

He relaxed and smiled back. "Small place. Not a lot of people here. Putting in some range time, sir?"

A shrug. "Beats staring at a wall."

"That it does. Just need you to sign in."

He flipped a log around and put a pen on top of it. I wrote my name and rank, the serial number of the rifle I was using, and how many rounds I had come in with. Simple enough.

"You got eyes and ears, sir?"

I checked my pockets and cursed. "No. Guess I forgot. I need to go get 'em?"

"No sir, got you covered." He reached into a drawer and pulled out a pair of safety glasses, yellow ear protectors, and a small box of foam earplugs. "Gotta wear double hearing protection if you're not running a suppressor. Small room, you know?"

"Fair enough."

There were seven lanes to choose from. I took one in the center and put down the rifle and ammo. On the opposite side of the room from the check-in desk was a low shelf loaded with range supplies including targets, small sandbags, and short stools. I grabbed three sandbags, a stool, and a paper target.

Since the M-4 I'd procured had never been fired, I put a hundred rounds through it to break it in. The shots grouped well, but wandered around a bit once the barrel heated up. I let it cool a couple of minutes and then set to work zeroing the rifle.

I fired the first group from a seated position with the rifle balanced on two bags in front and one beneath the stock. The group was less than an inch, but the gun was shooting high and left. I adjusted the front sight post for elevation and the rear aperture for windage, and tried again. This time I was on center.

The two types of ammo I would most likely be using—M193 and M855—have highly similar ballistic paths out to 250 yards with a hundred yard zero. To achieve this at 25 yards, I adjusted the sights until I was grouping shots between 1.5 and 2 inches below my point of aim. Not exactly precise, but close enough.

There were numerous small targets outside the man-shaped center target, to I sent groups at all of them. The rifle was accurate and did not malfunction. When I had burned through about five hundred rounds, the paper target was barely held together and I had grown bored. So I used one of the cleaning kits the range had on hand, lubed the rifle, and walked over to the desk.

"There any rules against me keeping this?"

"No sir," the private said. "Just need you to fill out a requisition form. Got a rifle you need to turn in?"

"I do, actually."

"Just bring it to the armory, sir. They'll take it off your hands."

I filled out the form, took the M-4 back to my room, and dropped my old rifle off at the armory. It occurred to me that as exotic as a top secret underground government bunker may seem at first blush, the reality of daily life here was depressingly similar to life in regular infantry. The principal activities seemed to involve eating, sleeping, training, and filling out paperwork. Not exactly movie of the week material.

Since I had nothing else to do, I took my combat optics—an ACOG and a VCOG—and zeroed them both at the range. Then I cleaned and lubed the gun again and turned in my unexpended ammo to the armory, signed another paper, and checked my watch.

It was only two-thirty.

I smelled food. I walked to the mess hall and found four older civilians putting what was left of lunch away. One of them, a woman in her late sixties, peered at me through a pair of glasses.

"You need a bite to eat?"

"If it's not too much trouble."

"Missed chow, did you?" a man said. He looked almost as old as the woman.

"Afraid so," I said. "But I won't make excuses. Take anything you got to spare."

The old woman went around the corner for a few minutes and came back with a plate of lima beans, collard greens, flatbread, and some kind of shredded meat.

"Not to look the gift horse in the mouth," I said, "but what kind of meat is this?"

"That would be *chevon*," the old man said, grinning. "Ever heard of it?"

"Chevon is French for goat, if memory serves."

The old man cackled. "'Fraid so. It's not bad though. A little stringy, but the flavor's good."

"Where does it come from?"

"There's goats galore back east," the old woman said. "Folks're farming them all over out there. Hell, you can shoot 'em wild. Meat's cheaper'n chicken these days. Army makes jerky out of it and air drops it every couple of weeks. Have to soak it overnight to make it edible. Ain't exactly prime rib, but it beats the hell out of survival rations."

I pinched a scrap between two fingers and tried it. As the old man said, it was a bit stringy, but did not taste bad.

"Thanks," I said, and walked over to a table.

I ate alone. It was quiet, save for muted conversation between the kitchen workers. The mess hall was not large, built for maybe fifty people at a time. The tables were sturdy, constructed of stainless steel and some kind of wood composite with a vinyl veneer, and the chairs were made of plastic and steel and were stackable. I'd seen them a thousand times at churches, schools, and government buildings all over the country. I wondered if the same company had made them all. I wondered how the kitchen workers wound up slinging hash down here in this remote bunker of indeterminate age. I wondered how long it would be before the final assault against the ROC, or KPA, or whatever the hell they called themselves, began.

My first couple of days in the bunker had been a nice break from the horrors of the surface world, but I found myself growing anxious. This place was not home. Miranda was home.

I wanted to get back to her.

*****

I lay down in the mid-afternoon, closed my eyes, and focused on keeping my mind empty. After a while, I drifted off and had a dream that jolted me awake. I sat up in bed and stared at the darkness, waiting for my heart rate to return to normal.

What did I dream about?

I searched and searched, but found nothing. Finally I lay back down and turned on the lamp next to my bed. Dim orange light filled the room, not quite reaching the far corners. I had a sense of urgency. There was someone I needed to talk to.

Stop it. Go back to sleep.

I gave it an honest try. But just as I was drifting off, a name entered my mind unbidden. I thought about what I had read of Freud's research regarding the sub-conscious mind. As I did, I sat

257

up and tied my shoes without realizing I was doing it until it was already happening.

Fuck it. Go with it. See where it leads.

I thought about what my step-mother had taught me as a kid about approaching strangers. Gifts were always a good way to break the ice. I thought about the man I was going to see. I thought about the couple of times I had walked close to him and smelled a faint hint of liquor. I thought about how his eyes had been bloodshot behind his glasses, and there were little blooms of ruptured capillaries beginning to form around his nose and on his cheeks. He was a drinker.

Takes one to know one.

I dressed, neatened my appearance, brushed my teeth, and grabbed my lock picks. There was a security door in the warehouse with a simple metal placard that read 'CLEANING SUPPLIES'. If I were stationed here and needed a place to stash booze, that would be my first candidate.

The lock was simple and took me about fifteen seconds to pick. Once inside, I closed the door and turned on a small flashlight I'd brought with me. The first pass revealed nothing. No hidden compartments, no bottles stashed under piles of rags or dirty towels, no boxes or other containers that didn't belong there. Which meant if there was booze in here, it was hidden in plain sight.

The light moved over bottle after bottle of cleaning liquids. Most of them I dismissed out of hand, but on a low shelf, tucked behind white boxes of Borax, I found six clear glass bottles. An upraised section of glass lettering said they contained one liter each. Plain labels listed the contents as 'HYDROGEN PEROXIDE'. I picked one up and examined it closely. Hydrogen peroxide usually comes in dark plastic bottles, and I had never seen one in full liter size. Furthermore, the bottle had a decorative swirl on its upper third that reminded me of the white distilled vinegar my stepmother kept around for cleaning purposes. A closer examination of the label revealed it had been printed out on standard paper and stuck to the glass bottle with cheap adhesive. I opened the cap and sniffed.

Definitely not hydrogen peroxide.

I took a small sip and swirled it around. Not bad. I'd had better, but I was reasonably certain it would not poison me or cause permanent loss of vision. I slipped the bottle in a small assault back I'd brought along and quietly stepped out of the room. Looked left, looked right. No one.

I approached the door leading to the area set aside for the Phoenix Initiative. The door was locked, but the lock was no more sophisticated than the one on the supply closet. I had it open in seconds and strolled casually inside.

There was no one in the hall. I kept up the slow, unconcerned saunter I'd entered with. When traversing areas one is not authorized to be, it is best to appear as if you belong there. Do it well enough and no one will question your presence.

At first, I was not sure how I was going to find my destination. But then I noticed the doors were labeled plainly. Water treatment lab. Infirmary. Chemical storage. Hazardous waste. Cleaning supplies. Electronic and electromechanical repair. At an intersection, I read a placard that said the restrooms and the dining hall were to my right, and living quarters were to my left. I turned left.

Red placards flanked me on both sides as I entered the living quarters. They read, 'Authorized Personnel Only'. I walked past them.

As it turned out, the rooms were numbered and had name labels next to each door. It did not take long to figure out there were only a few people living there, which made for a short search.

I knocked on the appropriate door. Faraday answered a moment later and stared at me.

"Captain Hicks."

"I was hoping to have a word with you," I said.

Faraday leaned out his door and checked the hallway. "I'm afraid you're not supposed to be here. How did you get in?"

I shrugged. "Door was open."

"That's odd. It shouldn't have been. I'll have to-"

"You got time for a drink?" I said, holding up the bottle. I had removed the hydrogen peroxide label.

"What's that?" Faraday asked, staring at the bottle. There was an avaricious gleam in his eye.

"Moonshine. Ain't the best, but it ain't the worst either."

Another check of the hallway. "Well...all right then," Faraday said quietly. "I suppose there's no harm in it. Please come in."

I entered. Faraday checked the hallway one last time and closed the door. I heard the lock click into place.

The room was almost identical to mine. I sat down in the kitchen and put the bottle on the table.

"Got any glasses?"

THIRTY-THREE

It did not take long to get Faraday drunk.

In the process, I learned that his first name was Alexander, call me Alex. He was born in Manchester, England, and had lived there until he was eleven. A few months after his birthday, his father brought the family across the pond to take a job at an investment firm in New York. I told Faraday he still had his accent. The more he drank, the thicker it got.

I kept the conversation light to begin with, mostly asking him about how he came to work for the Phoenix Initiative. He was guarded at first, but a few more drinks loosened him up.

"I don't know why I'm still so reluctant to talk about it," he said. "Most of it's been declassified anyway."

"Get it off your chest," I said. "You'll feel better."

Faraday drained his glass and reached for the bottle. I had barely taken a few sips.

"They approached me while I was at university," he said. "I was graduating in a few months and had already served an internship with the CDC. I suppose that's how they learned about me. Top marks, magna cum laude, letters of recommendation from several of my professors, all the accolades a young academic could ask for. Mum was quite proud. Father seemed to view the whole affair as a matter of course. He was like that. Perfect English reserve, stiff upper lip, kept everyone at arm's length, never too strong a praise nor too strict a condemnation for any behavior on my part, good or ill. I don't think he raised his voice once in his whole bloody life."

Another long pull of moonshine. "Miserable bastard."

Faraday was growing morose. Booze does that to some people. I did not want him going off on a tangent about how his father didn't hug him enough, so I decided to steer the conversation elsewhere.

"Who approached you?"

"Oh, a couple of bureaucratic types. You know the ones, ugly suits, federal ID badges, schoolboy haircuts. It was pre-9/11 America back then. If I'd joined the Initiative after that, it probably would have been Homeland Security knocking on my door."

"Who did they say they were with?"

"The Department of Health and Human Services."

"What were they recruiting for?"

Faraday drained his glass. I refilled it for him. "Cheers," he said, taking a long drink. "As I recall, they said it was a research position. Top secret research, mind you. An opportunity to be on the front lines of global pandemic prevention, they said. And of course I believed them. Why wouldn't I? I was one of the preeminent minds in my field, after all. That's what everyone was saying about me, and no one was more convinced of the truth of that statement than I was. I was so brilliant, in fact, that I signed the paperwork without even reading it. Couldn't quite see past the stars in my eyes, or the visions of my name being announced at a convention of Nobel laureates." He laughed bitterly and stared into his drink. "How quickly dreams fade."

"What happened?"

He did not answer for a while. He finished his drink and had another one. I was beginning to worry he would pass out before I could get anything useful out of him.

"Everything was all right at first," he said finally. "The job was exactly what they said it would be. I worked on a project that was the precursor to AIM-38. It was exciting for a while. But then months turned into years, and the proverbial rush of blood to the head faded, and I matured a bit and began to notice things were somewhat…odd."

"Odd how?"

"I'll give you an example. Part of the benefits package was paid housing. They put me up in a modest two-bedroom apartment not far from the research campus where I worked. The campus was in a small town in northern Virginia near Washington DC. Quite a few of my coworkers lived in the same building as I did. For the first year or two we barely spoke to each other. The labs were highly compartmentalized, you see, like silos. Cross-pollination was not encouraged. Sensitive nature of the work and all that. But there was this one girl that caught my eye, and I'm not embellishing to say I caught hers as well. We began seeing each other. Nothing too overt, just the occasional dinner at her place or mine, drinks, conversation, sex. It was a nice arrangement. We grew quite close. But then Patricia wanted to go out on proper dates. Began making overtures about moving in together. Said with our combined salaries we could afford to rent a proper house."

Faraday went to take another drink, but his glass was empty again. He gazed at it irritably and refilled it.

"And then, without warning, it all ended. I stopped on my way home that night and bought some good red wine and Patricia's favorite cheese and knocked on her door expecting my usual warm welcome. I received nothing of the sort."

Faraday stopped to pour another drink. Half the liter of moonshine was gone now. "She opened the door just a crack, kept it on the chain like I was a criminal or something. And that was exactly how she looked at me—like she was afraid. Her eyes were wide and frightened. She told me she didn't want to see me anymore. I laughed. I thought it was some kind of a joke. 'Come on, love. Let us in', I said. She shut the door in my face and locked it and told me to go away."

Faraday put down his drink and stared blearily at the wall. After a few seconds, he removed his glasses and let them hang from his fingers.

263

"I was gutted. Absolutely gutted. I couldn't believe it. How could she be so cold after all we'd shared? Just days before she wants to move in together, and now I can't get her to so much as look at me. I racked my brain trying to think of what I might have done to push her away. I begged and pleaded, and one day I knocked on her door and told her I wasn't leaving until she spoke to me. She called the police. I was drunk. I tried to fight them and wound up spending the night in jail."

He picked his drink up, drained it, and put his glasses back on. "My department head called me on the carpet when I returned to work. I was barely functional. She told me to go home and rest and come back in the morning. When I did, I was ushered into her office straightaway. She explained that Patricia was being reassigned to another project, but they wanted me to stay on there in Virginia. I don't think I've mentioned it, but my research was progressing very rapidly. My team and I were making breakthroughs on a regular basis. Much faster than other teams working on similar projects. I was the subject of a great deal of admiration by some, and envy by others. I accepted my employer's desire to retain me at face value and agreed to stay."

"Did you ever hear from Patricia again?"

Faraday shook his head. "No. Last year I checked the Archive in Colorado Springs and found her name on the M&D list."

"The Outbreak?"

"No. Breast cancer. Can you believe it? To survive the end of the world only to succumb to such a dreadful disease. Truly there is no God, and I tell you that as a statement of fact."

I sensed yet another philosophical minefield and chose to avoid it. "So what happened next?"

A shrug. "Life happened." Faraday drained his glass and began reaching for the bottle, then stopped. "I'm afraid I'm being terribly rude. I should probably ask first."

I picked up the bottle and poured. "You know, in Japan, it's considered impolite not to pour your friend's beer if you're having drinks together."

"Yes, I've heard that. Thankfully, we're not drinking beer. A man can grow old trying to get drunk on that stuff. Especially these days."

Faraday took another pull. He had reached the point where he wasn't really tasting the liquor anymore, so I knew my time was running out.

"You were talking about life after Patricia," I said.

"Oh, yes. I was terribly hurt, you know. Terribly hurt. For a while Patricia was all I thought about. I poured myself into my work trying to forget about her. And you know what? Eventually it worked. I moved up the ranks quickly. By the time the 9/11 attacks occurred, I was the head of my department. After the attacks, though, things got a bit…serious."

"You said before when you first started working for the government you noticed things were odd. We kind of got off that topic."

"Yes, I suppose we did. Well, the first odd thing was Patricia's sudden rejection of me. The next happened a month later. I was distraught, you see. I had lost faith in myself, in my work, in everything. One night, after quite a bit of wine, I packed a bag and got in my car and decided I was going to drive west until I found someplace to stop, and there I would start my life over again. Silly, now that I think about it. But at the moment I was quite serious. Not that it mattered. I'd barely made it a mile out of town before they stopped me."

"Who?"

Faraday looked at me. His eyes were bloodshot and his hair and beard were a frizzy cloud around his head. "The men in suits, of course. Two of them. One very tall and athletic looking, the other older and thin as a whip and entirely polite. The older man did all the talking. The tall one never said a word, just stood there staring at me. I think he would have been perfectly delighted to kill me."

"How did they find you?"

"GPS locator on my car. I had no idea they'd put it there. One minute I was driving, the next I was looking at blue lights in my rearview. I thought to myself, 'Well, you've done it now, Alex.' I was as drunk as a fly in a barrel of gin. I thought I was in for another episode of DUI theatre, but that wasn't what happened."

He went quiet. I waited until I thought he might be fading and bumped the table. Faraday looked up with a start.

"What happened?" I said.

Faraday ran a hand through his hair and pushed himself straighter in his seat.

"They put me in their car and drove me back to my apartment. Put me down on my sofa and took off my shoes. The tall man stood by the door while the older fellow pulled a chair close so he could speak to me in confidence. I don't remember everything he said, but the gist of it was clear—they owned me. I belonged to the government, and I would not be allowed to leave. If I needed a holiday, or a leave of absence, that could be arranged. They understood I was under a great deal of stress and were willing to make accommodations. But under no circumstances would I be allowed to leave my job and live life on my own. They needed me somewhere they could monitor me. My research was too important to allow me to quit in the manner I'd attempted. The implications of any further dalliances in that direction were absolutely clear, even in my inebriated state. When I woke up the next morning, there was a note on my door telling me to take the day off. I walked outside and my car was in its parking spot. That, oddly, was the most chilling thing. I never tried to leave again. My life became about my work after that."

"What were you working on?"

"Isn't it obvious? AIM-38. At least at first. After the World Trade Center came down, I was approached by agents of the newly formed DHS. This was in the early years, shortly after the passage of the erroneously titled Patriot Act. What a load of rubbish that was. I suppose the sitting president's notion of patriotism was granting the government carte blanche to detain and imprison anyone they wanted, invade the entire nation's privacy with impunity, and generally trample the constitution like a piece of trash in a dodgy neighborhood. But I digress. Anyway, the men in the ugly suits told me about the Phoenix Initiative and asked if I was interested in coming on board. I accepted immediately."

"What did they want you to do?"

"A better question would be, what didn't they? I had my fingers in dozens of projects over the years. Weaponizing AIM-38, engineering the inoculant thereof, organizing the building of new red facilities, field testing various biological agents. Nothing to tell the grandchildren about, I assure you."

"You said 'red facilities'. What are those?"

"Oh, of course. You don't know about those, do you? How best to explain." Faraday tapped his finger against his chin a few times. "You're a soldier. You probably know a thing or two about setting up a security perimeter, yes?"

I nodded.

"What's the key to setting up a good perimeter?"

"You're asking me?"

"Yes."

"That's an easy one. Layers."

Faraday snapped his fingers and pointed at me. "Exactly. Layers. The Initiative works the same way. Backup plans for backup plans for backup plans. Layers, in other words. Red facilities are one of those layers. For example, before the Outbreak, did you ever wonder where flu vaccines came from?"

"Not really, no."

"Well, we did. It was one of the many questions the Initiative had to address. Namely, what to do if those facilities were no longer available. Where would we get vaccines from, then? What about antibiotics? Insulin? Pain killers? How would society cope without those things?"

I thought about the hardship and suffering I'd seen since the Outbreak. "Not well."

"No. Not well at all. People dying of infections that would never have been lethal five years ago, diseases nearly eradicated

267

making a comeback, infant mortality rates skyrocketing. And this is only the beginning. That's what the red facilities were intended to address. Well, one of the issues, anyway. There were others."

"Like what?"

Faraday flipped a hand around to indicate the room we were in. At some point he'd poured another drink without me noticing. The bottle was only a quarter full now.

"Like this," Faraday said. "This place around us. It was built back in the 1950s and expanded over the years. This one and hundreds of others like it. There are at least three of these bunkers in every state. Not to mention the doomsday shelters and the vaults. My God, I hope you get a chance to see one of those someday. They make this place look like a cheap London flat."

Faraday tried to take another drink, but only managed to spill half the contents of his glass down his shirt.

"*Agh*. Bloody hell." He put the glass down and sighed. "Perhaps I should call it a night."

I gently took his glass, set it on the counter, and helped him stand up. It took a great deal of effort, but I managed to dump him on his bed. He rolled over onto his back and asked if I would be a darling and take his shoes off for him. I did. Faraday's eyes were closed and his breathing had grown slow and steady. I went back into the kitchen, cleaned the two glasses in the sink, dried them with a dish towel, and put them back in the cupboard. Then I slipped what was left of the booze into my assault pack and made my way to the door. Just before I opened it, I heard Faraday speak behind me.

"You know, it really was nice talking to you, Captain Hicks. It's so rare I get to just sit down and have a normal conversation with someone these days. I hadn't realized how much I'd missed it."

I stared at him for a long moment. He began to snore, and I felt a great swell of pity for the man. He was a much a victim as the people in the internment camps. Treated better, maybe, but no less a prisoner. I shut the door quietly, went back to my room, and lay awake long into the night thinking about what Faraday had told me.

The walls around me no longer brought a sense of comfort. I couldn't help thinking about how my situation compared to Faraday's. I wasn't here entirely by choice, and I doubted things would go well for me if I decided to quit the mission. I had learned a great many secrets I highly doubted the government wanted made public knowledge, and looking at it from a purely utilitarian standpoint, it didn't make much sense for General Jacobs, or whoever, to let me return to civilian life after I fulfilled the terms of my sentence. Jacobs was, above all, a pragmatist. To call him Machiavellian would not be an overstatement. He had let people die before to accomplish his goals. Lots of people. He had ordered assassinations. I knew this for a fact because I had carried out one of them. Something told me it would not be my last.

As I lay in the darkness, I remembered something my father once told me about assassins. He said it was a short-term line of work. When I asked him what he meant by that, he said, "The first rule of hiring an assassin is this: After the job's done, you kill the assassin. Dead men tell no tales."

The severity of my situation was beginning to set in. When offered this opportunity, I had jumped at it. I had let Jacobs play me like a violin. He'd known exactly what buttons to push, what leverage to use. Offered me rank, offered me autonomy, offered me better pay, better benefits, a chance to be closer to the real action, and, most importantly, a chance to have a life with Miranda. He'd struck all the right chords, and I'd danced to his tune like a good little monkey.

No more.

I've got your measure now, Jacobs, I thought to myself in the darkness. *Come what may, one way or another, I'm getting my life back. And God help you if you try to stop me.*

I closed my eyes, and after a few hours of fitful worrying, I slept.

269

THIRTY-FOUR

The morning after my conversation with Faraday, General Jacobs informed my team we would be getting support from a hand-picked JSOC team. Gabe asked who had done the hand picking. Jacobs said he and Grabovsky had made the selections. Gabe shook his head, but voiced no complaint. Jacobs gave him an impatient look, but there wasn't much he could say. Gabe was not military. He was a civilian working on a contract basis, and as such, did not owe Jacobs the decorum of military discipline. Gabe's obvious distrust for Jacobs' leadership got under the general's skin in a way I found immensely entertaining.

"Despite what he says, nobody works for the general voluntarily," I said to Gabe after we'd left Jacobs' office. "I'm willing to bet that includes this support detachment he's assigning us."

"Makes you wonder what he's holding over their heads."

"Yes, it does."

Introductions were made later that day in the mess hall. There were six of them, all Navy SEALs and long-time JSOC veterans, which told me they were from a certain SEAL team that did not officially exist.

The SEALs had served together since before the Outbreak, and it showed. There was a casual familiarity and verbal shorthand

270

between them that spoke of long association. They shared a bond of the impenetrable kind, forbidden to outsiders, forged by time and mutual hardship. Their hostile, walled-off comradery reminded me of a passage from an old Stephen King book:

You cannot friend a hawk, they said, unless you are a hawk yourself...

The SEALs were all NCOs, or the Navy equivalent. To be honest, I wasn't even sure if being an NCO was a thing in the Navy. From what Tyrel had explained to me over the years, it seemed as though E7 and above existed in a strata far beyond E6 and below. But then again, the Navy does everything differently than the other services. Instead of saying 'copy' or 'roger' they say 'aye aye', which sounds archaic as hell to me. And it gets worse. Left is port, right is starboard (unless you're facing the back of a ship—aft or stern or whatever the hell it's called—and then port and starboard are reversed), a rope is a line, candy is geedunk, a chow hall is a messdeck, a bunk is a rack, a toilet (or latrine, for die-hard Army types) is, for reasons I cannot explain, a head. And the list goes on.

During a meal together after our initial meeting, I asked one of the SEALs why a forecastle was pronounced FOK-sul, with the O being a long vowel sound, and not pronounced the way it was spelled. His response summed up the Navy's reasoning for following its outlandish traditions more succinctly than anything I could have articulated:

"How the fuck should I know?" he said. "People been calling it that for like, two-hundred and fifty years. Why change?"

Enough said.

But that's getting ahead of things.

The oldest of them was a master chief boatswain's mate named Gellar (boatswain being pronounced 'bosun'). He was tall, black, and possessed of about as much mercy as a pit viper. He was clearly the man in charge of his team, and would direct them when it came time to fight. Nonetheless, he was informed by Jacobs he would defer to Grabovsky as to our overall mission objectives.

271

Meaning it was Grabovsky's job to give the orders, and Gellar's job to make sure his men carried them out.

The other SEALs were no less surly than their leader. The next in line introduced himself as Smith, electronics technician first class. I was later reminded by Tyrel that 'first class' meant petty officer first class, the equivalent rank of a staff sergeant in the Army. I also learned that in the regular Navy an electronics technician's job was exactly what the title described. They were called ETs in the fleet, and normally worked on radar, radio, navigation, signal warfare, and other complex electronic devices, and the series of schools they had to go through to learn their jobs were intense and difficult and the failure rate was very high. In the SEALs, however, ETs killed people and blew shit up the same as any other operator. I told Tyrel it seemed to me like a waste of a perfectly good technical education. Tyrel said, "Yeah, well, that's the Navy for you."

Gunner's Mate First Class Lowell (again, no first name given) was one of the most average looking people I'd ever met. Average height, average build, brown hair and eyes, no distinguishing marks, neither handsome nor repulsive. But according to Master Chief Gellar, he was to explosives what Mozart was to a piano. After introducing himself, Lowell simply stood and stared at us, his expression mildly neutral. There was something disconcerting about the man. I had the feeling he was one of those people who only showed emotion when engaged in an activity that aroused his interest. And in Lowell's case, that involved blasting caps and detonation cord and the warm glow of bright orange fireballs.

Chief Engineman Miller reminded me very much of my old squad mate Isaac Cole. Big, black, and built like a fire truck. Unlike Cole, however, his demeanor was not affable and easygoing. Rather, he was stoic and cold and glowered at everyone in his field of vision as if they were targets to be eliminated.

The next man introduced himself simply as Petty Officer First Class Hemingway. That was it. No further comment. I detected a calmness about him that reminded me a lot of myself. Which is not to say I hold any immodest opinions regarding my personality. However, I have lived in my own skin long enough to understand how my general demeanor is perceived by others. Hemingway gave off the same vibe.

Last was Boatswain's Mate First Class Chavez. About my height, lean, and where his skin was visible, covered in tattoos. By examining them, I discovered he was from one of the less desirable neighborhoods of Los Angeles. His face was narrow and angular and had a chipped look to it, and he had slight cauliflowering around the edges his ears. I surmised he had seen more than his share of fist fights.

It was just after 1300 when our teams were introduced. General Jacobs informed us it was imperative we learn to work together, and as such, would be going out on patrol with a group of Resistance fighters at 1600 hours. Be ready. Dismissed.

We stood and stared at each other for a few awkward seconds. Finally I looked at my group and said, "We should get a bite to eat before we head out."

"Good idea," Grabovsky said.

"Our gear is still topside," Master Chief Gellar said. "We'll meet you there at 1530."

Grabovsky nodded curtly. "Will do."

*****

I expressed to Grabovsky some concerns about unit cohesiveness, being that we had never worked with Gellar and his team before.

"Don't sweat it," Grabovsky told me. "We all get trained pretty much the same. Pro is pro. You'll see when the time comes. Just remember your training, and everything will be fine."

It wasn't a satisfying answer, but it was the only one I was going to get.

We met Gellar and his men at the appointed time. A small contingent of Resistance fighters were waiting as well. Grabovsky shook hands with their leader, who introduced himself as Hopper,

273

no first name given. Hopper said he had been with Grabovsky's company the night the Resistance crippled the ROC's army. Grabovsky pointed a thumb at the young fighter and said, "Don't worry about him. He's good."

I observed the scars on the side of Hopper's head, the way he wore his weapons, and the steel in his eyes, and took Grabovsky at his word.

Three trucks were idling outside, one outfitted with an automatic grenade launcher, another with an M-240, and the last bearing a confiscated RPG launcher and a bag of rockets.

"Get in," Hopper said. "We're headed north."

Grabovsky's face lit up. "Lookin' for trouble, huh?"

"You know me," Hopper said, baring his teeth.

The roads we rolled over were rough and cracked, and in many places, runoff from heavy rains had washed them out entirely leaving behind tangled aggregates of mud and debris. Thankfully, the drivers were competent and the trucks were built for extreme terrain. Nonetheless, we set a slow pace. Tough as they were, the trucks were not invulnerable. If the drivers broke them, we would be on foot and the Resistance would have to send people out to attempt repairs. Operational vehicles were too valuable an asset to abandon no matter how severe the damage they sustained.

More than an hour went by before the lead truck turned off onto a dirt two-track and parked in a small open space canopied by gigantic cedars, maples, and cottonwoods. The air was still, humid, and stiflingly hot. I hopped from the back of the truck I was in and hauled my rucksack straps over my shoulders.

I was carrying my SCAR sniper rifle. It had a Nightforce scope mounted to the top rail and a pair of back-up iron sights offset forty-five degrees to the right. The rifle was heavy. I liked it. The weight was comforting. I knew what the weapon was capable of, and I knew what I was capable of with it.

Back in the First Recon, I'd often confiscated our squad's sniper carbine from my friend Derrick Holland, our designated marksman, and wreaked havoc with it upon marauders dumb enough to raid farms and small settlements within Fort McCray's area of responsibility. The practice had cemented within me the lessons of marksmanship I'd learned since the age of twelve: A sniper is a force multiplier. A good one can kill with near impunity. When the enemy sees one of their own go down in a spray of blood, the effect is immediately demoralizing. When more than one goes down, when the bodies start piling up, panic is never far behind. A few well-placed shots can often end a firefight before it starts, especially if the enemy in question is surrounded and a voice from out of nowhere tells them to surrender or suffer additional casualties. It is amazing how fast a big swinging dick raider loses confidence when faced with the possibility of someone blowing his heart out through his spine.

As I was clipping the rucksack belt around my waist, Hopper addressed the patrol team. "We go on foot from here. Five yard intervals, stay low and quiet. No sound. Hand signals only." His gaze turned to my group. "Just to be sure…"

He made a few hand signals. Tyrel spoke up for us, saying what they meant. When Hopper was satisfied we knew the language, we established call signs, covered the trucks with camo nets, and moved out.

The Resistance fighters took the right flank and Gellar and his men took center, leaving the left side of the skirmish line to my team. Hemingway was to my right. I put five yards between us and matched my speed to Hopper's as he set the pace. As we moved, I slipped past foliage and branches and ferns and felt the old instincts and muscle memory kicking in. It felt good. The part of me that revels in combat was happy to be on the move again, happy to be doing something aggressive. My ears strained, and I noted with satisfaction I made almost no noise as I passed through the forest. Gabe's form moved to my left, the big man somehow making his outline hard to detect even in broad daylight. He slipped through the undergrowth like a ghost, his passage swift and fluid.

He was at home here in the wilds.

So was I.

We covered two miles in just under an hour. The land rose up steadily until a ridgeline became visible up ahead. Movement to my right caught my attention, and I looked to see signals passing down the line. I knew the message before it reached Hemingway, but waited anyway.

Get low. Crawl to the ridgeline and stop.

I signaled affirmative and looked to my left. Gabe was already signaling Tyrel, who passed the message down to Grabovsky. I slung my rifle around to my back, pushed my spare mags lower on my waist, and did a high crawl to the ridgeline. Once there, I lay flat and still and let my eyes go unfocused, using them as motion detectors.

The terrain below sloped downward for hundreds of yards, thousands of trees standing like silent sentinels, the undergrowth beneath them concealing anything less than three feet in height. For all I knew, there was an entire platoon of ROC troops moving toward us, concealed by ghillie suits. With the amount of real estate in front of me, it would be difficult to spot them. I wished Eric Riordan were there. His uncanny eyesight had proved invaluable on numerous occasions.

Hopper turned out to be a patient man, a quality I admired. If the scars on his head were any indication, it was a trait he had come by the hard way.

We waited and watched, eyes straining. According to our maps, we occupied the best vantage point for miles around. If there was anyone moving our way, this was the best place to spot them.

Ten minutes passed. Then twenty. The wet smell of decaying organic matter filled my nostrils, bugs crawled on my skin, and the front of my clothes and MOLLE vest were absorbing water from the damp earth. I heard rodents and lizards skittering through the ferns and leaves, and in the branches far above, the shrill call of birds stirred the air.

Then, close to the thirty minute mark, the birds went silent.

Gabe noticed it at the same time I did. I looked at him and he made a signal.

Hostiles.

I acknowledged and turned to my right. From what I could tell, no one else had noticed anything amiss. I backed off down the hill, came up into a low crouch, and moved to Hopper's position. When I was a few feet behind him, I scratched gently in the leaves to let him know I was there. He jumped slightly, and I couldn't help feeling a sense of satisfaction at getting the drop on him. When he turned his head to look at me, I motioned for him to join me. He crawled backwards until we were less than a foot apart.

"You hear what I'm hearing?" I whispered.

"I don't hear shit," he said irritably.

"Exactly." I pointed upward. "The birds didn't fly away. They're still here."

He looked up, and after a few seconds, realization dawned. "Ah, fuck. You take left, I'll take right. Let everybody know we got trouble coming. Tell 'em to turn on their radios."

"On it."

My part was easy. All I had to do was move back to my position and signal Gabe. He took care of the rest. I settled into the same spot where I had been waiting before, the ground still warm from when I had lain there a few minutes ago. My eyes traced the slope, a warm sphere of anticipation building in my stomach. It had been too long since I'd had a good fight. The incident in the refugee district back in the Springs did not really count. My opponents had been overmatched. Now, I was up against real competition.

I thought about the photos I had seen of bodies burning in huge pits dug by the very people lying dead in them. I thought about the way Mike had aged a decade since I'd last seen him. I thought about the video of decimations carried out by KPA troops, and I thought about how all of it could have been avoided if the people who came in on the Flotilla had collaborated with the survivors they found instead of conscripting them into slave labor. I thought about Chinese assault rifles, and the Alliance, and the ROC troops stationed in Carbondale, and the man I had killed in cold blood as he lay sleeping and defenseless in his bed because doing so was the only way to prevent a bloody civil war from tearing apart what was left of my country. I thought about how the images of that night played in my head on an endless loop, over and over and over again, and how many times I had woken up smelling blood and cordite and seeing the startled, pale face of the woman who had been asleep next to him, her features round and waxen in the moonlight as she awoke to a faceless terror. A terror that had a name.

Caleb T. Hicks.

Think of what they've taken, I told myself. *Think of what they've done. Think of what they've made you give.*

I heard the crunch of boots on dead leaves. The sound was faint, like the mumbling voice of someone turning a corner as they walked out of a room. I closed my eyes and tried to figure out how many of them there were. It did not sound like a small patrol.

Moving slowly, I brought my rifle into firing position. We had the high ground, we were armed, prepared, and had the element of surprise. And soon, I would be looking down at a target rich environment.

I hoped they were complacent. I hoped they had patrolled this area a hundred times and never found anything of interest. I hoped there were a lot of them.

And I hoped they showed up soon.

THIRTY-FIVE

"Alpha One, Charlie Two. I got hostiles, over," I said into my radio.

"Roger, Charlie Two," Hopper said. "From my twelve o'clock, give me a bearing, over."

"Spread out from ten to two. Heavy camouflage. Looks like commando types. Over."

"Copy. All stations, look for movement, but hold fire until my mark. Charlie Two, give me targets."

I worked from right to left, searching for movement. If I had been a civilian, or even a regular infantryman, I most likely would not have seen the enemy coming. But Mike Holden, Tyrel Jennings, Blake Smith, and my father had spent four years doing their damnedest to spot me in the backdrop of the Texas hill country before I could spot them. They'd cleaned my clock at first, but by the time I was sixteen, I could beat them two times out of three. The guys down the hill from me were good, but not as good as the men who raised me.

"Alpha One, from your two o'clock, track low and left, big oak tree, cluster of ferns beneath. Look for a tree cancer."

"Got him Charlie Two. Good eyes. Bravo three, you got him?"

"I see a bundle of ferns that looks like its crawling next to a little red maple. That the one?"

279

"Affirmative, Bravo Three. He's yours."

"Copy, Alpha One. Standing by."

On it went. I spotted targets and called them to Hopper. He assigned them to shooters. Pretty soon, there were more targets than men to shoot at them. I glanced over at Gabe while I worked and noticed a small smile on his face. I had no doubt he had spotted the hostiles before I did, but had let me take the credit anyway. I was pretty sure I understood why. Gabe had street cred among these guys. I didn't. Showing off a little would inform the rest of the team I was no slouch, and that I brought something to the table other than youthful exuberance. I reminded myself to thank him later, assuming we both survived the next few minutes.

I informed Hopper we were facing no less than forty-two enemy troops. Platoon strength, in other words. Gabe chimed in and said he was pretty sure it was fifty-six and pointed out a secondary skirmish line I hadn't spotted. I did not begrudge him for it; I should have seen them myself, and in situations like these, ego goes out the window. There is no room for pride in a firefight.

Between my team, the six SEALs, and Hopper's Resistance fighters, there were eighteen of us. Which meant we were outnumbered better than three to one. The lack of bullets flying over my head told me we hadn't been spotted yet. I knew my group was solid, and had expected no less from Gellar and his SEALs, but Hopper's men had impressed me. I'd had my doubts about their capabilities, but those doubts were now laid to rest. The Resistance was no joke. They knew their business and did it well.

"All stations, this is Alpha One. Hold your targets and stand by. When I give the word, take your shots and fall back by fire teams. Cover each other's retreat, stay in your lanes, and for fuck's sake, maintain muzzle discipline. Alpha Four and Alpha Six, fall back to the trucks and man the heavy weapons. Everyone else, we'll lead 'em on a running fight back to the trucks. Once there, I'll give the order to hit the ground and my guys will lay the hammer down. This is gonna be danger close, so once you're down, stay there until you get the all clear. Alpha Four, when the time comes, make sure you keep those goddamn grenades well clear of our guys. All stations acknowledge."

280

The affirmatives went down the line in order, one man at a time, no one tripping over anyone else's comms. I'd seen experienced infantry platoons that couldn't do it as well. Again, I was impressed.

"All stations, Alpha One. Stand by."

I put the reticle on target. He was less than a hundred yards away. The 1-9x scope was dialed down to two-power, giving me a clear target picture. I put my finger over the trigger and kept my breathing steady, making slight adjustments as I did so to keep the crosshairs where they needed to be. My heart was a rhythmic drum, beating evenly, my finger twinging ever so slightly between beats. I wanted the shot to go off at the bottom of my breathing cycle between heartbeats. The SCAR's match-grade trigger was light with only a millimeter of take-up. I put slight pressure on it and waited.

The earpiece made a static sound. "All stations, Alpha One. Fire on my mark."

I breathed in.

"Three."

Lungs full.

"Two."

Let it out.

"One."

Lungs empty, reticle on target.

"*Mark.*"

My heart thumped inside my chest, and between one beat and another, I pulled the trigger. The rifle was suppressed, so instead of a tremendous, echoing *BAKOOOW,* there was only a medium-sharp *crack.*

I had loaded the cartridges for this rifle myself. I had used my black card to obtain fresh brass from the Army's diminishing supply. The powder and primers and projectiles were the best I could acquire. I knew precisely the muzzle velocity, trajectory, and energy delivered on target I could expect from each bullet I fired at

281

every distance from fifty to a thousand yards. The man in front of me was less than fifty yards away. Which meant the 175 grain projectile penetrated his chest cavity with over 2,400 foot pounds of energy. That kind of impact would have dropped a bull moose, much less a human being. I couldn't be sure, but I had a strong suspicion he was dead before he hit the ground.

Shots rang out to my left and right, and down the hill, men died. The troops below began shouting to one another in a language that I could only assume was Korean, and the ones still standing, which was most of them, raised their rifles and began returning fire. Bullets slapped the ground down the hill and clattered among the trunks and branches over my head. Wood shrapnel began falling around me like sharpened hail. I was now in ricochet country, a place for which I hold a deep and abiding hatred.

Only my team and the SEALs were running suppressors. The Resistance fighters had no such advantage, which meant as the enemy started shooting back, most of the bullets went their way first. The ones hitting over my head were just wild shots from frightened men trying to suppress anything on the ridgeline. Which, to their credit, was not altogether ineffective.

"Fall back, Alpha Team," Grabovsky said. "We'll draw 'em off while you take position. Cover us on the way by."

"Copy Charlie One. On our way."

I'm sure Hopper signaled for his men to haul ass back down the hill toward the trucks. I'm also sure he shouted something to them about closing intervals when they hit the ground to cover the SEALs' retreat. But I didn't hear or see any of it. I had my hands full trying not to get shot.

To my left, Gabe had a SCAR 17 battle rifle of his own. It wasn't as tricked out as mine, but his skill more than made up for the difference in accuracy. I'm good, but Gabe is great. There is a big difference between the two, and it showed as he went to work.

Crack.

A ghillie-suit clad man I hadn't even seen went down.

Crack.

282

Two men were trying to take cover behind the same tree. Gabe's bullet passed cleanly through the first man's torso and hit the man behind him center of mass, dropping them both.

"You gonna get to work or what?" Gabe shouted above the din. I didn't look at him, but I knew who he was talking to.

I caught movement in the foliage to my right. There was a lump of greenery where the rest of the ground was flat. I put my scope on it. The lump twitched and a fern in front of it swayed as if caught in a strong breeze.

Rookie mistake.

I put two rounds into the lump. It twitched and began to roll over, so I gave it one to grow on. The lump went still.

At best guess, we had put down between fifteen and twenty enemy troops without sustaining any casualties. Not yet, anyway. The rest of the enemy had taken cover, and despite our best efforts, we weren't making much headway against them.

I thought back to my infantry days and the tactics we used. When an infantry unit goes on patrol, they do so with the understanding they may be ambushed. If such a thing occurs, one needs to have the means to repel said attack. This is accomplished by the disciplined and coordinated employment of weapons with greater firepower than those being directed against them. As such, most squads have at least one machine gunner and at least one grenadier. The force we were up against was an entire platoon of fifty-six troops, which meant five to seven squads. The best we could hope for was to have reduced their number by a third, and whether or not we'd gotten any machine gunners and grenadiers was a question mark. As best I could tell, the two troops I'd taken had been riflemen.

As I was thinking this, I heard the unmistakable *rat-tat-tat-tat* of an RPK light machine gun cutting loose, soon followed by another of its kind, and then the distinct *phump-phump* of two grenade launchers going off at once.

"Fall back!" Grabovsky shouted into the radio.

I did not need to be told twice. Instead of getting up, I simply rolled backward a few times. As I did, thirty caliber projectiles fired by powerful 7.62x54mm cartridges slammed into the forest just above my head. One of the grenades fired by the men below wasted itself against the hillside, but the other hit close to the ridgeline where Gellar and company had been just a few moments ago. I didn't hear any screams, but then again, despite the earplugs I had put in before the shooting began, my ears were ringing so loudly I doubted I would have heard them anyway. Dimly, I wondered how much permanent hearing damage I'd accrued over the years, and what the long term effects would be.

Fuck your hearing! A shrill voice shouted in my head. *Run, you idiot*!

I ran.

THIRTY-SIX

There is nothing fun about a running fight.

Bullets fly back and forth, and you're never quite sure who fired the one that just whipped past your ear close enough to feel the turbulence of its wake and smell the vapor trail. You serpentine as you run, praying your movements are erratic enough to throw off anyone aiming at you, and when you've passed far enough behind the people laying down covering fire for you, you skid to a halt, find the best cover you can, try to remember how many rounds are left in your magazine, and start firing at anything pointing a gun in your direction.

We formed three groups: Hopper's fighters, Gellar's SEALs, and my team, which was led, ostensibly, by Grabovsky. Although at the moment Grabovsky's leadership consisted of the same activity as the rest of us—trying not to get his ass shot off.

We leapfrogged each other as we ran down the mountain, breaking up into fire teams and forcing our pursuers to divide their forces. On two occasions the enemy grenadiers tried lobbing grenades at us, but their ordnance succeeded only in rebounding off the thick stands of trees and exploding closer to the ROC troops than to us. After the second shot, they got the picture and stuck to sending hot lead at us.

About the fourth or fifth time it was my team's turn to stand and fight while the others ran, one of Hopper's men faltered in his steps, went down, and did not get up. Hopper yelled at him, but the

285

man didn't move. A steadily expanding pool of blood stained the ground beneath him, slowly running downhill.

"He's gone, Hopper," Grabovsky shouted. "Get your ass moving."

Hopper cursed violently, sent a volley of fire toward the ROC troops, and moved.

Now I was pissed. These ROC assholes had no right to be here. They had done nothing but commit atrocities since they'd arrived, and now they'd killed a man fighting to defend his home. The fear that had gripped me when that RPK first rattled back at the ridgeline left me. A coldness started in my stomach, spread to my chest and face, and steadied the muscles in my hands. There was no more shaking, no more panicked breathing. I took position a few feet behind a thick oak tree. A tree won't always stop a bullet, and taking cover close to one cuts off your field of view. Better to hang back a few feet and hope the wood withstands any bullets that come your way.

Two deep breaths settled me enough to steady my aim. The ROC troops were less than a hundred yards behind us. They came on with the hot-blooded zeal of hunters with their prey on the run. We'd whittled them down by a few, but they still outnumbered us two to one.

I raised my rifle and tracked a man carrying an RPK. He was short, maybe five foot seven and perhaps a hundred and thirty pounds soaking wet. He had the characteristic high cheekbones and dark hair and eyes of people from the Korean Peninsula. He looked like he might have been twenty years old. Maybe.

Christ's sake, it's been five years since the Outbreak. How young do they recruit these guys?

Not that it mattered. However old he was, this was the end of the line for him. I didn't care if he had joined the KPA voluntarily or not. I didn't care if he took issue with the things his forces had done or if he'd reveled in them. All that mattered was he was on one side, I was on the other, and if I gave him half a chance, he'd put a bullet in my head and keep right on running. In this situation, high-minded notions of mercy did not apply.

286

The SCAR kicked me in the shoulder and the bullet took him low in his chest. He screamed, fell, thrashed, and clutched at the place where he'd been shot, eyes bulging in pain and disbelief. I didn't understand what he was saying, but the plaintive tone was clear enough.

His RPK had flown from his hands when he went down and now lay ten feet down the slope from where he lay. I could have put another bullet in him to end his suffering, but I didn't. Cold logic dictated doing so was unnecessary. I had limited ammo, and he was out of the fight anyway. Furthermore, he was already dead, he just didn't know it yet. Where the bullet had struck was a complex junction of arteries and major organs. Even if the bullet and its wound channel hadn't destroyed his heart, he'd bleed out internally in short order.

Let him scream, I told myself. *Screams of dying comrades are demoralizing, and we need all the help we can get.*

To my right, Gabe squeezed off two shots. Another soldier hit the dirt face first, the top of his head a bloody, ragged mess. Beyond Gabe, Tyrel opened up with his IAR, forcing the troops on his side of the line to hit their bellies and scramble for cover. I saw a rifleman skid to a halt behind a tree and take aim in Tyrel's direction. I put the reticle on his head and pulled the trigger. Half of his cranium was missing when his corpse slumped to the ground.

"Charlie, fall back," Gellar radioed.

I had a bead on one more troop. Out of pure meanness, I put a bullet low in his guts. He would die, but he would be long in doing it and his dying would be pure agony.

Fuck him. Fuck all of 'em.

I fell back, making sure not to run in a predictable pattern. As I ran, my earpiece came to life.

"Sorry to say this fellas," Grabovsky said breathlessly, "but I'm out of ammo."

"I got the team," Gabe said. "Head back to the trucks. Get that RPG ready."

"Can fucking do."

Now we were three. I had ninety rounds left on my vest and twelve in the mag in my rifle. After that, I would be headed back to the trucks myself.

The rest of the journey down the long hill was a blur. I ran, I swerved, I counted steps when I passed Hopper's team, and when the time was right, I turned and picked off as many troops as I could—which wasn't many—before Gellar ordered the three of us to fall back. Tyrel informed us he was down to his last magazine. I still had sixty rounds left.

"Gabe, how are you on ammo?" I asked.

"Forty for my SCAR," he said. "But I got an M-4 on my back and sixty rounds for it."

"Roger. That should get us back to the trucks."

"Let's hope so. Make 'em count." Gabe's rifle cracked less than two seconds later.

I spared a glance behind me. The slope was beginning to flatten out, meaning we were only a few hundred yards away from the trucks now. We were in range of the heavy weapons, but too far away for them to do us much good. There were a lot of trees in the way, and even if there weren't, the enemy was too close behind us for the machine guns and grenades to force them back without risking hitting our own people. Hence the term 'danger close'.

The two-mile trip up the hill had taken an hour because we were being cautious, taking our time, and moving up a steep slope. But on the flight back to the trucks we were sprinting full-out, hopped up on adrenaline, and going downhill, a factor which lends speed to even the slowest of runners.

We'd been going for maybe fifteen minutes, and salvation was now close at hand. I was tired, sweating through my clothes, and my skin had turned red from overheating, but being in close proximity to escape was enough to lend strength to my tired legs.

Scanning up the hill, I estimated there were as many as thirty enemy soldiers still in pursuit. We'd racked up quite a score in this fight, and as far as I knew, had only lost one man. But that could change quickly if the enemy caught up to us.

To my right, I heard the chatter of Tyrel's IAR. He chewed through his last magazine in short bursts, forcing the enemy troops to take cover again. The pause in their progress allowed Gabe and me to pick targets and put bullets into them. I got two and Gabe hit one and missed another. But only by about an inch, and only because the target was on the run.

"I'm out," Tyrel said over the comms net. "See you at the rally point, amigos."

From the corner of my eye, I saw him sprint down the hill. *Good luck*, I told him silently. *And don't look back.*

"In position," Gellar radioed. "Fall back, Charlie."

"Moving," Gabe replied. I took one last shot that found its mark low. A grenadier howled and fell over clutching his groin. I grinned savagely and took off down the hill.

Die screaming, motherfucker.

Shots rang out as Gellar covered our retreat. As we ran, I realized there were shots ringing out from beyond Gellar's position as well.

What the hell?

The slope flattened the further I went and the trees began to thin out. I quickened my pace, ran around the side of a thick maple, and laughed triumphantly as I saw the trucks come into view.

And ran headlong into a tall Gray ghoul.

In the instant before we collided, I had half a second to bring up my SCAR in a two handed grip and hit the ghoul in the throat. After that, we were a tangle of living and dead limbs as we tumbled down the remaining slope. We had rolled maybe twenty feet when our progress was suddenly and jarringly arrested by the trunk of a cedar tree. Unfortunately, it was my back that hit the tree and stopped us rolling.

The ghoul was inches from my face, its terrifyingly strong fingers ripping into my shoulders. I screamed with my jaw clenched, spittle flying from between my teeth, and pushed the SCAR against its throat, keeping the creature's snapping maw at bay.

I was in trouble. I'd had the wind knocked out of me when I hit the tree, and it was only sheer mad-dog meanness that had kept me from dying in the first few seconds afterward. I was holding the ghoul off for the moment, but that wouldn't last. My strength would eventually wear out—the ghoul's would not. That is, by far, the worst thing about ghouls. They never, ever get tired.

I needed to do something, and I needed to do it quick.

As my lungs figured out how to breathe again, it occurred to me the ghoul was lying across my body. Back in my youth, when my father had me taking Brazilian jiu jitsu classes, we would have called this position 'side control'. I sincerely doubted the ghoul on top of me knew jiu jitsu, which gave me an advantage. But only for a short window of time.

On day one of any jiu jitsu class, the first thing you learn is how to move your hips while lying underneath an opponent, otherwise known as the hip escape. Once you've moved your hips away from your opponent and turned your torso toward him, you can begin working on either pulling guard, sweeping him over, escaping, or taking his back.

At the moment, I was far more concerned with escape. There isn't a ghoul in the world that will succumb to a chokehold, so taking its back was useless. Not to mention the fact it would take every ounce of strength I had to stay on its back and keep it from turning around and biting me. Its grip on my shoulders would make sweeping it an exercise in futility, and pulling guard would be flat-out suicide. My best option was to get away from the thing, create distance, and put a bullet in its head.

I planted both heels into the ground, bridged up with my hips, and turned my chest toward the ghoul, keeping the rifle between us as I did. The movement pulled my torso from underneath it, causing it to fall face-first onto the ground. It wasn't much, but it gave me the few precious seconds I needed to release my rifle and get to my feet.

One of the ghoul's hands slipped free as I stood up, but the other maintained its grip. I'd been in this situation before and knew how to handle it. I grabbed the outside of its palm with both hands, planted one boot on its face to keep it pinned to the ground, wrenched it's wrist sideways with everything I had, and leaned forward using my thigh as a fulcrum. The elbow snapped and the hand came loose. Now I was free.

I hopped back two steps and drew my Beretta. The ghoul began rising to its feet, its skeletal mouth open in a permanent, macabre grin. I put the barrel of the pistol against its forehead and pulled the trigger. The back of its head exploded, spraying the tree I had been lying against only seconds ago with black gore. Some of the ichor splattered my rifle.

Goddammit. Is anything gonna go right today?

I holstered my sidearm, picked the SCAR up by the buttstock and part of the handguard not covered in ghoul sludge, and ran as fast as I could toward the trucks.

On the way, more ghouls appeared out of the forest. Not good. Now I understood why there was gunfire coming from the trucks despite the fact the KPA troops were not in range yet. I cursed myself for an idiot. I should have known the sounds of combat would attract every ghoul for miles. Even a single gunshot is like ringing a dinner bell for the rotten bastards. A pitched battle is akin to setting out an all-you-can-eat buffet. It was a good thing we had the trucks. Otherwise, I'm not sure we would have been able to make it out of that valley alive, even without the KPA troops in pursuit.

I had been living too soft, I decided. Spending too much time in places where the infected had been eradicated or defenses had been erected to keep them at bay. It amazed me how easy it was to lose the old habits that had kept me alive for so long in the wastelands. If I survived the next few minutes, it was a deficiency I intended to correct.

I didn't dare bring the SCAR up to my face for fear of getting ghoul blood in my eyes, but I still had my pistol. Carrying the SCAR in my left hand, I drew my pistol with my right and slowed my run to a brisk jog. The ghouls were widely spread out, no doubt

291

because of the close proximity of trees in the forest, so I didn't anticipate having to shoot more than a handful before reaching the trucks.

Behind me, I heard the thump of grenades going off. I have heard a lot of grenades detonate since joining the Army. There is a difference in sound between the frag and concussion grenades used by Union forces and the little green balls used by the ROC and their marauder friends. The explosions behind me were definitely US made. Gellar had most likely let the KPA troops close to within throwing distance, tossed every frag grenade they had to force the enemy into cover, and were now beating feet toward the trucks.

I exited the treeline, dropped two ghouls in my path, and ran the last few yards to the trucks. Hopper's men were already there, one of them on the M-240, one on the MK-19, and the rest, including Tyrel, shooting calmly at the approaching horde of undead. In the third truck, Grabovsky crouched in the bed, the RPG launcher on his shoulder and a bag of rockets beside him. His gaze was intensely focused toward the approaching KPA troops. He reached down, picked up a box of ammo, and held it in my direction.

"Give us a hand with these ghouls," he said.

I gently placed my SCAR and rucksack in the bed of the truck. "I need an M-4."

"Take mine." Grabovsky handed me his rifle.

I took a moment to look it over. It was obviously a custom job: eighteen inch mid-weight free-floated barrel; ambidextrous charging handle, safety, and mag release; hand-machined muzzle brake, battery assist lever, and trigger guard; match-grade trigger; fifteen-inch aluminum quad rail; rifle-length gas system; A2 post removed in lieu of a low-profile adjustable gas block; folding BUIS; foregrip mounted under the lower picatinny rail; and what appeared to be a short length of bicycle inner-tube stretched around the pistol grip. The six-position stock was aftermarket—Magpul by the look of it—and the optic was a VCOG identical to the one I owned. This was not the weapon of a grunt. This was a custom built sniper carbine. I could only imagine what modifications Grabovsky had made to the internals.

There was a PEQ-15 laser sight mounted on the forward part of the rail. I tried the grip. The rubber inner-tube thickened it and gave it a firmer, more secure hold. I'd have to remember that trick.

"This thing zeroed?"

Grabovsky glared at me. "The fuck you talking to?"

"Question withdrawn."

I took the box of ammo and the three empty magazines Grabovsky offered from his vest. The ammo in the can was loaded on ten-round stripper clips. Like many infantry guys I know, I keep a stripper clip guide on me at all times. I affixed it to the first magazine, bent out the little brass tab on the edge of the stripper clip, slid the clip into the guide, put the bottom of the magazine against my chest, and pulled. Half a second later, ten rounds loaded. I repeated the process until all three mags were ready to go. The entire procedure took less than a minute.

During that time, Gabe and Gellar's team emerged from the treeline, dropping infected as they went. I wondered briefly what had taken Gabe so long, then figured he had probably stayed behind to help cover the SEALs' retreat. If I'd been a little less selfish, and a little less stupid, I would have thought to do the same. I intended to apologize to all parties involved if I lived long enough.

Gabe and the SEALs had the advantage of superior speed on their pursuers, and had put more than a hundred yards between them by the time they exited the treeline. To my left, Hopper spoke into a handset wired to a loudspeaker on his truck set to an earsplitting volume.

"Get down! Do it now!"

Our guys did not hesitate. They hit the ground face first and covered their heads with their arms. The KPA troops chasing them saw them go down, and almost in unison, looked up to see the trucks and the heavy weapons aimed at them. I imagine they had about a second and a half to think 'oh shit!', or the Korean equivalent, and realize they had been duped before the M-240 and MK-19 opened fire.

At least eight of them died in the initial volley. Grabovsky sent rocket after rocket among them, wisely blasting trees and showering them with shrapnel and falling timbers. RPGs are designed to destroy vehicles, so they aren't the best weapons to use against men spread out on a hillside. But Grabovsky's tactic of aiming at trees created a devastating effect. The troops on the hill had no place to hide.

I tore my gaze from the carnage and scanned where Gabe and Gellar's men waited for the explosions and flying bullets to stop. The KPA soldiers were not the only threat they faced. The infected had spotted Gabe and company and were shambling in their direction, heedless of the bullets and grenades flying toward the hillside. Many of them were torn apart by machine gun fire but continued their struggles nonetheless.

No head shot, no kill. Another trait of ghouls I do not find endearing.

The reticle of Grabovsky's VCOG was familiar. I lined it up on a ghoul's head and gently squeezed the trigger. It broke cleanly at maybe four pounds. The ghouls head snapped to the side, a gout of black stuff erupted over its shoulder, and it slumped to the ground. I searched for another target and soon found one. It was a little farther away, so I increased the magnification on the VCOG. When I looked through it again, I could make out the details of the ghoul in question.

She was young, maybe early twenties, and recently dead. Her clothes were mostly intact, her shoes were still on her feet, and she did not appear to be suffering from the abundance of injuries one sometimes sees on ghouls that were torn apart before they died. She may have even been pretty once. Now, her lank hair was matted and filthy, its color indeterminate, her skin a mottled gray, her eyes covered by a milky white film. She was wearing a flannel shirt and jeans and sturdy boots. Her sleeves were rolled up to her elbows. There was an ugly black oval on one of her forearms.

Got bit, didn't you? I thought. *Probably killed the ghoul that did it too. But you couldn't pull the trigger on yourself, could you? Or maybe you were out of bullets. Either way, happy trails.*

I put an end to her sad pseudo-existence, pushed down the tide of pity rising within me, and searched for another ghoul to kill.

"Cease fire!" Hopper screamed into his handset. "Cease fire!"

The M-240 and the automatic grenade launcher went silent. Grabovsky stopped firing rockets. I scanned the hillside with the scope, but saw no movement. I did, however, see a lot of dead KPA troops.

"Get to the trucks!"

Gabe and the SEALs were on their feet and running immediately. I picked up the mags and the box of ammo on the ground beside me, tossed them into the back of the truck, and hopped in. Gellar, Gabe, and the other SEALs arrived seconds later. All around us, ghouls were closing in.

"Get that machine gun up front," Hopper ordered. "Come on, let's move."

The trucks revved up and turned around on the loose ground, kicking up gravel and mud as they did so. In seconds, we were headed back toward the bunker. Despite the converging horde, the Resistance fighters showed discipline in their driving. We moved a little faster than on the way out, but not fast enough to risk disabling a vehicle.

Ghouls are slow, after all.

THIRTY-SEVEN

After debrief, the Resistance sent a team of scouts to make sure we had not been followed. Considering the size of the horde swarming in our wake, it seemed unlikely any KPA survivors would be foolish enough to attempt such a thing. But the Resistance had not survived this long by leaving stones unturned. A few hours later, the scouts came back tired, sweating, and footsore from fleeing the infected, but reported all clear.

The man who died was Hank Crowley. He had been one of the recruits sent to Idaho, and had participated in the first main assault against the ROC. Two other Resistance fighters suffered minor wounds, which Doctor Faraday treated, and one of the SEALs, Chavez, caught some shrapnel in the muscle over his shoulder blade. A medic removed the metal and cleaned and stitched the wounds. General Jacobs gave him the option to sit out the final assault. Chavez informed the general the wounds had been beneficial. His back was itchy before the attack, and the shrapnel had scratched it for him. He felt much better now. Jacobs smiled and said, "Very well."

We had a memorial service for Crowley the next morning in the mess hall. My group and I stayed toward the back. We hadn't known the man, but for a brief while, we'd fought side by side with him. We owed it to him to attend his wake, even if it was not our place to speak words over his passing. He had friends in the Resistance, including Mike, who took care of that part.

Afterward, everyone went back to work. Crowley was not the first comrade they had lost, and no one expected him to be the last.

According to Hopper, whom I spoke with after the wake, the patrol was considered a strategic success. Mike, Hopper, and General Jacobs had long suspected the KPA was sending patrols farther south into Resistance controlled territory, and now they had confirmation. Not only that, but we'd taken out as many as fifty-six KPA special operations troops at the cost of only one man. It was dreadful arithmetic, but by Resistance standards, this was considered a more than acceptable loss.

I mentioned that pretty soon the KPA would notice their patrol hadn't returned and send someone to investigate. Hopper said that was a good thing. Killing 'Kim', as he called the KPA, (apparently a reference both to the former North Korean dictator and the ubiquity of the name in Korean culture), was a lot easier if you could draw him out. I expressed concern about reprisals.

"Nah," Hopper said. "Kim already figured out that don't work. Besides, they need people to grow their food. Fuckers don't know shit about farming. They'd starve without the prisoners."

I stopped walking when Hopper said that. It gave me a thought so terrible I did not want to give it voice.

"Hey, you okay?" Hopper asked.

"Yeah, sorry. Just remembered something. I gotta go."

"All right. See you around."

I strode briskly to the warehouse, picked the lock to the Phoenix Initiative wing, and set about searching for Faraday.

"Hey," a young assistant called to me as I stormed past. "You can't be in here."

He ran up to me and grabbed my arm. I seized his hand, put him in a wristlock, bent his arm until he was doubled over, and dropped a hammer fist onto the back of his neck. His legs gave out and he slumped to the floor, eyes glazed. Throughout the process, I did not break stride.

I found Faraday in his office poring over paperwork. His door was open. He looked up when I stopped outside, and when he saw my expression, his face went pale.

"Captain Hicks, what are you-"

"Tell me we're not killing them."

His mouth worked a few times and his forehead wrinkled in confusion. "I'm sorry, I don't understand. Killing whom?"

"The prisoners in the camps. AIM-38. You said it was curable. You also said the KPA may have stolen the formula for the inoculant. If those prisoners die, the KPA starves. I want to know if the point of this mission is to kill the prisoners and starve out the KPA."

It took a few moments for the question to register. The confusion on Faraday's face could not have been manufactured, and I knew right then I had my answer. But I had come here and leveled the accusation, so I would stand there and listen to the reply. I owed Faraday that much, especially considering the assistant who was probably still laid out in the hallway.

After a few moments, Faraday's eyes cleared and his face reddened with anger. He stood up to his full height and glared at me in pure indignation. "Captain Hicks, whatever you may think of me, I am not the monster your friend Gabriel thinks I am. I have done a great many things I regret, mostly out of cowardice. I should have refused more assignments than you would believe. But I don't do that kind of work anymore. I realize you don't know much about the Initiative, but did it ever occur to you to wonder why a man with multiple doctorates in a variety of disciplines, and a former Initiative department head no less, is assigned to a hole in the ground on the front lines of a brushfire war?"

It was a point that should have occurred to me. I felt deflated. "No. I figured the Army needed a subject matter expert on AIM-38, so they sent the man who developed it."

"I wish that were so, but it isn't. There are literally dozens of people the Initiative could have sent to handle this assignment just as well as I. The truth is, this is a punishment."

Now I was the one confused. "Punishment? For what?"

Faraday ran a hand through his hair, a lost look shrouding his eyes like the shadow of an approaching cloud.

"For years, I grappled with the things I've been asked to do, with my role in the programs I've participated in. Over time, the guilt inside me grew and festered and ate at my conscience until it nearly consumed me. I was on every anti-depressant the Initiative had access to, and a few it did not. I drank constantly. I was on the verge of a breakdown. Rock bottom came when my superiors asked me to do something…beyond countenance. I'm not at liberty to say what it was, but believe me when I tell you, it was an atrocity even a jaded soul such as me could not stomach. So I told them no. I told them I was done. I'd had enough. I could not, *would not,* do their dirty work anymore. They told me I had no choice. I told them there was always a choice, even if it was a terrible one. I was then marched into a courtyard and forced to my knees and a man put a gun to the back of my head. The director of the Initiative himself stood next to me and told me I had one last chance. I told him to go fuck himself. At that moment, I honestly did not care if they killed me. I was ready. A few seconds passed, and then the man with the gun holstered his weapon and escorted me back to my quarters."

I swallowed and found I could not meet Faraday's eyes. He took a step closer to me, his tone softening.

"The director's assistant visited me the next day. She asked what I wanted to do going forward. I told her I wanted to do the opposite of what I had been doing. I wanted to help people, not use them like lab rats. I wanted to make a difference for the better. So they sent me here. And whether you choose to believe me or not, I *am* trying to make a difference. I know what we're doing seems like madness to you, but I assure you it is a calculated risk. I want those prisoners to survive. I want them freed. I want them to get their lives back, or as much of them as they can. It would be the first good thing I've done in a lifetime of villainy. So no, Captain. The plan is not to kill the hostages and starve their captors. This is, unequivocally, a rescue mission."

I nodded slowly, not meeting his gaze.

"Are you satisfied now?"

"Yeah. Sorry to bother you." I started to walk away, then stopped. "I, uh…one of your assistants…"

"He didn't try to stop you, did he?"

"Yeah. He did."

"Is he alive?"

"He'll be all right. Might have a headache for a while."

Faraday sighed, took off his glasses, and rubbed the bridge of his nose. "Where is he?"

I told him. He said he'd take care of it, and in the future, if I wanted to speak with him, to go through channels. I told him I would, and then I scuttled out of there with my tail between my legs.

THIRTY-EIGHT

In the days following the patrol and the ensuing battle, the resistance fighters acted differently around me. Before, they had regarded me with skepticism, probably wondering how someone my age could be as well trained as the other JSOC operators they had worked with. After seeing me in action, however, they seemed to have changed their opinions. While I was not exactly everyone's best friend, they at least acknowledged I could hold my own in a fight. This, apparently, held significant weight in their estimation, and they treated me accordingly.

The SEALs, on the other hand, remained unimpressed. While they acknowledged my capabilities, they showed little interest in getting to know me personally. All but one of them, that is: Petty Officer First Class Charles (Chuck) Hemingway.

Over chow one day, I asked him if he was related to the famous author with the same last name. He winked at me. "You never know. Guy got around."

I supposed it was possible. Chuck was tall, had square features, brown hair and eyes, a high widow's peak in his hairline, and was strongly built like his namesake had been.

"Ever get the urge to write literary fiction or pet a six-toed cat?" I asked him jokingly.

"Fuck no," he said, grinning. "I can barely spell my own name, and cats make me sneeze."

301

"Maybe not then."

Hemingway laughed quietly and went back to his meal.

At another juncture, while pouring over intel reports, I heard Hemingway refer to Chavez as Domingo.

I looked at him. "Domingo Chavez?" I asked.

He looked at me. "Yeah. What, you heard of me?"

"Sort of. Ever read anything by Tom Clancy?"

He squinted at me. "Who?"

"Never mind."

While waiting for the mission to start, we met with Master Chief Gellar and company on a daily basis. We poured over the same maps and read the same intel briefings and asked the same questions and worried about the same problems. It did not necessarily improve our standing as a fighting unit, but we at least got to know each other a little better.

The day before we were ordered to deploy for the final assault, Hemingway and I were in the warehouse above the bunker enjoying a respite from the underground warren. It felt good to see the sun again. The garage door was open, allowing in a cool afternoon breeze. Hemingway was good company. He spoke when he had something to say, stayed quiet when he didn't, and did not fidget or compose useless utterances in the midst of perfectly good silence. People like that are rare, and I consider it a privilege when I find them. Which is why I was surprised when Hemingway suddenly trudged into a question hesitantly, as if unsure of his boundaries.

"I want to ask you about something," he said, an edge of caution in his voice.

I looked at him. "Okay."

"You uh…I think you might know somebody I know."

"Okay."

"Thing is, I'm not supposed to know you might know them, or why you might know them. Know what I mean?"

I blinked a few times and shook my head. "No, Chuck. You're not making a damn bit of sense."

He scratched his head. "Okay, how about this. There's a guy out there. You might have run across him. Big guy. Apache Indian from Arizona. Name's Lincoln Great Hawk."

"Oh, okay. Yeah, I know the guy."

Hemingway looked surprised. At what, I wasn't sure. "So, like, you can talk about that?"

Ah, I thought. *Now I understand.*

"You know how it is," I said. "There's things I can talk about, and there's things I can't. As for Great Hawk, he quit whatever three-lettered acronym he was working for and settled down in Tennessee in a little town called Hollow Rock. Owns part of a mercantile there. I used to be stationed at the FOB near the place, Fort McCray."

"I've heard of Hollow Rock. Supposed to be pretty nice there."

"It is."

Hemingway was quiet a moment, then his expression became inquisitive. "Wait, so you were with the First Recon?"

"Yep."

"But they're regular Army."

"And tough bastards, in spite of it all."

"How'd you go from infantry to, you know, *this*." He held out his hands as if the forest around us were a metaphor for Joint Special Operations Command.

"Guess I shot enough people someone figured out I was talented."

Hemingway thought it was funny. I didn't tell him I was serious.

"So that thing in Illinois, you know what I mean?"

"Officially, no. I have no idea what you're talking about."

"Officially."

"Correct."

"But you know Great Hawk."

"I do."

"And Fort McCray was the closest FOB to Alliance territory back in the day."

"It was."

"And you were stationed there."

"Yep."

"And now you're here, and you have a fucking black card."

"I do. And you, Petty Officer Hemingway, have a wonderful talent for regurgitating known facts."

"Just seems like a hell of a coincidence, you know?"

"It does indeed."

Hemingway stared at me. I did not stare back. "So you and Great Hawk, that thing in Illinois…"

"What thing?"

"That's your story, huh?"

"And I'm sticking to it."

We sat quietly for a while longer. The sun moved behind the warehouse, casting us in cool, deep shade. A breeze picked up from the south, carrying with it the faint dusty smell of northern California. The sweat on my forehead dried and I relished the break from the day's heat and humidity.

"You're a goddamn liar, Hicks. You were there."

"I've been lots of places. You'll have to be more specific."

Hemingway threw up his hands and sat back in his chair. "Anyway, how's Great Hawk? You said he runs a store or something now?"

"Bought into a transport and salvage business. Mostly he runs the salvage side of things, but pickings are getting slim in western

Tennessee. A mutual friend told me he's starting his own private security business."

"What, like the Blackthorns?"

"Something like that, yeah."

"Jeez. Never thought he'd give up the life."

"I'm not entirely sure he did."

"What's that mean?"

I shook my head. "Nice day, don't you think?"

A pause. "Fuck you, Hicks."

Hemingway leaned back in his chair, extended his legs, and closed his eyes. He may not have been graceful about it, but he knew when to admit defeat.

THIRTY-NINE

Late the next morning, while I was sitting in my room reading a dog-eared copy of *For Whom the Bell Tolls*, there was a knock at my door. I put the book down and went to see who it was.

"Word just came down from Central," Grabovsky told me when I opened the door. "We got the green light."

"When?"

"Tomorrow night."

I felt an unexpected wave of relief. "About damn time."

"No shit. Briefing's at 1600 in the conference room. Don't be late."

"I'll be there," I said, but Grabovsky was already walking away.

Finally.

I closed the door and began packing my gear. When I was done, I opened a drawer on my bedside table and took out two dossiers. The other members of my team had copies as well, including the SEALs who had been briefed separately. I studied the faces in the various pictures, trying to commit them to memory so I could recognize the subjects from any angle when I saw them. I had been looking at the pictures every day since receiving them, but memory is an unreliable thing. It is best to keep important information at the front of the mind. As my father used to tell me, repetition is the mother of all learning.

306

I reread their files, then I studied the pictures again. If I did nothing else tomorrow night, I was going to find these two. And one way or another, by dawn the following morning, they were going to be in Union custody.

Either that, or I would die trying.

*****

Things move slowly in the military until it's time to destroy something. Then things move very quickly indeed.

I showed up early for the ops briefing. It was two hours of reiterating things we already knew, rehashing attack plans that had already been studied ad nauseam, and assessing data from intel reports we had all read and discussed extensively. The only new takeaway was the AIM-38 virus had already been airdropped over the target areas. By the time we arrived, the KPA troops guarding the prisoners would, presumably, be too sick to fight. Nevertheless, we were reminded to be on the lookout for troops and enemy officers that may have received the Chinese version of the inoculant, assuming they had actually made any.

In short, it was a review before the final exam.

There is usually a part of me that is apprehensive about going into combat. The battle lust does not typically kick in until the bullets start flying. Beforehand, my sense of logic is in the fullness of its power and warning me of the potential consequences. But not this time. There was no fear, no nervousness, no anxiety. I was ready to be done with this shit. I wanted those prisoners safe, inoculated, and on their way to rebuilding their lives. I wanted the KPA dead and buried. I wanted to find the people General Jacobs had tasked my team with capturing and get them on a helicopter back to the Springs.

Mostly, though, I just wanted to see Miranda again.

The briefing ended and everyone involved in the mission spent the evening preparing and re-preparing their gear, weapons, and minds. I deliberately stayed awake until two in the afternoon the next day so I could get a solid ten hours of sleep before assembling topside with the rest of the team.

I woke up at midnight, ate an increasingly rare MRE of unknown age, and drank three liters of water. Then I rounded up my gear and followed Gabe, Tyrel, and Grabovsky out of the bunker to the staging area. To my surprise, Mike was already there, looking incongruous in full combat gear with his shock of graying hair and silver beard.

"You coming with us?" I asked.

"Goddamn right I am," he said. "I started this thing, and I'm gonna see it through to the end."

"We're glad to have you," Tyrel said, patting his old friend on the shoulder. Mike gave him a tight smile.

The SEALs comprising our support detachment were there as well, along with close to a hundred Resistance fighters and more than a dozen special operations personnel. I recognized Sergeant Hathaway and nodded to him. He saluted me as I passed, and it took me a moment to remember that I was an officer now and was supposed to return the salute. I did, and I think I even managed to make it look casual. If I didn't, Hathaway had the good grace not to laugh at me.

General Jacobs did not show up. Orders came over the comms net as to which team was supposed to wait where for pickup. Ours was told to wait in a forest clearing half a kilometer from the bunker. Grabovsky consulted his tablet. After a minute, he closed the cover and slipped it into his pack.

"Come on," he said, setting out northward. "Let's get this shit over with."

*****

While waiting in the tall grass of a meadow in the middle of the night, I had a chance to ask Mike if he'd ever found his wife.

"I did," he said, his face going blank. "Made it to her family's place about six weeks after I left the Springs. Place was trashed. Bloodstains, broken windows, doors smashed in, you know what it's like. Infected had been there. I spent the next two weeks searching the surrounding area. Finally found her with a bunch of other infected trying to get to some poor fella they'd trapped on the roof of a gas station."

"Jesus, Mike. I'm sorry."

He shrugged. "Wasn't anything unexpected. I led the horde away, found some high ground, took aim at what used to be my wife, and did what I had to do. Then I went back and found the guy trapped on the gas station. You've met him. He's the coordinator for the teams in Washington."

"Romero?"

"Yep."

Grabovsky waved an impatient hand at us. "Quiet a minute," he said. He pressed his headphones against his ears. Smith, who had volunteered to be our radioman, squatted next to him, scanning the treeline with his NVGs.

We crouched in the clearing, waiting for word from Grabovsky. Each of us had a rucksack, body armor, and a full loadout of weapons and gear, including breaching charges. We also carried one LAW rocket per man, a single Carl Gustaf M3 recoilless rifle for the squad, and two crates with six shells each for the M3. Hemingway and Chavez would be the M3 team. Chavez would carry three shells, with the rest of his team dividing up the remainder among them. I was glad I wasn't asked to help. My gear was already heavy enough; I wasn't in a hurry to add to it.

"You've got the star shells," I heard Gellar tell Smith and Miller while they were distributing the M3 munitions. "Don't lose 'em. We might need 'em later."

"Aye, aye, Master Chief," they both replied.

I muttered quietly to Mike, "Fucking Navy and their weird-ass language."

Mike looked at me. "What do you mean?"

309

"Who the hell says 'aye, aye'? Seriously, it's like no one told them we won the war against the British and they still think they're fighting for King George."

That got a laugh out of the old man. It felt good to hear it. "Believe me, that's the least weird of their traditions. Ever heard of the shellback initiation?"

"No. What's that?"

"Weird. That's what it is."

"You assholes know I can hear you, right?" Tyrel said.

Mike smiled at him. "Am I saying anything that ain't true?"

Tyrel glared a moment, then looked away. "No."

"Hey, you hear that?" Hemingway said.

Everyone went quiet, straining their ears. After a few seconds, I heard the distinctive *whump-whump-whump-whump* of helicopters. Lots of them. Strangely, I had a vivid memory of the scene from *Apocalypse Now* where the Hueys are flying toward the Vietnamese beach and Robert Duvall is arguing with someone about whether heavy or light surfboards are better, and when they get close to shore, they start playing *Ride of the Valkyries* over a set of loudspeakers. And all the while, Martin Sheen is calmly looking around and chewing gum while the air cavalry start blowing up a Viet Cong village. At that moment, I felt like Captain Willard in that scene: calm, collected, and ready to kill something. Although perhaps without the same destructive sense of ennui. Not anymore, at least. There was a time.

One of the helicopters veered in our direction, circled the meadow, saw our IR patches, and descended a safe distance away. When it landed, one of the crew chiefs opened the door and waved at us to approach. I put on my combat goggles and braved the rotor wash and lashing, waist-high grass on the way to the Blackhawk. Gabe and Mike went in front of me while everyone else followed behind.

Between the eleven of us and the two crew chiefs, it was somewhat of a squeeze. I told myself it could have been worse. Eleven men in full combat kit and four aircrew, including pilots, is about as much as Blackhawks are built for. They can hold fourteen in a pinch, but you have to drop some gear to do it. As it was, there were only thirteen people in the cargo area and the two pilots up front.

The Blackhawk's rotors began to spin faster. We clipped our harnesses to the anchors recessed in the helicopter's deck and tried not to move around too much. We were equipped to rappel out of the bird, and looking around, I saw there were two lines set up on each of the two open sliding doors. I wondered how we were going to manage that when we barely had enough room to move.

Very carefully, my father's voice told me.

I remembered being twelve years old the first time he took me up in Black Wolf Tactical's helicopter and had me rappel out of it.

"It's just like going down the practice skid," he told me beforehand. "Just slide down the rope like you've done a thousand times."

It was most certainly *not* just like going down the practice skid. There was rotor wash, and incredible noise, and wind tossing the helicopter around, and it seemed as though we were impossibly high in the air even though it was only a hundred feet. I almost chickened out, but then I saw my father staring at me expectantly, his gaze unyielding, his mouth a thin, sharp line. His eyes locked with mine and he stabbed a finger toward the ground.

I had just recently read *The Gunslinger* by Stephen King, and Roland Deschain's poignant rebuke sprang to mind:

You have forgotten the face of your father.

So I clenched my teeth, screwed up my courage, and kicked off. Once I got going, it was actually pretty easy. I hit the ground, disengaged my harness, and when I looked skyward to give my dad a thumbs up, I was grinning so hard my face hurt.

As I remembered this, it occurred to me I had never been through any kind of training in the Army to prepare me for rapelling from a helicopter. Nonetheless, General Jacobs obviously had confidence I could do it. Which meant someone had been talking about me, and I was pretty sure I knew who. I glanced in

Mike's direction and decided my recruitment into the general's service no longer seemed quite so coincidental. Not for the first time, I had the feeling of larger, unseen forces moving around me and bearing me along in their wake like leviathans in a murky ocean. I did not care for it.

The flight was short. When we reached our destination two miles from the internment camp, the crew chiefs helped us attach our harnesses to the ropes. Gellar and Grabovsky went first, rapelling down the port side, while Gabe and Mike exited from starboard. When they hit the ground they held the ropes for the next man on rappel, one of those next men being me. I landed next to Gabe, detached from the rope, and helped him steady the line. In less than two minutes we were all on the ground. Above us the helicopter wheeled southward, gained altitude, and flew away into the pitch black sky.

I looked around. Through the grainy image of my NVGs, I saw we were in a forested area where the trees were spaced widely apart. Looking north, I could see the forest grew thicker in that direction.

Grabovsky checked his tablet. Mike stepped next to him and studied the screen.

"Where we at?" he asked.

"We're clear to move within half a klick. General Jacobs wants us to find a good vantage point and stand by until the other teams are in place."

Mike looked around at the assembled operators. "You heard the man. Let's move out. We ain't got all night."

"Yes sir," came the reply, in unison.

FORTY

"By the way," I said to Grabovsky as we walked toward the prison camp. "How are we on infected?"

"Not as bad as we could be," he said. "The prison camp is loud, but secure. There'll be ghouls when we get close, but it should be clear until we get there."

"Anything on satellite?"

"Satellites only see large hordes. If it's less than twenty or thirty they can go unnoticed. Especially if they're spread out."

"Which they will be in the woodlands."

"Yep. Once we reach the clearing they'll be bunched up, but that's a whole other problem."

"I imagine our good friend Carl Gustaf can help with that."

Grabovsky actually smiled a little. "I bet he can."

We took our time trekking through the forest. It was a dark night with a cloudy sky overhead and rain in the forecast for the next morning. The last thing we needed was to run into a horde and have to waste time and ammo fighting our way clear. Or even worse, having to abort. I'd kill the ghouls with a damn rock if I had to. I was not failing this mission.

When we were a mile out, the tell-tale groan of undead drifted to us through the forest. We all stopped, circled up, and scanned our surroundings. A low fog was drifting in, and it was getting difficult to see more than thirty feet or so.

"Switching to thermal," Gabe said.

Hearing him say it reminded me my night vision scope had a thermal setting as well. I flipped up my NVGs, switched it over, and scanned for infected. Unlike living people, who show up bright white in an IR imager, ghouls show up as a shadow among the gray background. They're hard to spot when they stand still, so one has to look for movement.

"Got six coming in on my side," Gabe said.

"Two here," Miller said.

I scanned again and saw movement. After a few seconds, I had a count. "Four my way."

"Anybody else?" Grabovsky said.

He got a round of negatives.

"Good. At least there ain't many of them. Switch to hand weapons."

Grabovsky, Tyrel, Mike, and the SEALs drew MK 9 ghoul choppers. Gabe produced his elegant falcata. I slid my M-4 around to my back, flipped down my NVGs, and unsheathed my fighting knife and a machete I'd requisitioned from the bunker. I had sharpened the machete with a set of steel files I'd borrowed from the bunker's armory, and while it wasn't a MK 9, it was good enough to get the job done.

Hemingway looked over at me. "Where's your MK 9?"

"Didn't bring one."

"They didn't have any at the bunker?"

I gave him a flat stare, the effect of which was lost behind my goggles. "If they did, don't you think I would have brought it?"

"Hey, don't get pissed at me. I'm not the one that told you to leave your chopper behind."

I opened my mouth to give a sharp reply, but Mike cut us off. "You two wanna shut up? We got incoming."

314

"Yes sir," I said, shutting my mouth. Hemingway did the same.

"Lowell, you're on anchor," Gellar said.

"Got it." Lowell activated his PEQ-15 laser sight, which produces a sharply focused beam visible only through NVGs. If any of us got into trouble, Lowell would bail them out. But only as a last resort. Even suppressed, M-4s make a lot of noise. We couldn't afford that right now.

"These fuckers on our side are closer," Grabovsky said. "Move in on 'em by twos, then we'll hit the rest. Hicks, Hemingway, you two watch our six."

"Roger that," I said. Hemingway acknowledged as well.

I tied my scarf around my mouth. The NVGs would protect my eyes, although I might have to wipe down the lenses after this.

The squad paired up and moved in. If the sight of eleven armed men heading in their direction alarmed the ghouls in question, they did not show it. Their progress remained steady as they lurched toward us. I noticed they were all Grays.

"Probably heard the helicopter," I said. "Came looking for a snack."

"Shouldn't there be more, then?" Hemingway asked.

"Not if they got distracted by the noise coming from the prison camp. Probably turned around after the bird left and went back the way they came. These shitheads must have gotten close enough to hear us walking in. Grays move faster than other ghouls."

"I've noticed that," Hemingway said. "Heard they can heal too."

"They can. I've seen it."

"Fuck's sake. What's next, ghouls that can run and climb?"

"Christ, don't even say it. They learn to do that, the human race can hang it up."

Our conversation ended when Miller decapitated a ghoul with a powerful backswing. Gabe went to work on Miller's left side, a swipe of his falcata sending a diagonal section of cranium spinning

315

one way and a body falling the other. Hemingway and I turned in the direction of the other ghouls. Lowell stood close to us, hanging back so he could get a clear shot if anyone got into trouble.

The two Grays Miller spotted were moving in fast. They must have been well fed; the usual two-to-three mile an hour shuffle was absent. These two were moving at a brisk walk, almost the speed of a slow jog.

"I'll take left," I said.

"Got the other one." Hemingway took a two-handed grip on his MK 9 and moved in.

The Gray coming toward me had not been a large man in life. At least I didn't think so—it's hard to tell after they shed their skin. All the putrefied fat goes with it. What stared at me was a scrawny nightmare of exposed muscle tissue, wide lidless eyes, and a gaping, skeletal mouth full of gnashing teeth. The face around the mouth was stained black with the gore of its last meal, and its fingers were bent into outstretched hooks. The urge was strong to say fuck it and shoot the damn thing, but I resisted.

When it drew close, I kept my dagger low and away from my torso, sidestepped, and lashed out with the machete. The ghoul's right arm fell to the ground, severed at mid bicep. When it turned to face me, I push-kicked it in the chest, knocking it back a few steps. It recovered quickly and came at me again. This time I dodged the other way and cut off its left arm, then danced backward to give myself space. The ghoul was undeterred. I was reminded of the scene from *Monty Python and the Holy Grail* with the black knight. I giggled thinking about it, despite the severity of the situation.

"It's only a flesh wound," I muttered as I push-kicked the ghoul again, slipped around to its left side, and chopped into the back of its neck. The blow severed its spinal cord and the ghoul slumped to the ground. It was disabled now, but it wasn't dead. As long as the brain was intact, it would remain in its undead state. I solved that problem via a carefully aimed stab with my fighting dagger. The blade slid neatly into the eye socket and scraped against the back of the creature's skull. I gave the knife a twist and pulled it free.

316

Looking up, I saw Hemingway had killed his Gray and moved back into position. I followed suit. The last four ghouls were still inbound. They would be on us in less than a minute. I glanced behind me and saw Mike split a ghoul's head down the middle like a melon before yanking his blade free.

"Come on," he said. "We ain't done yet."

We reversed positions with the others. I checked our surroundings with the IR scope, but saw no more infected. Gabe, Miller, Tyrel, and Gellar made short work of the last of the undead. Everyone looked around just as I had done, looking for threats. There were none in sight.

"Okay," Gellar said. "Clean your weapons and-"

"*GRRRGH!*"

We all jumped and turned toward the sound, weapons raised. Hemingway was fighting with something attached to his leg.

Oh shit, I thought. *Oh no.*

It was the ghoul he'd fought. There was a wide gash in its skull, but the blade had not penetrated deep enough to kill it. We all rushed forward at the same time. Gabe got there first and hit the thing in the back of the neck with his falcata. Its jaw released from Hemingway's calf muscle and it fell to the ground. The tall SEAL's face became a mask of rage and he began stomping the creature's head in impotent fury. We all took a few steps back and let him get it out. When he was done, the ghouls head was a pulpy mess. He stood staring at it for a few seconds, breathing heavily.

"Somebody look at my leg," he said, desolation in his voice.

Gellar activated a flashlight with a red lens, squatted down, and shined it on the bitten area. The fabric and a chunk of skin had been ripped away and blood was pouring down into Hemingway's boot. Gellar stood up.

"I'm sorry, Chuck. It got you."

Hemingway took off his NVGs and let the M3 slide to the ground. Then he dropped his pack and sat down on it, head hanging between his knees.

"It's my own damn fault," he said. "I should have made sure it was dead."

No one said anything for a while. It was Mike who finally spoke up.

"What do you want to do, son?"

Hemingway ran a hand through his hair. "It takes a while for the Phage to kick in, right? I probably still have some time. We could put a bandage on my leg. I could still help with the mission."

Gellar shook his head sadly. "Can't risk it, Chuck. You know that."

Hemingway looked like he wanted to argue, but stopped himself. He sighed and looked up with resignation written on his face.

"Sorry guys. I fucked up."

No one responded. There was nothing to say. Everyone knew what had to be done, including Hemingway. Chavez stepped forward, took a knee, and embraced the man who had been his friend for years, who had spilled blood in the same dirt and fought and hurt and struggled and shared with him all the hardships of surviving in a ruined world. Words are paltry and weak in such moments.

Sorry, brother," Chavez said, his voice choked. "Gonna miss you."

Hemingway hugged Chavez back, tears squeezing from between closed eyelids. "So long, amigo."

The rest of the SEALs took turns saying goodbye. I hung back. Gabe, Mike, Tyrel, and Grabovsky all gave their condolences as well. I was the last to approach.

"Been nice knowing you, Chuck."

He reached out a hand. I shook it. "Same to you, Caleb. You're good people. Wish we could have had more time."

"Same here."

318

When I was done, Gellar approached. His eyes glimmered wetly in the darkness. "How do you want to handle it?"

"You mind, Master Chief?"

"Not at all."

Hemingway nodded and looked at the ground. "From the side, if it's all the same. My sister will probably want an open casket. You're gonna come back for my body, right?"

"Soon as we can."

"Good. Let my sister know I went down fighting, okay?"

Gellar put a hand on Hemingway's shoulder. "No problem. You ready?"

The young man took one last, long look up at the sky. "Wish the stars were out tonight. Be nice to see 'em one last time."

He made a 'get on with it' motion with his hand. Gellar dropped his pack, produced a small .22 pistol, and threaded a long suppressor to the barrel.

"Good luck, brothers," Hemingway said. "Go save some lives."

"See you soon, brother," Gellar said. Then he aimed the gun and put a single round into the side of Hemingway's head.

The young man went slack. Chavez stepped forward, caught him, and eased him to the ground. Once there, he and the other SEALs arranged him carefully and folded his arms over his chest. Lowell stepped forward, closed Hemingway's eyes, and wrapped the fallen man's right hand around his MK 9 and his left around his dagger. When he was finished, he dug something out of his pack and put two coins on Hemingway's eyelids. Even in the dark I could see the unmistakable luster of gold.

"For your journey," Lowell said quietly.

"Anybody got anything they want to say?" Gellar asked. No one answered.

"All right then," Gellar went on. "Whatever you're feeling right now, put it in a box. We still have work to do. Miller, you're on the M3. Chavez, collect Chuck's ammo and split it up. Captain

319

Grabovsky, I need you to notify Central and send a GPS fix for this location."

"No problem."

"Let's clean our weapons and get moving," Mike said.

I wiped down my machete and knife with alcohol-soaked wipes I carried in my pack. That done, I checked Gabe's face for blood spatter and he did the same for me. We were both clean. I wiped my gloves down just to be on the safe side. The Phage was deadly and irreversible once inside a host, but outside a host, even a mild disinfectant such as soapy water, vinegar, or grain alcohol could kill it.

When everyone was finished, Mike asked Grabovsky to check his tablet.

"The other teams are on station," Grabovsky said. "We're holding up the show."

Mike turned and began walking. "Then let's not keep 'em waiting."

FORTY-ONE

The forest thinned and the ground sloped sharply downward. Mike ordered a halt when we reached the edge of the woodlands. He and Grabovsky covered themselves with a rain poncho to shield prying eyes from the light emitted by the ruggedized tablet. A few minutes later, they emerged and Mike motioned for us to gather close.

"We've gone over the plan before, but we're doing it again." He pointed at the field east of us. "There's two-hundred yards of waist high grass between us and the camp's field of fire. We'll get across that pretty easy. The hard part is gonna be the last hundred and fifty yards. Kim was smart when he built this place. All the fields are to the south where the irrigation ditches are. They use the slaves to keep the killing ground cut low so guys like us can't sneak up on 'em. But that's exactly what we're gonna have to do. And that's not the worst of it. When we get to the wall, we'll probably have infected to deal with. That said, we got a few things working in our favor."

Mike began to count off on his fingers as he spoke.

"One, they've been hit with AIM-38. Satellites have been watching close ever since. The slaves are laid up, and so are most of the guards. But about two dozen or so have been seen moving around, so we have to assume they were inoculated and the enemy knows what's going on. Two, they don't know when, or if, we're going to attack. They probably heard the helicopters, but General Jacobs has been making sure to keep plenty of aircraft flying

321

around here at night, so they might not think too much of it. But that's a big 'might'. Don't count on it. Three, no matter how many are left, we got 'em outnumbered. So remember, let the other units assault the main compound. Our job is to take out the guards on our side, breach the wall, and assault the command center. If we don't find who we're looking for there, we'll search this place inch by inch until we do. As soon as the assault starts, Blackhawks are going to be in the air searching for runners on FLIR. If we don't find our people here, we might have to chase 'em through the woods, so be ready for that. Everybody clear?"

We said we were.

"Good. Let's get it done."

I put on my ghillie suit, as did the others. When we were ready, Gabe, Mike, and I led the way across the field. Grabovsky, Gellar, and Tyrel came next, the remaining SEALs departing after them in pairs. Miller and Chavez hung toward the back with the Carl Gustaf. Between them, they had five rounds: two high explosive anti-structure munitions (ASMs), two fragmentation anti-personnel rounds, and one star shell. The star shell, otherwise known as an illumination round, could be fired into the air to cast light on the encampment. I'd seen them used before, and for the brief time they were in the air, they turned night into day over a small area.

It took us half an hour to cover the distance to the open ground surrounding the prison camp. Mike radioed for everyone to hold position. I looked over at him and saw him produce a suppressed sniper rifle he'd been carrying in a waterproof sleeve on the way out here. Now that I could see it, I recognized it as a bolt-action .300 Winchester magnum, or Win-mag, as it's commonly known. His rifle was more powerful and had better range than the 7.62x51 rounds Gabe and I were using. I also noticed the Win-mag was suppressed with a can nearly a foot long, which almost made me laugh. Even suppressed, .300 Win-mag is loud enough to hear at long distances.

Better than nothing.

There were about ten yards between us. From where we lay, we had a clear field of view of the western wall of the compound. The place looked much different at ground level than it did in the satellite photos. The wall was twelve feet high and built much like the one back at Hollow Rock. There was a deep trench on the outside from which I could hear the moans of infected. The trench sloped upward toward a double palisade of telephone poles. It occurred to me I had not seen a single roadside pole since arriving in ROC territory. Now I knew why.

The space between the inner and outer walls of the palisade had been filled in with dirt and gravel to reinforce the wall. There was a tightly packed berm butting up against the inner wall to buttress it against the weight of large hordes. The fact this place had been built in less than a year spoke to how hard the KPA had driven the prisoners trapped here. A familiar, red-tinged anger rose up and filled me with a desire to come to grips with the people responsible for this atrocity. I almost breathed a sigh of relief.

There you are. Been waiting for you to show up.

"There's four guards on our side," Mike's voice told me though my earpiece. "Gabe, you take the two on the north side. I'll take the guard tower in the middle. Caleb, you take the rover on the south side. You see anybody in the tower in that direction?"

"Wait one." I switched to thermal and used the zoom function to examine the tower. It was empty."

"Nope. It's clear."

"All right. Stand by. Gotta call the bossman."

Mike switched over to the command net and spent a couple of minutes in whispered conversation.

"Listen up," Mike said into our squad's channel when he was finished. "Switch over to the all stations net. Once we breach the wall, switch back to our channel. Acknowledge."

Everyone did, and then switched frequencies. The net was mostly inactive, only the occasional check-in between squads breaking the silence. There were six other squads positioned around the killing ground, all of us designated delta. We were Delta One, being that we had the senior man on the battlefield in our squad.

323

"All delta stations, this is Delta One. It's time to do what we came here for. Acquire your targets and sound off when ready. All other stations, maintain radio silence."

It took two minutes for the other delta squads to respond. I used that time to dial in my thermal imager so it had the same magnification as a scope set to six power. My view of the rover was crisp and clear, the imager producing resolution high enough to make out the features of his face, albeit indistinctly.

I'd felt bad using my black card to procure the NV/IR scope back in the Springs. The Army didn't have many of them, and they were in high demand. But considering the stakes I was facing, I was glad I had taken it.

"All stations, Delta One. Fire on my mark. Three, two, one, *mark*."

I fired. My target went stiff and stumbled back a few steps, but stayed on his feet. I fired again, and this time he went down, landed sideways, and fell into the interior of the wall. To my left I heard the muffled report of Mike's Win-mag and Gabe's SCAR. The latter fired three times. Mike looked over at me. I gave him a thumbs up. Then he looked at Gabe, who did the same.

"All delta stations, Delta One. Report status."

The other teams had all taken out their targets. I heard no sound of gunfire or explosions from inside the compound. So far, so good.

Mike switched over to the command net and had another whispered conversation, then switched back.

"All stations, Delta One. Initiate phase two."

There was a rustle in the grass behind me. I looked back and saw Miller's broad form standing next to Chavez's slender one. Smith was on his feet moving in their direction in case they needed additional shells. Chavez opened the breach, put in a shell, closed the breach, and slapped Miller on the shoulder. He did not bother to announce the back blast area was clear. If there was anyone behind us, they were enemies, and I sincerely hoped they ran face-first into the blowback from the Venturi damper.

Miller did not bother to announce three times that he was firing, nor did Chavez put a hand on his back to steady him. Chavez was smart enough to know what was about to happen, and a man Miller's size did not need someone to brace him. He was plenty strong enough to fire the M3 on his own.

I was glad I was wearing my earplugs when the M3 went off. The first shell, an anti-structure munition, covered the hundred and fifty yards in a blink and detonated against the wall. When the smoke cleared, the outer wall had been blown open on the lower half, spilling out a few tons of dirt and rocks, but had not been fully breached. Chavez loaded another shell and Miller sent it downrange. This one hit higher on the wall, causing a four-foot-wide section of the outer wall to collapse. As it did, a tidal wave of ballast spilled out, filling in a large portion of the trench below.

One more ought to do it.

I looked back and saw Smith hand Chavez another ASM. The M3 roared again, and this time when the dust cleared, I could see a path into the camp.

While all this was going on, I heard LAW rockets, mortars, and more recoilless rifles firing at other sections of the wall. The urge to charge headlong into the fray was almost overwhelming. Only the discipline instilled in me by over two-and-a-half years of military service kept me in place.

"All stations, Delta One," Mike said over the radio. "Proceed with phase three. Delta Two, you're in command until I get back on the net."

"Roger that, Delta One."

"All right," Mike shouted to us as he stood up. "Switch to the squad channel and drop your suits. Time to go to work."

We did not bother taking off our ghillie suits the proper way. The ten of us produced knives and cut our way out of them to save time. We could always make new ones. Once free, we did a quick comms check, then set out for the breach.

The final assault had begun.

FORTY-TWO

The SCAR was on a two-point sling with a pull tab that allowed me to quickly loosen or tighten it. I pulled it outward to loosen the sling and moved the SCAR around to my back. Gabe ran in my direction as I did so. I slowed my pace so he could peel off the Velcro straps holding a suppressed M-4 to my pack. When I had it in my hands, we switched places and I did the same for him. Mike had simply left his sniper rifle where it lay and switched weapons before we set out across the killing ground.

Despite the instincts roaring at me to go as fast as I could, I matched Mike's speed. He kept us at a quick but even pace. This was not because he was out of shape—he wasn't—but because he wanted Chavez, Miller, and the seals carrying M3 shells to be able to keep up. They did so with no trouble, and I had the impression they could go faster if Mike urged them to.

When we reached the towering hole in the prison camp's outer perimeter, Mike made us stop and scan the trench. There were infected visible from where we stood, but the ones immediately beneath the wall when it collapsed were buried under tons of rubble. The outflow of rocks and dirt had created a bridge across the trench that would allow us to avoid the undead completely.

"Those ghouls ain't made it up yet," Mike said over the squad channel, "but they will. When we get in there, watch your backs. Turn on your lasers and let's move."

I activated the PEQ-15 on my M-4 and followed Mike as he ran for the breach. Gabe was beside him on the left, and I took position on his right. I heard Tyrel curse at us as he caught up and took position on our six.

"You fuckers forget about me or something?" he shouted.

"Just waiting for you to catch up," Mike yelled back.

All further banter was forgotten as we reached the pile of rubble. To either side of us, undead eyes stared and clawed fingers reached in our direction. None of them were close enough to grab us, so we ignored them and focused on the path ahead. The slope up the berm was steep, and I had to put a hand on the ground at several points to keep my balance. The others seemed to have some trouble as well.

Gabe and Mike made it through the breach first and took up defensive positions. I made it in ahead of Tyrel and knelt five yards to Mike's right, covering the south side of the prison yard. On the southern and eastern walls I could see troops pouring in through other breaches, most of them even more heavily armed than my squad. The Army had spared no expense for this offensive.

I wondered how the Resistance forces and spec ops guys at the other internment camps were faring. I also wondered how long it would be before the F-18s from one of the Navy's last remaining aircraft carriers stationed two-hundred miles offshore began dropping JDAMs on outposts manned solely by KPA troops.

During the ops briefings, Jacobs had stated unequivocally he was not looking for a surrender. The North Koreans had been given ample opportunity to do so, and had steadfastly refused. The time for diplomacy was over. His intention now was to destroy the ROC, root and branch.

Initially, I'd had my doubts. The Army's history since Vietnam did not really bear that philosophy out. I could only imagine the political repercussions if the KPA surrendered and we killed them anyway. But it was clear to me now Jacobs had not been fucking around—he'd meant every word of it.

Behind me, I heard the rest of the squad make it safely into the compound. I looked northward toward our destination: the command building.

"Break off by fire teams," Mike said. "Miller, Chavez, hang back and-"

An explosion interrupted him. The light dampers in my NVGs kept the sudden illumination from blinding me, but it still hurt my eyes. I looked toward the explosion and felt my stomach sink.

"Shit," I said. "They're hitting the slave quarters."

In an instant, I dropped the M-4 and switched back to my SCAR. A pair of KPA troops were loading a shell into a mortar that was obviously zeroed where the prisoners slept. I flipped up my NVGs, took aim, and fired a shot at each man center of mass. Two more shots rang out to my left as Gabe opened fire on them as well. They were dead in seconds.

"All stations, Delta One, clear the net." Mike radioed. I wasn't on the all stations net, but I assumed the radio chatter stopped immediately. "All stations, Delta One. They're hitting the prisoners with mortars. All delta squads break off and search for heavy weapons. You see anybody come near 'em, you drop the fuckers. All EOD personnel get your asses to the prisoner's quarters and start searching for explosives."

Mike switched back to the squad channel and waved a hand over his shoulder. "Let's go. Our mission hasn't changed."

I gave one last look toward the prisoner's longhouses. People were half crawling and carrying each other outside away from the fire. They made it just far enough to get clear of the blaze and then collapsed to the ground. I wondered how many had died in the initial blast, and how many more were too weak to escape.

Can't think about that now. Get moving.

We set a hard pace toward the command building. It was a simple two-story structure, eighty feet by sixty feet, and constructed of cinder blocks, mortar, and other scavenged construction materials. Someone inside must have seen us coming because a window opened and a dim figure brought a rifle up to its shoulder. I stopped, aimed, and fired. The shot was rushed, and I only managed to catch him in the arm. But it was enough to get him to drop his weapon and retreat inside.

No one else tried to shoot at us as we approached. When we were within seventy-five yards, Mike ordered a halt.

"Smith, take out the front door."

"Yes sir." Smith unslung his LAW rocket. The rest of us put our earplugs in and went prone. Smith went down to one knee.

"Back blast area clear?" Smith called out.

"Clear," Chavez responded.

"Rocket out!"

The LAW made the deafening *crack-BANG* I'd heard so many times since joining the Army. Ahead of us, the front entrance to the command building disappeared in a cloud of smoke and flying debris.

"On your feet!" Mike commanded. "Let's go!"

Gabe, Tyrel, and I comprised one of the fire teams. Mike, Lowell, and Smith broke off together, as did Chavez and Gellar. Grabovsky and Miller were the last to pair up. Our original plan was to have Chavez and Miller work together, put Grabovsky in Mike's place, and Gellar and Hemingway would be their own fire team. But Hemingway was not with us anymore.

Not now. Plenty of time for that later.

We stacked up outside what was left of the entrance. The steel double doors were twisted scraps of metal strewn around the small reception area. I stacked up first on my side with Mike standing across from me. Most of the squad stacked up behind him as they arrived. Only Gabe and Tyrel stood on my side. Mike pointed at his eyes, then at me, and with his left hand, counted down three, two, one, *go*.

I entered the room, weapon raised, and broke right, sweeping as much territory as I could. Mike was right behind me covering the left side. The rest of the squad entered quickly. Someone stood up from behind the reception desk on my left and shouted something in Korean. I put the green laser on his forehead and pulled the trigger twice, but not before he squeezed off a short burst from an AK. The weapon had been pointed at Chavez, who had fallen straight to his back, aimed his carbine at the gunman, and let off four shots. The rounds fired from the AK flew harmlessly over Chavez's prone body and pelted the wall behind him. The gunman himself fell down dead.

"Well that was stupid," Gabe said behind me.

I agreed. He would have had better luck if he'd simply fired through the flimsy wood of the desk where he'd hidden.

"Thank God for idiots," I said. "It's a miracle he survived that blast. Fucker must have been stone deaf."

"Don't count on all of 'em being stupid," Mike said. "Or deaf. Let's clear the room."

We did, finding no further attackers waiting. It was not a difficult sweep. The only things occupying the room were the desk, a few ugly couches, soiled chairs, and debris from where the rocket hit the front door.

"Smith, Miller, you two stay here and watch our six. Everybody else, drop your gear behind the reception desk. We go in with guns, grenades, and breaching charges only. Miller, keep that M3 handy in case someone tries to ruin our party."

"Yes sir," Miller replied.

"Smith, it probably wouldn't hurt to have a LAW ready to go. Just don't shoot it in here."

Smith looked insulted. "I know better than that, sir."

"I know. Just makes me feel better to say it. Gellar, Chavez, you two are with me. Grabovsky, you're with Gabe's team."

"Yes sir."

We dropped our gear behind the desk as ordered. It made quite a pile, and I was glad to be shed of it for the moment. Moving through buildings is delicate work. Doing it while carrying a full rucksack, a sniper rifle, and a LAW rocket is just shy of suicidal. When I was done letting things fall to the ground, I was down to my M-4 rifle, Beretta sidearm, two frag grenades, four flashbangs, spare ammo, Ka-bar fighting dagger, and a Spyderco folding knife. I felt light as a ballerina compared to a few moments ago.

"We'll take this side," Mike said, pointing to the right side of the room. "You take the other door. Keep 'em on a swivel, you hear?"

"We hear," Gabe said.

I met Mike's eyes before he turned to leave. "Be careful."

"Same to you, son."

I turned and followed my team to the door. It was close to the wall on the right side, so we all stacked up to the left. Gabe searched the edges of the door, looking for signs of booby traps.

"You know what? Fuck this."

We all carried a breaching charge in a bag hanging from the back of our web belts. Gabe took his out, stuck it to the door, and activated it.

"Ten seconds," he said.

We all backed off and covered our ears. The charge went off and sent the door crashing into the wall opposite the lock. Gabe waited for the dust to clear, then peeked around the corner.

"Clear. Let's move."

Gabe took point, and the rest of us followed.

FORTY-THREE

We made fast progress down the hallway.

The doors to the rooms we passed were scavenged from surrounding houses, most of them nothing more than flimsy panels of thin wood and two-by-two struts. The firm application of boot to handle was all it took to open them. We found offices and storage rooms similar to those at any Army administrative building. After we cleared the last door, Mike radioed they were almost finished with their side. Gabe turned to look at us.

"Okay. If there's anyone in the building, they're upstairs. Shoot if you have to, but don't forget why we're here. If the people we're looking for are in this building, we take them alive. Understood?"

The rest of us nodded. If Grabovsky had any objections to Gabe taking control of the team, he did not voice them. The two had worked together in the past, so he probably knew as well as I did what Gabe was capable of.

The big man led the way up the stairs with Tyrel close behind, Grabovsky following, and me watching our six. Halfway up, Gabe raised a fist to signal a halt. He turned, pointed at his eyes, and then pointed downward. The hallway was dark, even through NVGs. Somehow, though, Gabe had spotted a tripwire. My father used to tell me there was no substitute for experience, and as usual, he was right.

"Delta One, Wolfman," Gabe said, using his prearranged radio handle. "We're in the south stairwell. Just found a grenade on a tripwire."

"Copy, Wolfman," Mike responded. "We'll keep our eyes peeled."

Gabe looked at Tyrel. "You're pretty good with booby traps, right?"

"That I am."

Tyrel crouched, followed the wire to where it connected to a grenade with the pin barely held in place, and disarmed the trap. When he was finished, he pushed the pin back into the grenade and bent it down to secure it.

"Just in case," he muttered to himself.

We moved slowly up the stairs, not wanting to risk hitting another trap. Finally we reached the door. Gabe tried it and found it locked. After carefully searching for signs of tampering, he motioned me upward.

"You got your lock picks?"

"Always."

I squatted down in front of the lock. It was a heavy steel security door held shut with a standard lock on the handle and a dead bolt above. Neither one was difficult to defeat. In less than a minute, I had them both unlocked.

"Back off a second," Gabe said.

I took a few steps down the stairs, as did Grabovsky and Tyrel. Gabe slowly opened the door, being wary of traps. After a few moments, he opened it fully and motioned us through. We walked the corridor, looking for traps or alarms. No one found anything. There were eight doors in the hall, most of them made of the same insubstantial material as those downstairs. One, however, was heavier and made of steel.

"So what now?" I asked.

Gabe peered down the hallway. "We let Mike get his team into position."

A minute or so passed. We stood quietly, minds and bodies on high alert, and waited. Finally the door opened at the far end of the hallway and Mike's team came through. Mike was looking through a monocular IR device. He gave his team the same instructions Gabe had given ours. When his people were in place, the two men met in the middle of the hall and had a brief, quiet discussion. Then both of them nodded and Gabe came back toward us.

"We'll do a tandem breach," he said. "Everybody pick a door."

"What about that one?" Tyrel asked, nodding his head toward the steel reinforced entrance.

Gabe hooked a thumb over his shoulder. Chavez was headed our way with a shotgun in his hands. The weapon had a jagged breaching muzzle on the end.

"Heard you need a locksmith," Chavez said.

"That we do," Gabe said. "Get your charges in place."

Both teams moved through the hallway sticking breaching charges to doors. When they were all in place, Gabe raised a hand.

"Set timers to ten seconds and stand by."

The squad complied. I put mine on the steel door's handle while Chavez chambered a breaching round and hooked the muzzle onto the top hinge.

"You good, Chavez?" Gabe asked.

"Ready when you are."

Gabe waited until everyone signaled they were ready.

"Chavez, when the timer hits five, blow the hinges."

"Roger that."

Gabe looked around, made sure he had everyone's attention, and dropped his hand. The squad activated the charges simultaneously and backed off. I stood behind Chavez, sidearm in hand. Chavez counted down in a whisper.

"Ten, nine, eight, seven, six, *hit it*."

The shotgun roared loudly in the enclosed space. The first hinge shattered, pieces of metal pinging to the floor. Chavez racked another round into the chamber and hit the lower hinge. It disintegrated as well. Shortly after the second shot, the breaching charges made a series of tremendous thumps, and the doors flew open. Chavez backed off to switch weapons. The rest of us took a knee by our respective doors, led with our sidearms, and looked inside. Behind me, I heard Gabe, Grabovsky, and Tyrel enter their rooms. I stayed where I was. Chavez started to enter, but I grabbed him by the pants leg and dragged him back.

"Stay here," I said. My tone brooked no argument.

I stayed kneeling by the door and looked around the room. It was big for an office, about twenty-five feet square. There was a bed to my left covered in rumbled sheets. A small wood-burning stove stood nearby, its metal chimney extending up through the ceiling, and a pile of firewood dumped haphazardly beside it. A dingy sofa took up the wall next to the door, and across the room, there was a highboy complete with water pitcher and bowl, a desk, bookshelves, and several file cabinets. There were no windows. A single chair stood behind the desk.

The chair was unoccupied, but the room was not.

A man in the uniform of a KPA officer stood behind a squat, pudgy, sweaty little man with a bald head and a thin, wispy combover. The desk and chair stood between us. The officer had his back to the wall and held the pudgy guy in place with an arm around his throat and a gun to his head. Both were obviously Korean.

"Either of you speak English?" I asked, keeping my gun aimed at the officer's head and my body as concealed as possible.

"I do," the pudgy man answered.

The KPA officer yelled something at him and drove the gun hard against his temple. The pudgy little guy replied in Korean. The officer seemed to think about it, then motioned in our direction with the gun.

"You know who I am?" the pudgy guy asked. I did, but studied his face a few seconds just to be sure.

335

"Park Heon-Woo, if I'm not mistaken."

"You here to find me, yes?"

"Yes."

"You not here to kill me?"

"Not as it stands, no. But the other guy is kind of pissing me off."

The KPA officer asked another harshly spoken question. Park answered as calmly as he could.

"What's he saying?" I asked.

"He say tell you to back off. He use me as hostage so he escape."

"That's not going to happen."

"What you going to do?"

"I need you to stand very, very still, Park Heon-Woo. Your life depends on it, do you understand? No matter what you see, *do not move*."

"Okay."

"Tell him we're backing off. Tell him we're willing to make a deal. Tell him we don't want to kill him, we'd rather he cooperate."

"You no understand what he told about you. He think you torture him to death."

"Okay, fine. Just tell him we're backing off then."

"Okay."

Park said something else in Korean. The officer yelled at me as if volume would increase my comprehension of a language I did not speak, then motioned again with his gun. Clearly he wanted me to stand back from the door. I lowered my weapon.

In my peripheral vision, I could see the others stacking up for a dynamic entry. Gabe was immediately to my right, Grabovsky and Tyrel behind him. Chavez stayed on my side, out of sight. I put my free hand back where the KPA officer couldn't see it and signaled for them to stay put.

"Remember Park. Do. Not. Move."

"Okay."

I began to ease away from the doorframe until I was out of sight. Then I stood up, leaned quickly back in, raised my Beretta, and fired once.

Park jerked as if slapped. The right side of his face was splattered with blood, but it wasn't his. The KPA officer went limp and slumped to the floor, the backside of his skull a shattered, bleeding mess. My shot had taken him in the forehead just right of center. I let out a slow breath and entered the room.

"You okay?" I asked Park.

He said something in Korean. The rest of the team entered the room. The little guy looked downright terrified.

"Hey," I said, grabbing him gently by the shoulders and giving him a little shake. "I wasn't lying. We're not here to kill you. But we do need access to your research. Do you have it here?"

"Y…yes. All here."

"Where?"

"There." He pointed at the row of file cabinets.

I gave him a hard glare. "Seriously? You're concocting a vaccine that could save the world from the infected, and you keep your research in a bunch of fucking *file cabinets*?"

Park shrugged. "Is People's Army. They always cheap bastards."

I stared at him a few seconds, and then shook my head. "Unbelievable."

"Kim Ji-Su," Gabe said. "Where is she?"

"You come for her too?"

Gabe stepped closer, looming over the little man. He flipped up his goggles. His face was a sculpture of hard angles, thin slash of a

337

mouth, and stony gray eyes colder than a Siberian winter. His lips peeled back from his teeth as he spoke.

"Where. Is. She?"

"Okay, okay. I take you. Okay?"

Gabe grabbed him by the arms, iron fingers digging into soft flesh. "Don't lie to me. Do you understand? You lie to me, and I will hurt you."

Park grimaced in pain. "Okay, okay. No lie. I take you."

Gabe released him. "Lead the way."

As we exited the room, Mike and his team came over. Gabe gave them a quick rundown.

"So you're the miserable little shit that started all this," Mike said.

His face was drawn tight and there was a look of barely contained rage in his eyes. The pronouncement startled me, as did Mike's boiling anger. I'd known the man most of my life, and I had never seen him this enraged.

"Mike, what are you talking about?" I asked.

Mike glared a few seconds longer. "Gellar," he said, "you and your men find some boxes or something and start gathering every piece of paper and electronic device in this place. If you need help, use the command net."

"Yes sir. Where will you be?"

"We're going to find the other one."

"Colonel, are you sure you don't want a couple of my guys to come along?"

"Yes, I'm sure. Do what I asked you to do, Master Chief."

Mike's tone was hard as granite. Gellar nodded once. "Yes sir. We're on it."

To Park, he said, "Let's go."

We left the building and set out for the north side of the compound with Park Heon-Woo leading the way.

FORTY-FOUR

We passed the remnants of what little fighting there had been.

Between the Resistance and the JSOC operators, nearly a hundred and fifty troops had descended on the Klamath Basin internment camp. At a glance, I guessed they had run into a force of less than thirty KPA troops still able to fight. Nonetheless, there were dead Resistance Fighters and a few wounded operators being loaded onto stretchers.

"Must have inoculated their best guys," I said.

Gabe turned his attention to where I was looking. "Seems that way. Put up a hell of a fight."

"For what good it did them."

A platoon of support troops had arrived and were setting up floodlights and medical tents. The special operations guys still on their feet were sweeping the base for survivors while the Resistance helped the prisoners forced to flee their quarters. The fire started by the mortar was burning itself out, but the wreckage created by the explosion was still throwing off a choking cloud of smoke. Through the smoldering haze, I caught the outline of a charred body.

A very small charred body.

I looked away.

Not now. Feel it later. Put it in a box and keep moving.

340

There was a small inner compound on the northern side of the prison yard. During the intel briefings we had surmised it was a prison within a prison, a place to torture those who committed whatever petty violations the KPA deemed worthy of punishment. People went in, bodies came out. The bodies were wrapped in sheets, and promptly burned in a large pit, so it was impossible for our satellites and spy planes to ascertain their condition. The fact that Park was leading us toward the inner compound led me to believe perhaps we had misjudged its purpose.

I looked up and saw banks of solar panels on the roof, enough to produce sufficient energy to power several pre-Outbreak households. I'd seen them before on satellite imagery, but had not thought much of them. I figured the KPA used it as a place to charge radios and allow officers to enjoy comforts the rank and file could not. Now I found myself wondering what their true purpose might be.

"What is that place," I asked, pointing.

Park looked like he didn't want to answer. "You see soon."

Gabe grabbed him and pinched a nerve in the little man's elbow. "I'd like to know too. Answer the question."

Park's face twisted in agony. "Is lab! Is lab for testing!"

Gabe released the nerve. "Can we expect any trouble in there?"

"Not sure. Maybe guards stay, maybe fight." Park pointed toward the pile of dead KPA troops.

"So Kim Ji-Su might not be there?"

Park shook his head emphatically. "She no leave. No place to go."

It was as strange pronouncement, but it had the ring of truth to it. Gabe and I shared a glance.

"Keep moving," Gabe said.

We reached the main entrance to the lab, and as expected, it was locked. The walls were solid cinder block with no windows. I studied the lock and shook my head.

"Don't have picks for that," I said. "We should radio for one of Gellar's men to bring the Carl Gustaf."

"No time for that." Gabe handed Park off to Mike and Grabovsky, both of whom put a hand on him in case he decided to run.

"Give me a hand," Gabe said, motioning to me. "We're out of breaching charges, but not grenades."

He produced a roll of 100 mile an hour cloth duct tape. I peeled off a few sections and used them to secure one of my frag grenades to the door handle. Gabe did the same with the hinges. When we were ready, we motioned for the others to get to safety. They moved to the side of the building and waited around the corner.

"We'll have four seconds," Gabe said. "When the spoons pop, run like hell and count to three. Then hit the ground in a tiny little ball and let your back plate take the hits. Okay?"

"Sure."

Gabe used a multi-tool to straighten the tines of the pins on the two grenades he'd set up. This was an important step; if he tried to pull them simultaneously without straightening them first, the grenades might dislodge from the duct tape. The pins in modern grenades are not easy to remove. When I watch old movies of John Wayne or someone pulling pins with their teeth, I laugh. If someone tried that in real life they would need a skilled dentist to repair the damage.

I grabbed the pin of the grenade I'd set and held spherical portion in place with my free hand. "Just for the record," I said. "This is a bad idea."

"Duly noted. On three."

I nodded. Gabe counted down, and on three, we pulled. The pins came loose and the spoons popped into the air. I turned right, Gabe turned left, and as my father would have said, we ran like our backs were on fire and our asses were catching.

Three, two, one.

342

I managed five long, running strides before I hit the dirt and curled into a ball with the back plate of my body armor toward the grenades. I was outside the kill radius, but not outside the range of shrapnel. As I slid to a halt, the grenades detonated. I felt the thump of explosives through the ground, the impact causing a hollow feeling to bloom in my chest. Something smacked into my back plate, and something else hit the sole of my boot. I waited a second, and then sat up. The first thing I checked was my boot. A piece of shrapnel had cut a furrow in the tread, but there was no other damage. Gabe got up and approached.

"Check my back," he said. I did. There were a couple of hits on his armor, but nothing on flesh.

"You're good."

Gabe did the same for me and let out a low whistle. "About two inches lower, and that could have been a problem."

I glared at him. "Next time you decide do some crazy shit like that, get someone else to help you."

"Quit you're bitching. You're starting to sound like Eric." Gabe keyed his radio. "Door is breached."

The door lay in pieces spread several meters around the empty hole where it once stood. The two of us stacked up outside the entrance and waited for the rest of the squad to arrive. When they did, we gave the cloud of smoke and dust a few seconds to clear, and then entered.

Like the previous building, there was a small reception area and doors leading to branching hallways. Mike hauled Park inside and shoved him into the lobby.

"Where is she?"

"You follow," he said, beckoning with his hands. He walked to a door on the right hand side of the room, produced a strange looking key on a string from under his shirt, and unlocked the door.

"You first," Gabe said, motioning with his rifle.

"Okay, okay."

Park went through the entrance. We could see illumination ahead, so we flipped up our NVGs. There were dark red emergency lights on the ceiling every twenty feet or so, casting the hallway the color of spilled blood. The air was hot and stuffy and difficult to breath. We followed Park down a plain corridor to another door at the end. The little man unlocked this one as well, entered a t-shaped passageway, and turned left. We followed him until the hall terminated at a double door.

"This Ji-Su office. She inside."

"What makes you so sure?" Gabe asked.

"She not in lab," Park hooked a thumb over one shoulder. I looked where he was pointing. There was a door there with an indicator box beside the handle. It looked like the kind that used a key card for entry. There were two lights on the box, both dark at the moment.

"What's in the lab?" I asked.

Park paled. "You no want to see."

"We'll deal with that later," Mike said, forestalling further questions. "Park, open the door."

He did, using the strange little key. Then he stepped back.

"You go. She inside."

Mike grabbed him and shoved him in first. "Lead the way, shitbird."

Park stumbled, then regained his balance and took a few tentative steps inside, hands raised. "Is safe," he said.

Mike and Gabe looked at me. My reputation for being the best pistol shot in the First Recon evidently preceded me. Gabe must have thought pretty highly of my skills in that regard if he was willing to let me go first. I stacked up on the edge of the door, and as fast as I could, stepped inside, raised my pistol, and took a knee.

The room was small. There was a cot, a desk, file cabinets, and a small wash basin. A woman of perhaps forty sat in a chair in front of the desk. In one hand, she held a picture. In the other, she held a Makarov pistol.

The rest of the squad filed in behind me. The woman looked up. She had a round, prematurely wrinkled face, stringy hair, and an expression of infinite weariness. Her eyes were the empty black pools of a person who knew only horror and suffering. She looked at Park and smiled weakly.

"Are they here to kill me?" she asked in perfect English.

"No."

"Interesting. Which one of you is in charge?" she asked, shifting her gaze to me, and then to the men standing behind me.

"That would be me," Mike said, stepping forward. I kept my pistol aimed steadily at her forehead. If that Makarov moved, there would be consequences.

"I assume I'm speaking to Kim Ji-Su?" Mike asked.

A nod. "You are."

"Ms. Kim, I need you to put that gun down, if you don't mind."

Her gaze lowered and she looked at the weapon. "When the guards left, one of them handed this to me. He said if they didn't come back to do my duty."

"And what would that be?" Mike asked.

Kim Ji-Su laughed bitterly. "What do you think, American?"

Very slowly, she placed the gun on the ground and kicked it away. "I'm not dying for them. Not after what they did to me for all these years. Not after what they *made* me do. They took everything from me, but I won't give them my life."

I lowered my weapon and stood up. Mike stepped forward slowly and knelt in front of Kim Ji-Su.

"We're not here to hurt you. We're here to rescue you."

The petite woman looked at Mike with those desolate eyes. "From what? Myself? Good luck with that."

"You're work, the vaccine. We can help you."

"How? By making me your prisoner instead of theirs?"

"No. By offering you a chance at redemption. And, if you want it, freedom."

"Freedom," she let the word fall from her lips. "I've been a slave since I was a young girl. The Party realized very quickly I was a bright student. A genius. They put me to work doing…this." She made a vague gesture toward the lab. "There is no freedom from the things I've done."

"You're wrong," Mike said gently. "You can't change what's happened, but you can make a difference going forward." He stood up and looked down at her. "I won't force you. If you don't want to help us, I'll walk you out of here myself and take you somewhere you'll be safe. Your life won't be easy there, but no one will force you to do anything you don't want to."

Kim Ji-Su shook her head. "I would not know what to do with myself. Freedom is for people who know how to live. I do not."

"Then come with us. Help us put an end to all this."

Mike held out his hand. Kim Ji-Su looked at it for a long moment, and I saw the faintest glimmer of hope kindle in her eyes. Then slowly, hesitantly, she put her fingers in Mike's palm. Mike closed his hand around hers and gave it a gentle pat.

"Come on, Ji-Su. Let's get you out of here."

FORTY-FIVE

In the darkness before dawn, the helicopters returned.

They brought with them crates of inoculant. Medical personnel immediately set to work inoculating the prisoners, and, to my surprise, the enemy troops laid up in their barracks. The latter were strip searched, forced to don ill-fitting orange coveralls and slippers, and secured hand and foot with prison shackles. Once restrained, the prisoners were held together by long chains connected to their ankles. Armed guards surrounded them, their dour expressions saying 'give me an excuse'. The KPA troops were too sick to fight at the moment, but I wondered how that would change once the AIM-38 virus wore off.

I asked Mike if I could go and help the medical personnel.

"No," he said. "Sorry son, but our orders are to stay here with these two until their transport arrives."

We brought Park and Kim to the lobby and had them sit together on one of the couches. They sat as far apart from each other as they could. I did not detect the bitterness of hatred between them. Rather, it seemed as if they were embarrassed to be in one another's presence. There was probably a story behind that, but I was too tired to ask. And I doubted they would have told me anyway.

Mike got on the radio and asked for Gellar's status. They were still busy packing up files in the other building. Mike acknowledged and got on the command net. I heard him give a sitrep and ask for assistance securing the contents of the two buildings. Shortly thereafter, I heard the searing roar of turbofan engines overhead.

Fighter jets. Interesting.

Their arrival was followed by a stealth Blackhawk touching down on the open ground in front of the lab building. The cargo door opened and a man with a colonel's rank insignia stepped out, along with four heavily armed soldiers. Judging by their aggressive bearing and obvious confidence, I was thinking Delta Force.

"Which one of you is Colonel Holden?" the officer asked.

"That's me," Mike said.

"Colonel Andrew O'Conner." The two shook hands. "I believe we've met."

Mike nodded. "I remember you."

"Are they here?"

"Right inside," Mike said.

"Do they need medical attention?"

"No. They came peacefully."

O'Conner nodded. "Good, good. Have your men bring them out."

Mike turned and motioned to Gabe and Grabovsky, who went inside and came back out with Park Heon-Woo and Kim Ji-Su in tow. O'Conner held a hand toward the Blackhawk.

"If you'll come this way, please," he said. He was being polite, but it was clear he wasn't really asking. One way or another, they were getting on that helicopter.

The two went along quietly and climbed aboard the bird. Just before the door shut, Kim Ji-Su looked back at us and gave a little wave. Mike waved back. Then the door shut, the pilot spun up the engines, and the Blackhawk disappeared into the night. The sound of the fighters overhead went with them.

"Fighter escort," Tyrel said. "They must be pretty damned important."

348

Mike was still staring in the direction of the departed aircraft. "You have no idea."

*****

With dawn came a light drizzle. The clouds overhead were growing darker, telling me there would be a downpour later.

General Jacobs arrived, and his retinue immediately set to work erecting his command tent. The floodlights were turned off, but the roar of multi-fuel generators continued to shatter the morning stillness.

When Mike saw General Jacobs, he told Gabe, Tyrel, and Grabovsky to stay put and wait for the general's people to arrive. When they did, the three of them were to direct the arriving troops' efforts boxing up the contents of the inner compound.

"What about the lab?" Tyrel asked. "I ain't going in there, I don't care what Jacobs says."

"No worries," Mike said. "Let the people in hazmat suits handle that part."

"Fine by me."

Mike set out toward the command tent, and to my surprise, he motioned for me to follow. "Come on, son," he said. "General wants to see you."

I went with him into the tent and was immediately assailed by squawking radios, rustling papers and maps, and the hum of people working busily and speaking in hushed tones. General Jacobs stood over a table with a bright light shining down on it. On the table was a large map of ROC territory. The general had a box of multi-colored markers near his right hand, and as reports poured in, he made notations on the map. He looked up when we entered.

"Colonel Holden, Captain Hicks, good to see you. How'd you make out?"

"One casualty," Mike said. "Petty Officer Hemingway."

349

Jacobs paused. "Shit. What happened?"

"We ran into some ghouls on the way in. Hemingway hit one with a MK 9, but didn't make sure it was dead. Got him on the leg when he had his back turned."

The general closed his eyes and lowered his head. "Son of a bitch. He should have known better than that."

I wanted to say something harsh, but didn't. The general was right, if not entirely tactful. Hemingway knew better. He got sloppy, and he paid the price. What I felt on the subject was irrelevant. The truth was the truth.

"The rest of your squad all right?" Jacobs asked.

"Fine," Mike said. "Cuts and bruises, nothing serious."

"Good." The general shifted his attention to me. "Captain Hicks, I'll need you to hang around for a while. Might have some questions for you."

"Yes sir."

Mike joined Jacobs at the table, and the two of them were soon in deep discussion over the events of the previous night.

I found an unused corner of the tent, requisitioned a folding chair, and sat down. I heard reports about the F-18s that had flown ashore during the night and rained down JDAMs in hellish profusion on KPA outposts from Washington to California. The effect on KPA troop numbers was devastating.

People buzzed in and out of the command tent over the next few hours, occasionally being sent by Mike or General Jacobs to ask me questions. Mostly those questions pertained to what I had seen inside the command building and the inner compound, and what was said to me by Park Heon-Woo and Kim Ji-Su. I answered the same questions ten or eleven times, and then people stopped bothering me.

When not being interrogated, I kept my mouth shut and my eyes and ears open. I gleaned from the conversations around me that the final assault against the ROC had been mostly successful.

Mostly.

There were more inoculated troops than expected. Resistance and Army forces faced hard fighting from KPA soldiers not downed by AIM-38. I remembered Doctor Faraday saying they were fanatics. Their actions in the face of overwhelming odds proved him right. Especially as regarded the prisoners.

Here in the Klamath Basin, the damage dealt to the prisoners had been minor compared to the other camps. We had gotten lucky. If Gabe and I had not seen that mortar crew when we did, things would have been much worse.

At the other sites, they were.

In battle, mistakes happen. They happened to my squad, they happened to the troops that assaulted the Klamath Basin internment camp, and they happened elsewhere. Somewhere north of a hundred Resistance fighters died liberating the camps. We also lost ten special operations personnel with another two dozen wounded. Three helicopters crashed due to mechanical failure, and a fourth was shot down by KPA troops armed with RPGs. None of the pilots or aircrew survived.

As bad as our losses were, the prisoners suffered even more. In total, nearly two hundred of them died in the fighting. The AIM-38 virus claimed over a hundred more.

I thought about Gabe admonishing Doctor Faraday about what effect AIM-38 might have on the sick, the elderly, and the very young. As it turned out, his concerns were well founded. Most of virus's victims fell into one of those three categories. Their battered, tortured bodies were just too weakened by abuse, starvation, and disease to survive the effects the virus wrought on them. As reports later showed, most of them died mere hours before the offensive began. And most of them were children.

It was a good thing for Doctor Faraday he was not present. I'm not sure I could have restrained myself.

Around mid-afternoon, General Jacobs caught sight of me and stopped short. I assumed he had forgotten I was there.

"Had anything to eat yet, Captain?" he asked.

Of course not, you fucking old dunce. I've been sitting here for the last nine goddamn hours.

"No sir."

"Go on, then. There's a chow tent set up that way." He pointed a thumb toward the east side of the compound and then went back to his endless supply of maps.

"Yes sir."

I got up and left. The first place I went was the nearest latrine. Someone had thoughtfully set up a tarp, and beneath it, placed a large jug of hand sanitizer made from distilled grain alcohol and some kind of thickening agent. After relieving myself, I washed my hands as well as I could and followed my nose to the chow tent. Once there, I stared at the goat meat, rehydrated potatoes, and pinto beans, and decided I did not have much of an appetite.

By that point, the command building and the lab had both been gutted, the contents thereof packed into sealed crates and loaded onto a procession of HEMTTs which, from what I had learned sitting in the command tent, had been kept hidden less than a hundred miles away for the last six weeks. The transports departed the camp and set out for a pre-designated staging area twenty miles away, otherwise known as the parking lot of a pre-Outbreak mega-mart in an abandoned town. They were accompanied by four Apache attack helicopters, six Bradley fighting vehicles, and six Stryker IAVs.

Three companies of infantry and two support platoons, including mechanics and aircrew, were on their way from Idaho to meet the convoy at the staging area. From there, they would begin the long journey back to the Springs. In the interim, two hundred Resistance fighters had been assigned to help keep the infected at bay until reinforcements arrived.

I wondered for a moment why the seized research was going to the Springs in ground vehicles and not aircraft. Then I thought about the three Blackhawks that crashed due to mechanical failure, and figured General Jacobs was playing it safe. The folks at Cheyenne Mountain undoubtedly wanted every letter of that research delivered undamaged into their eager little hands. Jacobs obviously was not willing to risk losing any of it to another crash. The same courtesy, apparently, did not extend to the two scientists he'd had us capture.

I walked to the command building. The clouds overhead had grown dark and angry, turning what should have been a bright afternoon into a sullen, humid gloom. Lightning flashed and darted from cloud to cloud, illuminating the ground below in flashes of neon blue. I stepped over the remnants of the door Smith had blown up and looked around. The entire squad had assembled in the lobby and sat on chairs they had scavenged from the surrounding offices. The muttered conversations going on between them stopped when I entered.

"Long time no see," Gellar said. "Been busy?"

"Not really."

"Learn anything interesting?"

"No."

Smith looked dubious and started to say something.

"Hey," Gabe interrupted.

Smith looked at him. "What?"

Gabe shook his head. Smith stared a few seconds, then shrugged and went back to whittling a stick with his fighting dagger.

I did not feel like talking. I did not feel like being around people who were talking. I dropped my weapons, vest, body armor, and everything else I could divest without disrobing. There was a sensation of my back and shoulders expanding that comes whenever I put down a heavy burden I've carried a long time.

I grabbed a chair and carried it outside, well away from the command building. I put it down in an open patch of the prison yard and took a seat. The world past the wall was visible only through the breach Miller had created the previous evening. The bodies of dead ghouls littered the ground nearby, most of them in pieces. They had scratched and clawed at the rubble blocking their way in until it tumbled down enough they could scale the sides, but by then, the fighting was over and the troops turned their attention to the undead. It looked as if they had used explosives to knock the ghouls down, then finished them off with small arms. The area was clear for the moment, but there would be more. There were always more.

The forest beyond the breach stood out in brilliant shades of green against the dull gray half-light of the coming rain. Lightning lashed down some distance away, followed several seconds later by a powerful crack of thunder that made the earth beneath me tremble. The wind picked up from the south, shaking trees and moving the long grass like the surface of a storm-tossed ocean. I stayed where I was, unmoved and unmoving.

I thought about the wildfires that chased me and my family out of the Houston area during the Outbreak, and how nice some rain would have been back then. I thought of my father putting his hand against my cheek and breathing out his last words. I thought about Sophia pulling shrapnel out of me and stitching the wounds left behind. I thought about the nights we had spent huddled together in our little shipping container, the warmth of each other's touch the only comfort we had in the sad ruin of an even sadder world. I thought about how I fell apart after I lost her, the drinking, the self-destructiveness, and later, the vengeance I brought to the men who killed my father. When I was done thinking about these things, I thought about my father warning me not to become exactly what I was—a man controlled by other men in positions of power who wanted to use me as a weapon.

The cold statistics announced over the radio every Saturday revolved in my head like refuse picked up by the wind. Less than three percent of the world's population had survived the Outbreak, leaving billions of people dead or turned into abominations that desecrated the sanctity of life and made a mocking sacrilege of the peace offered by death. I wondered if there really was an afterlife. If there was, I wondered if there was a wait to get in. Perhaps the beings tasked with processing dead souls had not foreseen the catastrophe in the world below, and were just as overwhelmed as the rest of us. If so, considering the staggering number of people who had died, the distance between life and death must be a storm of ghosts so powerful as to shake the foundations of heaven and hell and everything between.

I looked at the sky, and the clouds scudding overhead, and felt the wind tugging at me and bringing with it the scent of moisture on the air. Soon, the sky darkened until it was almost black and the world beneath was cast in deep shadow. Several fat droplets hit the ground nearby, a few more making wet slapping sounds as they splatted against my clothes and landed on my head. Still I sat, and did not move. The rain picked up and began falling harder and harder until it was a torrent so strong I could barely see a few inches beyond my own face. I heard Gabe yelling at me from the command building, but it was a faint sound and easy to ignore. Rather than seek shelter, I closed my eyes and let the storm wash over me. It was cold, and it hurt, but I did not mind.

Inside, all was quiet.

FORTY-SIX

There was a week of mandatory quarantine. After that, it took four days, a Humvee, a Blackhawk, a Chinook, a C-130, and a horse-drawn cart to bring me back to the barracks at Peterson Army Air Base where my room waited for me.

Gabe and Tyrel traveled with me until we arrived back in town. The three of us spoke little on the journey to Colorado, each of us wrestling with our own thoughts. When we departed the C-130, we walked together across the tarmac carrying our personal equipment and weapons. At the terminal was the usual collection of Franken-vehicles and carts drawn by horses and oxen waiting to charge fares to soldiers exiting planes. I said a brief goodbye to my two friends, promised to meet them for drinks a week hence, and caught a ride back to the barracks where an empty room waited for me.

It was stuffy, so I left the front door open and threw the window as wide as it would go. The civilian contractors who cleaned the rooms had visited, as evidenced by the lack of dust. I put my gear away and sat down on the bed and stared out at the living city in the distance.

"Now what?" I said aloud.

The room had no answer.

*****

There was not much for me to do.

I reported to the headquarters building at 0800 the next morning in a neatly pressed uniform with my captain's bars proudly displayed. It occurred to me on the walk over that being frequently saluted was kind of a pain. The lackadaisical salutes officer's usually returned to enlisted troops suddenly made sense. It gets old pretty quick.

I was greeted by a second lieutenant assigned to General Jacobs' staff. He gave me a brown envelope with something small and weighty in it, and a sealed message from General Jacobs. Then he left the room without a word. I sat down and opened the message first. It read:

CLASSIFIED

TO: Captain Caleb Hicks

RE: Instructions upon return to Peterson AAB

--DESTROY AFTER READING--

Captain Hicks,

First, let me commend you for your bravery and exemplary performance. You were an integral part of your mission's success. By now, you have undoubtedly figured out who recommended you for duty as a federal emissary (hereafter FE). Let me assure you, I am firmly convinced that his faith in you was not misplaced. Now that I have been fully briefed on the role you played in your mission's success, I will see to it you are awarded another Bronze Star to add to your collection.

Upon your return to Peterson AAB, the only requirements I have are that you maintain physical readiness, and use the authority vested in you as an FE to equip yourself as necessary

357

should any further missions present themselves in the near future. You are to report to JSOC headquarters at 0900 daily, including weekends. One of my staff will pass on to you any messages from me or other members of your chain of command. Before leaving base, notify my staff of your intended destination, and keep the satellite phone provided close at hand. Should your battery run low, notify my staff immediately of your location and a charged battery pack will be brought to you. Additionally, you will be relocated to base housing within the week.

As to maintaining combat proficiency, Tyrel Jennings was kind enough to offer an open invitation to the Blackthorn training facility. He may ask you to provide instruction to new recruits from time to time. I encourage you to take advantage of this opportunity and train as much as you deem necessary. If special instruction is needed for any missions you are assigned to in the future, I will have it arranged for you as required.

On a personal note, I made you a few promises, and I intend to keep them. When the young man who gave you this information returns, tell him to inform Colonel Wayland you have arrived. That should set things in motion.

Thank you again, Captain. You have done a great service for your nation.

Respectfully,

Phillip Jacobs

Major General

Joint Special Operations Command

Commander

I opened the second envelope. Inside was the aforementioned satellite phone. I activated it and checked the battery. It was at full charge.

There was a shredder in one corner of the office. I put the letter in it and watched it disappear. A moment later, there was a polite knock at the door.

"Come in," I said.

The young lieutenant entered. "Do you need anything else from me, sir?"

"Yes. Please inform Colonel Wayland that Captain Caleb Hicks has returned. He'll know what to do."

"Anything else, sir?"

"That will be all."

"I'll get right on it, sir."

"Thank you."

Efficient little fellow, I thought.

*****

On a bright afternoon in early August, Miranda stepped off of a C-130 onto the tarmac of Peterson AAB. I walked toward her at first, then broke into a run. She stopped and waited, her two duffel bags falling to the ground. She was wearing a yellow and white sundress with flowers printed on it, and her smile was every bit as beautiful as I remembered. Her skin had been tanned bronze by the hot summer sun. I picked her up and spun her in the air and breathed in her scent. Holding her made something inside me let go, and after months of living in a cloud of gray, the world regained its color.

Miranda's musical laughter stopped when I put her down and held her around the waist. Her arms went around my neck and her gorgeous sapphire eyes held me in thrall.

"You look good," she said.

I wanted to tell her she was the most beautiful thing under the sky, but I couldn't talk. So I settled for kissing her.

*****

"So how did Eric take it?"

Miranda did another lap around the living room. The house I had moved into was much too large for me alone, and most of it was unfurnished and undecorated. I knew Miranda would not let that stand for long.

"He wasn't happy, but he *was* understanding. He told me he was happy for me. Him and Great Hawk and Johnny Green and all the guys from your old squad came to see me off. They told me to say hi."

"Hi? Is that what they really said?"

"No. They were far more vulgar, but I think that's what they really meant. Except Derrick Holland. He said he hates you for stealing me away from him, and I think he actually meant it."

I laughed. "That's all right. He never hates me for long. Besides, how does he figure I stole you?"

Miranda shrugged. "I think he believed as long as I was there and you weren't, there was a chance."

"Was there?"

"Absolutely not. I like Derrick. He's a nice guy when he's not being a smartass, so I wasn't as cold with him as I was with some of the other soldiers. But no one could ever replace you."

I stood up, walked behind Miranda, and put my arms around her shoulders. She grabbed my forearm and leaned back into me, her head against my chest. I could smell the soap she had used to wash her hair.

"Believe it or not, Derrick's an optimist. For guys like him, hope springs eternal. Especially as regards pretty girls."

"He was persistent, I'll give him that."

We stood a few moments, a large square of sunshine pouring through the window and highlighting dust motes in the air. The sound of the base was a dim hum in the distance. Miranda cast her gaze around the room and pointed at the wall across from us.

"That's where we'll put the sofa," she said.

"I don't own a sofa."

"We'll have to remedy that."

"My trade is still back in Hollow Rock."

"Not for long it isn't. Great Hawk is on his way out here, and he's bringing it with him. In the meantime, Eric gave me a letter of credit. You can draw on it from any of his business partners here in the city. He signed as guarantor, so there shouldn't be any trouble."

I found the gesture touching. Eric was a hard man to read sometimes, but as they say, actions speak louder than words.

"Be nice to see Great Hawk again."

"I think he's looking forward to visiting. As much as he looks forward to anything, that is."

"He may be placid on the outside, but still waters run deep."

"So I've heard." There was a smile on Miranda's face as she turned around and kissed me.

"You're more talkative than usual," she said.

"You bring it out of me."

Her hands drifted down to my shirt and began unbuttoning it. "What else do I bring out of you?"

I picked her up, carried her upstairs, put her down on the bed, and showed her.

Several times.

It was well after dark before we stopped, both of us exhausted and sweating amid rumpled sheets. Her hand was warm on my chest as we lay next to each other.

"So what happens now?" she asked.

I looked out the window. The sky was clear and I could see stars over the shoulders of the Rocky Mountains. "Now I'd like us to get married."

She sat up and kissed me gently. "Of course. But what about after that?"

I let out a long sigh. "I don't know. I still have another year and a half left on my sentence."

"You mean your enlistment."

"Same thing."

Miranda was quiet for a while after that. Finally she said, "How much time are you going to spend away?"

"Probably a lot. I'll make sure Gabe and Tyrel know to look in on you. If you have any trouble, let them know. They'll take care of it."

"I can take care of myself, you know."

"I know. But everyone needs help sometimes."

"Even you?"

"Especially me."

"Then why don't you ask?"

"Don't have to. All the help I need is right here."

Miranda's gaze softened, the blue of her irises floating in the glow of a moonbeam shining through the open window. I felt myself falling, and I didn't ever want the feeling to end.

"Where did they send you?"

"West," I said.

"The Republic of California?"

"Former Republic of California."

"I heard the broadcasts. They said there are still KPA troops out there."

"About four thousand or so. More than enough to cause problems."

"How long do you think they'll hold out?"

"Probably about as long as KPA forces in the Midwest did after the Alliance fell apart."

"I also heard we seized their things. Weapons and oil and stuff."

"Yep."

"What happened to all the ROC troops out there?"

"Most of them are dead. Some of them were captured."

Miranda thought about that. "What's going to happen to them? The ones that were captured."

"I honestly have no idea. But whatever it is, I doubt it's going to be good."

"I'm not sure how I feel about that."

"Neither am I."

She looked quizzical. "I thought you hated them?"

"Hate is a powerful thing. It takes a lot of energy to maintain. Somewhere along the way, I decided not to spend mine on things that do me no good."

"Very wise of you."

"I'm not completely hopeless."

She smiled again, and then grew thoughtful. "The civilians, the ones that came over with the North Koreans. I heard they were relocated to Idaho," Miranda said.

"I heard the same thing."

"What do you think they'll do there?"

"I don't know. Grow potatoes?"

Miranda laughed, her voice like bells ringing. "I guess this all leaves one big question."

I rolled over so I could look at her. "What's that?"

"Why?"

"Why what?"

"Why come over here in the first place? Why make enemies of the Union? Why not try to live here peacefully?"

I thought about that for a while. "As to why they came over, I think they didn't have much choice. Things were a lot worse in Asia during the Outbreak than they were here."

"That's saying something."

"Yes, it is. As to why they antagonized us, I think it was the only way they knew how to deal with Americans. You have to understand, these people were brainwashed from birth to hate us, fed all kinds of lies about us. Near the end of the fighting, a bunch of KPA soldiers in Washington committed suicide rather than let themselves be captured. Cut their own throats 'cause they were out of ammo."

"That's horrible."

"It is. And it's not the action of someone who thinks there's hope in surrender. It's what you do to avoid an even worse fate."

"But the civilians surrendered."

"Maybe they didn't believe the hype. Or maybe they were just scared and didn't know what else to do."

"At the risk of sounding callous, I'm glad I'm not one of them."

"Me too."

Another silence settled into the room. We let it sit for a while until it grew bored and wandered off.

"So I repeat my earlier question," Miranda said. "What now?"

"Now I report in every morning like I'm supposed to, make love to you as often as you'll let me, and we build the best life for ourselves that we can. Sooner or later I'm going to get another mission, and I'll have to leave for a while. I'd like to promise you I'll always come back no matter what, but we're both grownups and we know that isn't how the world works. Bad things happen to good people for no reason at all. The good guys don't always win.

People like us don't always get what we deserve, because what you or me or anyone else deserves has no bearing on the equation. I'll do whatever I can to stay alive, and you'll do the same. And hopefully, one day, we can start over in a better place where I can put down my guns and not have to live like this anymore."

Miranda kissed the tip of my nose. "Sounds like a plan."

We lay entwined together long into the night. Miranda's skin was smooth and soft against mine. She laid her head on my chest, put a possessive arm around me, and eventually, we slept.

For once, I did not dream.

FORTY-SEVEN

Heinrich,
Eastern Colorado

Heinrich sat on the bench of his wagon, looked across the flat expanse of eastern Colorado, and thought it ironic the same private army that nearly destroyed him just months ago was now keeping him safe.

Maru sat on a stool next to the wagon tending a cook fire. A small pot hung suspended from three sticks, chicken and dried vegetables and barley boiling within. Beneath the pot, flatbread sizzled lazily in a cast iron skillet smeared with pig fat. The big Maori picked up a wooden spoon and stirred the pot, flipped the flatbread, and went back to staring at the fire.

"How long?" Heinrich asked.

"Couple minutes on the bread. Little longer on the stew."

"Getting hungry."

"Makes two of us."

The sun was setting to the west, painting the sky in shades of peach and lavender. Stars were already visible to the east, while farther south, a full moon hung low on the horizon. It would be a warm, bright night with plenty of breeze. The tall grass on either side of I-70 rustled and swayed in the wind. Behind where

366

Heinrich sat, a long caravan of wagons crouched in the middle of the interstate. In front of him, another caravan had also made camp farther westward. Blackthorns on horseback patrolled in both directions, eyes alert for signs of infected or encroaching marauders.

"Strange, the places life takes you," Heinrich muttered.

After leaving The Holdout, the Storm Road Tribe had made their way west through Kansas. It had been no trouble at all to pose as traders, and what few federal patrols they ran into gave them only a cursory inspection and sent them on their way. Heinrich decided there was something to be said for operating under a legitimate front. Perhaps he would have to rethink his strategy going forward.

Outside the Wichita Safe Zone, which they had bypassed lest they risk one of them being recognized (there were several Army deserters in the tribe), they crossed paths with another caravan heading in the same direction. As unspoken tradition dictated, Heinrich and his entourage had met with the caravan's leaders and shared a meal together around a fire. The caravan leader's name was Holloway, and he was a firm believer in safety in numbers.

"Got four Blackthorns working for us," Holloway said. "It's a fair haul back to the Springs. The more of us there are, the less likely we'll be attacked."

You're not wrong about that.

"How much do you want me to pitch in?" Heinrich asked.

They sat and negotiated for close to an hour. Finally they settled on a price they could both live with and shook on it. The two caravans had traveled together hundreds of miles since then, watched over by Blackthorns, the hard-eyed young men in their dark uniforms oblivious to who it was that traveled with them.

Heinrich had given his men strict orders not to talk to the Blackthorns, and if engaged by them, to simply walk away from the conversation. It turned out to be an unnecessary precaution. The Blackthorns had no more interest in talking to Heinrich or his men than they did in talking to a stone. They were hired to do a job, and that was what they focused on. Heinrich appreciated their professionalism. However, this sentiment did not lessen in the least his desire to kill them. And he *would* kill them, he determined. But that was a problem best addressed one step at a time. For now, the next step was moving into Colorado Springs, getting the lay of the land, and setting himself up as a legitimate business man. From there, he could make further plans.

Maru finished making their meal, then stood up and offered a plate to his chief. Heinrich accepted it and began eating mechanically, his gaze fixed on the road ahead. Maru looked around, leaned in, and spoke in a low voice.

"So what's the plan once we're in town?"

"We settle in," Heinrich said without looking at his second in command. "We gather intelligence, and then I'll put together a plan to take down the Blackthorns."

"Any idea where to start? Once we're settled in, I mean."

Heinrich looked at Maru, his eyes cold and empty. "Everyone has a button you can push, some kind of leverage you can use against them. We know who the leaders of the Blackthorns are. Tyrel Jennings, Hadrian Flint, and their head trainer…what was his name again?"

"Garrett," Maru said. "Gabriel Garrett."

"Right. Anyway, we find what buttons we need to push, and we push them. Hard."

"Those Blackthorns are tough nuts to crack. What kind of leverage would work against them, you reckon?"

"That's an easy one," Heinrich said, turning his attention back to the city lights in the distance.

"We go after their families."

The saga will continue in Surviving the Dead Volume 9
Coming soon …

About the Author:

James N. Cook (who prefers to be called Jim, even though his wife insists on calling him James) is a martial arts enthusiast, a veteran of the U.S. Navy, a former cubicle dweller, and the author of the Surviving the Dead series. He hikes, he goes camping, he travels a lot, and he has trouble staying in one place for very long. He lives in North Carolina with his wife, children, and overactive imagination.

Made in the USA
Las Vegas, NV
10 January 2022